THE
FORGOTTEN

THE
FORGOTTEN

CASEY KELLEHER

bookouture

Published by Bookouture in 2018

An imprint of StoryFire Ltd.

Carmelite House
50 Victoria Embankment
London EC4Y 0DZ

www.bookouture.com

ISBN: 978-1-78681-578-1
eBook ISBN: 978-1-78681-577-5

For Lucy
The gin to my tonic!
x

PROLOGUE

Picking up the framed photograph next to her bed, Marie Huston stared at the two smiling faces that gazed back at her.

The pain inside her was as strong as ever, despite the fact that it felt like a whole other world now. A different time completely.

Beautiful Cassie and her, both of them looking so happy and carefree.

The image of her father had been torn from the picture. Ripped into a hundred pieces. It was the only photo she had of her and her sister together – the image that they'd used in the newspaper reports.

The media had milked her family tragedy for all it was worth. Portraying them just as he'd have wanted. Their father. A happy little family. The widowed father, and his two darling daughters.

That's what it would look like, if you didn't know any better.

And no one had known any better. Their father had made sure of that.

Making sure to the outside world, to anyone watching, that no one knew their dark, sordid secrets.

And they'd had many, many secrets.

Secrets, that their father had said, if they'd spoken about to anyone, would get them sent away to a children's prison. He'd told them that people wouldn't understand. That people would think Marie and Cassie were bad.

And of course, Marie and Cassie had hung on his every word.

They'd believed all of his sick, twisted threats and mind games.

Why wouldn't they?

He was their parent, their father.

Why would he mean them any harm?

All those times when he'd sneaked into their beds at night and made them do all those disgusting things to him.

When he made them do all those things that they didn't want to do.

That was love. That's how they had to show him how much they loved him.

Marie gripped the frame tightly in her palm, her fingers turning white from the force of the hold.

She was glad he was no longer part of the picture. He didn't deserve to be there.

The problem their father had was that little girls grew up eventually.

They find out stuff. And at five years older than her younger sister, Cassie, finally Marie *had* found out. All those things that their father had subjected both of them to for all of these years had been wrong.

All those things he had done to them.

It wasn't love.

It was sick, and twisted, and evil.

Marie's only saving grace from the abuse had been puberty. Later than some of the other girls at school, Marie had been fifteen when she finally got her monthly cycle and her breasts had started to grow, and she'd been so happy because it miraculously meant that her father didn't want her any more.

The nightly visits suddenly stopped.

It had given Marie a sense of relief at first. But her respite soon became Cassie's sole burden.

Marie had seen it in her younger sister's eyes; each morning she'd recognised the pain and suffering behind them: the broken shell of a girl now that Cassie was their father's only release.

Her little Cassie.

The girl that had often danced around the kitchen like a maniac, giggling and laughing with Marie.

They always did that when it was just the two of them. Whenever they were free of him.

But now it was as if the light had gone out behind her eyes.

And when she did look at Marie, it was only hate that grew there. Resentment that Marie was getting off scot free. That she was the only one suffering.

Cassie had gone so far inside herself that even Marie couldn't reach her anymore. Her sister had started wetting the bed. Then her behaviour had started to change at school too. Cassie had started getting into fights. Lashing out at the people around her, to the point where she'd almost been expelled for punching one girl in the face and giving her a black eye.

That's when Marie had decided that she needed to do something drastic. Something to stop her father from hurting Cassie any more than she was clearly hurting already.

So, Marie had offered herself to him then.

Squeezing her eyes shut, remembering how she had lain in his bed one night, waiting for him. How she'd been so willing to give herself to him. A sacrifice.

Using herself as a bargaining card, just so that he would leave poor Cassie alone.

But her father had simply rejected her.

Not only that, but he'd got some kind of a sick power trip from humiliating Marie too. Turning her down and marching her naked from his room.

Then, later that night, she'd heard them.

Her father and her sister.

Those disgusting noises. Cassie crying.

Placing the photograph back down on the bedside cabinet, overwhelmed by memories, Marie Huston smoothed down her new, crisp, blue nurse's uniform before checking her hair was tidy in the mirror. Not a strand out of place.

She was determined to make a good first impression today at her new job.

After years of studying and training, she was working in the Burns Unit at Chelsea and Westminster Hospital.

Today was finally her fresh start, her new beginning. Something to focus on, which might, in some way, ease the burden that weighed so heavily upon her soul.

She glanced back one last time at the face of her beloved beautiful sister, Cassie, feeling her tears threaten once more, as she picked up the photo and kissed it gently.

Marie had never meant for Cassie to die.

PART ONE
2004

CHAPTER ONE

Nancy Byrne's body was soaked in a thick film of sweat. Her hair clammy, trailing down her face and sticking to her skin.

The pain in her body was so acute, so agonising, that she thought she was going to pass out. Or throw up again.

She could still feel the slimy film that coated her teeth. The rancid bitter taste of hot burning bile in the back of her throat.

All she wanted to do was collapse into an exhausted slumber and wake up when this was all over. Only there was no chance of that.

Not with the continual pain that was building inside her.

The feeling of her insides being ripped out of her.

'I can't do this!' Nancy screamed as another wave of agony washed over her, the intensity building with every contraction.

'You can, Nancy. Trust me. You can do this,' Jan Barker said as she squeezed Nancy's right hand to offer the woman some encouragement. Having worked as a midwife at King's College Hospital for the past decade, Jan was certain that the young woman was almost there. She just needed to keep her strength up. To stay motivated. 'A couple more pushes and that baby of yours is going to be here, Nancy. We're so close. You're almost there, darling.'

Nancy shook her head disbelievingly. Glad that the midwife, at least, had some faith in her.

'There's nothing left in me. Please. I really can't do this.'

Staring up at the clock on the wall, she'd lost track of time, but she knew she'd been in labour now for almost twenty hours.

Her mother was at her side too.

'Come on, Nancy!' Colleen Byrne piped up, placing a hand on her daughter's head to show her affection. 'The baby's almost here, you've got to focus, Nancy!'

In her element ever since the midwife had called her to the hospital as Nancy's next of kin, Colleen had been lapping up every minute of being involved with Nancy's labour.

And what a privilege that was, witnessing her first precious grandchild being born into the world.

Oblivious to the fact that Nancy didn't actually want her there, she smiled down at her daughter, offering her words of encouragement.

'This little baby is coming, Nancy, whether you like it or not. You need to be strong for your child, darling,' Colleen cooed, embracing the one opportunity she'd been given to finally be there for Nancy in her time of need.

Maybe this was her chance to fix things with her daughter. To unite them both and help heal the bond that they'd never really had between them.

'Strong for my child?' Nancy spat, her mother's words like a red flag to a raging bull. 'You'd know all about that, wouldn't you, Colleen? Mother of the bleeding year! And can you please stop rubbing my bloody head,' Nancy said, breathlessly, shrugging her mother's hand from her hair. Frustrated then as she bore down once more as another almighty contraction surged through her body.

Nancy let out a low, deep moan, grabbing at the tube for the gas and air before muffling her despair as she inhaled a huge lungful.

'It's all right! She hasn't got a very high pain threshold! I won't take it personally,' Colleen quipped to the nurse beside her, rolling her eyes. 'And I do know all about it, Nancy. This bit at least. I gave birth to you and your brother on my own too, you know. That father of yours that you insist on placing on a pedestal was nowhere to be seen both times that I was in labour. Too busy working, supposedly, to make it to the hospital in time for either of his children's entrances into the world. That was Jimmy, all right! I don't think he even met Daniel until your brother was almost three hours old…'

'Jesus, Colleen. The last thing I need to hear right now is you slagging off my dad…' Nancy warned the woman, her tone curt. This was hard enough without being reminded that her father wasn't here anymore. That he'd never meet his first grandchild. And the very last person she wanted mentioned today of all days was her waster of a brother. Trust Colleen to take her opportunity to get in her two pence worth and bring up Daniel once again.

The woman just wouldn't let it go.

Daniel had gone. Fuck knows where or what had happened to him, Nancy no longer cared. As long as she never had to set eyes on him again.

'There's a time and a place, Colleen! And trust me when I say, it isn't now.' Nancy winced then, the pain almost too much to bear. Between that and having to listen to her mother's bitter comments, it was all Nancy could do not to scream.

Sensing the tension between the two women, Jan Barker stepped in.

'I'm just going to check Nancy's temperature,' the nurse lied, sensing Nancy's discomfort at having her overbearing mother in the room with her, lecturing her. Colleen Byrne was only adding to her daughter's pain.

Jan ushered the woman further back from the bed, away from Nancy's direct vicinity.

Colleen continued talking through Nancy's contractions, oblivious.

'Well, it's not right, is it? That you're doing this on your own. What about the father, Nancy? Have you even told him that you're in labour?' Colleen asked now, tight-lipped, knowing that she was pushing her luck fishing for answers about the identity of her first grandchild's birth father, but also knowing her daughter well enough to know that Nancy Byrne wasn't going to tell her shit.

The girl could be so pig-headedly stubborn sometimes.

Colleen had no idea why Nancy was so adamant about keeping the father of her child a secret from them all. Though that was Nancy all over. She liked to do things her way, or no way. Just like Jimmy, she was. Her father's daughter through and through.

Though it was about time that Nancy told her who had fathered her first baby, and Colleen figured that the fact that her daughter was now off her head on gas and air might finally make her talk.

Though, of course, Colleen had called that theory wrong too.

Instantly putting Nancy's back up at her questioning.

'Please, Colleen.' Nancy spoke through gritted teeth. 'Not now, yeah?'

'Okay!' Colleen nodded. 'Though I don't know why you have to be so secretive about the whole thing, Nancy. It's 2004, you can do what you want. No one's judging you. If you want to be a single mum, and bring up a child on your own, who are any of us to stop you? I just don't think it's fair on the child. To not have a father.'

Colleen stared at Nancy then, the sudden realisation hitting her.

'Is that it, Nancy? Is that why you don't want to tell us? Because you don't know who the father is?'

'Oh, please! Get her out of here, will you? She's doing my head in,' Nancy shouted, as she felt yet another wave of agony wash over her. 'Please, I'm in enough pain as it is without her adding to my misery…'

'Mrs Byrne!' Jan Barker said then, her voice as stern as her expression. 'I think it would be a good idea if you waited outside.'

'What and miss my first grandchild being born?' Colleen screeched incredulously.

Though she couldn't help but feel tearful at the sight of her daughter lying in the hospital bed. About to bring her own child into the world. The fact that even this wouldn't bring the two women together. The damage that had been done between them over the years was irreparable.

She'd overstepped the mark, she realised that now. She was only trying to help. To get closer to Nancy by letting her know that she could confide in her.

'I'm sorry, Nancy. Please let me stay.' Colleen started crying then. Huge wracking sobs shaking her body. 'I just want to make things right. I just want to help! Be a good grandmother to this baby. Start as we mean to go on...'

Nancy faltered. A tiny part of her wanted that too.

Maybe it was the fear she felt about becoming a new mum? Or the fact that Colleen was one of the few family members she and this baby had left.

Her mother, her nan and grandad.

She wanted her baby to have a family, of course she did. Maybe she was being too hard on the woman?

'Look, Nancy has asked for you to leave, so if you don't mind,' Jan Barker said, as she stared at the monitors and noticed the sudden change in the readings. 'You need to leave now,' she ordered, as she guided Colleen Byrne towards the door.

'We should have gone private!' Colleen sneered, catching the look the nurse and her daughter exchanged. 'At least that lot know what they are doing. They get paid enough—'

'Colleen!' Nancy shouted then. No longer interested in her mother's opinions.

The pain inside her was so strong now that she couldn't physically bear it any longer.

'This can't be right?' she cried. 'This pain is killing me…'

'Nancy?'

Jack Taylor stood in the doorway of the delivery suite. His sudden presence making everyone turn to look at him.

'What's happening? Is the baby okay?'

Looking from Nancy to Colleen then back to the chaos of the room.

'Oh, please tell me you didn't call Jack,' Nancy groaned, her legs up in the stirrups now. Visibly distressed as it was, without Jack adding to it by turning up here unannounced.

She wanted to do this her way, but her mother's interfering had put paid to that.

'Well, I'm glad someone did, Nancy. I have a right to know.'

'I was excited, I just wanted to share the news.' Colleen apologised, shaking her head, confused at why Nancy seemed so angry suddenly. Jack Taylor had been like family to them all, and in the months since Jimmy's murder, Jack had gone above and beyond to watch out for this family. Especially Nancy.

Though Jack sounded angry, too, now.

Colleen was puzzled by his turn of words.

'"A right to know"?'

He looked as equally pissed off as Nancy did. As if he was somehow entitled to know what was going on. 'What do you mean you have "a right"? I don't understand…'

Reading Nancy's and Jack's expressions only confirmed what was suddenly dawning on her.

'Jack's the father, isn't he? Jesus Christ!'

It all made sense now.

Why Nancy had been so secretive about her pregnancy for so long, why she hadn't mentioned to a soul who the father was.

Jack had been acting strange, too, Colleen realised, recalling all the sniffing about the man had been doing. Constantly around at the house, even more so than usual. Always asking about Nancy and how she was doing throughout the pregnancy. Fussing over the girl.

Colleen had naively thought that the man was just looking out for them all, being a good, loyal friend. Especially after Jimmy's murder.

That he'd had all their best interests at heart.

Only Jack had been more than just a friend to Nancy. That much was now blatantly clear.

'Please tell me it isn't true?' Colleen snapped, incredulously.

The man was at least twice Nancy's age. Old enough to be Nancy's father.

Old enough to know better.

Before Jack could answer, Nancy let out an almighty scream, drowned out by the simultaneous sound of the alarms that were monitoring the baby's heartbeat.

'I think the baby's distressed!' Jan Barker shouted to the rest of the team, as pandemonium broke out in the room.

'What's wrong?' Nancy screeched, seeing the urgency and chaos breaking out around her. 'Please? Is the baby okay?'

The room was full of strangers all dressed in gowns and surgical masks, panicked looks etched on the obstetric team's faces.

From the sudden commotion all around her, Nancy already knew the answer.

Something was wrong, something was very wrong.

'It's going to be okay, Nancy.' Then, turning to Colleen and Jack, Jan Barker added, with urgency, 'You both need to leave.' This time it was an order. 'The baby's become a little distressed; we'll have to use forceps. We need to get him or her out. Now.'

'"Distressed"? What does that mean? What's happening? You can't make me leave. My daughter needs me.'

'Just get the fuck out, Colleen,' Nancy screeched. Done with her mother's dramatics. 'There's something wrong with the baby. Are you too fucking selfish or stupid to understand that? Get out!'

Nancy had slumped back against the pillows then. Her face void of colour. Her eyes screwed tightly shut as a searing pain consumed her very being. Crying loudly now.

'Come on, Colleen. Let's respect Nancy's wishes.' Sensing the gravity of what was happening around them, and how distraught Nancy was, Jack Taylor intervened. Taking Colleen by the arm, he guided her out of the room to the seating area in the corridor.

Stung by her daughter's words, by the pure hate in Nancy's eyes, Colleen Byrne finally did as she was told.

Taking a seat next to Jack Taylor just outside the room, they both sat in silence.

Waiting for some news, to hear the sound of the baby crying.

Waiting to hear anything.

The air was suddenly shattered by a piercing scream, followed by a silence so harrowing that Colleen wanted to cry herself, too, then. Only she knew she had to stay strong, for Nancy's sake.

She closed her eyes to stop the tears from escaping, giving up on the hope of hearing the sweet sound of her first grandchild's cry.

Bracing herself for the bad news, as the midwife stepped out of the room, Colleen clutched at Jack Taylor's hand for support.

She couldn't do this again.

She couldn't lose another member of her family. She just couldn't.

Only to her surprise, Jan Barker smiled.

'I think I have someone who'd like to meet you both.' Holding the door to the delivery suite wide open, she invited them both back in. 'Congratulations, Daddy and Grandma. Nancy has just given birth to a very healthy and very beautiful little girl.'

CHAPTER TWO

'Come on, girls. Stay out with us and have some fun?' Flashing the two girls his most charming smile, Trey Coleman failed to keep the desperation from his tone as he watched them flag down a taxi outside The Ten Bells pub. 'Or at least let us ponce a lift back up the West End?'

'Sorry! No can do,' the first girl said then, tartly, as she held the black cab's door wide open for her friend. 'We're meeting some friends; there won't be enough room for you two as well.'

Trey shook his head. He might be pissed but he wasn't stupid.

These two money-grabbing tarts had taken him and Digsby for a right pair of mugs. After plying the two girls with jugs of cheap and cheerful potent cocktails that were on the menu, as many as their greedy little hearts desired, convinced by the girls' unspoken promises that they were onto a sure thing, it seemed that wasn't the case at all.

Not now that the East End boozer that was standing behind them was shut and the two lads had barely a penny left to their names.

And the pub had been busy; heaving, in fact.

That was the most annoying thing about tonight. The Ten Bells, in Spitalfields, was one of the best little pubs in the whole of the East End. A sure bet if you wanted to pull a couple of fit girls; only Trey and Digsby seemed shit out of luck tonight and had picked a pair of wrong'uns.

Trey had blown his entire week's wages on these two trollops, to now realise that the only two people being played tonight had been him and Digsby all along.

They had been a right pair of gullible idiots.

'Oh come on, girls. What are we meant to do? We're both boracic now after spending out all night. At least give us your numbers.'

The first girl shrugged; then rolling her eyes up to her mate, she ducked inside the cab.

He eyed the second girl. His one, Mandy. They'd been talking and laughing all night. They had a connection.

Surely she wasn't going to be as hard-nosed as her mate?

She faltered, holding on to the car door, eyeing Trey with a small wry smile on her face.

'Okay. Have you got a pen?'

Tapping himself down, though he knew that he didn't normally carry a pen on him, he eyed Digsby. He was desperate to at least get this girl's number. That way the evening wouldn't have been a complete waste of time and money.

'Have you got a pen, Digs?'

Stuart Digsby shook his head.

'Ahh, well, that's a shame. Only, if you had one, I'd have told you to get back in it!'

The girl laughed then, before throwing the boys a cute little wave and jumping into the cab.

'What?' Trey looked at Digsby, the confusion all over his face. 'I don't get it?'

The joke going completely over his head.

'A pen. Come on, Trey, think about it.' He laughed then, catching his breath only to make grunting pig noises. 'A pig pen. She was taking the piss out of you.' Digsby smirked, despite himself.

The girls were a couple of money-grabbing cows, brazen as fuck too. Only the look on Trey's face now was priceless.

'Slags,' Trey said, trying to save face. Watching as the taxi drove off into the distance. He could feel a wave of heat creeping up his neck; his face burning with humiliation at being made such a mug of.

Worse than that, he had no money left, not a single penny.

He'd been well and truly fleeced.

Hoisting himself up onto the wall that ran alongside the front of The Ten Bells pub, sitting side by side with Digsby, he dug his heels into the brickwork.

'They were a right pair of stuck-up bitches anyway,' Digsby said, trying to make his friend feel better. 'Far too high-maintenance for us. Plus my one had a stonker of a nose on her. The only way she stood a chance with me, was for me to be paralytic. She probably knew that too. Wanted to make a fast exit before it started to get light or she'd turn into a gremlin or something,' Digsby joked, pretending that he had standards for once, when they both knew that Digsby would shag his own grandmother if the room was dark enough.

'Shit man, what are we gunna do now?' Trey said, annoyed, glancing at the pub behind them that now sat in complete darkness.

There was no one else around; the street was completely empty.

Trey, Digsby and the two girls had been the last ones out of the pub doors. They'd practically been marched out by the bar staff, who had all followed them out shortly afterwards. Making a swift exit home after their busy shift.

'I dunno mate.' Stuart Digsby shrugged, knowing full well that neither of them had any money left. 'We haven't even got enough to get a kebab, let alone a cab home.'

Trey shrugged. He couldn't be arsed to trudge his way halfway across London.

Not yet anyway.

Instead, he just sat there. His eyes lingering on the pub behind them, staring at the windows.

'This place looks creepy now, don't it?' Trey said with a shiver. 'Did you know that it used to be called Jack the Ripper back in the eighties?'

'Yeah, wasn't it because that psycho used to drink here or something?' Preparing himself for one of Trey's drunken history lessons about the place – Trey was always harping on about shit like this, more so when he'd had a few beers.

Digsby remembered hearing some kind of a rumour about the place, only he'd never paid that much attention to things like that.

'No. Jack the Ripper didn't drink there. But one of his victims did. His last victim in fact. My dad said that this place used to have loads of prossies hanging around out the front, touting for work. Black Mary they called her.'

'Oh yeah, your old man an expert on where all the prossies hang out then, is he?' Digsby chimed in, winding his mate up.

Trey gave Digsby a dig in the arm. Carrying on with his story then.

'It's fucked up though, isn't it? That they changed the name of this place just to drag the tourists in. Jack the Ripper pub. A woman actually got murdered and it was just treated like some sort of gimmick.' Trey shook his head. His tone disgusted.

'Well, there ain't no prossies hanging about out here anymore,' Digsby said, sounding almost disappointed as he eyed the empty street. 'And even if there were, unless they're happy with £2.60 and half a packet of chewing gum in return for a blowie, we'd both be shit out of luck.'

'My dad said that they reckon this place is haunted now. Apparently, Black Mary still roams her patch over there, where she used to tout for customers,' Trey said, pointing over to the dark shadowy entrance of the alleyway that ran along the side of the pub.

'Your dad sure knows a lot about this Black Mary. You sure he wasn't banging her, 'en all?' Digsby laughed then. 'Dirty old bastard. What did he do, get caught trying to bag himself a hooker, and then made out that he was really doing a bit of ghost hunting? I've heard it all now. Your dad's a right card, mate, I'll give you that.'

Trey shook his head. His mate never took him seriously.

'He didn't see her. He saw her ghost. I swear to God, Digsby. He saw her. I'm telling you. He looked terrified when he told me. I could see the fear in his eyes. He said it was really late one night. And that no one had been around. The street had been empty. Just like it is now. The pub looked abandoned. Empty. Then he saw her, a young woman standing at the entrance of the alleyway. He said that she was crying. He said he went over to see if she was all right…'

'Oh, I bet he did!'

'Only when he got near to her, she just disappeared. Right in front of his eyes. He said that he could remember the sad look on her face. The weird Victorian clothes she wore. He said that she'd been so real, he could have reached out and touched her.'

'Touch her? See…' Digsby laughed. 'Sounds a bit dodgy to me.'

A sudden movement in the alleyway behind them caught both lads off guard.

Trey let out a high-pitched scream. Lunging forward on the wall, he fell to the pavement with fright as a man ran out from the shadows, running down the road.

'You muppet,' Digsby said, shaking his head at Trey's failed attempt at trying to put the shits up him. 'You're only scaring yourself, you know, with all your stupid ghost stories. You know that I don't believe in all that spooky shit. Never have and never will, mate!'

'What the fuck is that?' Trey said then. His gaze still fixed on the alleyway that ran down the side of the pub.

There was another movement in the shadows.

A silhouette, swaying unsteadily. Only this time it was a woman.

'Ohh, here we go. This will be your prossie ghost on her way over to haunt us. Black Mary is coming,' Digsby said, laughing, as he clocked the fear on Trey's face at the sight of the girl slowly making her way towards them both.

Only, even Digsby sounded a bit uncertain.

What were the chances of Trey telling him one of his ghost stories, only to then see a woman emerging from the alleyway looking worse for wear?

She was half-naked, too, her chest fully exposed, bare white skin illuminated by the faint street lamp that flickered further down the road.

'Fucking hell, she ain't wearing no Victorian clobber though, is she? She ain't wearing much at all,' Digsby said then, staring at the woman's breasts. 'She's got her fucking baps out.'

Topless, with just a skirt around her middle, she staggered slowly towards them.

One of her shoes was missing, the other hanging awkwardly off her right foot.

Trey narrowed his eyes. She didn't look like a ghost.

'Look at the fucking state of it, mate. Do you reckon she was round there shagging that bloke?' Digsby continued as they both watched the woman struggling to stay upright, as she forcefully dragged one foot in front of the other.

'I dunno, she don't look right, does she?' Trey said, pursing his mouth, as he stared at the woman's stilted movements. Walking as if she was in a trance.

'No shit, Sherlock. She looks fucking wasted. Bet she had one too many ciders and then ended up rolling around in the fucking mud with that fella that legged it. Dirty cow. No wonder that bloke did a runner. She don't look the type that you'd want to take home to meet your parents, does she?'

'Something ain't right,' Trey said, straining to get a better look at the woman as she neared closer to them both. 'Is she crying?'

Her face twisted. Contorted with anguish and pain. He realised that she was crying. Her face a mass of blackened mascara-streaked tears, her red lipstick smudged all over her cheek.

Her mouth was moving, too, but her voice was barely a whisper.

Trey strained to hear what she was saying as she came closer, stopping just a few feet away from the two lads.

'Help me,' she whispered, collapsing onto the cold concrete floor at Trey's and Digsby's feet.

The two men looked down at the woman's body splayed out on the ground in front of them.

Even Digsby had the decency to stop talking then, both of them rendered silent as they stared down at the woman; their eyes taking in the streaks of mud that covered most of the skin on her back.

Only it wasn't mud at all they realised, taking a closer look.

It was blood.

Smeared all over her torso, dripping down the backs of her legs. Pooling out onto the floor around her from the thick jagged lacerations that stretched across the woman's back. The deep bloody gouges stripped of flesh.

Trey gagged then. The sight of the woman's body reminded him of a piece of meat you'd see hanging up in a butcher's shop.

Injuries that looked inhumane.

She wasn't moving now. Instead she lay completely still, face down on the cold wet ground.

'Fucking hell.' Trey's voice. High-pitched, laced with panic. Something else too. Terror.

Digsby's voice suddenly pulled him out of his trance-like state.

'Fuck, mate! We better call an ambulance. I think she might be dead.'

CHAPTER THREE

His eyes flickered open and he was quickly startled by the harsh brightness of the room. The glare almost blinding him.

Quickly he closed the lids again, taking a minute to let his vision adjust, before taking his time and slowly reopening them.

He hesitated, at first, as he tried to gather his bearings. Glancing around the strange room that he didn't recognise, flinching when he registered that he wasn't alone. That there was a woman standing next to him.

A face he didn't know, long brown hair twisted into a plait that ran down one of her shoulders. A warm smile spread across her face.

He had no idea who she was.

He was lying in bed, he realised. Only it didn't feel as if it was his at all.

Nothing felt real or familiar. Nothing gave him any feeling of comfort.

'Where am I?' he mumbled, eyes sweeping frantically across the white clinical room in which he lay. The panic inside him magnifying, as a low dull buzzing sound filled his ears, interrupted every few seconds with the loud shrill beeping of machinery.

He was in a hospital room, he figured. Surrounded by medical equipment and monitors.

Wired up to them.

Lifting his arm, he could see the cannula that was taped to his skin. The tubes that led to the intravenous drip on the steel stand the other side of him.

The woman was dressed in sky blue overalls. A nurse?

'I'm in hospital? Why? What happened to me?'

'It's okay...' the woman began, her words of reassurance not matching the concern that etched her face as she looked down at him, and then back to the monitors as he screamed out in pain once again.

Gripping the side of the bed, he experienced the piercing stab of what felt like a thousand needles penetrate his skin all at once. A dull ache rippling through him. Making him wince until it gradually subsided.

'What's happening to me?' he whispered. His voice, unrecognisable even to him. Just a dry, hoarse whisper.

So many questions. So many dark thoughts rattling around inside his brain.

'Why am I here?'

'My name is Nurse Huston. You can call me Marie if you like.' The nurse smiled.

A genuine smile that not only reached her eyes, but made them sparkle. She was staring down at him with so much intensity that it was almost unnerving. 'I've been looking after you. You're at the Chelsea and Westminster Hospital. You're a patient here in our Burns Unit. It's a lot to take in, I know. Here...'

Knowing the shock that her patient would be feeling right now, how disorientated he would be from being in a coma for so many months, Nurse Huston poured a beaker of water and brought it to the patient's lips.

'Have some water. Your mouth must be dry after having the ventilator tube in there.'

The man nodded gratefully as Nurse Huston held the cup to his mouth and tipped it back. He gulped back a large greedy mouthful.

The icy cold feeling as he swallowed it down made him shudder, as his dry, cracked lips soaked up the droplets from the rim of the cup.

'Burns Unit?' he said then, as the woman's words sank in.

Nurse Huston smiled, pleased at the patient's first signs of progress. Not only had he regained consciousness, he was drinking fluids too.

She should call the doctors or her senior nurse, now that the patient had woken. That was procedure; only part of her wanted this moment for herself. It was selfish, she knew that. But she'd been the one tending to this patient for the past nine months.

She just wanted these few first moments before the doctors and nurses would arrive and overwhelm the poor patient with all the technicalities and gory details of his ordeal.

She wanted to be the one to break it to him instead.

To tell him what had happened to him.

He had a right to know.

Taking a seat next to her patient, she was aware how frightened he must be feeling. This was a lot to take in. She kept her voice soft.

'Do you remember anything at all about why you are here?'

The man faltered, silently staring up at the ceiling, obviously deep in thought.

Finally, he shook his head.

'That's okay. How about your name? Can you tell me your name?'

Silence once more.

She watched as the man clenched his fists. The frustration and pain his memory loss caused him were clear to see.

She realised he couldn't remember anything. Not his name, not how he got here.

'It's okay. That's completely normal. You will remember in time.' The nurse reassured him with another warm smile. 'You were involved in an accident. A fire. You were badly injured, I'm afraid, but you're a fighter, let me tell you,' the nurse added with a small laugh. 'You were my very first patient I was assigned, do you know that?'

She thought back to her very first day on the job. How Nurse Langton had led her into the private room of the Intensive Treatment Unit, and she'd first set eyes on this patient. His body so badly burned, so damaged that the doctors had almost given up on him.

She'd honestly never thought that she'd see the day when he would open his eyes and actually speak.

Yet, he'd come through it all. Somehow, against all the odds, he'd survived and the fact that she'd been part of the process of nursing this man better, that she'd actually made a difference, made her feel ecstatically happy. Staring down at the man in the hospital bed now, a flurry of excitement swelled inside of her.

He'd finally regained consciousness.

He was talking. Moving around.

It was for the rare moments like this that Marie had trained to do this job in the first place.

'That was nine months ago now. I've been here every single day, caring for you while you were in a coma. I haven't missed a single day.'

'Nine months?'

Nine months? He'd been in coma for nine months?

She watched as he narrowed his eyes, recognising the pain returning to him. Building inside of him, surging through him.

She winced as he screamed out again, pushing down on the bed, as if to try and force the pain out of him, panic and confusion on his face.

Nurse Huston read his thoughts.

He must be wondering just how horrific his injuries were to cause this much pain nine months on.

'It's okay. You had another skin graft a few days ago. We've just changed your dressings. The pain always feels worse when the air gets to the wounds. I've just upped your morphine levels, so you'll be able to relax again shortly. I've been keeping a close eye on you,' Marie said then, wanting this man to realise that he wasn't alone. Not any more, despite the fact that they still didn't know who he was. He'd had no ID on him when he'd been brought in, and all the staff here had been able to hope for was that someone would try and find the man. That a family member might contact the local hospitals, or the police. But no one had claimed this man as their own. The entire time he'd been here at the hospital not a single soul had come here to visit him. No one had come looking for him.

That was part of the reason Marie had gone above and beyond her duties for this patient. Spending so much time with the man. She'd popped in to see him every single day, regardless, whether or not she was working. Sometimes she even stayed on after her shift, sitting in this chair next to him, reading to him. Or just talking about her day. Marie had started to rely on him, just as he relied on her as his nurse. In a funny way, he had become a confidante to her, especially as he didn't talk back. He just listened to her. That was all she needed.

'What happened to me? How badly injured am I?' the man asked.

He raised his hand and ran his fingers across his face. Flinching as he felt the material that covered his skin, the large gauze patch covering his left eye.

'It's a surgical mask. It helps with the healing process. Not exactly the height of fashion now, mind. So don't you be panicking when you take a look at it, but it does the job, trust me,' Marie said, not wanting to add that it was far less scarier than the alternative; the patient seeing their burned and blistered skin, their face no longer recognisable. The Lycra mask was a much kinder sight to bear.

'My eye?' the man said as he ran his finger further up and touched the pad that covered his eye. Realising then that his vision was slightly impaired.

That he was only looking out from one eye.

He knew even before the nurse spoke.

'I'm really sorry. We couldn't save it,' Nurse Huston said gently, placing her hand on the man's arm as a form of support as she broke the news.

She stared towards the doorway then, making sure that none of her colleagues could hear her talking to the patient so frankly.

The doctors were the ones to break news like this to the patients. Only Marie knew that they wouldn't be as honest and sincere as she would be.

To them, this man would just be another patient.

To her, he'd become so much more than that. She genuinely cared about him.

He deserved to know the truth. The ugly truth, rather than a beautiful lie. Rather than her playing it down.

She wanted him to know from this first moment that she would always be straight with him.

That he could trust her.

He went quiet then, the enormity of what he had just been told sending him into shock, as he lay there, obviously trying to process what he was hearing. 'What happened to me? The fire? How? I don't understand?' He sounded disorientated.

He'd lost an eye.

Gripping the sides of the bed once more, only this time not from pain. This time in a vain attempt to keep the room from spinning so violently.

'We don't know for sure ourselves,' Marie said, as she recalled the facts that had been given to her at the time. 'You were found by a dog walker out by an old abandoned warehouse, in King's Cross. By the old disused railway tracks,' Marie said then, hoping something she said might jog his memory even the slightest bit.

Still, nothing.

She could see by the pained look on his face that the man still had no recollection of his ordeal at all.

'Can I see?' he said.

Marie was apprehensive, peering out of the room into the abandoned corridor; she should really wait for the doctors. They would be able to talk the patient through his exact procedures and the implications of them with much more depth than she could.

But they didn't care about him. Not like her.

Maybe, if she showed him, it would feel less impersonal.

She nodded.

Cautiously, she lifted up the hand mirror and held it out in front of him. Waiting for a few minutes before she spoke again. She watched as he took in the harrowing reflection that stared back at him.

'You've had several surgeries including skin grafts and reconstructive facial surgery. The mask is to speed up the healing process and prevent any infection.'

He lifted up his eye pad then. Forcing himself to see the damage that was there.

He winced. The horror hitting him with full force as he processed how serious his injuries were. The man recoiled at the sight of the jagged, rough line. His eyelid sewn tightly shut.

'It's healed really well,' she said, sensing the shock that the man was feeling right now.

This was the hardest part of her job, she thought. The aftermath. Helping the patient come to terms with catastrophic injuries like this.

'From the fire?'

Nurse Huston shook her head.

'You had other injuries too. Ones that weren't directly linked to the fire,' she said, speaking with caution.

Her patient had a right to know the truth, to know what had really happened to him.

It might trigger his memory.

'We think that you were possibly tortured. Obviously we don't know anything for sure, but you had other injuries inflicted on you that led us to believe that.'

She remembered the conversations at the time between two specialists. Of how the patient's eye injury looked as if it had been caused by a much greater source of direct heat, like a blow torch or something similar. The other injuries that they'd recorded on his notes. The missing teeth, and toenails. The lacerations in his skin.

It was a lot to take in.

'I have to call the doctors in now so that they can check you over and make sure you're doing okay, now that you're conscious again,' Nurse Huston said as she heard the voices floating down from the opposite end of the corridor. 'But I'll be right here. Okay? If you need anything. I'm here.'

The man nodded, understandably dazed. She touched his arm lightly, with such gentleness, before making her way down to the nurses' station to inform the other staff that the patient was conscious again.

Their few stolen moments together over for now.

Her heart was beating rapidly inside her chest.

It was the strangest most wonderful feeling ever, and Marie Huston couldn't even explain it to herself.

But she'd felt it. She was sure of it.

That connection between them both. That link.

Call it fate, or serendipity. Whatever it was, this patient had been brought into Marie Huston's life for a reason, and she into his.

And now that he was awake, she would continue to be there for him in any way that she could.

The poor man still had no idea that he had no one else in the world to look out for him. That he was all alone.

That Marie was all that he had.

CHAPTER FOUR

'You all right, Nan?' Nancy said, smiling at her grandmother, breaking Joanie's trance.

'I am now, girl. Now I've met my beautiful great-granddaughter,' the older woman said, smiling back at her. Taking in the beautiful sight of her granddaughter holding her precious newborn daughter lovingly in her arms.

Scarlett Edel Byrne.

Right at this very moment, Joanie Byrne couldn't have been prouder.

'She's perfect, Nancy. Little Scarlett is just the blessing that this family needs.'

Especially after everything that they'd all been through.

'Motherhood is going to be the making of you, my girl.' Joanie smiled with certainty, watching Nancy place the tiny scratch mittens over Scarlett's small hands, so that the baby wouldn't tear and mark her skin with her tiny fingernails.

'Who fancies a cup of tea?' Michael said, barely able to drag himself away from the delectable sight of his great-granddaughter's presence, now that Jack had brought them both home from the hospital.

Joanie had been on tenterhooks all morning. Ordering the staff about to ensure that the house sparkled from top to bottom. The marble staircase had been swept and polished, the kitchen fully stocked up with all Nancy's favourite foods. Joanie had even instructed one of the gardeners to place some huge urns of red flowers either side of the large arched front door. It was almost as if Joanie was expecting royalty to arrive at the Byrnes' residence here in Richmond, not Nancy and her baby. Though the woman's excitement over their first great-grandchild coming home had been infectious; a completely new feeling for Michael.

'Tea?' Jack laughed. 'I think this one here deserves a bottle of champagne, after all the hard work she put in giving birth to our daughter last night,' he said proudly, shooting an admiring glance over to Nancy. Glad that their secret was finally out.

That the rest of the Byrne clan now knew he was Scarlett's father.

He understood why Nancy had wanted to keep it a secret from the family. Not telling a single soul that he was the father.

It was complicated. Scarlett was the result of one passionate night, a one-night stand in effect.

Though if Nancy would give him half the chance, Jack could be so much more to her. There would be nothing greater he could wish for than to be with Nancy, but he knew that he had to respect Nancy's wishes. She didn't see him that way.

Why would she?

He was more than double her age. A middle-aged friend of her father's. Jack had been on her father's payroll as a bent copper, way back when Nancy was born. Since then, he'd come into his own. Working his way up the ranks as a DCI for the Met. He'd been part of the family for years.

Jack was more like an uncle to her than anything else.

As far as Nancy was concerned, what had happened between them that night had all been one big mistake. A mistake that she'd initiated in a moment of weakness. All they could do now was pick up the pieces and be the best parents that they could be for Scarlett's sake.

Nancy hadn't told her family about him because she hadn't wanted any of their opinions or their negativity about her not being with him forced upon her.

Or worse than that, the opposite reaction, and Nancy's mother and grandparents turning against him. That they'd think he took advantage of her.

Though she needn't have worried about what any of them thought. Scarlett was here now, and the family seemed to have willingly accepted the news.

Whether they liked it or not, nothing was going to change the fact that Jack was Scarlett's father. And he was going to be the best dad that his daughter could ever wish for. He'd silently vowed that to himself when he'd first held his little girl in his arms, just minutes after she'd been born.

He would do whatever it took, whatever was needed, to see that Scarlett and Nancy wanted for nothing now. Even though he and Nancy weren't together, they were going to bring the child up together, as one unit. As a family – however unconventional that seemed to the rest of the Byrne clan, and Christ knew this lot knew how to do unconventional.

'You know she can't drink alcohol, Jack,' Colleen scolded the man. 'She's breastfeeding.'

'Yeah, Jack!' Nancy laughed, wagging her finger at him playfully. Knowing that Colleen didn't mean any harm in her reproach. She was just looking out for Scarlett. They all were. 'It's all right, Colleen. He's only teasing me. He knows I'm gagging for a drink, after being teetotal for the last nine months. But you all should have some. I insist. We need to wet the baby's head. It's good luck, isn't it? And we could all well and truly do with some of that.'

'Well, in that case, I say we get a couple of bottles.' Michael Byrne chuckled, not needing to be told twice, and got to his feet. 'Come on, Jack, Nancy's right, it's tradition. Let's go and pick up some supplies and leave the ladies to coo over little Miss Scarlett here.'

Jack smiled, checking with Nancy that it was okay. Nancy nodded.

'Go on. I'll be fine,' she insisted. Knowing that Jack was being more protective than ever of her now that she was officially the mother of his child.

It was a good feeling, she realised. Knowing that he was consciously looking out for her. That he actually cared. She just hoped that his enthusiasm lasted. Not every dad stuck around and faced their responsibilities. Though she was certain that Jack would.

Of course they should all be celebrating.

Today was the happiest day of Nancy's life. Scarlett may not have been planned, but she was very much wanted and loved by them all.

Staring down at her precious little daughter, her tiny strands of dark auburn hair on her head, eyes tightly shut as she slept, her chest rising and falling with each gentle, peaceful breath, Nancy had never seen anything more perfect in her life.

'God, I can't stop staring at her, Nan! It's like I'm obsessed or something. She almost doesn't feel real.' She giggled, after the men had left.

She sat back in the chair, still dazed at the fact she was a mother now, that this tiny baby that lay in her arms was her child. Her responsibility for the rest of her days. She wondered when it would ever really sink in.

Right now it felt like the most perfect dream.

'That's only natural,' Joanie said expertly. 'I remember being the same with your father,' she said, the sudden memory twisting at her heart. The ache inside her would never dull. She remembered it like it was yesterday. All those years ago, how she'd first looked down at her boy, Jimmy. How she'd felt the same surge of love for her child, just as Nancy was feeling for her own baby now.

The fact that he was dead in the ground hurt her heart.

That her son had gone before her would never sit right with Joanie. No child should ever go before their parents.

Oh, the endless, unforgiving, bittersweet circle of life.

Forcing back her tears, she vowed she wouldn't cry. Today was a happy day.

'I'm so glad you're home, Nan,' Nancy said, moving up closer to her nan on the sofa and placing her hand affectionately on top of hers. 'This place hasn't been the same without you. I couldn't have imagined bringing Scarlett back here without you being here to see her, Nan.'

'And I wouldn't have missed this for the world,' Joanie said now, the determination in her voice apparent. Glad to finally be home herself after spending the past eight months in a private psychiatric hospital.

In truth, she'd been ready to come home months ago, only she'd insisted on staying there a while longer than she needed to. Determined to get her head together properly. To have the time she needed to grieve properly for her son.

The specialists had told her that she'd had a mental breakdown and Joanie had been scared witless that she'd never get back to normal again. Only, somehow she had. She'd become strong again. Almost back to her old self, though not completely.

A part of her would always be broken now that Jimmy was gone.

The hospital had helped her greatly. Not only to heal, but in other ways too.

Joanie had started to remember things.

Things that had seemed so absurd and misconstrued inside her mind.

Things that she'd thought she'd conjured up in her own head, only she knew now with clarity she hadn't imagined anything.

Everything had suddenly become crystal clear.

She was back now. Home. Exactly where she belonged. And Joanie had no intention of going anywhere anytime soon.

'Jesus, would you look at all these flowers and balloons,' Colleen said, flapping around the place, tidying as she went to make room for all the vases of flowers everywhere. 'The place looks like a florist.'

She smiled then at her own words. Her eyes shining with fresh tears that she didn't need to explain to Joanie and Nancy.

She'd grown up in a florist. Those days had been the happiest days of her life. Flowers were her constant reminder of her dear old mum, Edel. Every time she looked at beautiful floral bouquets and neatly arranged potted plants, she couldn't help but think of the woman. Oh, how her mother would have loved to have met little Scarlett. She'd be beaming with pride up there in Heaven now, knowing that Nancy had named the beautiful child after her.

'Would you ever sit down, Colleen? Flying about the place like a blue arsed fly. You're making me dizzy, woman,' Joanie said, a glimmer of amusement on her lips.

Purposely ignoring Colleen's obvious grief.

Ignoring the fact that since Colleen had arrived here today, she hadn't even been able to look Joanie in the eye. Not once.

She was glad that the woman was seemingly nervous in her company.

And so she should well be.

Still, right now wasn't the time or the place for her to put the woman to rights. This was Nancy's and Scarlett's moment. Joanie wasn't going to spoil that for the girl.

Colleen's time would come, and Joanie had a feeling that the woman knew it too.

'Jack certainly hasn't scrimped on spoiling his two girls,' Joanie quipped, eyeing the beautiful bouquets of flowers and pink balloons. She was glad that the man seemed to be stepping up and taking his responsibilities seriously.

The revelation that Jack was Scarlett's father may have left Colleen lost for words, but personally Joanie could have called it months ago. She'd had her suspicions about Nancy and Jack for a while now. From way back after her Jimmy's funeral, when she'd seen them both together in the kitchen after Nancy had been attacked.

Jack had always watched out for this family, and Joanie knew in her heart of hearts the man wouldn't do wrong by Nancy. The girl could have done a lot worse; Joanie only had to look at her Michael to know that much.

'He's only got one girl, Nan, and that's Scarlett. We're not together. I keep telling you all that,' Nancy said, sounding almost defensive as she repeated herself for what felt like the umpteenth time.

'Whatever you say!' Joanie said waving her hand in the air; she winked at Nancy, as if she knew better.

Which, of course, she did. Always.

She'd seen the way Jack had looked at Nancy. The way that the man acted when he was in her company. He was besotted with her, and Joanie was sure that Nancy felt the same.

Though the pair of them were adamant that they weren't together. That they were purely friends and that they were going to bring the child up together without the added complications of a relationship.

Joanie would give that little notion six months max, before they both realised that they had it bad for each other. She'd lay her pension on it in fact.

Nancy was an attractive girl; she gained attention from men wherever she went, but it was different with Jack. It wasn't just lust that Joanie saw in the man's eyes. Jack genuinely cared for

Nancy. He loved her, and it was only a matter of time before Nancy worked that out too.

'Can I hold her, Nancy?' Colleen said then quietly. Staring down at the small baby as if she was the most delicate, precious thing in the whole wide world.

She'd been dying to ask Nancy if she could hold her, only she was frightened that Nancy wouldn't let her.

Frightened that the girl wouldn't allow her to be part of her grandchild's life.

But Nancy had no intention of being so petty.

'Sure,' Nancy said, passing the baby to her mother. She watched as Colleen stared down at the child, besotted.

'Oh, Nancy. She looks just like you when you were born.' Colleen spoke softly. Tears brimming in her eyes. 'Doesn't she, Joanie? She's the absolute image of her.'

Joanie nodded, her eyes narrow, as they fixed on Colleen.

So far, since she'd been home, she'd managed to control her temper with the woman. God knows how, but somehow she had.

Now wasn't the time to air her grievances, and grievances was an understatement.

There would be time for that later.

'I'm so proud of you, Nancy. You're going to be a great mother, and Jack will be a great father.'

'I hope so,' Nancy said. 'I know that it's not the norm, me and Jack doing things like this. But it just happened, and now that Scarlett is here, well, everything feels… I don't know. Better?'

Colleen knew just what Nancy meant.

She had a true purpose in life now.

No longer living solely to work, she was a mother. A child changed everything. Scarlett would bring Nancy joys that Nancy never knew existed.

'A little girl is just the thing you need, Nancy. You can step back from the business now, and concentrate on being a mum,' Colleen said, still gazing at the child with wonder.

'Why would I step back, Colleen?' Nancy said then, unable to hide the defensiveness in her tone. 'If anything I'll be working even harder. Especially now I have this one to provide for. I can do both you know.'

'I don't doubt that, Nancy,' Colleen said tentatively, aware that she was treading on thin ice when it came to offering Nancy any form of advice. The girl had no interest in her mother's thoughts or opinions.

'It's just… you're a mum now. Running brothels and Christ knows what else, it just doesn't seem right.'

'Oh, please!' Nancy said, shaking her head, annoyed that her mother would make an assumption simply because she was a woman. 'This is 2004, Colleen. I can be a mother *and* a businesswoman.'

'A businesswoman? Is that what you call it?' Colleen said, unable to help herself.

Nancy had taken over the empire that Jimmy had built, and Colleen knew all about that sordid world. The drugs, the brothels and the working girls. All of it hidden underneath a facade of the properties that they invested in and the fancy charity events that they attended, contributing large amounts of money to keep all the bigwigs sweet.

It was a dark and sordid world, and all the Byrnes' money was ill-gotten gains, that was the truth of the matter.

'It's hardly a world for a little girl to grow up in.'

'But it was good enough for me, right?' Nancy spat.

'Of course you can do both, Nancy. And being a mum is truly the most rewarding job in the world,' Joanie said, with a smile. Trying to ease the tension that was building between the two women.

'The most tiring job, too,' she laughed, catching Nancy stifling yet another yawn. 'Why don't you take the little one and go and get an hour's sleep? We'll put the champagne on ice when the boys get back, and have it when you're more rested,' Joanie said. 'Hospitals are never good for getting any sleep in. All the noises and nurses checking up on you every five minutes. You need your own bed.'

'You know what, I think I will,' Nancy said, only too glad to get away from her condescending mother. Not only that, but the idea of getting into bed and catching up on some sleep sounded like just what she needed. 'Don't let me sleep for too long though; I won't sleep tonight otherwise.'

'Get it while you can. You'll be lucky if you get a decent night's sleep now for months,' Colleen piped up again, nodding knowingly at Scarlett. 'This one might look the picture of innocence, but she'll soon have you exhausted.'

'I'll see you in a little while,' Nancy said, taking her child from her mother's arms, and doing as the two women advised.

Joanie waited then. Watching as her granddaughter carried her great-granddaughter from the room and closed the door behind her.

Then she eyed Colleen.

The woman's expression so full of raw emotion from holding her granddaughter for the very first time. Her eyes still wet with fresh tears.

'Oh, you play a good game, Colleen, I'll give you that,' Joanie said, glaring at the woman, her eyes colder than steel.

'What do you mean?' Colleen said, face visibly paling as she stared at the old lady.

She'd been waiting for this, convinced that the first moment they had alone together, Joanie Byrne would pull her up.

'You know exactly what I mean!' Joanie said, sitting back in her chair. Looking as bolshy as ever, as if she'd never been ill.

'Though, unlike you and your dramas, I won't be letting our little discrepancy ruin Nancy's day. This will keep,' Joanie said then. 'But you see all this, you living here in this house…' Joanie shook her head, defiantly, 'this won't be happening. After everything you've done, I want you out and I'm going to make damn sure that it happens too.'

She got up off the chair and left the room as Colleen sat down. Already defeated, rendered silent now by the venom in her mother-in-law's words.

Colleen stared around the empty room, left in no doubt that Joanie Byrne knew.

She knew everything.

Joanie Byrne was well and truly back, which meant that Colleen was now in for a whole world of shit.

CHAPTER FIVE

Sitting in Alfie Harris's kitchen, as Jennifer Dawson busied herself making them all a coffee, Nancy took in all the boxes stacked up around the room.

Moving, perhaps?

She wasn't about to pry. But still, she couldn't help but wonder what this was all about.

Alfie Harris suddenly summoning her here today, out of the blue?

She'd been nervous at first, given the history between them. She'd figured that perhaps Alfie had some kind of axe to grind with her, and she'd only managed to relax when Jennifer had greeted her on arrival. Opening the front door to her with a friendly hug and an offer of coffee because Alfie was running late.

'How's Megan doing?' Nancy asked, then. Figuring she was safer asking Jennifer this question than Alfie. Even if she was almost too scared to hear the answer.

It had been a year now since Megan's drink had been spiked with an overdose at The Karma Club.

'She's doing amazing, Nancy,' Jennifer Dawson said, placing the steaming hot mug down in front of Nancy, and taking a seat beside her. 'She's almost back to her old self.' She smiled then. 'It's been a really long, tough journey for Alfie, but it's changed him for the better in some ways. It's brought them closer.'

Nancy nodded, recognising the love in the woman's voice, the fact that she genuinely seemed to care about Alfie and his daughter.

She decided that she liked this woman very much. Jennifer wasn't like most of the women that latched onto men like Alfie Harris. She was a keeper, and judging by the huge sparkly rock on the woman's finger, Alfie had been wise to spot those qualities in the woman too.

'And you're a mother now, too, so I hear?'

Nancy nodded, smiling then, as she thought about her gorgeous baby daughter, how precious little Scarlett was to her, and was once again consumed by guilt at her involvement in poor Megan Harris's harrowing situation.

'I am, indeed. She's an angel. Barely even two months old and already showing so much personality.'

'Ahh, I bet she's beautiful,' Jennifer said warmly, just as Alfie Harris strolled into the room.

'Nancy!' Alfie said offering a smile to the woman, letting Nancy know that she was here on good terms, whatever they may be.

He planted a kiss on Jennifer's cheek, saying, 'Sorry I'm late. I was just dropping Megan over to a friend's house. The traffic out there is dire.'

'Jennifer was just filling me in. She said that Megan's doing really well? I'm so happy to hear that, Alfie. Truly,' Nancy said, genuinely.

'She's done amazing. Really amazing.' Alfie nodded.

Neither of them mentioned the elephant in the room between them.

Nancy's brother, Daniel.

Nancy had thought about asking Alfie. Enquiring as to what had happened to him on that fateful night that she'd given her brother up for his reprisal, when she'd handed Daniel over and let him take the fall for what happened to Megan.

Only she knew better than to start asking questions.

They'd made a deal. Nancy had served up her brother to the man and Alfie had taken care of the rest.

He'd got rid of Daniel once and for all, and Nancy didn't need to know the ins and outs of it all.

Daniel was gone, just as she'd wanted. They'd both got their revenge.

'That's why I asked you here today actually. We've got some big changes ahead of us.' He indicated all the boxes.

'You're moving?' Nancy asked.

Alfie Harris nodded.

'We are indeed. Out of the country. London isn't for us anymore. We're off to sunnier climates, ain't we, babe?' he said, taking Jennifer's hand, and squeezing it tightly.

'We're moving abroad, to Spain. The three of us, starting afresh. Megan's really excited about it, in fact. It's just what we all need.'

Nancy smiled. She could understand that. Though she still had no idea why Alfie had asked her here today if everything was going so well.

'I want to sell the club, Nancy. To you, if you'll have it?'

Nancy raised her eyes, taken aback.

Not sure what she'd been expecting today, but being offered to buy out The Karma Club had certainly not been it.

'You want to sell it to me?' Nancy said, then. Unsure what to say.

A year and a half after opening, The Karma Club remained one of London's biggest on the clubbing scene. The venue was a sensation, drawing in A-list celebrities and the best DJs from all around the world. And Alfie Harris had raked in a fortune from the place.

'I'm putting my girls first,' he said then, as if reading her mind. 'The club has been one of my greatest successes, but I hate it, Nancy. I hate being there, I hate what it represents. I hate that I have to think about what happened to my Megan every time I walk through those doors. And that I'm just waiting for it to happen again, to some other poor unsuspecting young girl. Because it's only a matter of time, isn't it? Drugs and clubs go hand in hand.'

Alfie Harris shook his head.

'Gem Kemal's been running the place for me. And for a while it was all going smoothly; though lately I've had word that he's got himself involved with some fucking scrotes. Some lads from Manchester that think they are the big I am. They're all about Ecstasy and acid. They've been causing a bit of trouble here and there.'

Alfie drank his coffee, his expression deadly serious.

'And do you know what? I haven't got the fucking energy to deal with the fuckers. I'm happy just to walk away from it all.' He laughed then. 'I never thought I'd say that. Maybe I'm getting old, eh!'

He winked at Jennifer. The age gap between them had always been their little joke.

'The truth of the matter is, my heart isn't in it anymore. But I don't want that place to turn to shit. Not after how hard I worked to get it where it is today. I want someone who can run the club as it should be. Someone who isn't afraid to get their hands dirty and take care of the shit that needs sorting. Someone like you.'

'Me?' Nancy said, remembering only too well the deal she'd made with Gem Kemal.

She'd handed the man all her father's contacts for his drug runs and he had been using all the drop-off points to bring gear into the country and sell it in the club. Seemingly behind Alfie Harris's back. Though from what Alfie had just told her, Gem Kemal was making his own way in the world now and he was no longer being inconspicuous about it either.

That wasn't a good sign.

'Who are the Mancs? Do you know?'

Alfie smirked.

'Some fucking wide boys, plastic gangsters. You know the type. Their chat is much louder than their presence, let's put it that way. And Gem's in deeper than he cares to admit with them. Between the lot of them they are going to run that place into the fucking ground.'

Nancy nodded, getting a clearer picture of what was being offered here. It didn't sound like it would be plain sailing. There was work to be done, and a huge fucking problem to sort out in the process.

Alfie Harris could sense her doubt.

'I want to do a good deal on the place, Nancy. With you, because I trust you.'

Nancy sipped her coffee. Swallowing it down, along with her guilt.

Her heart was hammering inside her chest. He trusted her. After all the lies, all the deceit.

'It's a lot to think about,' Nancy said, wondering if perhaps she should run this by Jack. Though she already knew his thoughts on the matter. How he thought she was mental just to hand over the drugs side of the business to someone like Gem Kemal.

Jack had always thought she'd acted in haste, making that decision without running it past any of them. Handing her father's business, the business that he and Alex Costa had built up over decades, to some Turkish degenerate in a moment of fucking madness.

Though of course she had her reasons, reasons that Jack didn't know about nor would he understand.

She'd told Gem he could have it all. That he could run the drugs side of it, and that she'd wanted no part of any of it. Her father's business that he'd built up from nothing – he'd made himself and the rest of the family an empire – and through guilt and fear of what she'd done to poor, young Megan Harris. Nancy had been so desperate to cut Daniel out, to get her revenge on her brother that she hadn't thought that anyone else would get caught up in the crossfire. When Nancy had heard about Megan, about the child being in a coma from an Ecstasy overdose, she had been willing to walk away from it all. So consumed by her guilt, that she'd been willing to cut off such a lucrative supply of money for them all.

And now, Alfie Harris was giving her the chance to get it all back and then some.

The drugs *and* the club. Nancy could have it all.

The properties she had in her name now, inherited from her father, and the brothels she ran all pulled in a substantial income, but the truth was, their income had taken a huge loss by cutting out the drugs side of the business.

'Can I have some time to think about it?'

Alfie Harris shrugged. Showing his irritation.

'Time is something I don't have, Nancy. We're leaving in a couple of weeks. Tell you what, let's talk figures, and then maybe you'll have a better idea about how serious I am. I want the club off my hands, and I need it sorted out ASAP. You'd be a fool not to bite my arm off for it.'

Nancy nodded. Alfie Harris was offering her a serious earner here. A goldmine, in fact, and the mere fact that she was even considering turning down such an honour was a huge insult to the man.

The club would bring enormous revenue, and Gem Kemal and these Mancs that were hanging around the place would be easily sorted.

It was a no-brainer when she thought about it. Adding The Karma Club to her already expanding list of properties and brothels, getting the drug runs back, too, would be just the thing to put the Byrnes back on top, where they belonged.

Nancy smiled then, a genuine one this time, as she nodded.

'Well, in that case, Alfie, consider me all ears. Let's talk business.'

CHAPTER SIX

Gem Kemal stared at the scene in front of him with a look of horror on his face.

His head barman was sprawled out on the floor of the main bar, a cut on his forehead, blood running from his nose. His once white shirt was now peppered with a spray of deep dark red. Paul Charlton and his men stepped over him, helping themselves to drinks from the optics.

This was getting way out of control now.

It was all too much.

'What the fuck have you done to him?' Gem said, crouching to the floor and checking for any signs of life. Thinking the worst, that these men had killed him, he was relieved when he felt the man's pulse throbbing beneath his fingertips.

'Ahh, come on, our kid. It's no mither, Gem. The bloke was just being a fucking wanker, so I had to have a word with him, didn't I!' Paul Charlton said, rolling his eyes at the lads all sitting at the bar who smirked alongside him, all of them drunk and drugged out of their minds. And despite the fact that the club had closed two hours ago, none of them looked as if they were prepared to call it a night anytime soon.

'I've got to close up, Paul,' Gem said, his voice sounding almost pitiful.

He'd meant to sound harder, in control, only he sounded as if he was asking for permission instead.

Which only made Paul Charlton play up to the fact.

'Home to your lovely wife, and those three kiddos of yours? Oh come on, Gem, relax mate. Lighten up. We're having a little private party. Come on, stay. Have some fucking fun for once. You had a laugh the other night, didn't you?!' Paul smirked then, as Gem looked down at the floor, ashamed of himself, trying to push the other night from his memory completely.

He still didn't know how it had happened; how he'd managed to get so drunk.

How he'd even contemplated cheating on Miyra with another woman.

Though *woman* was a bit of an exaggeration; the girl he'd had sex with had been seventeen at the most. Not even old enough to legally be in the club, he suspected.

And the only reason Gem even remembered what she looked like was because Paul had been winding him up, showing him the video of their steamy little encounter up against the bar that he'd filmed on his phone.

It was evidence to use against him. Paul Charlton hadn't said as much, but the underlying threat had been there and they both knew it.

The video was Paul Charlton's ticket now to do and act as he pleased and what was Gem going to do about it?

Say no, and risk his wife finding out all his dirty secrets?

Lose his family, for the sake of what? A few private parties, and few rounds of free drinks.

Though this lot would soon drink the club out of alcohol at the rate they were going at it.

'Come on, lads. Not tonight, Paul, mate…'

Paul Charlton laughed once more, the cocaine he'd just snorted hitting him with its full force.

Wired now, he had no intention of going anywhere and Gem Kemal was finally about to learn that they were anything but mates.

The past few weeks he'd spent buttering the cunt up, to get his foot in the door, had worked.

Gem Kemal was too thick and too arrogant to work out that the only thing Paul wanted was in on this club, and tonight he was going to make sure that this fat Turk in front of him finally realised the score.

'See, here's the thing "mate". See our kid, there. He's my pal, and so's he. And him,' Paul Charlton said pointing to his friends all standing around the bar. 'You, you're nothing more than a divvy cunt.' Picking up the bottle of beer, he smashed it down onto the bar top, before turning and embedding it into Gem's face.

Screaming in agony then, Gem Kemal dropped to the floor.

The pain in his left cheek, just under his eye, horrific.

Though his first thought was, thank God it had missed his eye.

His second, was that no one was coming to his aid.

They all just stood around him then, laughing and drinking and making jibes about him, calling him names.

Not giving a shit that his face was carved up.

Even the group of young girls that the lads had invited to stay in the club with them, none of them seemed to care.

They were all too drunk and drugged up to give a fuck.

And as Paul Charlton began repeatedly kicking the crap out of him, punting him in the stomach with his foot, Gem Kemal realised that he'd made a very grave mistake trying to befriend this psychopath, in the hope that he could bring in some more muscle into the club, now that he was coining in the money from his drug distribution.

But his generous offer of bringing Paul and his men in with him, to let them be part of the club, was being used against him.

He was now at Paul Charlton's mercy.

*

As the lights turned on and the club was lit up with a harsh bright yellow hue, Paul Charlton finally left Gem Kemal alone.

Thinking that it was the police, at first, he stepped back from the Turk's now battered body, eyeing the figure standing in the doorway.

Seeing the attractive redhead standing there, Paul Charlton instantly relaxed.

'Can I help you, darling? You taken a wrong turn or something? Only this is a private party,' he said. She was a bit too posh-looking for his type, but he liked a bit of variety every now and then. 'Though, I'm all up for you being my plus one!'

'Oh, I do love a party!' Nancy Byrne said with a wry grin, before staring down at the bloody mess on the floor, which she recognised to be Gem Kemal.

The man looked as if he'd already taken a beating, and judging by the horrific state of him, Nancy had turned up just in time.

She might be turfing him out of the club tonight, but in doing so she'd save his life.

Small mercies and all that.

'In fact, I've got just the thing you boys need to really get this party going.'

She looked at Paul Charlton then, keeping eye contact, letting him know that he didn't intimidate her. Not one bit.

'Oh, is that so. Sounds interesting,' Paul Charlton said, still trying to work out who this cocky bird was. Glad that she seemed so up for it.

Nancy nodded.

Alfie Harris had been right about these lads being plastic gangsters. They didn't have a clue who they were messing with.

It would be their biggest downfall.

This lot really did make a lot of noise, but they were all mouth. With no knowledge or kudos to back any of it up with.

Stepping aside, Nancy let her workforce of trusty men walk into the room before her. Jack Taylor too.

All of them tooled up, and ready to take these fuckers down.

Nancy followed them into the room.

Instantly sobering up now, Paul Charlton realised that this was trouble.

Unprepared for the fallout, all he could do was front it out.

'And who the fuck are you lot then?' he said, clearly wondering what was going on here, wondering if Gem, the sly fucker, had somehow managed to call for backup.

'I'm the owner, babe!' Nancy said then, smiling now that the formal introductions had been made. That was all this piece of shit needed to know.

'And I'm here to get every one of you skanky pieces of shit out of *my* club.'

PART TWO
2008

CHAPTER SEVEN

'I don't bloody believe it.' Holding the phone to her ear, as it rang continuously, Nancy Byrne was seriously pissed off.

'That's just great, isn't it! I paid top whack for a decent company to come in, only to end up with a bunch of cowboys. They only installed the new system this morning. Did they not even bother to check it was working before they left?'

'It was all working, Nancy,' Bridget Williams said earnestly, hoping that Nancy didn't somehow blame her. She should have checked, she knew that now. But she'd been so busy unpacking the mountains of boxes that were all stacked up around her that she barely had time to think straight let alone babysit the workmen who were on the premises too.

Besides, like Nancy, she figured that the company knew what they were doing.

They were specialists after all.

'Maybe it's just a fault with the system?'

'No shit, Sherlock!' Nancy said raising her eyes at Bridget's glaringly obvious diagnosis. Then realising that she was taking out her bad mood on her friend, she added, 'Shit, I'm sorry, Bridge. It's not your fault. I'm just so stressed out right now. This system's cost me thousands and already on the first day it's gone on the blink. I haven't got time for all this! I've got so much to do…'

Bridget nodded. She understood. Nancy was under it.

They all were, but it was her friend that had everything riding on the place.

Nancy had invested so much of her time and money into the project and since the renovations had started, the fancy Mayfair house had taken on a complete life of its own, becoming bigger and better than any of them could have imagined.

Of all the vast businesses that she ran, The Karma Club, the drug running, the numerous properties she'd invested in that were dotted all over London, the house was truly hers. Her baby.

Having known for years that her father and Alex Costa ran what had been, to all intents and purposes, seedy brothels, this was finally Nancy's chance to give these girls that worked for her something so much more than that.

Somewhere to be proud of, just as she was too.

The place was shaping up to be every bit as spectacular as Nancy had envisaged. All eight large double bedrooms had been fitted with luxury en suites, roll-top baths for two, and shower rooms in each one. As well as numerous reception rooms and a big sweeping staircase that took up the entire main entrance hall. The basement had been completely remodelled too. So much so, that it looked like a state of the art spa, with its Grecian-inspired decor, a hydrotherapy pool surrounded by a host of private steam rooms and saunas, along with a fully kitted out gymnasium.

Nancy wasn't just running a brothel anymore, she was offering her punters an exclusive, luxury private members' club, with a fully stocked champagne bar, and an onsite chef providing a fancy menu of meals and snacks for the punters during their stay.

Nancy had gone all out, transforming the house into something spectacular, employing only the best girls in the trade and ensuring that they were all trained in numerous therapies, like Hot Stone Therapies and Thai Massage. She wanted to give the customers the ultimate five-star experience, so that the clients would be completely relaxed. All of which would be followed by a very happy ending. That, of course, went as standard.

'I take it we paid them already?'

Bridget nodded, which only made Nancy sigh.

'Of course we have.'

'Hey, chill. You're probably worrying about nothing. It's an oversight that's all. And the reason you can't get anyone on the phone is because it's Friday night,' Jack Taylor said then, wading into the conversation and trying to calm Nancy down, as he placed the last of the boxes from the removal van in the corner of the kitchen. He knew full well that the woman had a lot on her plate lately with trying to get this place up and running in time for next week's grand opening. To say that Nancy was stressed out was a major understatement. 'You're not going to get hold of them at this time of the evening. They've probably all got a life, Nance. Not everyone is a workaholic like you.' Jack grinned, teasing Nancy, hoping to lighten the mood; though the look on Nancy's face soon told him that she wasn't in the mood for Jack's jibes tonight.

No matter how playfully he meant them.

'Well, that's not good enough,' she declared, picking up the phone once more and trying the number one more time. Determined to get hold of someone tonight. 'We paid them to do a job, and they haven't bloody done it. So they can either get their arses back out here and get it sorted out pronto, or I'll get a more capable company in and bill these cowboys accordingly.'

She waited. Listening to the dial tone.

Still nothing.

'Look, it's only one night. I'll call them first thing in the morning and get it sorted, okay? I promise,' Bridget said, feeling guilty that she hadn't been thorough enough to check the system before she'd handed over the money.

'Well, I suppose we haven't got much of a choice, have we?'

Throwing the cordless phone down on the kitchen side, Nancy grabbed the bottle of wine from the end of the counter. It was lukewarm. She didn't care. After the day she'd had, she needed a drink.

Not bothering to waste time searching through the stacks of boxes all around them that still needed to be unpacked, she held up three china mugs.

'Cup of wine anyone?'

'Oh, go on then.' Bridget smiled, gratefully, secretly hoping that a drink might chill Nancy out a bit. The woman was like the walking Antichrist lately, and Bridget more than understood why. This place might have set her back a small fortune but money these days wasn't an object to Nancy. No, the woman was a perfectionist when it came to making sure everything was done just as she'd envisaged, and she'd pay way over the odds if she had to, in order to get it done her way.

Bridget and Jack had done as much as they could to try and help her out, so that they could take a bit of the pressure off her, but the woman looked fit to kill this evening.

'Good, all this moving malarkey has left me gasping.' Nancy raised her eyes to Jack, hoping that he'd stick around for a drink too. Christ knows the man had earned it today, lugging the entire contents of Bridge Street over here in the removal van for them.

Only he shook his head.

'Not for me thanks. I've got plans this evening.'

Nancy nodded.

It was her time to tease now.

'Of course you do. Who's the lucky lady tonight then, Casanova?'

'Just a dinner date, nothing serious,' Jack said, visibly uncomfortable then. Unsure if he could sense an undercurrent to Nancy's tone. 'I can cancel if you want? I don't mind. If you want me to stay here? If you're worried about the place?'

'No, it's fine. Don't change your plans on my account.'

'Look why don't I just stay here tonight?' Bridget interrupted. Staring at all the tea chests piled high around them, their contents – the accessories and finishing touches for the place – still packed away neatly inside each one. 'It'll probably take me half the night to sort this lot out anyway.' Bridget had been hoping to rope some of the girls in to helping her unpack, though none of them had been anywhere to be seen this evening.

They were all too busy off out celebrating, saying goodbye to Bridge Street, and hello to this new, swanky place instead.

The only girl who'd bothered to stay behind was Felicity, who was currently upstairs, doing the mammoth task of sorting out all the bedding for each of the bedrooms, bless her.

'Here, tell you what, pour a mug out for Felicity too. I'll take one up for her and see if I can bribe her into staying on a bit later and giving me a hand. Honestly, it's no problem, Nancy. I can keep an eye on the house. You've got nothing to worry about.'

'Are you sure?' Nancy glanced up at the clock. 'Shit, is that the time already? There's still so much to do, but I promised Scarlett I'd be home in time to have dinner with her and read her a bedtime story. I can't cancel on her again this week. I've barely seen her as it is,' Nancy said, recalling the previous night's conversation with Colleen, when her interfering mother had got on the phone and read her the riot act. Berating Nancy for working all hours that God sent when she had a child waiting for her at home.

Nancy's only saving grace was that her mother had made the decision to move out a few years back, declaring that Nancy could probably use the space; though Colleen still came to the house every day and helped out with Scarlett. Thankfully the woman had gone back to her own flat by the time Nancy got home at night, which suited Nancy just fine.

Colleen was the last person Nancy would take parenting advice from, but her mother had informed her that Scarlett had been inconsolable when Nancy hadn't come home in time to tuck her into bed like she promised, and for once Nancy couldn't argue with that.

She'd been working around the clock lately trying to get this place ready, and it wasn't fair on Scarlett. She had barely seen the child all week.

She couldn't let her down again tonight.

Downing her wine, she felt irritated again.

The pressure of running a business and being a mother. Worse still, being lectured about motherhood from Colleen, of all people, was the ultimate insult as far as Nancy was concerned. The woman seemed to constantly pull Nancy up on the way she was raising Scarlett, seemingly having a knack for making her feel guilty for working as hard as she did.

It was a hard task to maintain a balance in her life. Juggling work and being a mum. A constant battle that she never seemed to get right.

Someone had to work though. That was what Colleen just didn't get.

The woman didn't have a clue how important Nancy's work was to her.

How much this business that her father had built for himself, for all of them meant to her.

And ultimately, this was all *for* Scarlett.

Her mother seemed to completely miss that point. Scarlett was the reason Nancy was doing this in the first place; she was the reason she was working her arse off.

This place would one day be her daughter's legacy, just as Nancy's father had bestowed his legacy to her.

Yet all Colleen harped on about was the time that Nancy was missing out on with Scarlett, the moments that she'd never get back.

What galled Nancy more than anything was that Colleen was right. Nancy needed to make more time for her daughter, she knew that, and she was determined not to screw up for a second night in a row. For Scarlett's sake. And her own too. The last thing she needed right now was another call from her mother, another reading of the riot act. She could do without that earache again, especially after the day she'd just had.

'Course I'm sure. I wouldn't offer otherwise. Besides, as of tomorrow I'll be officially living here anyway. What's one night earlier?' Bridget grinned, only too happy to make tonight her official moving in night. She was still positively beaming over the fact that she was going to be living in this house. After spending the past four years running Bridge Street alongside Nancy, she'd been over the moon when she'd heard that Nancy was buying up this place.

A posh mansion in Mayfair – and posh was an understatement. The house was a palace in comparison to what Bridget had been used to. With its long winding driveway at the front of the property, the place was set back from the road enough so that they would get the privacy that they needed with an establishment like this.

Which is one of the reasons Nancy had bought it in the first place she figured.

'A Champneys for misfits', that's how Nancy had described it to Bridget when she'd first talked the woman into running this place for her. And when Nancy had offered Bridget the chance to live in too, Bridget had almost bitten the woman's arm off for the opportunity.

The two women had struck up an unusual friendship over the past four years, despite being so completely opposite. There was

Nancy, with her fancy, private school education. Well-spoken, dressed in head-to-toe designer clobber. Hard around the edges and didn't take any shit from anyone. Whereas with Bridget, what you saw was what you got. She wore her heart on her sleeve. Loud and brash, she said it how it was. Proud of her Irish roots, and she had a mouth on her that could rival the Dartford Tunnel. And the language that came out of it... she could swear for the whole of England and Ireland combined.

Yet, somehow it just worked.

Nancy seemed to appreciate that there were no airs and graces with the girl. That Bridget was always straight down the line with her.

It was the same with Bridget; she knew that underneath that cold, hard exterior of Nancy's, the woman had a heart of gold. The tough exterior was all bravado. Nancy's way of protecting herself from the world.

Though she'd let her guard down a bit with Bridget, finally opening up about things that she'd never speak of to anyone else. Things about her father, the notorious Jimmy Byrne. About his murder.

She spoke about her family too. How she adored her grandmother, Joanie, while only tolerating her haphazard mother, Colleen.

The only thing that Nancy never, ever spoke about was her brother, Daniel.

Bridget had only ever heard the man's name acknowledged in conversation very rarely between Nancy and Jack.

That subject was completely off bounds, and Bridget could see why.

The fact that her brother had disappeared completely almost four years ago, that he'd never even seen his little niece, must cut the woman so deeply.

According to Jack, from what Bridget could make out, Daniel had upped and left England one day. Gone travelling abroad, which, judging by the family's reaction, was probably for the best.

No wonder Nancy didn't even like to hear her brother's name mentioned.

Still, who was Bridget to pry? Nancy was good to her, more than good, in fact, the woman was a diamond.

'I can't wait to move in if I'm honest!' Bridget laughed. 'Little old me, swanning around in this big, old mansion. It's the dream, isn't it?!'

'Oh, hark at you, Lady of the bleeding Manor here. And I see you're starting as you mean to go on, with your mugs of wine! Keeping it classy.' Jack laughed, nudging Bridget on the arm playfully, sensing the girl's excitement. 'See, Nancy, it's all in hand. Stop stressing, okay? Between the three of us, we've got it all covered.'

Nancy nodded. Knowing that Jack was right. They could sort the alarm system in the morning.

'Good. Well, now that's all sorted I'm going to leave you ladies to it. Bridget, I'll be over first thing in the morning to give you a hand, okay?' Kissing Nancy on the cheek before he left, he winked at Bridget and shot her a friendly smile.

'Cheeky bugger. Lady of the bleeding Manor indeed.' Bridget raised her eyes then as she clocked Nancy flush a deep crimson. 'Steady on, girl, you're blushing right down to your feet.' She grinned then. 'So, who do you reckon the lucky lady will be tonight?' Bridget said raising her eyes towards the door where Jack had just left.

Nancy could bury her head in the sand all she wanted, but Bridget could tell that Jack going on yet another date was bothering her.

'Who knows? I've lost track of the whos and wheres. There's always someone with Jack…' Nancy said glugging back the last of her wine.

Then, seeing the smirk on Bridget's face she added, 'What? He's a free man, Bridget. It's got nothing to do with me.'

Bridget couldn't help herself then.

'If you say so!' She giggled.

Nancy sighed, and sensing her friend's dubiousness, she added. 'Seriously, Bridge. He can do as he pleases, and why wouldn't he? He has women throwing themselves at him. I'm sure he's not complaining. He's a bloke after all. Good for him.'

There it was, thought Bridget, hearing the hint of jealousy to Nancy's tone.

For a smart woman, Nancy really was completely clueless when it came to Jack Taylor. He might be out on the town with a different woman every night, but it was Nancy he wanted. The man was head over heels in love with her. Even a blind person could see that.

Which only made her think Nancy could see it too. Yet, typical Nancy insisted on keeping Jack at arm's length. Maybe she was telling the truth when she said that she just didn't feel the same.

Maybe? Though Bridget wasn't completely convinced about that.

This was what Nancy did. She shut people out. Kept them at arm's distance and that's what she was doing with Jack too, Bridget was convinced of it.

This was Nancy's way of protecting herself, so that she wouldn't get hurt. Christ knows she'd had enough heartache to last a lifetime the past few years. It was no wonder why she cut herself off from everyone; her little daughter included, unfortunately, though Bridget would never say that out loud. Especially not in Nancy's earshot.

As much as deep down Nancy loved and adored her child, she came across as detached. Letting her family and Jack do the bulk of the work bringing the little girl up.

But that was none of Bridget's business, and she had no intention of making it hers.

'Strange though, isn't it, that none of these dates that he goes on ever seem to work out? I don't think he ever bothers seeing any of the women twice.'

'Maybe he's just fussy?' Nancy said then, knowing too well what Bridget was implying. Her friend was convinced that Jack was in love with her, and that that was the real reason he'd never moved on.

Blah, blah, blah. Nancy had heard it a million times before, despite Nancy telling her friend until she was blue in the face that her and Jack would never work out. That they'd just been a one-night stand, as cold and crass as that sounded. They'd only spent that one night together.

The night Scarlett had been conceived.

She said that sleeping with her dad's friend and confidante – a man more than twice her age – had been a mistake. A mistake that Nancy had no intention of repeating.

She'd always made that crystal clear from the minute that Scarlett had been born that the only thing she wanted from Jack was for him to be there for Scarlett. For them to both work together as their daughter's parents. To give Scarlett the best start in life that they could.

Relationships only complicated things as far as Nancy was concerned, and Nancy had had enough of dysfunctional families to last her a lifetime; she didn't want the same disappointments and complications for her daughter too.

'Oh, he's fussy all right! You know what the problem really is? None of those women are you!'

'Well, that's tough luck then, isn't it?' Nancy said, finishing her drink, before picking up her keys and handbag from the side. She grinned. 'Because it's never going to happen. Besides, Jack's not the only one with a hot date lined up, you know!'

'Bollocks?' Bridget screeched, almost dropping her mug in shock at the 'Ice Queen' – as the other girls secretly called her behind her back – confessing to a date? This was a first. Judging by the smug look on Nancy's face, the girl wasn't winding her up either.

'You kept that bloody quiet! Go on then, who is he?'

'She! It's a she, actually.' Nancy laughed then, enjoying the look of shock on her mate's face.

'Who?' Bridget shook her head confused.

'And when I say hot date, I mean smoking. It's all happening. Smiley Faces and Chicken Dippers, the works. Who knows, if I play my cards right, by about 8 p.m. I could be snuggled up in bed reading her a bedtime story too.'

'Scarlett?' Bridget rolled her eyes then, kicking herself that she'd almost fallen for Nancy's wind-up.

'Damn right, Scarlett. I haven't got the time or the patience for any man in my life right now, Jack included. So get any wild fantasies you have about the two of us out of your head. It ain't happening. All right?'

Bridget smiled again, still not wholly convinced, but Nancy chose to ignore it.

'Right, doll, I'll see you in the morning. You sure you're going to be all right here?'

'Er, let me think about that. Little old me, living it up in this big old beautiful house. Yeah, I think I'll cope.' She laughed. 'Seriously, don't you worry, Nancy. I'm going to ply Felicity with the rest of this wine. Get her drunk and rope her into unpacking the rest of these boxes with me.' She winked, walking Nancy out and closing the door behind her friend as she left.

Bridget took a deep breath and stared around the kitchen at the carnage everywhere.

The place was a bloody tip, but the sooner she got stuck in, the sooner she could fall into bed.

Her bed.

In her new stunning home.

Shaking her head once again, as she started sifting through the boxes, Bridget still couldn't believe it.

Things were well and truly on the up these days, and Bridget had every intention of making the absolute most of it all.

CHAPTER EIGHT

'The girls have all gone to The Paradise Club. I said I'd go and meet them,' Felicity Monroe said, standing in the bedroom doorway and watching as Bridget Williams smoothed down the curtains she'd just hung. 'You should come for a couple too, bet you could do with a drink?'

The two women had been working flat out for hours. Unpacking boxes and making up the beds just so, but the place was still nowhere near finished.

Even so, Felicity was eager to get out of there.

She'd said she'd give Bridget a hand, but she also wanted to join the rest of the girls for a drink too, seeing as they were all out celebrating tonight.

Bridget couldn't begrudge any of them that.

They should be celebrating. It was the end of an era. Bridge Street had officially closed its door, and as of Monday they would all be working in this swanky new place. If it was ready in time, of course.

'Go out? What? And miss out on all the fun of staying here on my tod and unpacking the rest of these boxes? Nah, you're all right. You go though, Felicity,' Bridget said then, glancing up at the clock and seeing that it was almost midnight. 'I don't know how you girls do it. Going out so late at night. I'm getting too old to be going out clubbing at midnight. This is about the time I'd be thinking of calling it a night and coming home if I was out.'

'Jesus, Bridge. You're in your thirties, not your nineties. No one goes out early anymore. Anyway, you forget, we're used to going out late after working all night at the flat. It's good to have a drink and let your hair down once in a while. Christ knows we all bloody earn that much, at least.'

Bridget nodded. She could understand that. The girls worked bloody hard for their money, they deserved to let off some steam every now and then.

'No wonder you're all out celebrating. You lot are going to miss Bridge Street like a bleeding hole in your head, compared to working in this place,' Bridget reasoned, totally getting why the girls were all so excited.

They'd made it.

Nancy had only kept on the best-looking, hardest-working girls. She wanted high class. Girls that were happy to learn a trade in massage and holistic therapies. Eventually, she wanted to branch out to offer an escort service, too, for the new wealthy punters that she wanted to attract.

Knowing Nancy, she was bang on the money too, and if these girls played their cards right, they'd also be raking in a fortune. This was the noughties and while running a brothel might still be illegal, there was no crime in opening up a private member's spa, was there? And that's all Nancy was doing. Adding a bit of class to the sex trade, which was normally considered a seedy and dark industry. There was big money to be made and Nancy Byrne wasn't missing a trick when it came to cashing in, but she didn't just want to make money for herself. She wanted to give her girls a chance to earn decent money too.

If they didn't work for her here, they'd only be out working their trade somewhere else. At least here, Nancy could offer them a safe environment. She was a Byrne and that name guaranteed protection. They'd be looked after properly.

Bridget grinned then.

'I can't believe that I actually thought I'd made Bridge Street look anywhere near half decent.' She laughed. Remembering how when Nancy had first handed over the reins to her, Bridget had been so eager to put her stamp on the place, to make it look stylish: 'more modern'. Slapping up silver glittery 'wag' wallpaper and draping faux fur throws strategically over every available chair in a fruitless bid to make the place seem more sophisticated. Who had she been kidding? 'You couldn't polish a turd, you could only roll it in glitter!' Wasn't that the saying? Well, that's exactly what she'd done.

Bridget had done the best she could, but it didn't matter how much they decorated the place, or cleaned it up, at the end of the day the flat in Bridge Street would always be just a grotty little knocking shop in the middle of Soho, nestled between a dodgy pizza place and a cheap and cheerful off-licence. This place, though, was something else entirely.

She sensed Felicity's impatience as the girl stood by the doorway, foot tapping against the solid oak floor, coat wrapped tightly around her, her bag on her shoulder.

'Go on, you go. You've been a diamond staying on and helping me out tonight. I really appreciate it, Fliss!'

Walking back downstairs to see Felicity out, she stopped in the lounge and picked up her handbag.

'Here, have a drink on me,' she said, rooting around inside, looking for a couple of ten-pound notes. Groaning as she saw the red money bag tucked down inside her handbag.

'Shit! I meant to give Nancy the week's takings earlier!'

It was all still there, bagged up. A week's worth of money from Bridge Street. A stupid amount, in fact, to have lying around in her handbag. Near on ten grand in total. But with everything she had going on today, she'd simply forgotten to do the handover.

'Don't worry, babe. Sort it out tomorrow.' Taking the notes from Bridget, and smiling gratefully, Felicity shrugged. 'Are you sure I can't tempt you to come along? I bet you could do with a couple of glasses of wine. You might get a second wind?'

Staring at the stacks of boxes piled up around them that she hadn't even opened yet, Bridget was more than tempted to down tools and go out and have a bit of fun for a change. Only she couldn't. She promised Nancy that she'd get this place sorted and she wanted to prove to the woman that she was good for it.

She shook her head.

'A couple of glasses of wine at this time of night and all I'll be fit for is my bed. Nah, you're good, Felicity. I need to get this lot sorted. You go. Go on, I insist.'

Leading the woman out towards the front door, they both stopped suddenly as they heard an almighty bang coming from the back of the property.

'What the fuck was that?' Bridget said, her voice almost a whisper, thinking that something had fallen and smashed against the marble tiles that adorned all the floors on the ground floor of the house.

'Did you hear that?' They looked at each other, neither of them daring to speak as they stood in silence, listening. A second almighty crash came a few seconds later, letting them both know that the noise was nothing accidental.

'Someone is trying to break in? Shit!' Felicity whispered, her face white with fear as the third loud crash came, sounding like force was behind it.

'It sounds like someone's bashing the back door down!'

Bridget nodded in agreement. That was exactly what it sounded like. Somebody was trying to force their way in here.

'Shit. Come on, we need to move,' Bridget said, thinking fast on her feet as she made a grab for the bag of money and the cordless phone.

'Get your arse in the kitchen now, Felicity,' Bridget ordered, ushering Felicity into the kitchen, before switching the lights off. Plunging them both into darkness. The two women squatted down behind the kitchen table.

Bridget dialled Nancy's number, her hands shaking as she held the phone to her ear, anxiously waiting for the woman to pick up.

Another bang.

This time the sound echoed down the long main corridor that ran through the centre of the house. She could hear footsteps then. Inside the house.

'They're in…' she whispered to Felicity, placing a finger on her lips to let the girl know they needed to stay quiet. Then, pointing at the floor, she instructed Felicity to stay down out of sight.

Aware that it was stupid o'clock in the morning, she willed Nancy to pick up the phone.

Finally, the woman did.

'Nancy, it's me. Bridget! We've got trouble at the house. Someone's broken in,' she said bravely, staring out through the gap in the doorway.

She eyed the shadowy figure just off in the distance, at the opposite end of the hallway, their silhouette moving about the front room, as they began searching through boxes.

Whoever it was, they were looking for something in the front reception room. Going through the desk and the cupboards by the sounds of it. Dragging everything out, ransacking the place.

Bridget could hear the sound of the furniture being kicked and shoved across the room.

Another loud crash. Glass?

'Shit, Nance,' Bridget said now, her voice barely a whisper as she watched the dark stocky figure walking down the corridor towards her. 'I can see someone. A man I think. He's got something in his hand? A weapon?'

Bridget felt physically sick then. Whoever this was, they clearly meant business. She and Felicity were in real danger.

'What the fuck do I do?'

'Where are you?' Nancy said, picking up on the fear in Bridget's voice. She tried to remain in control.

'We're in the kitchen. What shall I do?'

'Stay where you are, okay. Don't move, and don't make a sound. Try and stay out of sight. I'm on my way over. I'll bring backup.'

The phone went dead, leaving Bridget's ears filled with the dull, final sound of the tone, quickly replaced with the loud hammering of her heart. The blood rushing inside her ears. Then the heavy footfall of the intruder, getting louder as whoever it was came closer now.

'Shall we make a run for it, Bridget?' Felicity whispered.

Bridget shook her head.

There was no time for that. The man was heading this way.

Staring over at Felicity she once more placed her finger over her lips, telling the girl not to make a sound. Whoever this man was, he was armed and clearly dangerous. It wasn't worth taking the risk and running.

Sensing the fear on the younger girl's face, Bridget reached out and squeezed her arm. The poor girl looked as terrified as Bridget felt.

Shit! she thought then, remembering the takings that she'd shoved inside her handbag. She'd left them up on the table.

That's probably what this bastard was looking for, she realised.

He'd tear this place apart looking for them, and probably find her and Felicity in the process.

Where the fuck was Nancy?

Closing her eyes in despair, Bridget felt sick with fear. By the time the woman got here, it would be too late.

She needed a Plan B.

Searching the kitchen sides for something she could use to protect herself, she spotted the bread knife by the sink that she'd been using earlier to slice through the masking tape of the endless boxes. Grabbing it, her hand skimmed the cordless phone and she stared in horror as it spun across the kitchen worktop and fell to the floor. Smashing against the new marble tiles.

The house was plunged into silence then.

Bridget was frozen to the spot. She stared at Felicity.

The intruder suddenly went silent too. He'd heard her.

Waiting, she couldn't hear his footsteps and braced herself for the onslaught that she knew for sure would now follow. Then the footsteps started again; this time, with a purpose. Stomping towards the kitchen. Towards them.

Bridget held the knife out in front of her, standing in front of Felicity. Shielding the younger woman, just as the kitchen door burst open.

A man. Dressed in black, a balaclava pulled down over his face to conceal his identity.

All Bridget could see were his cold, callous eyes staring straight at her.

She held the knife up higher, directly out in front of her. Fighting the violent tremor of her shaking hands.

Determined to show the man that she would use it if she had to.

'What the fuck do you want?' she shouted, trying so desperately to keep her shit together as she locked eyes with the masked assailant.

His hand raised then too, a metal crowbar held tightly in his locked fist.

Raising it high above his head, he stepped towards the two women.

CHAPTER NINE

'Come on, Jack!' Nancy Byrne cursed impatiently.

Her car had been abandoned in the middle of the private road.

She stood at the end of the long winding driveway, scanning the deserted street in hope of a glimpse of the man's arrival. Praying silently to herself that he would hurry the hell up.

That Bridget and Felicity would be okay.

That was the problem with being set so far back in the grounds of such a large plot of land: there was no other fucker around to hear if there was trouble going on. Without the alarm system working, none of the neighbours around here would have the slightest clue about the commotion that was going on inside the house. The irony being that had been exactly the appeal of the house that had made Nancy want to buy it in the first place. Privacy. And this place gave her that in abundance.

She'd had a gutful of people sticking their noses into her business over on Bridge Street. Despite the fact that most people around there knew her and her family well enough to know better than to start asking questions, it didn't stop people talking behind her back. Casting their own opinions on the Byrnes' businesses. Spreading rumours that always found their way back to her.

Especially after everything that had happened with her father. With Daniel too.

This was supposed to be a fresh start. A new beginning for her and her family. Something she could build entirely on her own, and actually be proud of.

No one would be watching her, or judging her, or interfering around here. Because there was no other fucker about.

Recalling the panic in Bridget's voice when she'd phoned her, Nancy knew that she didn't have time to stand around on her own out here like a spare part, waiting for Jack and some of the other men she had on her payroll to magically appear.

She had to help her friend.

Nancy made her way down the long winding driveway, careful to stay in close to the hedgerow to avoid being seen. She contemplated going in through the front door, which she would have done, had she not been alone.

At least she was armed, she thought to herself as she snuck around the back of the house to where Bridget had told her the intruder had got into the house. Reaching into her handbag as she went, her fingers frantically searched the bottom of the bag.

The gun? Shit!

In her hurry to get here, she'd forgotten to retrieve it from the safe.

If it wasn't for Scarlett, Nancy would have kept it in her handbag, close to hand at all times. Only, she couldn't do that with a child in the house.

She stalled when she reached the back door, which had been left ajar and, judging from the state of what was left of it, had been kicked in with brute force. She studied the splintered, jagged bits of wood that jutted out from the split doorframe. The metal lock had been forced out. Discarded, now, on the floor.

Inside, she could hear shouting.

A male voice. Aggressive and bellowing orders.

Nancy took a deep breath; with no way of protecting herself against this lot, her only hope was that her presence alone would be enough to deter whoever these fuckers were. To catch them unawares and make out that she'd turned up mob-handed. That her men were with her too.

'Fuck it!' Nancy said, eyeing the back gate once more in the vain hope that Jack might suddenly appear from the shadows.

She would have to do this alone.

She made her way inside as quickly as she could amongst the darkness, and eyed the state of the place.

The back of the house had been completely ransacked. The desk and a handful of chairs that dressed the room had all been tipped over and kicked across the floor. There was paperwork everywhere too, strewn all over the carpet.

Following the sounds of the shouting and crying, Nancy made her way down the hallway, towards the front of the house, to the kitchen.

The noise was getting louder now.

Female voices. They sounded distressed.

She was in way over her head. She knew that; but what choice did she have?

All she could do was pray to God that Jack got his arse here soon.

Nancy stopped in her tracks at the sudden noise that filled the entire house, recognising the sound of the blood-curdling scream.

Like a wounded animal.

That voice?

It was Bridget.

*

Raising the crowbar above his head, the man placed his finger over his lips as a warning to the girls not to make a sound.

His eyes going to the bag on the table.

'Give me the money, and no one gets hurt,' he said then, his tone shaky and desperate, despite the threat that lingered there.

Bridget shook her head.

She couldn't do that. She couldn't just hand over the takings.

It was near on ten grand.

The girls had worked their arses off, literally, for this money.

Sensing the woman's hesitation, the man gave her one final chance.

'Give me the bag,' he repeated.

His tone was harder, his eyes flashing with fury through the slit in his balaclava.

But Bridget wasn't about to give him the money. 'No!' she said, snatching the bag up from the table before the man could get to it.

There was no way that she was going to hand over a week's worth of takings. Nancy would be here soon. With backup. All Bridget had to do was stall this fucker until then.

She held out the knife then too. Showing the man that she meant business. Her arm dead straight, aimed straight at him. Determined to stand her ground.

No one moved.

Bridget and Felicity were both cornered at the back of the kitchen. The large kitchen table stood between them and the door. The masked intruder was there too, blocking the only way out. There was no way to escape.

She couldn't back down, not now.

Stepping slowly towards the man, defiantly. Only instead of taking his cue and backing off, the man came closer too.

He wasn't frightened of her. Blade, or no blade.

He should be, Bridget thought, as she took her chance and struck out, slicing through the air as she lunged forward.

The man was quick to dance out of her way. Ducking to his side, defensive now, he smashed the crowbar down on Bridget's tiny frame.

Bridget screamed out in pain as the metal bar impacted her arm. Hearing the crack of bone just as the pain ripped right through her.

Felicity screamed too.

Bridget had no choice but to fight for her life now.

It was this man or her, and there was no way that Bridget was going to let it be her.

She pounced once more. Thrusting the knife towards the man with everything she had.

She missed.

Then to her surprise, he made a grab for the weapon. Twisting his hands around the handle, and squeezing her fingers with all his strength so that she'd drop the knife.

Wincing at the acute pain which forced her to cry out once more, still Bridget wasn't willing to let go.

'Felicity!' Bridget screamed. 'Help me…' she shouted, catching a glimpse of the girl in the midst of her struggle, as she continued to single-handedly fight off the masked intruder for possession of the knife.

Only Felicity didn't move. She couldn't.

Rendered silent and frozen to the spot, she looked as if she'd gone into shock. Staring at Bridget wrestling with the intruder, her tiny form being overpowered by his, Felicity's eyes were full of terror.

But Bridget couldn't hold him off on her own. She was no match for the man. He was too strong.

'Let it go,' the man ordered Bridget through gritted teeth.

He had the knife then, firmly in his grasp again. His hand gripping tightly around the handle. Only Bridget was still holding it too. Twisting her body towards the man to gain more leverage, as she tried to retrieve it from him. But her hand slipped free and for a second only he held it.

She faltered as if she'd been struck.

He'd punched her?

The sudden pain in her side stopped her in her tracks.

It felt like a punch at first. Except harder. Sharp and searing, causing her hand immediately to go to the place of acute pain.

To hold and protect it.

That's when she felt the blade penetrating her side. Protruding from her skin. A warm liquid seeping out through her fingertips.

She held her hand up and stared at the dark red fluid that covered her skin.

Blood?

She felt weak then. Faint. The room spinning silently as she rapidly crumpled to the floor.

Somewhere in the distance now, she could hear Felicity's voice too. The girl finally speaking up.

Too late to help now, but screaming hysterically at the scene that had unfolded before her.

'You've stabbed her? What have you done? What the fuck have you done?'

*

Hearing the harrowing scream echoing down the hallway towards her, Nancy ran.

Ignoring all the instincts that told her to wait for Jack to get here, so she'd at least have some backup. Nancy didn't have time for that.

Bridget and Felicity were both in trouble. They needed her.

She shouted, hoping to call the intruder's bluff.

'Bridget? Are you in here? I've got Jack Taylor here with me and some of my men.' Shouting now, as she neared the kitchen doorway.

It was all bravado, but bravado was all that Nancy had right now.

Reaching the kitchen doorway, she was met by the sight of the masked assailant standing in the middle of the kitchen, as if he was frozen to the spot, and Felicity standing at the back of the kitchen against the sink. Hugging her arms tightly to herself as she continued to bawl, her eyes transfixed on the floor in front of her. As if she was in a trance.

Nancy followed her gaze, a small gasp escaping her lips as she saw her friend splayed out on the floor, clutching her side, hands covered in blood.

'Bridget?' Nancy said, stepping around the intruder, immediately going to her friend.

Dropping to her knees, she realised that Bridget was unconscious. The knife was still inside her, her hand pressing at the wound as she lay sprawled out on the kitchen floor.

Nancy glared at the man in the mask.

'What the fuck have you done to her?' she said then.

Show no fear to your enemies, only contempt. Isn't that what her father always said? Only Nancy's contempt was real, suddenly enraged at what this animal before her had done to her friend.

Though he looked just as shocked as Nancy was, her words suddenly snapping him out of his daze.

She watched him falter. Taking in the carnage before him. His stare wavering as he took in the sight of the woman lying motionless on the floor, a pool of blood seeping out around the knife.

He'd stabbed her?

He needed to get the fuck out of here, and fast. Quickly, he made a grab for the bag down on the floor at Bridget's side.

Nancy shook her head, disgusted at the realisation of what was happening.

Money. That's what this was all about.

That's why Bridget was splayed out on the floor with a knife sticking out of her, that's why this place looked as if it had been torn apart.

This bastard was robbing her.

He'd stabbed Bridget.

The money meant fuck all to her now, but there was no way that she was going to let him get away with hurting her mate.

Springing to her feet, Nancy stood blocking the doorway. Her hands holding on to the doorframe. Her eyes flashing with defiance.

If this fucker was going to do a runner, he'd have to go through her first.

It was stupid of her, desperate, but she had to do it.

He moved quickly. Too big and too fast for her, trampling towards her like a rhino on a stampede. He grabbed at Nancy's shoulders and slammed her backwards with such force into the wall behind her that he was surprised when she didn't leave a dent.

Instead, she slid down the paintwork, crumpling into a heap on the floor, her expression dazed as he jumped over her, as if she was nothing more than an inconvenience. Just a piece of dirt on the floor.

The tightening in her chest made her breath wheeze. Nancy took one last parting shot, in the hope of stopping the man in his tracks. Grabbing at his leg, she hooked her hands around his thighs and used all her body weight to try and pull him down. It worked; the bastard lost his balance. Falling like a hot sack of shit, he slammed down onto the floor next to her. Wincing, she heard the crack of his jawbone as his face took the impact of his descent.

Nancy made a grab for the handbag on the floor next to her and tossed it back into the room, into the far corner, towards Felicity.

Another tactic to stall the fucker, until Jack got here.

Only the man wasn't going to stay down for long. Already getting to his knees. Nancy picked up the pot plant that lay on its side, discarded on the floor from where it had been previously thrown or kicked. Holding it high above her head, she brought it down vigorously on the man's skull. Watching as the ceramic pot smashed into several large pieces.

She hoped to knock the man out, but somehow, Christ knows how, the man still managed to get back up. Stunned now, unsteady on his feet, but up on them all the same.

Ten out of ten for persistence, she thought. Nothing was keeping this fucker down.

Sensing that Nancy wasn't going to give up without a fight, he lunged at her, punching her hard in the stomach. Winding her. Sending her straight back down to the floor.

Then he ran. Back down the hallway, towards the back of the house.

Just as Jack Taylor and some of Nancy's men came hurtling through the front door.

'Nancy?' he shouted. Reaching the woman and checking that she was okay while signalling to the other men to get after the intruder.

Seeing her pale face, eyes wide with worry and shock, he asked, 'Jesus, Nancy? Are you okay?'

She indicated towards the kitchen, to where Bridget was lying, bleeding, the knife still inside her.

Finally Nancy Byrne spoke, her tears coming then, despite herself. 'That bastard stabbed her, Jack. She hasn't moved. We need to call a fucking ambulance! Now.'

CHAPTER TEN

'You stupid fuck!' Dennis Watkins shouted, incredulous now at what he was hearing. Running his fingers through his sparse, thinning hair.

He stared over at his mate, Louis Blackwell, and shook his head, before cursing loudly to himself, at the enormity of the situation that Kyle Boyd had just brought to his doorstep.

Literally.

The two men hadn't been able to work out what the fuck had happened at first, when Dennis had opened the front door to find Kyle standing there. In the middle of the night, crying and mumbling. Making no sense.

His face pale, his clothes covered in blood.

He initially thought that Kyle had been attacked. Instinctively wanting to help the lad, he'd quickly ushered Kyle inside.

Into his cramped little kitchen, of his Clapham flat.

Only as the story unfolded, they soon learned that the stupid fuck hadn't been attacked at all. This was all his own doing. He'd taken it upon himself to do a job on the sly without them, and somehow he'd managed to completely fuck it up.

'What the hell were you thinking?' Dennis Watkins growled. Seriously pissed off now at the complete audacity of the kid. 'Going back on your tod and doing the job alone? What's that all about? Ain't I paying you enough?'

All the work they'd done. All the jobs they had set up and, in just one night, Kyle Boyd had managed to jeopardise everything that they'd all worked for.

Dennis and Louis had the perfect little operation. A home security company. Installing CCTV and state-of-the-art security systems. They targeted some of the richest houses in London.

Only what their rich clientele weren't aware of was that they always made a note of the key codes and access points while they were at the property.

Then they bided their time. Waiting weeks, sometimes even months, to strike. Careful not to arouse anyone's suspicions that they were involved in the scam.

They would break in to the property when no one was home and deactivate the alarm system. Resetting all the data that the boxes recorded on their internal memory, so that it didn't look as if the machines had ever been tampered with.

If there was ever any fallout as to why the alarm system hadn't been triggered, and did the job it was supposed to have done, they could prove to the victim of the burglary that the alarm had been working perfectly. That the evidence of when the alarms had been activated and deactivated had all been recorded as expected, and that the customer had clearly just forgotten to set it.

It was a foolproof system, as long as they all stuck to the rules and stayed professional and discreet.

Only Dennis had fucked up, it seemed. He was the one who had given Kyle Boyd an in on the job too. Having met the kid on a legitimate call-out at a big apartment block, and sensing that Kyle Boyd would go far with a bit of direction, Dennis had given the kid a break. Though he'd gone against his better judgement, it seemed now. And this is what he got in return. Zero fucking loyalty.

Not only had he gone behind his and Louis's backs and taken this job for himself, but Kyle-divvy-bollox-Boyd then had the barefaced cheek to bring this shit back to his door. The kid really did have balls, Dennis had to give him that much at least.

Turning up here and expecting Dennis and Louis to somehow bail the fucker out.

The whole situation was just one great big head-fuck.

'I just can't get my head around the fact that you just took it upon yourself to go back, on your own. What were you thinking? That's not how we fucking work, and you know it.' Hoping that Kyle had some sort of explanation. That he hadn't just purposely cunted Dennis off, after everything Dennis had done for him.

'I'm sorry, Dennis. Truly I am,' Kyle said now. His body violently shaking as he continued to hold a cloth under his nose in a bid to stem the blood flowing from his newly acquired broken nose.

Though his nose was the least of his problems for now.

He'd stabbed someone tonight. He hadn't meant to. He truly hadn't.

He didn't even think anyone would be there at that time of night. He thought the place was empty.

By the time he'd realised there were two birds inside the house, it was too late.

One of them was brandishing a knife, and had come at him with it, too.

All Kyle had done was try to defend himself. He'd meant to get the knife off her. To twist it away from her, and out of her grasp.

Only it hadn't worked out that way and he'd ended up stabbing her by accident in the struggle that ensued.

Now, every time he closed his eyes all he could see was that shocked expression on that woman's face, as the knife had plunged into her flesh. The way she'd slumped lifelessly down onto the floor.

The knife handle sticking out of her, circled by a ring of deep red blood.

Leaning over, Kyle threw up the contents of his stomach all over Dennis Watkins's kitchen floor.

'What if I've killed her, Dennis?' Kyle Boyd was openly crying now. Aware of just how pathetic he looked; only suddenly he no longer cared. 'Shit! What if she's dead? What have I done? I didn't mean to do it, it just happened. She just launched herself at me. Shit, I'm so sorry, Dennis.'

'Oh, you're sorry?' It was Louis Blackwell's time to talk then. Dennis's flatmate and business partner was done with sitting in silence while Kyle sat there blubbering and begging Dennis for forgiveness like a fucking pussy.

Kyle Boyd wasn't getting an ounce of sympathy from him, not one.

'Well, why didn't you just say that in the first place? 'Cause sorry makes everything okay, doesn't it?' Louis spat, Kyle's abysmal attempt of an apology pushing him well and truly over the edge.

This was typical Kyle all over.

Fucking things up, and then crawling back here begging for forgiveness and knowing how soft Dennis was with the kid, how Dennis saw something in the kid that Louis couldn't, 'potential', the cheeky fucker would probably get it too.

He knew something like this would happen eventually.

Of course it would: Kyle Boyd was a liability.

Louis had never liked him from the off, and he'd made no disguise of the fact.

The kid was way too full of himself. Acting the big I am, trying to worm his way in with Dennis. Which only riled Louis further – that Dennis couldn't see what was staring him in the face.

Maybe now Dennis would realise what a fuck-up the kid really was.

'I'll tell you what he was doing going back there on his own. He wanted the money for himself, ain't that right?' Louis spat, clenching his fists tightly at his sides, to stop him from launching them into Kyle's snivelling mug as Kyle shook his head

Denying that was the reason why.

'Bullshit. You know whose fucking house that was, don't you?'

Kyle nodded.

Of course he did. They all did. It was Nancy Byrne's place.

Everyone knew the Byrne family. They were notorious, and Kyle had heard an earful of stories from Dennis and Louis from the second that Nancy Byrne had called the job in. The drugs, the clubs, the brothels.

Kyle had seen it all first-hand, how much money the woman was clearly making, now that she'd bought herself that big, fancy gaff over in Mayfair.

The stories must all be true.

Which didn't bode well for him at all now that it had all gone tits up.

'Well, I hate to tell you this, Kyley-boy, but you are fucked, mate. I mean stealing from a Byrne is bad enough, but you carved up one of Nancy's girls! Are you fucking insane! Nancy Byrne has probably already put the word out on him, Dennis. Half of London will be on the lookout for him now. The best thing we can do is stay the fuck away from this prick before he drags us down with him.'

Kyle threw up again. Heaving until there was nothing left inside him.

Louis was right, he was in a whole world of shit now. The type of shit that he wouldn't be coming back from anytime soon.

There would only be one outcome from his actions tonight. He'd either get a capture from the law, or a capture from Nancy Byrne and her cronies. And given the choice between the two,

Kyle could only secretly hope that the Old Bill caught up with him first.

And even if they did, chances were that Nancy and her men would still find a way to get to him eventually.

He was screwed.

Eyeing Dennis, pleadingly then. Searching the man's eyes for a flicker of empathy towards him. Something. Only it wasn't to be.

Dennis simply shook his head.

His mind well and truly made up.

'Louis is right,' Dennis Watkins said as he paced the kitchen. 'We should never have let you in on the job. I took too big a risk on you.'

'Oh finally!' Louis said, glaring, as Dennis was only finally realising what Louis had been telling him all along. That Kyle wasn't up to the job. That the kid was a liability.

Dennis had insisted on learning that the hard way.

'But, Dennis. Please. I'm sorry. Honest to God, I'm so sorry,' Kyle said, his face burning with humiliation as he felt his tears start again then too.

He wanted to explain. To try and make Dennis understand. He was heart sorry, genuinely. Sorry that he'd been so stupid and gone back to the house. Sorry that he'd stabbed someone. A woman, no less. But more than anything he was sorry for letting Dennis down.

The man believed in him. Or at least, he had done up until tonight.

Only Kyle had fucked all of that now. Dennis deserved an explanation.

'I know I shouldn't have done it. It was stupid, I know that now. But I overheard one of the girls saying that they were all going out tonight. I thought the place would be empty. I wasn't going to do anything. Honest to God, Dennis. It's just...' Kyle stopped himself. Babbling nervously, he realised he'd said too much.

'Just what?' Louis said, instantly picking up on Kyle suddenly cutting his words short, mid-sentence.

'Only, when I told my girlfriend whose house it was, and that I'd seen the bag of money, she told me that I should do the job. On my own like…' Kyle looked at the floor now. Unable to look the two men in the eye. 'She said that this was my chance to take a shot at Nancy Byrne, and that if I didn't take it, then she'd end it with me.'

Unable to believe that he was admitting out loud to these two men what his girlfriend had threatened him with. How pathetic he sounded now that he was repeating her ultimatum.

How weak and feeble he must be coming off.

But they didn't know Jess.

'Your girlfriend *told* you to do it?' Louis wrinkled up his nose in disgust at what he was hearing. Of all the excuses, this really was a joke.

'You don't know how forceful she can be,' Kyle cried. 'Her and Nancy go way back. Jess has got some personal vendetta against Nancy Byrne. It's like she's obsessed. There had been no way that I could have said no to her. She would have left me.'

Jess had been insistent that tonight was the perfect opportunity to get to that bitch, Nancy.

'Jesus! I've heard it fucking all now, haven't I?!' Louis exclaimed, shaking his head at Kyle, incensed. 'Is that what this boils down to, is it? When the shit hits the fan, you blame your missus! Fucking hell, you really are a fucking degenerate, ain't ya!'

Unable to control his temper any longer Louis lunged at Kyle; grabbing the younger lad by the tops of his arms with both hands he threw him on top of the kitchen table. Wrapping his hands tightly around the kid's throat, squeezing the life out of him.

'You jeopardised everything we've worked for and now, by coming here and laying this all on us, you've royally fucking stitched us up too. You prick.'

'I didn't mean to. I swear to God, Louis…' Spluttering now, fighting for breath, as Louis Blackwell's grip tightened around his throat, with his every plea.

Kyle kicked out, struggling to get the older man off of him.

He was almost six-foot tall himself, but Louis was a man mountain in comparison. The bloke weighed at least double what Kyle did.

Kyle didn't stand a chance.

He couldn't breathe.

His lungs were screaming for breath, his chest wheezing.

He felt as if he was going to pass out. As if he would die right here on the kitchen table.

Dennis Watkins finally stepped in.

'Enough, Louis!' he shouted, grabbing hold of Louis's hands. Prising the man's tight grip free from the kid's throat. Sensing that if he didn't intervene soon, Louis would end up throttling the life out of the silly bastard. 'I said, that's enough.'

Restraining the man, he waited as Kyle rolled out from under Louis and scuppered across the table. Gasping for air as he went.

The tension between the men in the room palpable now. The room completely silent then as the enormity of Kyle's fuck-up tonight was at the forefront of all their minds.

Finally Dennis spoke.

'Tonight was a fucking abortion, of that there's no doubt. But the last thing I need now is you two fucking killing each other too.'

Dennis eyed Louis then, giving the man his final warning.

'The damage is done, so just leave it. All we can do is make sure that we don't get fucking dragged any deeper into this shit than we already are. We need to keep our heads down for a bit. Make sure the heat is well and truly off us.'

'I really am sorry,' Kyle said then, wiping the dripping blood off his face. Relieved that Dennis was still prepared to back him up after everything he'd done.

With Dennis onside, at least Kyle didn't have to worry about facing Nancy Byrne and her crew alone.

Only Kyle was reading it all wrong. Dennis wasn't planning on doing jack shit for the kid.

'You're damn right you're sorry,' Dennis Watkins said with a nod of his head. 'You fucked up tonight, big time. A lesson learned for you. And for me too.'

Kyle looked confused then.

'That's it, Kyle. You're out. We won't be working with you again, not after this. Louis was right all along. I should have fucking listened to him. You're not up for the job, and taking you on has nearly cost me everything. Chances are, we still might lose the lot because of you,' Dennis said, with all seriousness, wanting no more involvement with Kyle Boyd now he'd fucked them over. 'If Nancy Byrne and her lot catches up with you, you are going to be a very fucking sorry kid, indeed! Now get the fuck out of my house, and anyone comes sniffing around asking questions our names better not leave your fucking mouth, do you hear me?!'

Kyle nodded and got up from the chair, like a man defeated.

He followed Dennis Watkins to the front door, unsure what else he could do now.

'And tell that girlfriend of yours that whatever her beef is with Nancy, I hope tonight was worth it. She's started a shit storm for you now, lad! So I hope she was worth it 'an all.'

Slamming the front door, Dennis Watkins leant up against it, and closed his eyes.

Taking a deep breath, he knew that there would be repercussions for tonight's actions, without a doubt, and Louis was right: there was no way that they were going to allow the kid to pull them down into the shit alongside him.

Not when those mad bastard Byrnes were involved.

Kyle Boyd was well and truly on his own now.

CHAPTER ELEVEN

'You did fucking what?' Jess Green sat up in the bed and glared across the room incredulously to where her boyfriend stood lingering in the bedroom doorway.

Unable to believe what he'd just told her.

Though the culpable expression on his face confirmed that he was telling her the truth. That and the fact that he was standing there awkwardly, like a scolded child, about to be told off.

Jess glanced over to the clock on the bedside cabinet. It was almost five thirty now.

She must have fallen asleep.

She'd waited up most of the night for him to come home; only he hadn't and now she knew why.

'You're a fucking moron, do you know that, Kyle!' she said then, taking in the sight of his red puffy eyes from where he'd clearly been crying. The dry congealed blood at the end of his crooked-looking nose. His clothes, too, covered in blood. Only it wasn't his blood, was it? Well at least not all of it. Not if what he was saying was true and the stupid fucker had only gone and stabbed someone. 'Jesus, Kyle. Look at the state of you!'

Shaking her head in disgust, as she swung her legs out of the bed, wrapping her dressing gown tightly around her before stomping past Kyle Boyd and out of the room.

'I think I've broken my nose?' he said, following her down the stairs, hoping for at least a tiny bit of understanding.

Though the pissed-off expression on his girlfriend's face was more than enough to confirm what he already knew. He'd be getting zero sympathy from Jess any time soon.

She looked furious, and she hadn't even heard the worst of it yet.

'A broken nose is the least of your worries right now. Let me tell you…' Jess said with a snarl, making her way into the kitchen and switching the kettle on. She reached for her pack of cigarettes then, lighting one up and taking a deep drag, before pointing it towards Kyle.

'Can't you do anything right? Anything without causing some kind of drama? Do you know how much shit you'll be in now that you stabbed one of Nancy Byrne's girls, do you? That cow is a heartless bitch. Trust me, I know that from experience! She'll do her nut over this.'

Kyle Boyd looked as if he was going to cry again.

Nervously moving from one foot to another. Anxious now, at Jess's words. He knew that she wasn't just saying any of this to shut him up. He was in trouble. Big trouble.

Somehow in just one night, he'd managed to single-handedly piss everyone off around him. Nancy Byrne. Dennis. Now Jess.

Feeling thoroughly sorry for himself then, he wiped his nose as he felt a trickle of blood start to trail down his skin once more.

'It won't stop bleeding,' he said, his eyes pleading with Jess to have some sympathy towards him.

Though the only thing Jess gave him was a tea towel.

Grabbing it from next to the sink, she tossed it to him, hitting him straight in the face with it.

'You're getting blood all over the floor!' she said, with irritation, before turning her back on him and making herself a strong coffee. Not bothering to offer Kyle one. He could sod off if he thought he was getting anything from her, ever again.

'Where have you put the money?' Jess asked then, expectantly, glancing around for the bag of cash that he'd told her about on the phone last night.

Ten grand at least, he'd told her when he'd rang her to tell her what sort of a house he'd been working in.

Ten grand, just lying around on top of a cabinet in one of the rooms.

'That's how much money these people have,' he'd said, trying to impress her.

'Too fucking much. I tell you, you want to see the place, Jess. It's like a palace. You'd love it. A huge townhouse in Mayfair, with a fancy looking swimming pool and expensive gym gear all set up in the basement. I don't think much of the woman who owns it. Right flash cow she is, properly loves herself. Dennis said she's the daughter of some has-been gangster. Jimmy Byrne? You heard of him? Dead now apparently. Murdered. You should see this Nancy bird, proper rates herself…'

'You're working in Nancy Byrne's house?' Jess had said, her ears pricking up at Kyle's words, suddenly very interested in the conversation.

'Yeah. You know her?' Kyle said, realising that this Nancy was the same Nancy that Jess was forever harping on about.

The infamous Nancy from Jess's past that had royally screwed the girl over.

Kyle didn't have a clue what the bird had done to Jess, as Jess refused to talk about it, but whatever it was it was bad enough for Jess to be obsessed with the woman.

And the fact that he'd managed to gain access to Nancy Byrne's house, to her money, had been like adding fuel to Jess's raging fire.

That's when Jess told Kyle that he needed to take the money.

That Nancy Byrne owed her big time.

She insisted that he didn't swipe the money before he left, as Nancy and her lot would work out that it was him before he even made it to the front gates. Jess had it all planned out in record time. Kyle needed to go back there tonight, and take the lot. That there was probably other money lying around too. He needed to do this job, alone. Without Dennis or Louis. Just him, so that Jess and Kyle could pocket the lot.

'You did get it, didn't you?' she said then, her stare burning through him.

'I did, but then Nancy turned up and, after she broke my nose, she took it back,' he said, looking down at the floor. Knowing full well that Jess would lose her shit at that.

He cursed himself for leaving empty-handed.

The money would have softened the blow. It would have made his fuck-up tonight worth it.

Instead he'd come home with fuck all to show for himself yet again.

A prize prick, just as Jess always called him.

'The woman's a flaming nutcase, Jess. She took one look at the Irish bird sprawled out on the floor and just lost it. I'm lucky I got away at all. She went crazy. Smashing plants over my head, the lot.'

'An Irish bird?' Jess pursed her mouth. Wondering if the woman was Bridget Williams. What would be the chances of that?

After all these years. She was probably still there. Working side by side with Nancy, her head so far up the woman's arse that she could no longer see daylight.

'Do you think you killed her?' Jess asked, part of her hoping that he had. That would have been something.

'I don't know. Oh God, Jess. I really don't know. She wasn't moving. She was just lying there.' Kyle lost it then.

He'd been desperately trying to hold himself together, not to cry in front of Jess. But he just couldn't help himself.

'Shit, Jess. I didn't even realise what had happened until I saw the knife sticking out of her side. She'd just launched herself at me. The next thing I knew she was on the floor. I barely even touched her, I swear to God.'

Kyle sank to the floor then, unable to bear the guilt of what he'd done tonight.

Stabbing a woman.

'What if she's dead? They'll do me for murder. I'll do a life stretch for that.'

'Chance would be a fucking fine thing,' Jess sneered under her breath.

'Dennis and Louis lost their shit with me too. I'm out, Jess. They don't want to be associated with me now. I've lost my job, too, on top of everything else.' He mumbled something under his breath then.

Only, Jess caught the tail end of it.

'You what?' she said, getting riled now. 'Say it again.'

'I said, that it's not just my fault.' Kyle repeated himself. Feeling more desperate than brave. He just wanted Jess to be a bit more understanding. This was her fault too.

She'd told him to do the job.

This wasn't just down to him.

'You told me to take the money. You said that she fucking owes you? That this was your way of getting back at her? For what?' He was eyeing her then with a pleading look in his eyes. Begging her to let him in, to tell him what this was all about. What he'd risked everything for.

Jess just shook her head. Turning her back on the man, she stirred her mug of coffee. Drinking back the scalding hot liquid so that she wouldn't have to talk.

'I would never have gone back there on my own like that. You told me to do it,' Kyle said, quietly then.

'Oh, come on, Kyle. You're a grown man. I'm sure you can make decisions for yourself. You've got a brain in there somewhere, haven't you?'

Kyle crouched down on the floor. Dizzy, body feeling weak at the sudden realisation that he was really on his own now. That this all came back to him.

No matter what Jess had told him to do, he'd done it. Him.

He'd be the one taking the fall for his actions tonight too.

'I need to lay low for a while, Jess, just until the heat's off,' he said, the panic evident in his voice.

'Yeah, I think that's a good idea. You should go back to your mum.' Jess nodded in agreement. Finally something they both agreed on. 'I don't want you here.'

Unable to stomach the sight of the feeble, weak man before her.

Kyle looked up at her questioningly. Seeing the cold hard expression on her face; she was telling him, not asking him, to leave.

So he did what he always did when Jess dished out the orders. He did as he was told.

Going back upstairs to the bedroom and throwing some of his clothes into a holdall, he came back a few minutes later, hoping that Jess would change her mind. That she was just angry with him, that this would all blow over. Only she seemed even more resolute than ever.

'I mean it, Kyle. I want some space. I can't do this with you anymore.' Sitting down at the kitchen table, her hands wrapped around her coffee mug. Glaring at him, as if he'd done everything tonight purposely, purely to piss her off.

'I'll see you then,' he said, his voice full of regret. Hoping that maybe in a few days' time, when she'd calmed down, she'd realise that she'd made a mistake.

Closing the door behind him as he exited the house, he left Jess alone with her thoughts.

She drank down the rest of her coffee. Cold now. Deciding that it was too early in the morning to have a joint or a glass of wine, she lit up another cigarette instead and hoped that the caffeine she'd just consumed would be enough to settle her nerves.

The angst building inside her at just the thought of that bitch, Nancy Byrne.

Somehow that woman always got off scot free.

Always managing to somehow dodge the bloodshed and chaos all around her.

Jess's hands shook: the memory of that harrowing night a few years ago flooding back to her now. Wincing, she tried to block all thoughts of what happened to her out of her head.

Of course, she couldn't though. It was always there.

Haunting her. Taunting her. Lurking just beneath the surface. Always there just willing and waiting to raise its ugly head and torment her.

The money tonight had meant nothing to Jess, not really. It wasn't about that.

This was about revenge.

Revenge on Nancy.

Jess had a score to settle with the woman, and tonight had been the first opportunity she'd had at finally getting close to the woman.

Only Kyle had fucked it all up. Proving himself just as useless as always.

Even if he had stolen the money, it wasn't enough. Not really.

Nancy wouldn't miss a wad of cash going missing; she had that in abundance by the sounds of it.

And stealing Nancy's money nowhere near matched the pain and hurt that Jess had suffered in Nancy Byrne's hands.

That bitch needed a much more brutal lesson bestowed upon her.

Jess closed her eyes then, hoping that somehow it would help her block out the pain. The images and memories that were running through her mind would taunt her all day.

That's what happened.

Once she let Nancy Byrne back in.

Kyle may have fucked everything up last night, but one thing he had managed to do was show Jess that it was possible to get close to the woman. That there were ways.

Maybe now was the time to exact her revenge on Nancy once and for all, for everything she'd done to her. For everything she'd made her suffer.

Only there would be no room for any more fuck-ups. Jess was going to dish out her revenge personally next time.

And that bitch was going to pay, if it was the last thing she ever did.

Jess would make sure of that.

CHAPTER TWELVE

Standing at the foot of the hospital bed, Nancy Byrne was doing all she could to hold back her tears.

Last night had been a living nightmare and, for a moment there, seeing her friend on the floor like that, hurt, she'd been convinced that Bridget was dead. That the bastard who'd broken in had murdered her.

Just the thought of not seeing the woman, or speaking to her ever again, had terrified Nancy.

'Please tell me that you didn't stay here all night?' Bridget said, stirring from her restless sleep, her face breaking out into a smile as she saw Nancy looking down at her.

Wincing as she pulled herself slowly up and sat back against her pillows.

'Jesus, Bridge. You look bloody awful,' Nancy said ignoring her friend's question, too busy taking in Bridget's sickly pale complexion. Her eyes puffy and yellow.

Placing the fancy box of chocolates she'd bought her friend down on the table beside them, she eyed the drip that led from Bridget's arm. Assessing the situation.

'Oh, well that's charming, isn't it? I hope you're not making a dig about this beautiful negligee that the nurse put me in. Tell you what, we should bring a couple of these back with us, the punters would love them. They tie up at the back, but somehow manage to still flash everything you have. Trust me when I tell you that I know that from experience. I've had the pleasure of old droopy arse over there, bending over and showing me what she's had for dinner last night every time she bends down to put her slippers on,' Bridget said nodding over to the elderly woman in the cubicle opposite her, not caring that the elderly woman was glaring her way, listening in to their conversation.

'I can bloody well hear you, you know,' the woman snarled across the ward. Tapping at her hearing aid.

'Good!' Bridget replied. 'Well, why don't you take the hint then huh? Maybe next time you need to put your slippers on, you could face the other way then, so I don't have to stare at your hairy arse crack.'

'I'm switching you off. Had enough of listening to you bloody moaning, I have.'

Clearly annoyed, the older woman twiddled with her hearing aid, before flipping Bridget her middle finger. Then turning onto her side in a strop, she carried on reading her book.

'Bridge!' Nancy laughed then. Glad that her friend was just as feisty and gobby as normal. The doctors had said as much, only this was all the sign that Nancy needed to believe that Bridget was really okay. 'You're clearly not as bad as you look then…'

'I'm fine,' Bridget said, shaking her head. 'To be honest, I'm more embarrassed than anything else. I really thought I was a goner, Nancy. Imagine how mortified I was when they told me that the knife had only nicked my skin. That it was only a flesh wound. Trust me to bloody faint. I can't even handle a nosebleed… Anyway, you can talk about me looking awful. You don't look so shit hot yourself.' Bridget grinned. She meant it too. She might be the one lying in a hospital bed, but Nancy looked terrible.

Huge dark circles under her puffy eyes. Her skin, devoid of her usual face of make-up, dull and sallow.

She looked like a completely different person. The complete opposite of her usual immaculately turned out persona. In the past few years that she'd been working as Bridget's boss, Bridget couldn't recall a single time she'd seen Nancy with so much as a strand of hair, or smudge of eyeliner, out of place. Perfect hair, perfect make-up.

'You look like you haven't slept a wink all night.'

'I haven't,' Nancy admitted, taking a seat next to her friend then. 'I was so worried about you, Bridge. We all were. Even when the doctors told us that you were going to be okay, and that I should go home and get some sleep, I didn't believe them. I kept thinking that the minute I left you, you'd…' The raw emotion thick in her voice as she spoke honestly.

The lump in her throat, constricting, causing her to be unable to finish her sentence.

She didn't have to.

They both knew how lucky Bridget had been.

The attack could have been so much worse than it had been.

'Jack took me home in the end. He insisted that there was no point staying here, that you needed some proper rest. I think by the time I crawled into my bed and finally got some sleep it was almost 6 a.m., and Scarlett woke me up wanting a wee about half an hour after that. Typical huh!'

'Well, you don't need to be worrying about me, Nancy.' Reaching for her cup of water on the tray beside her. 'Shit!' Bridget winced. Holding her side that the nurses had placed some dressing over.

'Are you sure you're okay? Do you want me to call the nurse?'

'No, seriously. I'm fine,' Bridget protested, holding her hands up to stop Nancy. 'It's just a bit sore, that's all. If I start complaining to that lot, they'll only insist on keeping me in here for longer, and I just can't, Nancy. The food's bad enough as it is, especially when I've got to try and eat it while old Hilda Ogden over there keeps insisting on flashing her gash at me too. It's no wonder I've lost my appetite.'

'Well, if you're sure,' Nancy said, not entirely convinced but knowing how pig-headed Bridget could be when she wanted to. She passed her friend her cup of water, before sitting back down again.

'I'm positive, Nancy. Seriously. The face on you! Would you stop looking at me like that…'

'Like what?' Nancy said, holding her hands up to protest her innocence.

'Like you're about to burst into tears. Seriously, Nancy, it's a little nick of the skin. The doctors are only keeping me in to make sure that it doesn't get infected. I'll be back at the house later today, you can bet your life on that. We'll get everything done in time for Monday still.'

'Er, the last thing you need to be worrying about right now is work, Bridge. We'll manage. I've already spoken to Felicity. She's rounding up some of the girls and they are all over there to give me a hand to unpack the rest of the place. They all send their love. All you need to worry about is making sure you're feeling better.'

Bridget nodded gratefully.

The last thing she wanted to do was let Nancy down. The woman had given her such an amazing opportunity to run the new house, and instead of being back there overseeing everything was up and running in time for the grand opening on Monday, Bridget was stuck here in bloody hospital.

'How is Fliss doing?'

'She's okay. A bit shaken up, you know. It must have given you both a fright, someone breaking in like that.'

Bridget nodded.

'Has Jack managed to find out anything yet? Who it was?'

'No, not yet.' Nancy shook her head sadly. Wishing that she could have said different. That they had some sort of lead. Only the truth was, they had absolutely nothing to go on.

Whoever it was that had broken in last night had managed to get away without a trace.

Which only made Nancy more furious.

'I should never have listened to you and Jack. I should have insisted that company came back out yesterday evening and fixed that bloody security system, no matter how late it was. We would have caught the fucker that did this to you red-handed if the cameras had all been working. At least then we'd have something to go on. I told Jack to read them the riot act when we finally manage to get hold of them. Right now we have nothing to go on, fuck all.'

'The security system would have made no odds, Nancy. The bloke was determined to get in, and he'd made sure that no one would recognise him. Hence the balaclava. It could have been anyone,' Bridget said with a shiver. Recalling the icy cold look in the man's eyes.

The knife in his hand.

How everything had happened so fast.

The fear she'd felt; the struggle between them.

Poor Felicity looking so scared, cowering behind her.

'You were caught off guard. It won't happen again,' Nancy said, regretting that she hadn't put her security staff in place before the official opening. Though she'd never figured she'd have to. The place wasn't up and running, and her staff were only there to protect the girls. To make sure that there was no trouble while they worked. 'I'm going to put some men in place at the property full-time now. There'll be security on site at all times. So, when you come home, you won't ever be put in that position again, Bridge. I mean it. I'm so sorry,' Nancy said, riddled with guilt.

She couldn't even begin to imagine the fear that Bridget had felt, being confronted with the intruder.

'Hey, it wasn't your fault, Nancy. You couldn't have known that some idiot was going to break in. None of us could. I mean what's the chances? And the fact that he was alone too. He's got to be either really fucking ballsy, or really fucking stupid.'

'Well, he purposely fucked with me, so I'm going to go with the latter,' Nancy said, still visibly annoyed that someone would dare to walk into her property and single-handedly try and rob her. Not to mention what he'd done to Bridget. 'When we catch up with him, which we will do, he's going to wish to God that he'd never set foot in my house. I'll fucking kill him myself for what he did to you,' Nancy vowed. 'I promise you, Bridge. Jack will find him.'

''Course he will. Good old Jack, eh!' Bridget smiled then. The faith in her words genuine. Jack was a rock to them all. If anyone could find the bastard that stabbed her last night, he would. She had no doubt about that.

'Anyway, enough of all the depressing stuff. Tell me about tomorrow? The children's gala. You're still going, aren't you?'

Nancy nodded.

''Course we are. We wouldn't miss it for the world, couldn't even if we wanted to. It's all Scarlett's spoken about all week. You wanna hear her talking about all the Disney princesses that she's going to meet. They certainly know how to throw a party, huh!' Nancy said with a grin.

Keeping up appearances, as always, as one of London's most successful businesswomen and property tycoons, following in her father's footsteps, Nancy Byrne had done so much for the children's wards at St George's Hospital that she had been given the honorary role of ambassador for one of them.

As exhausted as she was with everything that had been going on the last few days, she had to make an appearance. Her donation to the hospital was so substantial this year, and she knew that a lot of important, influential people would be at the event too.

Not only that, but giving back to that hospital in particular helped to ease her guilt at what had happened to poor Megan Harris a few years back.

Even though Alfie Harris's daughter had gone on to make a full recovery, Nancy had never truly got over how close she'd come to throwing that poor young girl into the firing line. Just so she could reap revenge on her brother, Daniel.

'Oh, I bet Scarlett's going to be in her element surrounded by all the Disney princesses and characters there. She's mad for them. That last time I babysat for her, she made me watch that *Little*-poxy-*Mermaid* on repeat. Five hours of my life I'll never get back! I think I went to bed that night with 'Part of Your World' still playing out in bleeding stereo inside my eardrums.' Bridget laughed, affectionately.

It was no secret how much Bridget doted on the child. Always telling Scarlett that she could call her Auntie Bridgy, while constantly showering the child with little gifts and sweets every time she saw her.

Another reason why Nancy liked Bridget. Not only was she a good friend to Nancy, but she really cared about Scarlett too. The woman was the salt of the earth.

'Oh, don't. She's obsessed with that bloody Ariel,' Nancy said, rolling her eyes. Only too familiar with Scarlett's latest fixation. 'You know why, don't you? She said that they both have the same long red hair. She's managed to convince herself that that's all part of the criteria and that she's actually part mermaid too. My poor nan couldn't get the little madam out of the bath yesterday. She was in there for over an hour and a half, apparently. Joanie said she'd had to keep topping up the hot bath water to stop Scarlett from turning blue and that by the time she'd managed to coax her out of there, she'd looked like a wrinkled prune.' Nancy laughed then. 'I tell you what, the pair of them are hilarious to listen to. Always butting heads with each other, but they adore each other really. They're just two of the same. Stubborn as you like. Scarlett's just like Joanie. And my dad,' Nancy said, a tiny tremor of emotion behind her words. Which caught her still, even after all these years, every time she thought about the fact that the two most important people in her life would never meet each other.

That her father would have so loved Scarlett. The man would have adored the girl.

It was a pain that cut deeply.

'Oh, yeah. Because we don't know any other stubborn, fiery redheads that she might take after, do we?' Bridget smiled at Nancy. Stating the obvious that Nancy seemed to forget that Scarlett was the woman's mini-me. 'And I'll tell you what, you think you have trouble on your hands with her now, you wait until she gets older, Nancy. That one's going to give you a right run for your money.'

Nancy nodded in agreement.

She'd been thinking the same herself. Scarlett was only four, yet already the child was as stubborn and strong-willed as ever. Christ knew what she was going to be like when she hit her teenage years. Already Nancy was dreading it.

'So this event, it's just the three of you going?' Bridget teased, interrupting Nancy's thoughts. 'Like a proper little family outing.'

'It's a family event.' Nancy laughed, rolling her eyes at the fact that Bridget just never let up.

The woman was forever convinced that there was much more to their unconventional relationship than Nancy let on. She was like a hungry dog in search of a bone, always looking for little clues that there was more than just a friendship going on.

'Seriously, Bridge. If there was something going on between me and Jack, don't you think you'd know by now? You know the score. We're her parents. That's it. No hassle, no dramas, no complications. It's purely platonic, and it works. I don't see Jack that way.'

'Well you must have at some point, otherwise Scarlett wouldn't be here, would she?' Bridget said, still not convinced. Still, getting any real information out of Nancy was like getting blood from a stone. So instead, she changed the subject.

'Here, let's crack open that box of chocolates you bought me,' Bridget said then, pointing to the tray table beside her, visibly perking up at the fact that Nancy was staying for a while and keeping her company. 'We might as well put them to good use.'

'Are you sure you're allowed chocolates while you're on a drip?'

''Course I am. They've only got me on this for my blood pressure, Nancy.' Then smirking, she added sarcastically. 'Seriously, Nancy, if I can survive a near-fatal stabbing, I'm sure I'll survive a box of posh choccies!' Bridget insisted.

'Well, you may not be nil by mouth, Bridge, but I bet old Hilda Ogden over there, wishes that you bloody were.'

Nancy laughed then, as the two women shot a glance across the ward to the bed opposite them, where the old lady lay, still shooting them both daggers over the top of the book she was reading.

Chuckling to herself, Nancy did as she was told and opened the chocolates for her friend, glad that Bridget was back to her usual gobby self.

Popping a chocolate in her mouth, she smiled at Bridget. Playing down the fact that she was seriously pissed off that someone had the blatant audacity to break into her house and harm one of her girls. To try and rob her of her hard-earned money.

This would never have happened if her father had still been here, running things.

This was because she was a woman, in a man's world.

People still saw her as weak. As an easy target.

Nancy Byrne was anything but. Whoever did this to her friend would be found and, when he was, Nancy was going to take great pleasure in making an example out of him.

No one fucked with her. No one.

CHAPTER THIRTEEN

'Grandad!' Throwing her beloved doll down onto the floor without a second thought for it, as soon as she clapped eyes on her great-grandad, Scarlett Byrne ran towards the man, screeching with excitement.

'Hello, my little pickle.' Bending down Michael Byrne opened his arms widely and scooped the child up. Hugging her to him. 'Ahh, who's my favourite girl in the whole wide world?'

'Oh? Is it not me then? Charming!' Joanie Byrne chuckled as she sat in the armchair with her hand wrapped around her warm mug of tea.

'Poor Nanny.' Winking at Scarlett so that the child knew Nanny Joanie was just winding up Grandaddy Michael.

'Okay, okay. My two favourite girls then.' Michael beamed at Joanie.

They'd been getting on so well lately, and he knew exactly how to butter the woman up. Especially seeing as he had made plans today. Michael lived for his time alone with his precious great-granddaughter.

'No, no. No,' Scarlett screeched. 'Just me. I'm your favourite girl, Grandaddy. Me.' Scarlett giggled, pretending to pull her great-grandad away from her nan Joanie, just as he bent down and attempted to plant a kiss on his wife's forehead.

'Oh, of course you are! Come here,' Michael said, earnestly, tickling the child, who in turn squealed with delight at the attention she was receiving.

'You two!' Joanie pretended to scold them both, as she turned up the TV, secretly in her element at the little bond the two of them had with each other.

The love between them both was so pure, and so genuine, that it almost made Joanie want to cry with joy. Michael Byrne had well and truly redeemed himself these past four years.

Ever since Scarlett had come along, he'd been a changed man.

He may not have been much of a father to their Jimmy, in fact if anything he'd barely given their only child the time of day. Michael was far too busy for any family stuff, back then, when Jimmy had been a boy. He'd been too preoccupied with chasing bits of skirt, as Joanie had referred to all her husband's indiscretions over the years.

Michael had only ever looked after number one.

Only these days, he'd become the dedicated family man. A fantastic great-grandfather to Scarlett. Nothing was ever too much for his precious great-granddaughter, and Joanie was made up for the man.

Finally, he got it. Just how much children could mean in his life. How much joy and love they brought with them.

He'd missed out on so much when their Jimmy had been small. Joanie realised that now, and she also had to acknowledge that not all of that had been entirely his fault either. She'd been selfish too. Wanting to keep her Jimmy all to herself.

How she'd relished turning him against Michael.

She wasn't about to make the same mistake with Scarlett. If anything she encouraged the bond that the two of them had between them.

Playing the good cop, bad cop, just often enough so that Michael would come out looking on top. She loved Scarlett more than life itself, but Scarlett adored the very bones of her great-grandad and Joanie would never step in the way of that love.

'I can barely hear my programme with all that noise you two scallywags are both making.' She laughed.

'Nanny said that we're going to the park again, Grandaddy? Can we go now?' Scarlett asked, jumping from one foot to the other, as her great-grandad placed her back down on the floor again.

'You may as well.' Joanie waved her hand at her husband playfully. 'You take your Grandaddy to the park, Scarlett, at least that way Nanny Joanie will get some peace and quiet while you're both gone.'

Michael glanced at his watch. Acting coy now, as if he wasn't fussed either way.

Before grinning down at Scarlett.

'Go on then, go and get your shoes on.'

'Yay! Come on, Grandaddy!' Scarlett squealed again, as she ran to get her coat and wellington boots from where she'd left them from yesterday's little adventure with her Grandaddy. 'Shall I wear my boots and we can jump in puddles again? Like we did yesterday?'

'Only if you don't splash me, you little monkey.' Michael laughed as he bent down to kiss Joanie on the head, in a bid to say goodbye, just as they both heard the sound of the front door go.

'Hello, Nanny Colleen!' Scarlett called out. 'I'm going to the park with Grandaddy. Look, I've got my pink wellies on.'

'That's lovely, darling,' Colleen said with a grin, though secretly she was a little miffed that the child was going out, when she'd only just got here.

She'd only managed to see Scarlett once this week, and that was purely to put the child to bed and read her a story because Nancy had been running so late.

They were supposed to be all equally sharing Scarlett's childcare, though Joanie and Michael always seemed to have their own plans for the child, now that Colleen wasn't living here anymore.

Colleen was left with only the scraps it seemed.

'Yesterday, Grandaddy kicked a puddle at a cat, and the cat ran off and we laughed. Didn't we, Grandaddy?'

'Michael!' Joanie reprimanded the man, just as Colleen walked in, stopping just inside the lounge doorway.

An outsider, forever looking in.

'Well, that's not a very nice thing to do to the poor cat, is it?' Colleen said, shooting a glare at her father-in-law. 'Not the greatest thing to teach a four-year-old, is it?'

Michael looked at Scarlett and rolled his eyes playfully, which Scarlett only mirrored. Rolling her eyes up at her Nan Colleen; only she wasn't as subtle and Colleen caught her, which only made Scarlett giggle some more.

Catching the look the two exchanged, and realising that she was the butt of their joke once again, quickly put Colleen's back up. She knew all about the not so private little jokes and jibes they had about her. Making out as if she was always moaning about something. As if she was the one at fault here.

'I was going to do some arts and crafts with Scarlett today. I told you that the other day. You remember, Scarlett? I said I'd be up on Saturday morning, and that we'd do some painting and sticking together. Just you and me.'

Scarlett shook her head.

'I don't want to, Nanny. I want to go to the park with Grandaddy.'

'Well, maybe you should go to the park another day. It looks as if it's about to rain. And I haven't seen you for a couple of days, darling. Wouldn't you like to have fun with your Nanny Colleen?'

'NO!' Scarlett squealed, shooting Nanny Colleen a filthy look as she stamped her feet. The child's mouth twisted into a scowl, making her look even more like her mother than ever. 'I don't want you. I only want Grandaddy.'

Colleen eyed the child's fiery red hair, those mischievous green eyes.

It could have been Nancy when she was that age. The child was the image of her mother.

Nancy had dismissed her back then, too, in favour of Joanie, and now it was happening all over again.

'I've promised her now,' Michael Byrne said to Colleen apologetically. The sight of the child's crestfallen face at being told she couldn't go suddenly was too much for him to contend with. 'Don't worry, Colleen. If it rains, we'll be all nice and wrapped up. Scarlett's wearing that lovely big pink coat you got her. Besides. We're adventurers, aren't we, Scarlett?' Michael winked at the child. 'A little bit of rain doesn't bother us!'

Scarlett whooped loudly again at that. She loved her secret adventures with her Grandaddy.

'Okay, darling. Well you have fun with Grandaddy, won't you? I'll come up and see you tomorrow instead,' Colleen said, desperately trying to keep the bitterness and disappointment from her voice. If only for Scarlett's benefit if nothing else. She was sick of always being portrayed as the bad one.

So instead she put on her biggest smile.

'Say goodbye to Nanny Colleen and Nanny Joanie,' Michael Byrne said, pulling on his coat, before taking Scarlett's hand.

Doing as she was told, Scarlett blew kisses to her nanny Joanie, and then to her nanny Colleen. Quickly hurrying out the door before her bossy nanny Colleen could say anything else.

*

'That child is obsessed with Michael,' Colleen Byrne said tartly, still standing in the doorway. Stung by the child's indifference to her. 'She completely idolises the man.'

'Yeah well, I guess someone's got to.' Joanie chuckled. Aware of the bitter undertone to her daughter-in-law's words but deciding not to feed into it.

Colleen was jealous, that much was obvious.

Blaming her and Michael for the fact that Scarlett just didn't want to spend time with her. As if it was their fault somehow. Which was a completely ridiculous notion; but then Colleen always seemed to have a problem these days.

'Well, it's not on. I think you both need to be more supportive of me. If I make plans with Scarlett, then you should both help me to enforce them. Otherwise, I'll never get to see her.'

It was Joanie's turn to roll her eyes then.

'Oh, Colleen. It's only a trip to the park. Seriously, you're making a big deal out of nothing.'

'Am I?' Colleen said glaring at Joanie now. The anger inside her bubbling away. 'He's too soft on her. He lets her do and say as she pleases. She's only four years old, she needs boundaries and discipline. He's going to turn her into a spoiled brat otherwise.'

Just like you did to Nancy and Daniel when they were kids, she thought. Though Colleen didn't voice that out loud. She wouldn't dare give Joanie the ammunition to use against her. Running back to Nancy and telling her such things.

'Oh please, Colleen,' Joanie said now, trying to keep the irritation from her tone. 'Can you hear yourself, love? Scarlett has years ahead of her to abide by the rules and do as she's told. Let the child have some fun.'

Good old Joanie, the voice of reason, Colleen thought, staring at the woman, and seeing straight through her.

This was all just an act. Joanie was secretly enjoying every second of Scarlett's rejection of her. Even straight-faced, there was a light that danced in her eyes as if she was mocking her.

'Fun? It won't be fun when that child comes home full of cold.'

Joanie bit her lip, afraid of what would come out of her mouth if she spoke. She turned the volume up on the TV remote, but still the woman didn't take the hint.

'I'm not stupid, Joanie. I know what you're doing,' Colleen said, her voice steady and in control, surprising even her. 'The child acting so indifferent towards me. She's got to be picking up on someone else's words and behaviour.' Colleen glared at Joanie. Making it blatantly clear who she was directing that comment at.

'You mean *me*?' Joanie laughed then. Throwing her head back, and cackling loudly. 'Oh come on, Colleen. You seriously can't be implying that I'm trying to turn Scarlett against you? Are you mad?'

Colleen pursed her mouth. Narrowing her eyes at the woman. Typical Joanie.

She always did that. Belittled her. Made her doubt herself.

But Colleen knew that's what was happening here. Why else would the child be so dismissive of her? Even if Joanie wasn't about to admit it anytime soon.

And it wouldn't be the first time that the woman had made her question her mental well-being either, making out that she was acting crazy and paranoid, when they both knew what was really going on here.

'I take it Nancy's out working, again!' Colleen said, not bothering to hide the disregard in her voice that Nancy had left Scarlett at home yet again. 'I thought she said that once this new knocking shop of hers was up and running that she was going to step back a bit. Be around a lot more for Scarlett.'

'It's not a knocking shop, Colleen. It's a private members' spa,' Joanie said, biting her lip now as Colleen went into one, yet again, about the amount of hours that Nancy seemed to be leaving the child in Joanie and Michael's care.

It was as if lately it had become some sort of personal contest between the three of them: who spent the most time with Scarlett. And whatever the outcome, Colleen was never happy.

The fact that Nancy was actually at the hospital this morning, seeing to poor Bridget, after the poor woman had been stabbed last night, was news that Joanie decided to keep to herself.

Christ knew that Colleen didn't need any more ammunition to throw at Nancy about her line of work and the risks involved. She'd have a bloody field day with that snippet of information.

'A private spa, my arse,' Colleen spat. 'That girl's away with the fairies. Such grand illusions, just like her father had. It's a brothel, Joanie, and it doesn't matter how much money she throws at the place or how much she dresses that fact up, that's all it will ever be. I thought that now she had Scarlett she'd stay away from places like that. She'd want to be a better role model.'

Joanie saw red then.

'A better role model. How dare you! Nancy's not out there doing the whoring herself for money, Colleen. She's out there working her arse off, so she can pay the bills and keep a roof over her child's head,' Joanie smarted. 'It was good enough for you, wasn't it? Spending Jimmy's hard-earned money quicker than the man could earn it on all your expensive fur coats, fancy jewellery and your next bottle of vodka. You weren't bothered where the money came from then, were you? Nancy has stepped up. She's doing a sterling job, too,' Joanie said, the pride in her voice evident. 'She's a businesswoman and a bloody great mother. She loves the bones of Scarlett. Even a blind person is capable of seeing that.'

'A businesswoman? She's pimping out young girls.'

'Bollocks,' Joanie said, glaring at Colleen as she wondered when the woman had suddenly become all sanctimonious. 'She's giving those *young women* a decent wage, in a safe environment too. She's even sent the girls off to do lots of courses. Given them the chance to get real qualifications in Holistic Massage and Hot Stone Therapy. Where else would those girls get a chance like that?'

'And whose benefit do you think she's doing that for? The girls? Don't be so naive, Joanie. She's doing all that so, if the Old Bill go sniffing about the place, she's just covering her arse.' Colleen shook her head. 'Besides, you're missing the point. My gripe isn't about where she works: that's down to her. It's about the hours she keeps. She's a mother now. And her working every hour that God sends means she's missing out. Trust me, I of all people know that. She won't get this time again. She should make the most of it. Make the most of Scarlett before that child is grown too,' Colleen said, the emotion thick in her voice. 'It's not right leaving Scarlett here all the time.'

'With me and Michael you mean? Her great-grandparents?' Joanie said now, well and truly losing her patience with Colleen.

'Do you know what, Joanie, forget it. You'll never understand,' Colleen said, shaking her head sadly. 'You make out as if you love Scarlett, but the only person you really care about is yourself. As long as you get Scarlett all to yourself, who cares what's better for the child. Who cares what's better for Nancy? It's all about Joanie Byrne with you. Clinging on to those around you for dear life. Like some desperate old has-been,' Colleen sneered, feeling suddenly braver than she had done in years.

Joanie Byrne was riling her up, and it had well and truly worked this time.

'Well I won't let you do this to me again, Joanie. I won't let you keep my blood from me, do you hear me.'

'Keep your *blood* from you?'

How Joanie didn't jump out of her chair and launch herself at the woman right then and there, Joanie couldn't quite fathom. It was taking everything she had to contain her temper, every bit of strength she had inside her.

The woman was forever the victim, acting as if butter wouldn't melt. As if she couldn't do any wrong – only Joanie knew better. Joanie knew everything.

Colleen, the foolish woman, knew that too.

For years their little secret had gone unspoken between them.

Colleen had done as Joanie had told her and moved out of the house and, in return, she had got Joanie's silence. A high price to pay.

Only, the truth always came out in the end, and maybe today Colleen had pushed the woman too far.

'I think that it's high time you and me had a little chat, don't you?'

She tapped the chair next to her. Indicating to Colleen to take a seat. It was an order, not an invitation.

Colleen did as she was told. Recognising the twisted look of hate and anger on the older woman's face, she knew exactly what the onslaught would be if she didn't do as she was told.

'Don't even think about sitting there in front of me, and fobbing me off, Colleen,' Joanie Byrne spat. Her words as cold and hard as ice.

Now that the two women were alone, Joanie wasted no time in getting straight to the point.

'You want to talk about keeping blood from people, then let's you and me talk about what you did to me, shall we? The elephant that's been in the room for the past four years.'

'I thought that we dealt with this. I did what you asked. I moved out,' Colleen Byrne said, reminding Joanie that they were both still playing the game.

It had gone unspoken between them both. What Colleen had done all those years ago, when Joanie had been carted off to the looney bin. After some time away from her home, away from Colleen's special concoctions, she'd managed to get her head together and her memory had returned to her.

Joanie had been okay with Colleen when she first visited her at the psychiatric hospital. Friendly still, if a little subdued and confused at what was going on. Though as time went on, she became cold and distant with her.

Then her visits were stopped completely, and Colleen was told that Joanie didn't want to see her anymore.

Colleen hadn't even questioned Joanie's decision; she didn't have to. She'd known then, with certainty, that Joanie had worked it all out.

How Colleen had been drugging her.

That her daughter-in-law had sought out her revenge by driving Joanie into thinking that she was mad and that she'd lost the plot.

It had worked, too, for a time. Until the rest of the family had stuck their noses in and insisted on sending the old bint off to a psychiatric hospital.

Colleen had waited patiently for the onslaught that she was certain would follow, once Joanie made the revelation to the rest of the family. She'd love that. Turning the family against her.

Only Joanie hadn't told any of them.

Instead she'd held that little nugget of truth over Colleen's head since the day that Scarlett had been born. Using her knowledge to her advantage and blackmailing Colleen.

She'd made her move out of the family home.

Still a first-class bitch through and through. That steely glint in her eyes and raw hatred radiating from her. The old woman had come home from hospital and had somehow seemed to have found her strength again. Despite being in her early seventies, the woman's mind and tongue were both sharper than they'd always been. Cutting and scathing all at once.

Even more so now, four years on.

And today, it seemed, was going to be the day that Colleen was going to be told a few home truths whether the woman liked it or not.

Today, Joanie was officially done with all the pretence.

'Let's talk about all those times when I thought I was losing my mind. It was you. Feeding me with bullshit. Manipulating me. Spiking my food and drink with medication.'

Colleen didn't answer. Instead she sat deadly still. Her silence speaking volumes.

What could she say in her own defence?

Deny what they both knew was true?

A few years back, Colleen had almost chanced her luck. Convinced that even if Joanie did tell, the rest of family might not believe her.

It would have been Colleen's word against Joanie's. Poor, fragile, confused Joanie.

Only Joanie didn't seem to be any of those things now.

If Joanie spoke up now, none of them would question the woman twice.

'You pushed me down the stairs,' Joanie said. Pointing her finger directly at Colleen. Her eyes boring into the younger woman's. Reminding Colleen of the same steely glazed look that her late husband Jimmy used to have when he was angered.

'I remember. I remember it all. How you told me that my Jimmy's murderer was coming to get me. That they were going to kill me too. You messed with my head. Deliberately making me paranoid. I was a quivering wreck because of you.'

Joanie kept her glare. Her eyes not leaving Colleen's. Determined to have her say and let her daughter-in-law know that she was on to her.

That she'd had Colleen's card well and truly marked for years.

'When I tried to run, you tripped me. I remember that too. Looking down at the steps beneath my feet and seeing your foot, too, before I tumbled down the staircase. I could have broken my neck…'

I wish you fucking had! Colleen thought.

Clasping her hands together tightly on her lap, Colleen still didn't speak; she didn't dare. She'd been foolish to lose her temper with Joanie and call the woman out. Cursing herself now for her stupidity. For letting her anger get the better of her. She needed to play the game, to let Joanie get this out of her system while the others weren't around. She couldn't risk riling the woman up worse than she already was; she couldn't let the rest of the family find out.

Nancy would never forgive her if she knew the truth. She'd keep Scarlett from her.

Colleen had too much to lose, something that Joanie was all too aware of.

'Don't worry, Colleen,' Joanie said, her eyes narrowing, her glare not leaving Colleen. 'I forgave you years ago when you packed your things up and moved out of *my* house.'

She smirked then, triumphantly.

'Besides, it was nothing that I hadn't already done to you.'

Joanie didn't waver.

'You took me for being old and senile, Colleen, and you still do. And that's where you make your biggest mistake. Thinking that you could take advantage of me at my weakest; only I'm not weak anymore and you won't ever get the opportunity to disrespect me in that way again. And I certainly won't have you disrespecting Nancy, do you understand?'

The cutting edge to Joanie's words were clear for Colleen to hear.

'She's a good girl. And a great mother. Something that you most certainly can never claim to be.'

Joanie pursed her mouth, laying it all out in the open between them. Making it clear that the two women would only ever be rivals. That the stagnant, putrid water than ran deep between them was too great to ever bridge.

'If Nancy finds out what you did to me, she will hate you even more so than she does now. She'll stop you from seeing Scarlett.'

There it was.

They were both clear now. Both aware of the mutual hatred that lingered in the room between them.

'I won't stop you being a part of that child's life unless I have to. So, whatever happens, Colleen, this is all down to you. If you ever, EVER, slag off Nancy's parenting or question myself and Michael's involvement with Scarlett's upbringing again, you will live to rue the day, do you understand?'

'Perfectly,' Colleen said at last. Her mouth pursed. Her eyes blinking back fresh tears as she got up from the chair slowly, as if she'd just had all the air knocked out of her.

She'd never win against Joanie Byrne, she knew that now.

Christ knows how she ever thought she could.

CHAPTER FOURTEEN

'Wow look at how pretty your mummy looks!' Jack said warmly, later the next evening as Nancy Byrne waltzed into the kitchen, unaware of just how breathtakingly beautiful she looked as she tugged down the material of the floor-length royal blue dress she was wearing.

'Really? Do you think it's okay? I feel a bit overdressed,' Nancy said tugging self-consciously.

'Okay? You look a million dollars, Nance!' Jack said, genuinely. 'And besides, we're going to a Disney princess ball. I'm sure that given the theme, you'll probably be the most conservatively dressed woman there.' He laughed then as Nancy rolled her eyes.

'Honestly, you look stunning,' Jack said reassuring the woman, unable to take his eyes off Nancy, even as Scarlett came screeching into the room to see what her father was making such a fuss about.

'Wow, Mummy, you look like a real fairy princess. Just like Cinderella,' the child said, stopping in her tracks and looking up at her beautiful mummy.

'Oh, great! That wasn't the look I was going for.' Nancy laughed, then rolled her eyes at Jack once more as Scarlett only confirmed what she'd already been thinking. 'I'm going to change. I knew it looked too much.'

'Don't you dare! Honestly. Wear it, you look sensational,' Jack said. He meant it too. Right now, standing in the Byrnes' kitchen looking at the mother of his child and his tiny daughter, he couldn't have been any prouder of the pair of them.

'What about me, Mummy? Do you like my dress?' Scarlett shouted doing a twirl in her deep blue and gold dress adorned with a huge red bow.

'Snow White? What about Ariel? I thought she wanted…?' Nancy said, staring at Jack and wondering why he was discreetly doing a cut-throat signal to her. The penny dropping, Nancy changed tact. 'Wow, you look super beautiful, Scarlett. I bet you're going to be the prettiest princess there.'

'Yep!' Scarlett said with a huge grin. 'And Daddy said that all the princesses will want to have their photos taken with me. Look what Daddy bought me, too,' Scarlett said, holding up her brand-new plastic doll.

'Oh, lovely. Another Ariel mermaid doll. Haven't you already got that one though?'

Scarlett shrugged, shooting a guilty look her father's way.

As Jack laughed and shook his head, realising that he'd been duped by his own child.

'Yes, but Daddy said if I stopped crying, that I could have anything I wanted in the whole shop. And all I wanted was my Ariel doll, 'cause I love her so much,' Scarlett reasoned with her parents, as they both stared down at her. Nodding at her as if she was talking perfect sense. 'So now I have two. Can I bring both my Ariel dolls with me, Mummy? Pretty please? They want to come and meet the princesses too,' the child said, excitedly, barely stopping for breath between words.

Nancy grinned.

''Course you can. We're leaving in ten minutes though, so you'd better be quick if you want to get your other one.'

Happy with this, Scarlett ran off in pursuit of her other doll.

'You said she could buy anything in the entire shop?' Nancy said, still grinning. Though she playfully narrowed her eyes at the man.

Enjoying winding him up now that they were alone.

'Seriously, Jack, that child can wrap you around her little finger and she knows it too!'

'Don't,' Jack said rubbing his hand through his hair, in total agreement. The memory of his shopping experience with his young daughter just a few hours earlier still painfully fresh at the forefront of his mind. 'They didn't have any Ariel costumes left. So it was a choice between Snow White, or Buzz Lightyear and Woody from *Toy Story* and, let's just say, that news didn't go down well with Madam. She kicked off. Big time. Threw herself on the floor in front of everyone in the shop and had a massive paddy,' Jack said, recalling the humiliation he'd felt when half the shop had stared at him, almost accusingly, as if he'd personally upset the child somehow himself. 'I didn't know how to make her stop, so yes I admit it.' Jack held his hands up, laughing now, at how easily played he'd been by the kid. 'I used bribery and it worked a treat. Or at least I thought it had; only it turns out little Miss Scarlett was playing me all along. What a little madam.'

Nancy nodded in agreement; she certainly couldn't argue with that.

She was smiling at the child as she returned to the kitchen, both dolls in her hands now. Joanie and Michael both walking into the kitchen behind her. Laughing and chatting away to Scarlett as she showed off her brand-new doll.

'Oh, they are both very lovely. Like twins,' Joanie said, pretending to be impressed.

'So, if that one's Ariel, what are you going to call the other one?' Michael chipped in.

'Ariel number two, silly Grandaddy!' Screwing her face up as if the answer was obvious, Scarlett dramatically rolled her eyes at her great-grandad, which only made him laugh harder.

'Oh, wow, Nancy,' Joanie said, stopping in her tracks as soon as she set sights on her granddaughter. 'You look incredible. Doesn't she, Michael?'

'You look breathtaking,' Michael said, nodding in agreement as they both stared at their granddaughter. Nancy Byrne was a vision indeed.

'We need a photo,' Joanie said, shooing Michael off to grab her camera from the lounge. She stood with her hands over her mouth. Taking in the sight of the beautiful couple in front of her. Nancy dressed in a beautiful gown. Jack wearing his smart grey suit. She couldn't help but think what a lovely couple they both made.

Granted, Jack was twenty years Nancy's senior. But that had never bothered Joanie. What was age, if but a number?

'Scarlett, go and stand with Mummy and Daddy. Nanny wants to take a picture of the three of you.'

'There's no need, Nan,' Nancy said, waving her hand in protest. 'It's a high-profile event. I'm sure the paps will be out in force tonight like usual. There'll be enough pictures floating around the newspapers tomorrow morning,' she said, knowing full well that the press were bound to try and take pictures of her tonight. The press couldn't help themselves. She was Nancy Byrne, daughter of the infamous, late gangster, Jimmy Byrne. They tried their hardest to portray her as some kind of socialite. An It girl, as they were known these days. Turning up and looking pretty for the photos. Just a bit of eye candy; though Nancy was anything but and she'd played the press back at their own game, proving to them all time and time again that not only was she beautiful but she was also busy making a name for herself these days as a successful businesswoman too. Owner of the prestigious Karma Club, and a whole host of properties across London. Her legitimate businesses: keeping her real money-spinning business well under wraps of course. Nancy Byrne had really come into her own. And, what's more, she publicly donated a huge amount of money to certain charities too. St George's, in particular.

The press didn't really know what to make of her, which suited Nancy down to the ground.

'I don't want that kind of smut.'

Joanie wrinkled her nose.

She knew as well as Nancy did that the paparazzi would be there in force tonight indeed. That lot were like vultures, always trying to get their hands on the 'money shot'. Snapping their cameras at awkward angles, just when Nancy was getting in or out of a car. Commenting on her bust and her bottom, as if she was nothing more than a piece of meat. As if she was just some kind of bimbo airhead that looked pretty.

It was beyond disrespectful.

Still, this was the age they lived in now, she guessed. It may be 2008 but as a race they hadn't really evolved at all. That lot still ran around in packs like depraved animals seeking out their prey.

The press had been bad enough, years ago, when her Jimmy had attended any public events, but Nancy was a whole different kettle of fish.

Young and attractive, the media couldn't seem to get enough of her.

It was just a shame that they didn't have more bloody manners and paint Nancy in a better light. But then, they were just going with what sold well to the public.

'I want a picture for us. For the family album. Not something cut out of those tacky newspapers, with some smutty journalist commenting on the size of your arse, or making some other sexist jibe,' Joanie said, getting annoyed.

'Ooh, arse is a bad word, Nanny Joanie,' Scarlett said, looking up at her nan with an expression of both shock and amusement.

Her Nanny Joanie never swore. At least not when she thought that Scarlett was listening.

'Scarlett! Nanny Joanie didn't mean that word. She meant to say bottom,' Nancy said, raising her eyes at her grandmother, teasingly. 'She just gets a little bit angry sometimes.'

'Angry,' Joanie spat. 'I could say a lot worse trust me.' Then looking down at Scarlett, Joanie decided not to mention the paps again. She'd only say something she'd really regret otherwise, and little Scarlett didn't need to hear any of that.

'Don't you be repeating what comes out of your nanny's mouth, okay, Scarlett?'

Scarlett nodded.

'Right here we go,' Michael said, coming back into the kitchen, holding the camera up in front of him. 'I tell you what, Joanie, how about I set up the timer and I get one of all of us? A proper family shot,' he said, knowing that his Joanie would love that. The woman was forever taking pictures of Scarlett. To get one of all of them together, as a family, would positively make her day.

'What about Colleen?' Nancy said, looking up at the clock and realising the time. 'The car's going to be here in a minute. I thought Colleen said she wanted to see Scarlett before we left? She could have been in the photo?'

'Lord knows where that one is,' Joanie said, with a shrug. Secretly not overly fussed where Colleen was today. Or any other day for that matter. Especially after the words they'd both had with each other.

As far as she was concerned it was high time that the woman made some sort of a life for herself outside of this family.

Long overdue in fact.

'She's been acting ever so strange lately, hasn't she, Joanie?' Michael said. 'She went off on one yesterday about not being able to do arts and crafts with Scarlett, as she'd promised. Made a right big deal about it, and after all of the fuss she made, she hasn't even bothered turning up today?'

Joanie shook her head. Not bothering to correct her husband and mention that Colleen had phoned to see if she could see Scarlett, earlier today, but Joanie had told the woman that Scarlett had gone out for the day, shopping with Jack. That she'd get her to phone her when she'd got back; only Joanie had managed to forget to mention that to Scarlett. Accidentally, on purpose. Which would have no doubt pissed the woman off no end.

Colleen was probably at home right now sulking.

'Your nan reckons that she's got herself a fancy man, don't you, Joanie? All of a sudden she's too busy for us all.'

'Well, I don't want to talk bad of Colleen, but if she is putting a new man before her family, then she's got her priorities all wrong,' Joanie said again, trying to convincingly sound as if she was put out by Colleen's behaviour. Though the blatant truth was, whatever Colleen's reasons were for staying away, they suited Joanie just fine.

The less she saw of the woman the better.

'Colleen has a boyfriend?' Nancy said, screwing her face up. 'Do you reckon?'

Seeing the shocked expression on Nancy's face only made Jack laugh.

'Don't look so surprised. Your mother's bound to move on eventually.'

'I guess,' Nancy said, knowing that it was inevitable really. She couldn't even picture what sort of man her mother would go for. Not after she'd been with her father and nor was she overly keen on the idea of another man coming into their lives.

Though to be fair her parents' marriage had been far from perfect.

And Colleen did deserve happiness for herself. Of course she did, especially after years of being trapped inside a loveless sham of a marriage.

Spending two decades married to a man who was secretly gay and in love with his business partner. Her mother had sure known how to pick them.

'I haven't really thought about it that's all. I mean, as long as she's happy…'

'Exactly!' said Michael, ushering everyone over to the edge of the breakfast island, so that they were standing side by side. 'Now talking of happy, I want you all to look at the camera and on the count of ten I want you to say, six sizzling, saucy sausages.'

Michael winked at his granddaughter, who giggled at her great-grandad's funny turn of phrase.

Clicking the remote button on the camera's device, Michael ran to join the rest of the family. All of them staring into the camera. Smiling happily as the white flash filled the room. Capturing them all so beautifully.

The Byrne family.

All together. For one last time.

Each of them blissfully unaware that, in just a few days, their world would be turned upside down.

That for each and every one of them, nothing would ever be the same again.

CHAPTER FIFTEEN

'I'm exhausted.' Nancy grinned, as Jack Taylor led her and Scarlett out of the main doors of London's Roundhouse. Glad that they were leaving early, knowing that Scarlett was tired.

The rest of the partygoers looked as if they'd only just begun, arranging for their army of live-in nannies to collect their children so that they could stay on and party long into the night. Only that was Nancy's idea of hell; personally she couldn't wait to get home and into her bed.

The past few nights, what with getting the Mayfair house all ready and what had happened to Bridget, had left her feeling completely drained.

Still, she was glad that she'd come tonight. Not only were St George's charity balls always spectacular, but this had been the first year that Nancy had been able to include Scarlett in the celebrations too.

It felt good. Giving back and helping others.

As if somehow she was carrying on the tradition. Her father had always been involved with local charities. She even remembered him taking them all to a few fundraisers over the years, when she'd been little. Her mother, and Daniel too.

Though back then the events had been nothing like the scale of tonight's festivities had been.

Each year, the hospital's galas and balls were getting bigger and better. More and more extravagant every time. Ensuring that it was as popular as ever, she supposed, so that people kept coming back for more.

'It's hard to believe this place used to be an old railway engine shed, isn't it?' Nancy said in wonderment as she stared up at the huge circular building set on the edge of London's Chalk Farm Road, still wowed by the Grade II listed building's interior. The place was always stunning inside, but even more so, she suspected, after the event organisers had completely transformed the decor into a magical Disney princess wonderland for all the children to enjoy.

The place had looked sensational with a million twinkling starry lights adorning every ceiling and an incredible three-dimensional painted backdrop of wonderlands and fairy castles.

The venue had been packed to capacity too. Hundreds of guests had attended. And a whole host of celebrities. Jack had been in his element at mingling with them all, having been almost as excited as Scarlett was over the Disney princesses when he'd spotted his idols Mick Hucknall and Rod Stewart.

'Did you have a lovely time, Scarlett?' Nancy said, as Scarlett trailed behind them rummaging around in the party bag she'd been given as they left, knowing full well that her daughter had. The child was exhausted. So much so that Nancy would bet money on her falling asleep in the car on the way home.

'Yes, Mummy,' Scarlett said, through a mouthful of sweets. Not even bothering to look up.

Nancy laughed at how independent her little girl was becoming.

She'd hardly seen her all evening. Scarlett had been whisked away by the entertainers, happy to make new friends with the other children there. All of them kept busy with a live interactive theatrical show, while the adults had been treated to a champagne reception and a sumptuous three course meal, before taking part in the charity auction.

'I'd say that they raised a shitload of money this year,' Jack said, still buzzing from the excitement and energy of the evening. 'Did you see that fella from that pop band? How much he paid for those football boots? Bloody mad,' Jack said, shaking his head. Still shocked at what they went for. 'Though I don't know why I'm so surprised. Of course he's mad. Man United fan, wasn't he?' Jack laughed then. 'And what about David Beckham's first car? Nine grand for a Volkswagen Golf? In turquoise.' He shook his head then. 'That fella was robbed.'

'Well, at least it all goes to a good cause.' Nancy laughed in agreement. Glad that her donations would not only be put to great use, but that she'd managed to bid on two gigantic beautiful matching antique vases for the new house. They'd look amazing down in the new spa area, on the columns either side of the steps that led down to the pool.

'I had a great evening,' Jack said then, seriously. He'd been in his element tonight, in Nancy and Scarlett's company.

'Oh I bet you did. Surrounded by all those beautiful women,' Nancy said, playfully. Trying to hide the fact that she'd felt a slight twinge of jealousy at all the attention Jack got from most of the single females there tonight.

Some of the married ones, too, in fact.

Nancy and Jack might not have been together as a couple, but they were here as a couple tonight. A family. And it had shocked her how many women were quick to try and muscle in on what to anyone on the outside could clearly see was her territory.

Though some of them really didn't care. Too desperate, and too eager to bag themselves a man like Jack. They all flirted shamelessly with the man every time he left her side.

Whereas Nancy had experienced the complete opposite.

Aware of all the admiring glances she got from the vast majority of single men at the event tonight, none of them had dared to come within five feet of her, for fear of stepping on Jack's toes no doubt.

At least, that's what she figured.

It was either that or the cool, closed off exterior she gave off in waves. Keeping men at arm's distance at all times.

Life was easier that way.

'Oh, am I sensing a slight twinge of jealousy there, Miss Byrne?' Jack said, laughing then as Nancy immediately blushed.

'Of course I'm not jealous.' Cursing herself for saying anything now. She'd drank too much bloody champagne. 'I'm just making an observation that's all.'

Her defensive tone only made Jack laugh harder then, as he held his hand up, instructing their chauffeur to make his way down the road towards them, to pick them up.

'Fucksake!' he said, his voice low in front of Scarlett, as he spotted a few lingering paparazzi hanging around nearby, lingering down the side of the Roundhouse building.

They'd spotted Jack and Nancy, too, then, and had started making their way over.

Rushing towards them, cameras in hand.

'Scarlett, darling, come and stand by Daddy,' he said protectively, annoyed that this lot had no consideration for the fact that they had a young child with them, as they surrounded them now. Cameras going off in every direction.

'Nancy, over here,' one of them shouted. As the bright lights of the cameras flashed in a flurry all around them, Jack picked Scarlett up in his arms, keeping his child close.

Scarlett buried herself in his shoulder, wondering what all the commotion was about. Why all these people were trying to take photos of her and her mummy and daddy. They were scaring her.

'It's okay, baby!' Jack said, stroking Scarlett's hair and kissing her on the forehead.

'Just give them their shot, Jack,' Nancy said, resigned. Knowing full well how these vultures worked.

They'd hound them until they got it anyway.

The three of them stood still for a few seconds, begrudgingly.

The infamous Nancy Byrne and her perfect little family.

Grateful when the car pulled up in front of them, Jack shooed them away.

'That's your lot,' he said finally, not prepared to stand there for a second longer. He opened the car door and ushered Nancy and Scarlett safely inside, before jumping in beside them both and closing the door behind them.

'Bloody vultures,' he said, as the car drove off.

Scarlett, now safely in the car, instantly forgetting all about the paps, rummaging around inside her party bag once more.

Nancy smiled, leaning her head back against the black leather seats.

'I'm not interested, you know,' Jack said then, touching Nancy's hand, and looking almost relieved when Nancy didn't pull hers away.

She'd drank way too much tonight. Her head was feeling blurry.

She narrowed her eyes, not sure what Jack was talking about.

'Back there. You said about all those other women. I'm not interested in any of them,' he said then, looking at her intently. 'You know why.'

Nancy stared at Jack, aware of what he was saying. Of the enormity of his words.

'Daddy will you do a puzzle with me?' Scarlett said, interrupting them both before Nancy could reply.

Jack nodded.

His eyes still on Nancy. Drinking her in.

Before turning his attention on to Scarlett then. The moment lost.

Nancy watched for a few minutes as Jack fussed over his daughter. Tickling her and chatting away, with such tenderness it made her want to weep with joy.

He loved Scarlett just as much as she did.

He loved her too.

That's what he was saying, wasn't it?

Nancy leant her head back against the seat again, and this time closed her eyes, her heart hammering inside her chest at Jack's advances.

Recalling Bridget's words, time and time again about how Nancy was too pig-headed and stubborn to admit it, even to herself, how she really felt about him.

How she was too scared to let her guard down.

Only that wasn't it at all.

Nancy wasn't pretending, and she wasn't hiding her true feelings.

These were her true feelings.

She'd never allow a man close to her, not like that.

Not really.

Not after years of watching her mother's and father's pretence.

The lies and heartbreak that went on between them both. The games they'd both played.

And who had suffered the most?

Her and her brother Daniel.

It was any wonder they both had issues.

An absent father who loved her, lavishing her with gifts and the best of everything to compensate for never seeing her. And a mother – Colleen – who was there in body only, with her mind ravaged by booze.

A dysfunctional family at it's very finest, something that Nancy was adamant she would never repeat with Scarlett.

She couldn't allow herself to get caught up in anything with Jack, even if he did genuinely care about her and Scarlett.

She wasn't able for it.

Her heart was completely numb to it all, deep down. Because she knew, the second she let someone in, really let them in, that's when they could break her.

For good.

And Nancy would never allow that to happen, no matter what the cost.

CHAPTER SIXTEEN

'I would have rung ahead to arrange this meeting, only you haven't been returning any of my calls and we were starting to feel concerned about you,' Derek Wheelan said apologetically, sensing Robert Parkes's initial unease at him just turning up here unannounced.

Derek sat down in the armchair opposite the man, aware that the man was still silently glaring at him, though he pretended not to notice.

Instead he smiled, while secretly eyeing the flat. Taking in the man's living conditions, in search of some clues as to how Robert Parkes had really been.

The Drakewell Estate in East Twickenham was notorious for being overrun by gangs of youths. The place was rife with poverty and domestics, but Robert had been lucky. Social Services had worked alongside the local council and managed to allocate the man his very own flat.

Albeit compact. When he closed his front door, this was all his. His space.

It was a tiny flat, but Derek couldn't help but notice how bare the place was. The room was dressed with two brightly coloured monstrosities of furniture that had been donated to Robert by a local charity when he'd first moved in four years ago. A mismatched second-hand sofa bed in a deep teal green, and a pink and orange floral armchair that Derek sat upon. The bold splurges of colour looked almost intrusive against the rest of the drab, magnolia-painted room. As if they didn't belong to the cold, sterile surroundings.

In the corner of the room stood a rickety-looking clothes hook, with a neat row of uniform black and grey coats hanging from it.

That was it.

There was no television, he noted. No photographs or personal items of any kind anywhere. Even out in the kitchen, there was nothing on display. No food. No signs of any dirty crockery.

No clues to what sort of a person Robert was.

The only personal item was down at Robert Parkes's feet. A laptop, Derek noted. Eyeing the computer that had been shoved down on the floor and was just poking out from underneath the chair.

Progress.

The laptop was something, he figured. At least Robert had some kind of gateway to the outside world.

'How are you doing, Robert?' Derek said, lightly. Still sensing the man's unease at the unexpected intrusion.

Robert Parkes shrugged.

At first, he'd refused to let Derek into the flat, and he'd only begrudgingly agreed once Derek made it clear that if Robert sent him away again, he'd only come back again.

Something was up.

Derek was convinced of it.

Though he needed to keep the conversation as neutral and non-judgemental as possible.

Knowing how volatile this client could be, how Robert Parkes had been assigned four caseworkers in as many years, and in time each of them had point-blank refused to work with the man in the end. Due to Robert's uncontrollable temper and rage.

So far, Derek had been lucky enough to not experience that himself first-hand, though he could tell that Robert was on the edge today.

'I just wanted to check in with you and make sure that you're doing okay?'

'You mean, check up on me, more like!' Robert spat, not falling for the man's bullshit. He might look like some horror movie reject, but his brain was working perfectly fine.

He knew damn well what was really going on here.

This lot were keeping tabs on him: the so-called social workers and outpatients team from the hospital. All of them working together and pretending that they actually gave a shit, when the truth of the matter was, Robert was just another job on their checklist. Another statistic to record on their poncy computerised graphs. Just another number in the system.

'I see that you haven't been to your counselling sessions for over a month now, and you missed your last assessment appointment with me too.'

'So, you are checking up on me?' Robert laughed. The sound mocking and humourless.

'I'm not keeping tabs on you, Robert, not like that anyway. I just wanted to see for myself that you're okay. I know how hard it must be. Without any form of support. We still haven't had any luck locating any family members for you,' Derek said regretfully, shifting awkwardly in his chair.

Unable to even imagine how it must feel to wake up from the kind of trauma that Robert Parkes had woken from and to be completely and utterly alone in this world.

To not remember who he was or who his family were.

And worse than that, the fact that there seemed to be nobody looking for the poor man.

Derek Wheelan coughed then, clearing his throat.

He'd been keeping tabs on Robert, but only out of concern. That was the truth of the matter.

For the past few weeks, Robert Parkes had been living well and truly off the grid. Choosing to distance himself from any form of help that had been offered to him, the man was living in almost complete isolation. He hadn't turned up at any of his appointments or meetings, nor had he returned any of Derek's team's calls.

'We just want to help, Robert. To make sure that you're coping okay.'

Only Derek could clearly see that Robert wasn't okay.

He noticed that the man's hands were shaking.

Robert noticed it too then. Catching Derek's stare, he clasped them together tightly and placed them down on his lap.

Derek paused. Wondering if the man was taking something. Something other than his subscribed medication. Drugs?

He was acting more paranoid and jittery than usual.

His leg, bouncing up and down, as if he was nervous about something. Or just plain agitated.

Derek had seen it a thousand times before.

It wasn't unusual for patients to do this. Swap their recovery programme for some other type of release. Something that gave them more instant gratification, like alcohol or cannabis.

It was understandable given the circumstances. Everyone needed their vices, he got that. Something to help them deal with their angst and depression. To block out what they'd been through.

Only it was Derek's job to make sure that Robert was given all the help and resources he needed to ensure that he was properly rehabilitated, the correct way. So that he could live a normal life.

As normal as it could possibly be, given the circumstances.

Only Robert didn't seem very forthcoming with Derek's offer of help.

Stoney faced and defensive. He looked as if he couldn't get rid of Derek quickly enough. Still, Derek persevered.

'What about the support groups? Are you still going to any of them?'

Trying to keep his tone light as possible, Derek Wheelan skimmed over the previous social worker's notes, knowing full well that Robert Parkes hadn't attended a single support group or counselling session in almost five weeks.

'There's no point. They're all a waste of my time,' Robert said with a shrug, not bothering to lie or make up excuses about the fact that he hadn't gone.

'Well, that's a real shame,' Derek said nodding understandingly, as he simultaneously made a note in his notebook.

He'd only taken over the case a couple of months ago, so while he couldn't relate to everything that Robert Parkes had been through, he had studied Robert's notes extensively.

Robert had been admitted to Chelsea and Westminster Burns Unit just over four years ago, after being burned so badly in a fire that he almost died. His injuries had been horrific. Suffering almost sixty-five per cent burns to his body, by rights the man shouldn't even be here now. The doctors had only given him a thirty per cent survival rate. Spending months in intensive care, and almost a year in hospital, Robert Parkes had then needed over twenty operations and facial reconstructive surgeries. Not to mention the intense vigorous physiotherapy that he'd endured. His injuries had been so astronomical that the fact the man was even here, physically sitting across the room from Derek right now, was nothing short of a miracle.

Robert Parkes had proved all the specialists wrong and survived his ordeal.

That showed that he was a fighter.

Though, Derek knew that the man's recovery had been a long and gruelling process, and that he still wasn't completely out of the woods yet.

In fact, his rehabilitation was proving his toughest challenge yet.

Robert Parkes had lost his memory. He had no idea who he was. No idea where he was from.

The doctors had hoped, at first, that the memory loss was only temporary, and that their patient had been showing all the symptoms of Post Traumatic Amnesia, caused by the shock and trauma of the ordeal he'd suffered.

He couldn't remember anything at all, not even his own name.

One of the nurses in the ITU had given the man the pseudonym – Robert Parkes – until his memory returned to him. Only, as time went on, four years in fact, Robert had shown no sign of improvement and, with a lot of help from a notary and the Home Office, the name had legally become his own.

The doctors also now suspected that Robert had suffered what is medically termed as a neuropsychological impairment of the brain, which meant that he might never regain his memory again.

It must be terrifying for the man.

He didn't even have any recollection of what happened to him either, of what he'd been through, which Derek had decided was probably a good thing after seeing the extensive medical report stating that not only had Robert suffered greatly from the fire, but the man had been tortured too.

He'd lost his eye, which the doctors suspected was a horrific injury caused by a blow torch or something similar. He'd been missing fingernails, and toenails. Teeth too. According to the report.

Someone had been out to get this man. They had wanted to leave him for dead. But Robert Parkes, whoever he really was, had defied all odds and survived his ordeal, but he had other challenges that he needed to face now, challenges that Derek wanted to help him to overcome if only Robert would allow him.

'You're suffering from acute Post Traumatic Stress Disorder, Robert. It's important that you keep going to your appointments,' Derek advised.

Robert needed to conquer the psychological damage that had been caused by his harrowing ordeal. Not just the physical aftermath, but the mental damage too.

Whatever had happened to Robert Parkes was locked away deep inside his subconscious. So far from his reach, but still there teetering just underneath the surface. Tormenting him.

And then there was the not knowing.

Not knowing who he is, who he was.

Not knowing who his family and loved ones were.

No one had claimed him. No one had looked for him.

He clearly didn't have a criminal record either, as there was no DNA held on file to give the police, hospital or social services any clues as to who this man really was.

Derek was concerned that Robert was depressed; that that's why he'd taken to avoiding all of his appointments and shutting himself away in his flat all alone, using the place as some kind of fortress for him to hide away from the rest of the world. Only really it was a self-made prison. The man was living like a recluse and it was Derek's job to help the man now. Whether Robert Parkes wanted that or not.

'You've done so well to make such a strong recovery as you have, Robert, overcoming sixty-five per cent burns is just incredible. You're a survivor, Robert. A true survivor!'

'Am I?' Robert screwed his face up, shaking his head, clearly not in agreement. He wanted to laugh then, at this man's stupidity. To launch the fucker out of his flat. He had no clue what he was talking about. None at all. 'Is that what you'd call this? Festering all alone in this flat? Surviving! Live or die, they were the only options I had; very limited, don't you think? I didn't really have much choice.' Robert seemed to be challenging him now. His tone agitated. 'And look what I got for my efforts. Look at the state of me. Look at me!' Robert shouted, his voice echoing around the sparsely furnished flat. 'I should have just given up and died. Only, that would have been the easy way out, wouldn't it? And I guess whoever the fuck I really am clearly doesn't do easy!'

Derek didn't speak. He knew not to.

This was Robert's time to talk. To vent as he must so need to.

Derek Wheelan couldn't even imagine the frustration that the man must be feeling.

He waited, patiently. Listening to the bitterness and discontentment in Robert's voice, letting the man get it all out of his system before he spoke again.

'I know it's difficult for you, Robert, really I do…'

'Do you, though. Derek?' Robert Parkes said then, his voice raised. Irritated by this jobsworth's upbeat tone. The man knew nothing of Robert's harrowing plight. 'Give me a break. You don't know the half of it. Where are you off to after here, huh? You going home, are you? Let me guess… To your two-up two-down little house in the suburbs. With your frumpy wife and your two point four kids? Idyllic for you – Mr Fucking Average! You wouldn't know difficult if it smacked you in the face. You have no idea about my life, so please stop pretending that you do.'

'I'm trying to help,' Derek Wheelan said then, honestly, feeling the tension and hostility radiating from the man. This conversation was not going to plan. 'We really think that it's paramount that you continue with your counselling sessions and your support group meetings if you're to make a full recovery. I know it's hard to talk about the trauma you've been through,'

Derek said, believing that he could somehow get through to the man. He'd worked as a social worker for almost twenty years and to say that Robert Parkes was one of the most severe burn survivors he'd come across was an understatement. None of this was going to be easy, but it would be a damn sight easier if Robert Parkes at least complied and accepted their offer of help and support instead of constantly shunning every opportunity that came his way.

'Talk about it? Oh, I can talk about it. That bit's easy. Where should I start? Shall we talk about my night terrors? The ones that plague me every time I close my one remaining eye. That make me unable to sleep, so then I'm awake all night. Suffering with insomnia. Alone with my thoughts. Wondering what the fuck happened to me. Who the fuck did this to me. Then to spend my days exhausted and in excruciating pain. Every part of me aches. My muscles, my bones, my skin. How's that for talking, Derek? Who did that help? Me or you?' Robert shook his head. 'Talking doesn't change shit.'

'But the groups might help you. Talking about what you went through might trigger a memory. It's an important part of the healing process, and it reminds you that you're not alone.'

'Why aren't you listening to me, Derek? None of you are. That's exactly what I want. To be left alone.' Robert had heard enough of the man's spiel now. He was getting angry. Pissed off with always being spoken down to, preached to, by people that didn't have a clue what he'd been through.

His face a bright puce. Spittle spraying from his lips as he shouted.

'I don't want your help. I've told your lot a thousand times over, I don't want any of it. Why won't you listen to me? Why won't you all do what I ask? Leave me alone, so I can live my life without you lot always sticking your fucking noses in.'

Again Derek didn't respond. Instead he wrote something else down in his notebook.

More notes.

'What was that?' Robert asked then, pursing his mouth, his face twisted with curiosity.

He knew when he was being judged and that's what Derek Wheelan was doing. Judging him, scribbling bullshit down on a bit of paper about things that this prat didn't have a first-hand clue about. 'What did you write down, just then?'

Incensed. What the fuck did any of these social worker busy-bodies know about what he'd been through. About his suffering?

'I'm just making some notes that's all,' Derek said, ignoring the steely glare that Robert insisted on throwing him. Knowing that Robert Parkes could be very angry and volatile when it came to having these sorts of review meetings.

He'd attacked a social worker before.

It had all been in the man's notes. How Robert, even with his limited mobility, walking with a limp, had managed to pin the man up against the wall and shout abuse at him. That's why none of his department had wanted to take Robert's case on. That's why they'd handed Robert over to Derek to deal with. Derek had thicker skin than a rhinoceroses hide, although he'd be lying right now if he said he wasn't starting to feel intimidated by Robert.

Tapping his pen against his notebook as he persevered, determined to be the one that made a difference, he couldn't just give up on him.

'Our only aim is to help you live a full life again, Robert? Don't you want that?'

Robert bit his lip, silent then. His anger subsiding.

'Are you getting out at all?' Derek asked, wondering how Robert Parkes spent his days. 'Do you have any visitors?'

Robert shrugged again. Bored with the questions now. He knew the drill.

'What about work? Have you been actively looking for a job?' Derek said, glancing down to the laptop on the floor. 'That's another part of your rehabilitation, Robert. Getting you working once again. So you can be financially independent and contribute to paying your own way again…'

'That's why you're here, isn't it?' Sitting forward in his chair, his hands clasped together. Robert nodded then, as if finally understanding.

The cheeky fucker had been trying to catch him out. Turning up announced and seeing what Robert had really been up to.

Robert looked at Derek intently, so that the man would be in no doubt about Robert's 'life plan' when he left here today.

He would say this only once.

'Who do you think's going to want to employ me, Derek?' Robert leant in. His voice laced with anger once again. Annoyed that Derek Wheelan seemed to be under the illusion that it was as easy as that for him to simply just apply for a job. As if no one would notice. No one would say anything. 'Look at the state of me. Who the fuck wants to employ this huh?' Robert said, slapping himself hard on the forehead. 'What would I do, huh? Serve up Happy fucking Meals to little kids. Me – Mr-fucking-Crispy with one fucking eye. I'd terrify the poor bastards at first sight.' Robert was shouting now.

This was what the meeting was really about, he realised. Why Derek Wheelan was here today. They were trying to get Robert off the system. All this rehabilitation bollocks was really about Robert paying his own way in the world again.

They wanted rid of him.

'No one wants to employ me. I look like a fucking monster.'

Robert was glaring at Derek now. Willing the man to come out with some bullshit to say differently. When they both knew it was true.

Even he struggled to look at himself in the mirror most days.

The horrendous sight of his unrecognisable wrinkled, scarred face staring back at him. His left eye gone, the eyelid sewn shut. Just a jagged line of scar tissue there now.

A monster was an understatement.

He looked alien. Like nothing of this world.

'What about a job working behind the scenes. As a cleaner or something?'

'I can't work with chemicals. My skin reacts to everything. It's painful enough as it is,' Robert said losing his patience now. Derek just wasn't taking no for an answer.

'Perhaps an office job?' Derek persisted. 'We have a scheme set up with a couple of big companies. I'm sure we could find you a placement there. Nothing too strenuous. Office work mainly. Filing and photocopying etc. That kind of thing…'

'I said, I'm not interested,' Robert said. His voice low, but his tone defiant.

Derek Wheelan made another note in his notebook.

Tapping his pen against the page, his following silence speaking volumes.

'What did you just write?' Robert said, sensing the man's disapproval.

He was up and out of his seat then. Making a grab for the notebook, the two men struggled for a few seconds before Robert managed to overpower Derek. Grabbing the book from the man's hold he scanned the notes that were scrawled across the page.

His eyes staring down at the underlined words on the page.

Depressed. Non-compliant. Difficult.

Igniting Robert Parkes's anger then, like a red flag to a bull.

'This is you being understanding, is it? This is you showing me your support,' Robert spat, now. 'Coming around here and looking down your nose at me. Judging me. So what if I don't leave my flat? So what if I don't have any visitors? That's my choice,' he bellowed. 'My fucking choice for my life. I just want to be left alone. Is that too much to ask?'

'But shutting yourself away in your flat like this, it's not healthy.'

'Healthy?' Bored of the patronising conceited tone the man was using. Talking down to him as if he was a child. As if he wasn't capable of thinking for himself.

'Read your notes, mate, I've got life-changing injuries. My face and body are completely unrecognisable. I've been forced to wear a surgical mask for the past three years, and I have restricted movement in the left-hand side of my body. I lost my fucking eye. I look like I've just stepped off the set of a horror movie and you're sitting there telling me you're worried about my health?'

Robert threw the notebook back at the man. Slamming it into his chest.

'I can't even remember my own fucking name. I have no idea who the fuck I am or where the fuck I've come from, and you're telling me I need to get my arse out there in the world and file some fucking paperwork? Why? So it looks good on *your* fucking paperwork. So you can be the smug bastard in your office that feels as if you've made some kind of a difference. So that you can go back to your superiors and get some brownie points of your own?'

Derek Wheelan looked suitably ashamed of himself then, as Robert Parkes saw right through him. Of course he wanted to help Robert. That was his job. But there was a small part of him, too, that wanted to be the one that made the breakthrough. The small part of him that thought he could do better than his colleagues had done in getting through to Robert.

If his superiors were to hear about Derek's progress with Robert, it would only go in his favour too. He was so close to a promotion.

He backtracked.

'Look, if you're not ready to go back to work then I understand. But the counselling, it might help. It might jog your memory. Don't you want to remember who you are? Who your family are? Don't you want to find them?'

'All I want is for you to get out of my flat and leave me the fuck alone.'

He lost it then. Grabbing Derek Wheelan roughly by his collar, Robert Parkes hoisted the man up and off the chair. Frogmarching him to the front door, before launching him out onto the balcony.

'I really think you should persevere with your counselling, Robert. I think it would help you,' Derek Wheelan said, in one last-ditch attempt to get Robert to listen to him as he rubbed his throat with one hand. His notebook still clutched tightly in the other.

'And I think you should persevere with fucking off away from my doorstep and not coming back here again. Ever,' Robert bellowed before slamming the door in the man's face, glad to finally get rid of the nosey bastard.

Robert Parkes had far more pressing matters to attend to. Alone again, he picked up his laptop.

His hands were still shaking, he realised, as he clicked on the keyboard so that the screen lit up, revealing the photo he'd discovered just seconds before Derek Wheelan had rudely interrupted him.

Derek Wheelan was wrong.

Robert Parkes didn't need him; he didn't need any of them. He'd managed quite well on his own.

Finding out stuff about himself that even that bunch of social services degenerates couldn't, so it seemed.

Robert stared down at the screen, taking in the sight of the picture-perfect family staring back at him.

The woman wearing a royal blue floor-length gown, her vibrant red hair trailing down behind her shoulders. Those piercing green eyes looking back at him.

Cutting right through him.

Next to her, a man. Dressed in a smart grey suit, his arms leaning down and touching the child's shoulder who stood in between them.

'St George's Hospital's charity ball', the article said.

He knew these people?

The revelation caught him off guard, ripping through him, as if he'd been physically struck. The photo had triggered something in the dark, buried recesses of his mind.

He felt as if his brain had suddenly been launched through space and time, as a million thoughts and questions ran through his mind.

It was too much.

All of it was too much.

Running for the bathroom, he made it to the toilet just in time to throw up, emptying the contents of his stomach until nothing but bile burned in the back of his throat.

Holding onto the wall then, as the blood rushed around inside his ears, his heart pounding inside his chest.

And suddenly, Robert Parkes remembered it all.

CHAPTER SEVENTEEN

'Babe.' Shouting now as he crouched down on the cold tiled porch floor and lifted up the letterbox to see if he could see any sign of Jess.

Kyle Boyd knew that she was home.

He'd only left here two days ago. And even that had proved too much for him. Being away from his Jess.

He hated seeing her this angry. She was just doing her usual and ignoring him. Shutting herself away from him. Punishing him for fucking everything up the other night.

'I know you're still annoyed with me, Jess. And I'm sorry. Truly I am. But I need to talk to you, babe. Open the door!'

Nothing.

Just as he'd expected.

The girl was only too happy to leave him standing out here in the pissing rain.

He knew he had his work cut out for him, turning up here after she'd turfed him out and trying to get Jess to see him. His girlfriend wasn't exactly the forgiving type and Kyle had been calling her non-stop, over a million times in the last hour alone, all of which calls Jess had completely ignored. Switching off the phone in the end so he'd get the message.

Only, Kyle Boyd had no intention on just giving up.

Jess was angry with him, but it wouldn't last. It never did. She always forgave him in the end. Which was just as well, because as much as Jess could be a cold-hearted cow sometimes, Kyle loved the very bones of the girl.

He loved everything about her. How over-opinionated she was, how she always thought she was right. How she didn't take any shit from anyone, not even him. Especially not him.

And even if she did sometimes boss him about and call him the odd name, he knew that deep down she didn't really mean it.

It was just her way of letting him know his place.

Jess was as feisty as they came, he got that. The girl had to be. She'd been left with no choice.

From what he'd been able to gather from the tiny snippets she'd allowed him to know about her life, it had been tough for Jess. Really tough.

The poor girl had the scars to prove it.

Horrendous disfigurements that had been gouged out in her flesh. Huge lacerations inflicted all over her body. Marking her forever.

Scars that Jess had desperately tried to hide from him the first few times they'd gone to bed together, insisting on wearing a T-shirt or top of some sort. When she'd finally given in and let him see her body fully, he'd been sickened. Not by the sight of them, to him her scars only made her even more beautiful in his eyes. But for what she must have been through.

He'd been sickened at the thought that someone so sadistic and twisted had thought that it was okay to inflict that kind of pain onto somebody.

To hurt them so badly, to leave them so broken.

She said that she was damaged goods. Kyle had said she was a warrior.

She didn't believe him though.

Jess had been angry about them, full of rage, in fact, and no matter how many times Kyle had tried to broach the subject with her, she'd always refused to tell him how she'd got them. Just the mention of them made her completely clam up.

Quickly, Kyle had learned not to push the matter.

That Jess would tell him in her own time; only, as stubborn as ever, she never had.

Whatever had happened to her, whoever had happened to her, the fucker had royally fucked the girl's head up too.

Jess had become hardened. Wary of everyone.

That's what she'd told him.

Though of course, Kyle couldn't imagine her any other way. The way she was, was all he'd ever known.

Cold. Unforgiving.

She preferred it that way, she'd said. Keeping people at arm's length. Determined not to depend on anyone ever, she'd only ever look out for herself.

Only eventually, she'd allowed Kyle in.

And Kyle had naturally grown very protective of the girl.

That's what you did when you cared about someone. You protected them, and Kyle cared about Jess more than anything else in the world.

Which is why Kyle was here now. He had to make her see that she couldn't just give up on him.

He'd fucked up, yes. But he'd make it up to her.

He just needed one more chance.

And if he had to beg and plead with her, then so be it.

'Come on, Jess. I know you're in there. Please, let me in. I'm bloody soaked through.' Lifting the letter box and staring through, he thought he could see her standing just behind the glass panel of the kitchen door. The outline of her silhouette leaning up against the glass.

She was listening, that was something at least.

'Jess, please. Look I fucked up. I know that now. Seriously though, you need to open the door. I've been thinking about what you said, and I've found a way for you to get your revenge on Nancy. You're going to want to hear this, trust me, babe.'

Kyle waited.

He could hear her footfall then, padding across the laminate floor in the hallway.

Standing up, just as she opened the door. He stared at her with his puppy-dog eyes.

Droplets of water running down his face. His hair stuck to his head.

The rain was pouring down now, and still she didn't invite him in.

Instead she leant against the doorframe with her arms folded across her chest. The look on her face said that already her patience was wearing thin, so Kyle took his chance.

'I'm sorry, babe, really I am,' Kyle said, taking his shot at begging Jess for forgiveness. 'I know I messed up. It won't happen again. I'm going to make it up to you though.'

Then grabbing the folded newspaper from inside his jacket pocket, Kyle tapped the page.

'Here, look at this.'

'What is it?' Jess said, not convinced that Kyle even had a brain inside his head, and if he did, he'd probably be dangerous.

She just wanted him off her doorstep, aware that some of the neighbours' curtains were twitching now. That Kyle was once again drawing attention to himself, and to her, when the idiot should be anywhere else but here. Laying low like she told him. Jess decided the quicker she heard him out, the sooner she could get rid of him.

Only Kyle seemed hyper, convinced he had the solution to all her problems.

Standing there grinning at her like an overgrown oaf as he held out the newspaper and pointed to the photograph on the entertainment pages.

'She's got a kid, Jess.' Kyle tapped the page, his finger hitting the picture of Nancy Byrne.

He'd read the article. It was some charity ball for a kids' hospital. She was there with some bloke called Jack Taylor he'd recognised from when he'd fitted the alarm system at the house. A small child in between them.

There'd been no sign of the kid at the house when he'd been there, but she definitely had one. It said it right here in black and white.

'That's how we get to her.'

Jess was all ears now. Suddenly interested, she snatched the newspaper off him and scanned the page.

'You want revenge? Well, I reckon that this,' he pointed to the child, 'is worth far more to Nancy Byrne than a measly ten grand, don't you? I reckon we could rinse her dry. Get to her by using her kid. Hit her where it hurts the most,' Kyle said with a huge smug grin.

He had her now, hook, line and sinker.

He could see it in Jess's face, that look of determination in her eyes as she took in what he'd told her.

This was their shot.

A real shot.

They could fleece this Nancy Byrne for everything she had.

'See, told you I'd come right for you, babe; now are you going to let me in or what? My kecks are soaked through, and I'm freezing my nuts off out here. Literally.'

CHAPTER EIGHTEEN

Taking a seat on the bench just inside Richmond Park playground, Michael sat watching as little Scarlett Byrne ran from the roundabout to the climbing frame, positively in her element at being out with her great-grandad.

The child loved the freedom of the park. Being outdoors, in the fresh air, just as Michael did. He could sit here all day just watching her.

Though sometimes his heart was in his mouth at the way she swung herself off the apparatus so fearlessly.

'Careful how you go, Scarlett!' Michael warned with a giggle as he watched Scarlett take the steps to the climbing platform two at a time, before sitting down on her bottom at the top of the slide. Raising her arms above her, high in the air, she squealed with delight as she hurtled down the slide with speed.

'Look at me, Grandaddy. Did you seen how fast I could go?'

'I did, darling. You're like a little pocket rocket.' Michael beamed. Opening his newspaper, he was also in his element here at the park. He loved his little outings with his great-granddaughter. The child was a real tonic.

Who'd have thought it, after years of being an awful father, and not really having any bond with his own son, Jimmy? Michael adored little Scarlett.

His great-grandchild was the light of his life. Until she'd come along, Michael had never known a love like it. Not even with

Joanie if he was being honest. The love between him and Scarlett was really something else. A true bond. And the really amazing thing of all was that the child simply adored him too.

Smiling, he watched Scarlett wave at him before running back up the steps to have another go on the slide. She was already playing with another little girl about the same age as her. The two of them chasing one another around the playground. Giggling in unison. Michael couldn't help but feel a swell of pride inside him.

'That's my girlie!' Michael laughed, placing his newspaper down on the bench beside him, as he continued to watch the child in awe.

Scarlett coming along really had changed everything, for them all.

These days, even Joanie was almost back to her old self. That alone was a huge weight off Michael's mind. Suffering a breakdown just before Scarlett was born, there had been a time when Michael had truly believed that his wife would never be the same again.

Oh, she was back now. Though there was a definite softness about her that he'd never seen before. Especially when it came to Scarlett.

Still bolshy and over-opinionated, mind, she hadn't completely changed personality and, in all honesty, Michael wouldn't have it any other way.

Things were easier between them these days and it helped that they both had something to share that they loved and adored.

Oh how they both doted on their great-granddaughter.

Colleen did too, in her own way.

Though lately the woman was acting resentful towards them both. Michael had noticed it, though he was keeping his own counsel about the matter for now. Observing Colleen, he could see that she was somewhat obsessed with the child.

He could understand that, though, he guessed, seeing as Colleen had opted to move out of the family home just after Scarlett had been born.

Strange, that the time when Nancy would have needed her around more than ever, the woman had decided to leave. And no amount of persuasion could change her mind; lord knows, Michael had tried. Only Colleen had been determined to go, to live on her own. Insisting that she'd visit Scarlett daily.

Though, she hadn't stuck to her word, and lately when she did visit the child she seemed angered and bitter. But Michael couldn't understand why.

This had all been her own doing. Stepping back from Scarlett, just as she had done with Nancy and Daniel. Missing out on their upbringing too.

Though, of course, back then there had been much more to it.

He knew that deep down. How it must have been hard for Colleen.

Lately he could see it all starting again. His wife and his daughter-in-law constantly competing with each other for the child's time and attention. It was like Nancy and Daniel all over again. Like all those years ago, when Colleen was caught up in her own little world of pills and booze, allowing Joanie to actively push the woman out. It was as if history was repeating itself, without the medication and drink this time. Just the two women in some kind of power struggle.

Not that Scarlett seemed to notice.

These days the child had them all running about after her, vying for her time and attention and, because of that, Scarlett didn't want for anything.

Except maybe her mother, Michael thought sadly to himself.

Colleen was right about some things.

Aware as they all were at how little time Nancy spent with her daughter.

Though they were all too scared to voice that to her, of course. Too worried that if they said anything she'd see it as them poking their noses in, or figure that looking after Scarlett was a burden to them.

Of course, she was anything but.

Michael and Joanie didn't mind mucking in and doing their bit. In fact, if anything, having so much involvement in raising their grandchild was a privilege.

'Beautiful day!'

Seeing the younger, attractive woman approach the bench to sit down, interrupting his thoughts, Michael smiled and moved his newspaper out of the way to make some room.

'It is indeed.' He grinned, before turning his attention back to Scarlett as she stood at the top of the climbing frame. 'Scarlett, darling, hold on to the handrail,' he shouted, as Scarlett did as she was told and carefully walked along the wobbling bridge.

Michael chuckled then. The child was such a little cherub.

'Is that your daughter?' the woman said, following Michael's gaze to where the little girl sat now, at the top of the slide. Slipping down it, giggling, before racing back up the steps again, in order to have another go.

'You having a bit of jip with your eyesight, or are you just sweet talking an old man?' Michael laughed, secretly flattered that the woman thought he might look young enough to have a daughter of barely four years old.

'She's my great-granddaughter. Scarlett.' The pride evident as he spoke.

'What a beautiful girl.' The woman smiled, following the child with her eyes as she raced around the playground. 'She looks like a lively one.'

'Oh, she certainly is,' Michael said. 'Mad as a box of frogs and every bit as hyper! Wouldn't have her any other way though. How about you? Which one's yours?' Happy for the conversation. Especially seeing as it wasn't every day that he befriended such an attractive-looking lady.

'Oh, I don't have any children.' The woman shifting uncomfortably in her seat at the question. 'I can't…'

'Oh, I'm sorry to hear that…' Michael could see the sadness in her expression as she answered; he'd clearly hit a nerve. Instantly regretting starting a conversation that suddenly went so deep. He wasn't very good talking about women's things. Especially with a complete stranger he'd only just met.

And one that looked so close to tears too.

'No, please. It's fine. Really. I'm just having a moment.' The woman shrugged. 'I know it sounds a bit weird, but sometimes I just sit in the park for a bit, you know, and pretend, I guess. Just watching the children running around and laughing. For a few minutes I get to feel what it could have been like to be a mum…'

Embarrassed now, as she got a tissue from her pocket and wiped her eyes. Looking away from the older man, not wanting to read his thoughts on her.

She smiled then, shaking her head. Trying to lighten the mood.

'God, I probably sound like a right nutter now, don't I?'

Michael laughed then too. To be honest, he had been starting to think that.

It was a bit odd. But he could see that the woman was genuinely upset.

Having never been paternal himself, and he'd certainly never been a good parent when Jimmy had been growing up, but now he was a great-grandad, he got it. He understood what it was to have a child in your life.

Something this woman next to him would probably never experience. Who was he to judge her?

In fact, if anything, his heart went out to the poor girl beside him.

'I tell you what, I was just about to grab myself and Scarlett a nice hot chocolate from the kiosk over there. How about I get you one too?' Michael Byrne offered. Not wanting to dwell on the conversation and upset the woman anymore.

Then seeing the woman's reluctance to accept his kind gesture, he added: 'It's no trouble. I'm getting one for my great-granddaughter anyway. It's our tradition. Go on, I'll even ask for extra marshmallows? They are ever so good.'

The woman grinned then. Grateful of the offer.

'That's really kind of you. Thank you, I'd love one.'

Making his way over to the kiosk, Michael Byrne couldn't help but grin to himself as he carried out his good deed for the day.

Another perk of having such a cute little great-granddaughter, wherever he went, he was never short of attention from the yummy-mummies. Or women in general, even the childless ones, as today had proved.

Seeing a man with a child, seeing that paternal bond, it was like a magnet to women.

If only he'd realised that years ago.

Still, this was all perfectly innocent, he reminded himself. Nothing more than a friendly chat with a lady in the park, as they both drank their hot chocolate.

Nothing more than that, he told himself, looking back at the woman and wondering just how many years stood between them.

The woman was certainly a stunner that was for sure.

Easily thirty years his junior, maybe even forty.

Still, Michael Byrne may be married and well into his seventies but there was plenty of life in the old dog yet.

And who knew, he might be in with a chance?

And there was certainly no harm having a bit of a flirt in the process, was there? In fact from where Michael was standing there was no harm at all.

CHAPTER NINETEEN

Slamming down the phone, incensed, Colleen padded her way across the lounge of her small flat and stared out of the window.

That bloody Joanie.

She'd only called today to let them know that she'd be around to see Scarlett, yet the woman had sounded so smug as she'd informed Colleen that, yet again, Michael had taken Scarlett to the park.

There was always something, despite their conversation the other day when she'd told Joanie in no uncertain terms that she wouldn't allow the woman to keep her away from Scarlett.

Though Joanie obviously hadn't taken heed of her warning, Colleen thought, as she felt the anger building inside her once more.

The problem was, she didn't have any of the power. Joanie had all of it, just like always.

She could feel her heart then, thumping loudly inside her chest as she recalled the smugness in the woman's voice at the other end of the phone line. Joanie hadn't even attempted to hide the fact that she was laughing at her behind her back, revelling in the fact that she was deliberately trying to hurt her.

That bitch.

Colleen took a deep breath. Holding on to the window frame, she stared down onto the busy Upper Richmond Road. Desperately trying to focus. Anything to try and distract her from wanting to scream out loud and bang her head against the bloody glass in rage.

The road was already bustling with shoppers, as expected for lunch time on a Monday afternoon, she thought, as she eyed the long queue of traffic that stood at gridlock. The only movement for miles were the bicycles that dipped in and out of the vehicles that they passed, and the hordes of people blocking up the pathways.

Colleen watched then. Noting to herself all the yummy-mummies that were out in their usual force, milling through the designer boutique shops and fancy overpriced delicatessens. Remembering how the estate agent who had first shown her this flat had told her that East Sheen was so up and coming. That with the excellent schools nearby and touch of celebrity status associated with this part of Richmond how the property wouldn't be available for long.

Colleen had snapped it up. Though, not for any of those reasons, of course.

Her school run days were long over and she'd had more than her fill of the celebrity lifestyle after being the candy on Jimmy Byrne's arm for her entire marriage.

That life meant nothing to her. It was all fake.

The lifestyle, the status. None of it was real. Not really.

What Colleen wanted now was anonymity. To blend in to the background unnoticed.

The flat may have been pokey, but it was ample size for her to rattle about in, and it was in the right location too. The estate agent had been spot on about that.

Only a ten-minute walk from the house.

From her Scarlett.

Modern and nicely decorated, affordable too, not that money mattered to her. As Jimmy's widow, she'd never have to worry about money again.

That was the only thing that her Jimmy had got right. Ever the fucking righteous, of course he'd seen his wife was well provided for. It made him look good, even dead.

And the lying, cheating bastard owed her this much at the very least.

The mortgage all paid for. A nice lump sum in her account so that she needn't worry about finances.

That had been a huge relief, though for her it had never been about the material things. This was all about convenience. This flat and the money just meant two less things to worry about.

Colleen gazed down at a mother below, dressed to the nines and tottering down the high street in her designer outfit and skyscraping heels. Her perfectly blow-dried hair bouncing off her shoulders as she walked. A young child in the pushchair.

Colleen bit her lip. They were picture-perfect, as if the woman had just stepped out of a magazine.

Though, Colleen could see, even from up here that the young child in the pushchair was crying. His little face bright red, big fat tears streaming down his cheeks. Yet the woman seemed totally oblivious. Not even bothering to so much as offer the child any words of comfort; she was far too busy admiring her own reflection in a nearby shop window.

Colleen pursed her mouth and looked away.

Some people really didn't deserve the kids that were born to them.

She clenched her fists. Feeling fractious once again, as her thoughts turned to Nancy. Her daughter was not much better than that woman down there. Though she may not be obsessed with her appearance, she was obsessed with work and it was little Scarlett that paid the price for that. Always being left up at the house, in the care of Joanie and Michael, while Nancy busied herself, working all the hours that God sent. And Jack wasn't much better. A DI at the Metropolitan Police, but more bent than a corkscrew.

His hands had never been clean either. Between the pair of them, they really were a shit show. What with Nancy running whore houses, and bringing drugs into the country – all underneath the pretence of being a successful businesswoman.

It made Colleen sick to her stomach that her daughter couldn't see what was right in front of her eyes. That instead of spending time with her child that she'd been so blessed with, she chose to spend her time in a seedy brothel, pimping out young women.

Nancy was no better than Jimmy.

For the pair of them, it had only ever been about money and notoriety.

Christ knows, Colleen had tried to talk some sense into the girl. To make her realise that she would deeply regret her actions one day, when it was too late and Scarlett had suddenly grown up. That's when she'd realise the damage she'd done, all the important things she'd missed out on by putting work first. Like tucking her child in at night and reading her bedtime stories, or taking her to the park.

What had her daughter done when Colleen had tried to help?

Shunned her, that's what.

Nancy had told Colleen in no uncertain terms that she would be the last person in the world that Nancy would ever take parenting advice from.

She'd meant it too.

Her words cutting Colleen deeply.

Colleen hadn't pushed it after that. Stung and hurting, she'd only been trying to help.

Their relationship these days had become just as distant and awkward as always; but at least Nancy had never stopped her from seeing Scarlett.

That was something, she supposed.

Colleen wasn't going to jeopardise that, not when her daughter was finally including her. Even if her efforts were only for Scarlett's sake, Colleen was eternally grateful that Nancy had let her in at all.

She loved the very bones of her granddaughter and, what's more, Scarlett loved her back. Colleen could feel it.

Only lately there was a distance starting to form between them all.

Colleen could feel that too.

This was all Joanie's doing. That woman!

She was turning Scarlett against her. Colleen was sure of it.

'Shit!' she said, slamming her hand against the windowpane before turning and marching back across the lounge into the open-plan kitchen.

Finally giving in.

She needed a drink.

Joanie would love that, wouldn't she? To know how she'd driven Colleen back to drinking again; only Colleen couldn't seem to help herself. Alcohol was the only thing that helped her to cope with waking up every day to this huge, formidable void in her life. The feeling of loneliness magnified with thoughts of her family. All of them together at the house without her.

Grabbing a glass from the side, she unscrewed the top from the bottle of vodka and poured herself a generous measure as she recalled the smile on the shopkeeper's face as he had served her.

That knowing look. As if they had an unspoken agreement that when she popped in to buy a bottle of alcohol early in the morning, he would pretend that it was normal. Act as if she had merely come in to pick up her early morning newspaper.

Discreetly tucking the bottle away for her inside a dark blue carrier bag. As if he was doing her some kind of favour. Shielding her secret from the world. Before holding out his greedy hand, only too happy to take an alcoholic's money.

Bringing the glass to her lips with shaking hands, she tried and failed to steady them. Slopping the liquid up the side of the glass, she closed her eyes and quickly drank it down in one.

Aware of how bad she was getting again, that she was a slave to her addiction once more. Only today she didn't care.

Joanie Byrne had succeeded once again in pushing Colleen so far out of the family that by the time Colleen realised what had happened, it was already too late.

She was firmly on the outside desperately trying to look in.

And to think that Colleen had almost been grateful to the woman all those years ago, just after Scarlett had been born. For Joanie not ever telling the rest of the family what Colleen had done. That she had been the real reason behind Joanie's breakdown. That she'd drugged the woman.

Of course, Joanie hadn't told anyone.

Instead the woman had used their little secret as collateral, as leverage to ensure that Colleen always knew her place.

And according to Joanie, Colleen's place was as far away as possible.

She poured another measure of vodka. Knocking it back and closing her eyes as she got her first fix of the day, savouring the burn in her throat as the liquid instantly spread a tingling warmth all down through her.

Anticipating the numbness that would shortly come. How it would immobilise the thoughts that swam around her head. All day and all night, consuming her. Filling her with rage and anger.

That evil bitch, Joanie Byrne had already ruined her life once. Back when Nancy and Daniel had been little. Turning her own children against her. Making her look incompetent. Incapable.

And now she was doing it all over again; except this time it was her precious granddaughter that was the pawn in the woman's wicked game.

Colleen should have killed the old bitch while she'd had the chance. Christ knows how she'd tried. She'd almost succeeded, too. Sticking her foot out and making the old hag tumble down the staircase.

Drugging her. Filling her head with fabricated lies and stories. She'd made Joanie feel as if she was having a mental breakdown. Made the woman unable to establish fantasy from reality. Sent the woman mad.

Only Joanie had more lives than a bionic cat, it seemed.

Getting up from the many falls she'd 'accidentally' encountered, always covered in bumps and bruises.

The last fall had been a bad one though.

Michael had heard her. Slamming down the marble staircase, landing in a dazed and battered heap on the floor.

She'd almost broken her neck, Michael had exclaimed.

Chance would be a fine thing, Colleen had thought as the man had fussed over his wife, at last admitting what he'd been choosing to ignore. Acknowledging Joanie's strange behaviour. Finally looking beyond his big crooked nose and seeing what was happening, what had been happening for months, right in front of his eyes.

Joanie wasn't well. At least, that's how Colleen had made it look.

Her plan had been playing out just perfectly up until then; only Michael had to go and ruin it, didn't he? Involving the rest of the family, alerting them all to the fact that Joanie was having some kind of a breakdown, that she was a danger to herself.

And they'd all believed him. Of course they had.

Every one of them.

Then they'd packed the old bint off to a psychiatric hospital.

Making a huge fuss over wanting to get the old woman well again, as if she was Saint bloody Teresa. As if the woman could do no wrong.

And Colleen had no choice then but to let them admit the woman, even though she knew it was only a matter of time until

Joanie's fogged, clouded mind started to make sense of what had happened to her.

But she deserved everything she got.

None of the rest of the family knew the real Joanie, not the way Colleen did.

She'd spent a lifetime on the receiving end of the woman's malice. Learning first-hand just how sadistic and nasty the woman could be.

The rest of the family were all too damn stupid, too ignorant to see it themselves. Instead, they were blinded by the woman's facade, all of them under Joanie's spell.

They didn't know the lengths that the woman would go to, to get her own way.

To stop Colleen from wading in on what she claimed was hers.

Driving a wedge between her and her own children.

Nancy didn't have the time of day for her, that was the truth of it.

And Daniel. God knows where her Daniel was. Four years he'd been gone.

Jack had told them all some cock and bull story about how her son had been spotted out in Ibiza. That he'd found his credit card details had been used in a nightclub and a room to rent. Then a boat.

That was the story Colleen was meant to believe, that her Daniel, her boy, had gone off travelling the world.

Though in her heart of hearts Colleen knew that it wasn't true.

This family, and all the sick and twisted lies.

Something had happened to him. She was sure of it. Convinced. A mother knew that kind of thing. It was like a sixth sense. Like a force within her.

Though, with nothing to go on and no one to turn to for help, what else could she do but pray that, one day, her Daniel would find his way back to her?

Colleen poured herself a third glass.

Swirling the liquid around this time. Sipping it. Relishing it.

Colleen was done with them all. Liars and crooks the lot of them.

That was the one thing that Old Joanie hadn't factored in this time: that Colleen was much stronger these days, especially now that she was standing on her own two feet.

She'd spent a lifetime letting that old bag manipulate and belittle her, and she'd vowed that she'd never take any shit from Joanie Byrne ever again.

Her granddaughter, Scarlett, was everything to her, everything.

If Joanie thought for even a second that she could try and take the child away from her too, she had another think coming.

Finishing her third measure of vodka, Colleen smiled to herself, as the heat finally trickled through her.

She was resolute.

Colleen Byrne would do anything to be part of her grandchild's life. Anything. And no one, but no one, would stop her. Especially not Joanie.

Colleen would sooner see the woman dead first.

CHAPTER TWENTY

'Hey!' Walking into the flat, Marie Huston took her coat off and hung it up on the hook on the wall.

Turning, she eyed Robert. The man seemingly too busy to even bother to acknowledge her presence. Sat on the sofa, glued to the screen of his laptop, as per usual, the machine balanced expertly on his thighs.

'Earth to Robert! I said hello!' Marie said, instantly irritated at the fact that she'd had to repeat herself, and even then, Robert had simply nodded in her general direction. His eyes staying fixed on the screen.

Such disrespect and disinterest. After all she did for the man.

She'd only been in the door a few seconds and already Robert had managed to put her back up.

He was doing that a lot lately.

Winding her up, making her angry.

He knew how it annoyed her when he ignored her, yet still he insisted on doing it.

Clenching her hands into tight fists, she could feel that familiar fury inside of her. The anger that she tried so hard to hide.

Breathe.

Reminding herself not to start yet another row with the man.

Not tonight, when she'd promised to cook Robert a special meal. To make up for all the rowing they'd been doing lately. Arguments that Robert could easily prevent if he just let her in.

That's all she wanted. A proper relationship.

Like when she'd first met him. When he'd first woken up from his coma.

He'd been nice to her then.

Kind, almost. When she'd been his only visitor. The only person that made the effort to sit and talk to him each and every day. To spend time with him. Even when he'd been ready to leave hospital, Marie had done her upmost to help him. Working with social services and the notary to get his new name officially registered, so that he could be put back in the system once again.

So that he could get his finances sorted and to get housed.

Marie had helped the man get his life back.

Thinking that this was just the start for them. That Robert would want a relationship with her, once she'd shown him how committed she was. How loyal she could be.

But Robert wasn't having any of it.

Adamant that he didn't want a relationship with anyone.

Of course, he'd given her a key so that she could come and go as she pleased, but he'd forbidden her from even thinking about moving in with him.

He was far too independent for that. Far too determined to label himself as in a relationship too. And then there was the fact that he couldn't even abide being physically touched in any way, let alone capable of being intimate with anyone.

So Marie had settled on the very little that he did offer her.

A friendship, of sorts.

Though, these days, it was barely even that.

Something had changed in the man. Something that Marie couldn't quite put her finger on.

It was as if he didn't need her so much anymore, as if he was happier without her.

He acted as if she irritated him. Just her presence. Just her being here.

Marie closed her eyes, squeezing out the thoughts before they stayed inside her head and tormented her any more than they had already.

What was she thinking?

She and Robert were fine.

He had his strange ways, she'd give him that, but her love for Robert went far deeper than just physical affection. She didn't need to be part of a 'real' relationship in order to define what they had together.

They were soul mates, meant to be.

Even though Robert would never say so, deep down, she knew that he felt the same.

She needed to remind herself of that sometimes, though; otherwise the dark thoughts took over.

And that wasn't going to happen tonight: tonight, nothing was going to spoil her mood.

'I thought I'd make your favourite. Steak and ale pie,' she said, as she picked up the carrier bags and walked over to the kitchenette. Exhausted after her shift at the hospital, but still wanting to make an effort.

They needed this.

Some good food, some stimulating conversation.

Unpacking the ingredients she'd just bought from the shop on her way home, she smiled to herself, recalling that very first day on the job. The day she'd first met Robert.

How nervous she had been that day, arriving at the Burns Unit of Chelsea and Westminster Hospital. How everything had seemed so huge and daunting.

But then she'd walked into Robert Parkes's room and from that very instant that she set eyes on him, she knew that everything in her world had changed for ever.

Robert was special.

And chance had brought them together.

Robert had been her very first patient; though, very quickly, he'd become so much more than that.

He'd consumed her, somehow, taking up all of her working hours, and most of her free time too. Marie had felt their special bond, his pull to her, instantly.

Even unconscious, she'd known that he could sense her near to him. That he was glad of her presence. Of her company.

Robert had become as important to her as the air she breathed. He was like a drug that she craved, needed in order to survive.

After he'd been discharged from the hospital, Marie had visited Robert in his new home. Bringing him extra medication to help him with his pain, and to enable him to sleep.

He'd seemed to appreciate that, too.

So Marie brought him more. Only enough for a couple of days, mind. Never too much that he would start taking her for granted. Forget the hand that fed him, so to speak.

So Marie had lied to the man, telling him that she couldn't bring more than a few days' worth of medication or else somebody would notice.

Her plan had worked out perfectly too. Enabling Marie to see Robert almost on a daily basis. Until he was completely dependent on the extra medication.

Sleeping pills, painkillers. Uppers, downers. You name it, Marie Huston had got it for Robert.

And when his own doctor had refused to write him any more prescriptions, four years after his initial trauma, knowing that Robert's dependency on the prescriptions had become an addiction, well, that's when Marie knew that she had him good and proper.

Robert was all hers.

Before long, she began not only bringing the meds, but food and drink too. Doing his weekly shop, so that he wouldn't have to venture out to the shops. Knowing how self-conscious he'd become, even when he was wearing his special face mask. How aware he was of the people staring, as he dragged his leg that lagged just a few beats behind the rest of him as he walked. The left side of his body didn't have his full range of movement.

Cooking his meals, washing his clothes, doing all the chores around the house.

She'd quickly made herself indispensable. Nothing was ever too much.

And Robert had let her.

Because he needed her, and he loved her. He'd finally allowed her into his life.

He felt the same way as she did, she was certain.

'What's this?' Marie asked, dumping down the pack of braising steak on the kitchen side as she spotted the dirty crockery that had been abandoned in the sink. Picking up the plate, she stared at the remnants of what looked like a microwave meal. The last scrapings of bright orange sauce congealed to the plate.

'I ate already,' Robert said, not bothering to look up from the screen to see the scowl that he knew would be crossing Marie's face.

Marie leant back against the sink. Her arms folded across her chest now.

'But I said I was going to cook us a special meal,' she said, annoyed. All the effort she'd gone to, walking all the way down to the 7-Eleven on the other side of the estate. Spending her hard-earned money on all the expensive ingredients, when she could have just picked up a poxy microwave meal.

And the fact that he hadn't even bothered to give her a second thought.

He only ever thought about himself.

Oh, she knew what he was doing tonight.

He was trying to get rid of her.

This was all part of his little game. If he pissed her off enough, they'd have another row and then she'd scream at him and then he'd scream back. Demanding that she leave.

He always did that.

Demanded that she give him some space. Accusing her of being clingy and needy of his company.

His company.

The audacity of the man.

She steadied herself then before she spoke again. Took a few seconds, calming the swell of fury inside her.

'You know I wanted to make you something nice. I told you this morning, didn't I? That I was going to cook you something special. Something really nice.'

'Well, I forgot, didn't I?' Robert spat, finally looking up from the screen. Interrupting the spiel that he knew was coming. 'You're not my keeper you know, Marie.'

He shook his head then, that irritated look back on his face that he seemed to wear so often these days.

Ignore it, she told herself. *He doesn't really mean what he's saying. This is all part of his recovery. Part of pushing people away from him so that he won't get hurt.*

If only he'd realise that Marie would never hurt him.

She knew him, him and all of his funny little ways.

Always saying that he couldn't breathe around her, that she was suffocating him.

This was what he did.

He said these horrible things to her because he loved her. That's what they say, isn't it? That you lash out at the people you loved the most.

And he must really love her the way he spoke to her sometimes.

But not as much as she loved him.

No one could love anything or anyone as much as Marie loved him, that would be physically impossible. Robert was her life.

Even if he had nothing nice to say to her, even if at times he treated her with such contempt. He couldn't help it. He was stuck here, in this flat. Caged in. And Marie could see that he was in enormous pain.

The want and need inside of him, to find out who he was, where he really belonged.

He still didn't get it, did he?

He belonged here with her.

She smiled then, patiently. Even though deep down, she didn't feel very patient at all.

She wouldn't let him get to her, not tonight, she resolved.

She wouldn't let him ruin another evening.

'Never mind. I'm sure by the time I cook the pie, you'll be hungry enough.' She turned her back on him then. Hiding the tears that threatened to fall.

She was being oversensitive. She would not cry.

She would not.

'Did you get me my pills?' he called out, but Marie didn't answer, chopping up the onions loudly, pretending not to hear.

Typical. He acknowledged her now, didn't he? Now that he wanted something from her.

She should lie, she thought, say that she hadn't been able to get any for him today. That there had been too many doctors and nurses milling around for her to be able to steal anything. That would teach him for not showing her any attention and for always taking her for granted. Maybe then he wouldn't be so quick to treat her as if she was just here at his convenience. Maybe that's what he needed: a little reminder of how much he did actually need her.

'Marie? Did you get them for me?' he repeated himself then, the urgency clear in his voice. The want. The need. They both heard it there.

''Course I got you them,' she said finally, turning and shooting him a smile. Doing her upmost to hide the tremor in her voice, so that it wouldn't give her away.

She didn't want him to know that she was upset. That he'd done it to her again. Instead she pursed her mouth.

Sometimes, not often, she secretly preferred him when they'd first met. Back when he couldn't talk back. When he hadn't been so full of anger and rage.

'Good,' he said simply. The look of relief flickered then on his face. As he relaxed and slumped back in his chair.

Back to his precious computer.

Marie picked up a carving knife and started hacking at the meat.

*

'Are you not going to at least try and eat some of that?' Marie said, scraping up the last bit of meat and pastry off her plate and popping it into her mouth. Robert could sit there with a face on him, pushing the food around his plate as much as he wanted. She knew that she had made a blinding meal. It was just a shame that Robert wasn't in the mood to appreciate her efforts. 'It's such a waste to leave it.'

'I told you already. I'm not hungry.'

'Well, I'll wrap it up and put it in the fridge for you. You can have it tomorrow lunchtime instead of one of those manky microwave meals. Full of salt those things are, and chemicals.'

Marie drummed her fingers on the table top. Still put out at Robert eating earlier without her. Satisfied that she'd made her point now.

She stared at Robert.

He was acting strange tonight, stranger than usual, only Marie couldn't put her finger on what the matter was.

He seemed wired. On edge about something. He'd barely even bothered to taste the food she'd cooked for him, preferring to drink only the wine she'd bought instead.

She'd only sipped at her glass, while he'd almost finished the whole bottle.

'Have you taken your meds?' She wondered if that was it, whether the alcohol interfering with his pills had made him drunk.

'No. Not yet. I'll take them later.'

He didn't want them yet? Marie narrowed her eyes. That was unheard of.

Normally Robert couldn't get them off her quickly enough, taking a double dosage to block out the pain, or send him off to sleep. Normally he'd swallow them down before she'd even taken her coat off.

Something was definitely wrong. Tonight, his mind was clearly elsewhere.

His gaze still studying the laptop that he'd placed on the table beside his plate.

He hadn't left that poxy thing alone all evening.

Tapping away. Ignoring her. As he gulped down his wine.

Fuck this!

Marie slammed her cutlery down on the plate. No longer giving a shit if she caused a row now. The evening was ruined anyway.

'I worked a twelve-hour shift today. Then I walked to the shop to buy everything, fresh. I came home and spent two hours cooking. For you,' she said now. Her voice low, but her tone cutting, as intended. 'I know what you're doing, Robert. And it won't work.' She got up from her chair, taking his plate away from him. Stomping over to the bin and scraping the food away, she then started filling up the sink, all the while still talking.

'You want me to be pissed off with you. You want me to storm home, and leave you alone. Well, I'm not going anywhere.'

Again, nothing.

Marie turned to look at him, but he wasn't even listening to her. His head was down, once again engrossed in that fucking laptop of his.

Marie lost it completely then; launching herself across the table, she snatched the laptop up.

Wanting to see what it was that was so much more important than her.

What Robert was obsessing over.

Though the image before her instantly made her wish she hadn't looked.

A woman. Stunningly beautiful with vibrant red hair, and piercing green eyes.

The sort of woman that Marie Huston was well aware she wouldn't stand a chance against.

'As if someone like her would be interested in you!' she said then, unable to help herself. as her chest started to constrict. Her heart pounding away inside her.

But her words didn't seem to sting as she intended. Instead, Robert didn't bother to reply.

He was on his feet then. Making a grab for the laptop. Slamming Marie into the wall behind her as they struggled. Snatching the laptop out of her grasp as she slid down to the floor.

Winded then, but not from the blow. Marie looked up at him through her tears.

Cursing herself for being so weak and crying, when inside she was fit to kill him.

'Is she the reason why you're so fucking preoccupied lately?' Marie said, a tremor in her voice as she spoke. The hurt inside her like nothing she'd felt before. 'That bitch. What is she, your new fucking girlfriend?' Marie spat now, as she felt the surging rage inside her. Jealousy eating her up.

'You think that she'd like you?' Marie said with a nasty, bitter laugh as Robert didn't reply. The hurt inside her so overwhelming that she wanted to be sick.

She wanted him to hurt too.

'That she'd settle for someone like you!'

Robert slammed the laptop shut and flung the machine down on the table top.

Still he didn't speak, instead he slumped down on the chair.

He could hardly deny it, could he? His fascination with the woman on the screen. She'd seen the image with her own eyes, she knew his secrets.

Whoever the fuck this slag was, she appeared to already have Robert firmly under her spell.

Marie got to her feet then. Pacing the small dining area as she felt the rage inside her building. Growing so large inside her that if she didn't do something, she'd physically explode.

'It's not what you think,' Robert said, his eyes still low.

'Isn't it?' she spat. Aware now that he couldn't even look her in the eye.

The rotten, using bastard.

Taking the piss out of her, all the while he was lining up his next fucking love interest.

What the fuck did he think she was? Someone that would allow a man to mess with her like that. Someone who would just go without a fight?

Marie looked over at the kitchen side. Her eyes resting on the carving knife from earlier, propped up, abandoned on the side of the pie dish.

She'd kill him, she thought.

That's what she'd do, if he attempted to leave her.

If he *dared* to leave her.

'What is it then?' she challenged, getting to her feet.

Her palms sweating as she talked herself into picking it up. About how she would plunge it so deeply into his chest.

If she couldn't have him, no one else would either.

Instead she'd be the one that watched as his life blood poured out of him, as he breathed his last breath.

At least she'd have that.

'Tell me!' she screamed.

She needed him to say it. To confirm her deepest fears. To give her the reason to do it.

To kill that fucking bastard right here and now.

'That's Nancy…' he said, his eyes wide. The expression on his face as if Marie would know what that meant somehow. As if somehow he'd proved himself.

'I don't give a fuck what the bitch's name is—' Marie started, only Robert interrupted her.

'No, Marie. Don't you understand? It's her. I remember now.'

'Remember what? Who the fuck is she?' Marie shook her head, confused.

His girlfriend. His wife.

That would be just her fucking luck.

Indignant now, the rage inside her all-consuming.

Nancy?

Robert had never mentioned anyone's name before. Marie would have remembered.

She didn't know any 'Nancy'.

Robert laughed then.

Manically, sounding strange and hollow as it left his mouth.

'What the fuck is so funny?' she said then, staring at the man as if he was deranged.

He must be.

He was laughing so hard now that he had to hold onto his sides, as if he suddenly couldn't contain himself.

Laughing hysterically at a joke that she'd been clearly left out of.

Doubled over, he stood in front of her, his whole body shaking.

Then, sinking down to his knees he grabbed her by her hands.

Looking up at her earnestly, as if a light bulb had gone off somewhere inside his head.

As if finally he could see.

'I know who I am, Marie. I remember everything. My real name. I'm Daniel Byrne. And that woman on the screen. Nancy. That's my cunt of a sister.'

CHAPTER TWENTY-ONE

'Take a seat, darling,' Nancy said, guiding Bridget Williams to the sofa, before placing the bunch of flowers she'd bought for her friend down on the coffee table in the centre of the room. 'Put your feet up, that's an order. I'm going to get one of the girls to bring you in a nice pot of tea and something to eat. You are not to move off this sofa, okay? Felicity is on her way over and she's going to keep you company.'

'She's going to babysit me you mean?' Bridget said, eyeing Nancy. 'I've already told you, Nance, I'm fine, seriously. They wouldn't have discharged me if I wasn't. And despite the way you're mollycoddling me, I've still got the use of my arms and legs, you know. I can manage.'

'I know you can.' Nancy looked at her mate, noting that she did look a lot better today. Smiling and chatting the whole journey home. She had some colour back in her cheeks again too. 'I just want you to take it easy for a bit, that's all. At least indulge me a bit, Bridge.'

'But I don't want to put my feet up. I want to help. It's the opening night and I told you I'd be here to oversee everything ran smoothly. No matter what.' Bridget grinned, triumphantly. Insisting that she'd be back here tonight no matter what; even if the nurses hadn't let her go home, she'd have still found a way. She'd been adamant about that.

'Well, I'm glad you're "home".' Nancy smiled then, genuinely. Glad that Bridget really was doing okay. 'But I really just want you to take it easy, Bridge. The girls will all be in later, and they all know what to do. If you need anything, Felicity will be right on it. If there's any trouble, call Jack. He's at home with Scarlett tonight, but he can be here quicker than you can put the phone down. Okay? I mean it, Bridge. Tonight you are to do nothing that doesn't involve keeping your feet up and getting some rest.' Switching the TV on, Nancy passed her friend the television remote and a pile of magazines. 'You must be knackered.'

'Yeah well, if the nurses had given me a private room instead of sticking me on a ward with a load of geriatrics I might have got some sleep. I tell you, Nancy, some of the things that I've seen and heard on that ward the last couple of days… have left me scarred for life! Those old people really did let *everything* hang out, and the noises they make. Half the time I wasn't sure whether the sounds were coming from their mouths or their arses.' She shuddered at the memory.

'Oh, I can imagine,' Nancy said, not wanting Bridget to enlighten her with any of the finer details. 'I bet you're already missing your old mate, Hilda. Aren't you?'

'Hmm, well she certainly won't be missing me! Not after I told the old battleaxe where she could shove those slippers of hers that last time she bent over and flashed her crack at me. I swear she was doing it on purpose, just to make me gag.' Bridget giggled. Suddenly glad to be away from the place.

Home.

That's what this place was to her now.

Looking around at the plush furnishings and impeccably decorated room, Bridget decided that she could quickly get used to it.

Then, sinking back on the settee she shook her head in wonderment at Nancy. 'I'm so glad to be home though, Nancy. And this place looks amazing.' Glancing at the immaculate lounge.

This part of the house was off bounds to the punters. It was purely Nancy's and Bridget's domain. Tastefully decorated in subtle tones of beiges and creams. Simple but stylish, exactly as Nancy had envisaged.

'You did it, Nancy. Can you believe it? You actually did it. All of this.'

She grinned at her friend then, proudly.

She was seriously blown away.

Somehow, even with everything going on this weekend, the girls, Nancy and Jack had all clubbed together and managed to get this place ready just in time. The piles of unpacked boxes had all been sorted out and the last of the furniture had been delivered. The builders had finished all their last little jobs and touch-ups on the place.

This was it.

It was full steam ahead from now on.

'We got a different security firm in to fix the alarm system now,' Nancy said, still annoyed that she couldn't get hold of the cowboys that she'd paid to sort it out in the first place. 'And I've got security on site around the clock. We'll be taking no chances of anything else happening here. I want you and the girls to feel totally safe.'

Bridget nodded, knowing that Nancy felt partly responsible for what happened to her, only it wasn't her fault. It wasn't anyone's fault but the arsehole that had broken in here that night.

'Has Jack had any luck, tracking them down?'

Nancy shook her head. Wishing that she could say different. But it looked like whoever it was had got away with it. Thankfully, not killing Bridget or getting away with the money in the process, but that still wasn't the point.

Despite the fact that Nancy had managed to break the bastard's nose, and had droplets of the man's blood on the hallway floor, and all over her top – she'd been convinced that Jack could trace the fucker through that, through his DNA, only it had come back without a match.

Whoever it was, didn't have a criminal record.

So now they had nothing to go on. Nothing at all.

Jack had told her that the chances of finding the fucker were slim to none.

Though she had no intention of telling Bridget that.

'Right, I'm going to go and check on the girls and make sure everything's ready to go, then I'm off out for some champagne.'

'Ooh, 'ark at you! I was going to say, that's a lot of effort you've gone to tonight, just to chauffeur me home from the hospital. Who you all dolled up for?' Bridget said narrowing her eyes. Suspicious now.

She'd been feeling crap as it was after lying around in hospital the past few days, but following Nancy out to the car as the woman tottered in front of her wearing a designer fitted dress and patent Jimmy Choo heels had only made her feel even worse. Especially when she'd seen all the admiring glances Nancy had been getting from every male they passed, while Bridget trailed behind, in a scruffy grey tracksuit and Ugg boots, her hair unwashed, scraped up on the top of her head in a messy bun. Completely invisible, it seemed, in Nancy's shadow.

Not that she minded really, of course. Now she was home she couldn't wait to get a nice hot bath and feel clean again.

'Well, as it happens. I've got a date,' Nancy said, acting coy now.

Knowing the interrogation that was sure to follow.

'You've got a date? Nancy Byrne, "the Ice Queen"!' Bridget laughed making fun of the nickname that Nancy knew everyone called her behind her back.

Coming from Bridget, Nancy just laughed, knowing that her friend meant it playfully to wind her up.

'Who is it?' Bridget said then, narrowing her eyes. Certain that Nancy hadn't even hinted at anyone's name lately. 'Do I know him?'

The woman hadn't mentioned anyone, ever, in fact. Not in the four years that Bridget had known her. Dedicated only to Scarlett and her job, Nancy always claimed she didn't have time for men.

'Jesus, Bridge. Steady on with the Spanish Inquisition, babe. It's just dinner and a few drinks. I am entitled to a bit of male company every now and again,' Nancy said, regretting even mentioning it to Bridget now. Her friend was already chomping at the bit to find out all the details.

'If you must know, his name is Philippe Augustine. He's a business associate. You don't know him, but he's really nice.'

'*Nice*?' Bridget said, pursing her mouth. 'That's all I get? Nice? You gotta give me more than that, Nancy. Have you been out with him before? Does he know about Scarlett?'

Realising that Nancy was picking up her bag now, ready to leave. That she was just going to leave Bridget here in limbo, Bridget shook her head.

'Oh, no, no, Missy! You can't just leave me hanging like that, Nance. Come on, give me something at least. You can't just announce that you're off out on a date and not tell me anything else.'

Standing at the door, thoroughly enjoying herself now. Glad that her personal life seemed to be doing the trick of taking Bridget's mind off the shitty couple of days she'd just endured.

Instead she just grinned and shrugged her shoulders.

'Don't wait up for me, babe, I might be very, very late.' She winked then.

'Okay, what have you done with the real Nancy Byrne?' Bridget squealed. 'You filthy mare! Oh, don't you worry. I'll be waiting up for you. There's no way I could sleep now, knowing that you're out on a hot date with someone.'

Nancy turned on her heel, chuckling to herself all the way down the hallway, on her way to meet the very handsome Philippe. Son of one of her father's old contacts.

Nancy had been resisting Philippe's advances for months, but after the conversation she'd had with Jack in the car on the way back from the charity ball, Nancy had finally decided to take the bull by the horns and put the man out of his misery.

Surprising even herself when she'd picked up the phone and called him. Inviting the man out for dinner, under the pretence of helping her celebrate the success of her new spa venture's grand opening tonight.

Nancy knew that Bridget wouldn't be able to help herself but mention it when she saw Jack tonight, and the truth was, Nancy wanted Jack to know.

Their conversation had left her on edge somehow, and she wanted Jack to know, for once and for all, that his feelings weren't reciprocated.

That they never would be.

Phillip Augustine was just the man to get that point across.

A wealthy businessman, who just happened to be drop dead gorgeous to boot.

The man was just the distraction Nancy needed.

And as much as Nancy didn't need the complications of a new man in her life right now, that didn't have to mean that the 'Ice Queen' couldn't have a bit of fun every now and then, did it?

CHAPTER TWENTY-TWO

'Could I have a word?' Staff Nurse Langton said, eyeing Marie Huston as the woman approached the nurses' station, clutching her large handbag tightly under her arm.

In a hurry to rush off home after her shift no doubt. *Two guesses to who she was rushing home to*, Louise Langton thought wearily as she walked into her office, holding the door open to allow Marie Huston to follow her.

Which, of course, the younger nurse did, without question.

The tension between the two women was palpable. It had been for weeks. Since the rumours had started and Nurse Langton knew that she'd been skirting around this issue, but it was high time that she dealt with it.

Especially seeing as the other nurses working here were becoming suspicious of Marie Huston too.

'Please. Sit.' An instruction, not an invitation, Marie Huston noted as she sat down on the chair opposite her superior. Recognising the serious tone to the woman's voice.

Something was clearly up.

Nurse Langton had been acting off with her for some time now.

Sharp and snappy. Instead of any real conversation, the woman was constantly throwing orders at her.

Whatever Nurse Langton's problem was, Marie just hoped that she hurried up and got it off her chest, so that she could get out of here.

She was rotated off for the entire weekend, and she couldn't wait to get home.

Get back to Robert. *Daniel*, she corrected herself.

'Have I done something wrong?' Marie said then, earnestly. Not in the mood for a lecture tonight, which is no doubt what Staff Nurse Langton had called her into her office for.

'Well that depends,' Nurse Langton said, looking over the notes that were sprawled out on the desk in front of her. The requisition that she'd requested from the pharmacy.

Marie Huston's signature scrawled on almost every other column down the page.

Part of her wanted Marie to come up with a viable, logical explanation, but she knew that the chances of that were slim to none.

It was clear what had been going on here.

'It's been brought to my attention that you have been requesting a lot of medication, Marie. Far more than the required amount that we would issue out to our patients on this ward?'

Nurse Langton's tone was short, clipped.

Studying the long list in front of her, the sleeping tablets and extra strong painkillers that had been issued out.

She had her suspicions of exactly what was going on here, only she wanted Marie Huston to say it. For once, just once, she wanted the woman to be straight with her.

After all the training and opportunities that Louise Langton had given Marie Huston since she started working here at the hospital, the truth was the very least the woman could give her.

'I've signed for medication. Of course. If patients need a certain dosage…'

Nurse Langton shook her head. Cutting Marie's hapless excuses dead, mid-sentence.

'No, Marie. This is far more medication than is needed. Much, much more and, looking at the inventory, this has been going on for months. Well over a year in fact… probably longer than that.' Nurse Langton pursed her mouth.

Four years, Louise Langton guessed. Ever since Robert Parkes had been discharged from their care.

Her eyes bored into Marie's, as if she was willing the girl to think twice before trying to fob her off with any more lies, giving her one last chance to tell her the truth. To come clean. Maybe then Nurse Langton could help her.

'I want to know if you're taking any of these for personal use, Marie, or perhaps if you're taking them on behalf of somebody else?'

Nurse Langton let her question hang in the air between them.

Say it Marie. Admit it.

'Of course they're not for personal use. They are for the patients, a hundred per cent. Hand on my heart.'

She knew, Marie Huston thought, as she shook her head. Her face a picture of confusion and shock at what she was being accused of.

The old bitch knew about her and Robert.

That's what this was really about.

Robert – Daniel, damn it – was no longer a patient here. He was none of Staff Nurse Langton's concern. And what Marie did in her own private time was of no concern to anyone here.

'Is there something else, Nurse Langton?' Marie said then, challenging the woman to come clean about what this was really about.

Nurse Langton eyed the younger woman then.

Marie Huston might think that she had everyone here at the hospital fooled. That none of the nurses knew about her shacking up with one of their patients, but people did know. Of course they did.

How could they not?

Marie Huston had been obsessed with Robert Parkes.

The man had been on the ward for almost a year in total, and Marie had spent all of her free time visiting the man, and most of her working hours too.

So much so, that she'd nearly lost her job over him.

Louise Langton remembered how Nurse Huston's fixation on Robert Parkes had worsened once the patient had regained consciousness; the woman's infatuation with the man had become like a drug.

Nurse Langton had tried to help the nurse back then, too. Taking it upon herself to do Nurse Huston a favour, she'd moved the woman to another hospital.

Claiming that St Andrew's Children's Burns Unit had needed extra staff, at the time.

And as much as Marie had protested about going, Nurse Langton had insisted on the transfer. Letting Marie know that the temporary move wasn't in any way negotiable.

'I don't feel that the relationship you have with your patient is a healthy one, Nurse Huston,' Nurse Langton had said at the time. Truthfully. Nurse Huston had let her feelings get in the way of her professional outlook. 'I think you may have crossed the patient/carer line. It happens sometimes. We get attached, I understand that. Especially in cases as intense and unique as this one. I appreciate that you care about your patients and that you are only trying to help, but I really don't feel that you can offer the best nursing care to your patient when you get this involved, on such an emotional level. I think we need to put some distance between you.'

'But you can't...' Marie Huston had protested. Shaking her head in disagreement. Outraged that Nurse Langton could make such a decision without even consulting her. 'How can me caring about a patient possibly be a bad thing? I don't understand? I know that I spend more time with him than any other patient, but come on! Robert Parkes hasn't got anybody! In the nine months he's been here, he hasn't had a single visitor. Nobody is looking for him, nowhere on earth gives a shit about him…' Marie Huston had raised her voice. Her temper getting the better of her. Instantly annoyed by Nurse Langton's unfair misconception of her.

She'd been doing her very best by her patient.

How dare the woman punish her for caring too much? For just doing her job.

Robert Parkes had only just woken up from his coma. He needed her now. Nurse Langton couldn't transfer her.

'So what if I go the extra mile? So what if I genuinely care for my patients? That's the whole point, isn't it? That's why we do what we do. He needs me. He hasn't got anyone else…'

'He doesn't even know you, Marie. He's been in a coma ever since we brought him in nine months ago. He has no idea who you are.' Nurse Langton's words had stung her.

'I'm doing you a favour, Marie,' Louise Langton had said, finally being completely straight with the younger nurse. 'You are an excellent nurse. Truly. I just feel that your focus has become obscured of late. Please trust me, this is for your benefit. The last thing I want to happen is for you to damage your career, or worse still lose your job completely…'

Lose her job? Was this woman threatening her?

'The children at St Andrew's Burns Unit, in Essex, would benefit greatly from having you on board, Nurse Huston. It will be great for your working portfolio, and it's not forever. A month or two at the most. The ward sister is very excited about working alongside you.'

It hadn't been an empty threat either.

Nurse Langton had meant every word of it.

Her mind had been well and truly made up then. She was the nurse in charge here; it was down to her to make sure that her staff were working to the professional standards expected.

Louise Langton had really thought that that would be the end of it all.

Some time and distance between Marie and the patient would put pay to Marie's constant preoccupation.

And Marie had had no choice but to go.

Only, she had soon found another way of staying close to the man.

She'd started visiting him outside of the job and rumour had it that she was now in a full-blown relationship with the man. It didn't take a rocket scientist to work out where all the drugs were going to.

Four years on, Marie's obsession had just gone from bad to worse it seemed.

'I've given you the benefit of the doubt on a number of occasions, Marie,' Nurse Langton said then, unable to hide the disappointment in her tone. 'I've let things slide that I wouldn't have done for any other nurse. But I can't let this go. Not this time. I want you to empty your bag,' Nurse Langton said, shifting in her chair uncomfortably, now that she'd finally made the accusation.

'My bag?' Nurse Huston said, defensive suddenly. She'd been expecting to lie, to protest her innocence. To fob Nurse Langton off with some spiel about another nurse perhaps taking the meds and signing them off in her name. The last thing she'd expected was to be searched. Not when she had a bag full of vials of pills and bottles of capsules. 'But why? I haven't got anything. I already told you.'

Nurse Langton pursed her mouth, waiting.

The silence between them was suddenly glaringly loud in the room.

Marie Huston was cornered. Caught red-handed, she had nowhere to hide now.

She stared out through the glass panel in Nurse Langton's office door, nervously eyeing the other nurses that all seemed to be loitering around the nurses' station.

They all knew too, she realised.

All of them, so nosey and desperate to listen in.

Suddenly she recalled some of the strange looks that had crossed her colleagues' faces lately when she'd been in their company. The raised eyes, and whispered voices. All talking in code.

About her.

This was just one great big conspiracy.

They were all against her. All of them. They always had been, from the very start. Condemning her for wanting to help Robert.

Or Daniel Byrne, as she now knew him, though he'd always be Robert to her.

These women were just jealous because they didn't have what she had.

They never would.

'Fine,' she said then simply. Her voice shaking as she tipped the contents of her bag out onto the desk top; staring down at the floor, too ashamed to look the senior nurse in the eye as the boxes and pots of pills spread out across the desk between them both.

But her shame was that she'd been so careless as to get caught out, not because she'd taken them in the first place.

'You're taking these for Robert Parkes, aren't you?' Louise Langton said, knowingly.

That was the reason Marie Huston was risking her job and her reputation. The man that she was so obsessed and consumed by.

Marie didn't bother lying then. She knew. Marie had been careless; she'd fucked everything up.

Work, home. Everything was just one big mess.

She'd lose her job now, just like she was losing Daniel.

He'd finish with her now – now that she wouldn't be able to get him any more medication.

He was already losing interest.

She could feel it more than ever. Now that he remembered who he was, where he had come from. It was as if suddenly, right before her eyes, he'd become a complete stranger to her.

No longer wanting his medication, he'd told her he needed to stay alert, and focused. So he could remember everything.

So he could piece it all together.

Spending all his time on the computer, stalking that bitch of a sister of his.

Obsessed with his so-called family.

The same family that hadn't given so much as two shits about the man since he was burned in the fire. The same people that had never once bothered getting in touch with Daniel.

She was the only one who had ever cared about him.

The only one who had tried to help him, and what thanks did she get?

None.

If anything, he was drifting further and further away from her.

She'd lose him soon if she didn't act fast. That's why she'd come up with her own plan. Keeping him drugged without him knowing.

'I'm sorry that it's come to this, really I am,' Nurse Langton said then, her voice loaded with regret. 'But I have a duty of care to not only my nursing team but to this hospital too. You know that I can't just let this one go?' She glanced at the clock then, before looking back at Marie. Her expression plagued with regret, though she really hadn't been left with any other choice. 'I'm going to have to report this, first thing in the morning. For now, you're dismissed from the hospital.'

Marie Huston nodded. Getting up from the chair, she smoothed down her blue overalls, before tightening her ponytail.

Inside, her stomach bubbled with rage like that of a volcanic explosion about to erupt, but somehow she managed to keep her cool.

To not show the woman how much she hated and despised her right now.

Instead she simply walked out of the office without saying another word.

Nurse Langton was going to get her struck off. The interfering old bint was going to lose Marie her job over this.

The police would probably get involved.

'I'm sorry that it's come to this, I really am. I hope you understand,' Nurse Langton called out.

Only Marie Huston didn't bother to reply.

She understood just perfectly.

Louise Langton didn't know the first thing about being sorry, not yet anyway. But she'd soon learn.

CHAPTER TWENTY-THREE

He's trying to lift his hands, but realises that he can't. His arms are too heavy. His skin taut, tied behind his back with thick plastic cable ties that cut into his flesh each time he moves.

He's strapped to a chair, he realises.

Unable to move. He can't even lift his head now. Exhausted, as if even opening his eyes is too much effort.

He should give in to it. That's all he had to do. Close his eyes just one last time and this horrific ordeal would all be over.

Instead he was fighting it.

Every part of his body screamed with pain, every part of him hurting.

His eye. Fuck! That heat! That smell.

The pain so intense that he was gone again. Away into the blackness, the nothingness.

Only to wake again, to that godawful sound.

A creature wailing in agony, somewhere off in the distance. Only the noise was coming from him, he realised. From somewhere deep inside him.

He could feel a cool liquid then, trickling down his body. Offering a few seconds of cool, blissful relief from his torture before the stinging sensation started. The burning as prickling liquid entered his slashed, exposed skin.

That heady, intoxicating smell. He recognised it. Petrol?

Then came the heat.

The most intense heat he could imagine. Explosive. Engulfing his entire body.

Fight or flight. Live or die.

MOVE!

Sitting bolt up in the bed, as his vision adjusted to the darkened room, it took him a moment or two to realise he was safe.

It was just a dream. A nightmare.

Though still his heart hammered loudly inside his chest. He was covered in sweat too. Perspiration trickling down his body, the bedsheets stuck to his clammy skin.

He gulped back the acidic bile that rose at the back of his throat.

He remembered everything now, every last detail.

On his feet then, he ran for the bathroom. Making it to the toilet just in time to throw up.

His stomach empty, he turned and leant over the sink. Holding his hands underneath the cool flow of water, before splashing his face.

All the while resisting looking up. Avoiding the mirror right in front of him.

In fear of what he knew he'd see staring back at him.

Fuck it! he thought. What was some more torture to add to his already never-ending pain?

He looked then. Recoiling the second he caught sight of his mottled, scarred face.

Quickly he looked away.

He tried to steady his breathing that poured out of him in quick erratic bursts.

Through the nose, and out the mouth. Slow and steady.

Forcing himself to look again at the monster staring back at him.

Eyeing the long, jagged scar that ran the length of his face. The thickened fold of skin that left a puckered ravine down the centre of his face. The scars that he'd been left with for all the world to see.

His face had healed well considering that every inch of his burned skin had been scraped off to protect him from infection. It was amazing to think that the once-seared tissue on his face had swelled to more than twice its normal size.

Now, half of his head of hair was missing. The hair follicles damaged beyond repair. Scar tissue growing over where his hair shafts should be.

He forced himself to stare at his left eye then. The eyelid sewn up.

He'd lost his fucking eye!

He was supposed to wear a patch, that's what the doctor had advised.

More aesthetically pleasing, apparently. For whom?

Let people look at him. Let them stare. They were going to look anyway, how could they not?

This was it now.

His face, his body. Ruined for all eternity. Leaving him trapped inside this mess of a body. Barely functioning.

Riddled with panic attacks and flashbacks.

He rarely even attempted to leave his flat. Preferring the solitude of a simple, secluded life.

All he had was Marie.

Annoying, clingy, fucked-up Marie.

As if he wasn't being punished enough.

Still, she had her uses. He put up with her for now.

Until he worked out what he was going to do.

Turning the bathroom light off, Daniel made his way back into his lounge and picked up his laptop and settled back down onto the settee.

There was no point trying to go back to sleep. Not now.

Instead he just stared at the screen, at the image of his dear older sister, Nancy Byrne. Taking in everything about her. Her face, her expression. Her body language.

She looked happy, genuinely. Smug almost, as she stood there arm in arm with that traitor Jack Taylor. That lying, cheating piece of shit.

How pathetic she was, to still not know Jack Taylor's many secrets.

Daniel looked at the child nestled between them. That vibrant red Byrne hair. The same as his mother's. Nancy's too. Those striking green eyes. 'Scarlett Byrne. Aged 4,' the article said.

Born around the same time that he'd woken up from his coma.

His niece. His blood.

They looked like the perfect little family.

But looks could be very deceiving indeed.

How he'd love to rip her world right out from under her. To take it all away from her, just like that.

And he could.

He had that power.

He smirked then, glad that he finally remembered who he was.

Not this pathetic needy shell of a man that he'd been for almost the past four years. That wasn't him. He was somebody. Someone.

He was Daniel Byrne.

She'd done this to him. Nancy.

She'd taken everything away from him.

And very soon, Daniel was going to repay the favour.

That was the very least he could do.

His bitch of a sister had been living on borrowed time – but very soon that shiny little bubble that Nancy lived in was going to burst in spectacular style.

CHAPTER TWENTY-FOUR

Pulling her coat up under her chin to protect herself from the cutting wind, Louise Langton stepped out through the main entrance of Chelsea and Westminster Hospital and briskly made her way across the customer car park and out towards the main road.

Keeping her head down to shield herself from the heavy downpour, she'd thought about waiting for it to ease off before she made a dash for her car, only it didn't look as if it was about to stop anytime soon.

Hurrying to reach the narrow overflow car park further down the road, tucked away behind a small row of shops, she shivered, soaked through. Her wet clothes, her coat, too, drenched. Sticking to her skin.

For a second she wished she'd parked closer. In this weather and at this time of night, it was a pain in the arse to have to trudge to it.

Still, in hindsight, she'd rather have to contend with a bit of wind and rain than her brand-new car getting battered by some ignorant imbecile, had she parked in the main hospital car park while she'd been on shift. She'd only end up coming out to find that the paintwork had been scraped, or that some idiot had taken a chunk out of one of her doors.

The overflow car park wasn't as well known about, and even those people that did know of its whereabouts were often too lazy to be bothered to do the short ten-minute walk to get there. Though as far as Louise was concerned the short walk was more than worth it, purely for the peace of mind it brought her. Especially now that her husband had only gone and given her the surprise of a lifetime for her fiftieth birthday, a couple of weeks ago, and traded in her trusty old Ford Focus for her dream car.

A Mercedes-Benz SL-Class. With cream leather seats and top-of-the-range CD player. Her husband had gone all out. Leaving no expense spared.

Gordon was a diamond like that.

Crossing the main road, Louise turned into the narrow car park and immediately spotted her pride and joy. Sitting way back in the far corner, all on its own. A nearby street lamp lightly illuminating the pristine bodywork in all its glory.

The fact that there were no cars either side of it, no cars that end of the car park at all, pleased her no end.

She couldn't wait to get inside now.

She'd put her new heated seats on. *God, how had she ever lived without them?* And stick that new CD of hers on too.

It might be almost midnight, but at least she'd have the delectable Michael Bublé to keep her company on her ten-minute drive home.

Bliss!

Routing around inside her handbag for her car keys, she recalled Gordon's earlier phone call. How pleased with himself he'd sounded when he rang her this evening on her break, to tell her that he'd just finished his latest project: transforming the small decking area in their back garden.

He'd sanded it all down and installed some hanging baskets ready for their trip to the garden centre tomorrow on their day off.

But now she was going to have to come into work first thing in the morning to get this problem with Marie Huston reported officially.

It was a headache of sorts, but now that she'd finally confronted the girl, it was also a weight lifted from her shoulders.

She could be home by 10 a.m. and she and Gordon could still have their day together.

Louise was looking forward to buying some beautiful brightly coloured flowers and plants to fill them all, and he'd promised to treat her to a nice pot of tea and a scone in the little cafe there too.

The simple things in life, that was what life was really all about.

Enjoying each other's company, and Gordon was always good company, Louise thought, as she neared her car.

Stepping in towards the edge of the car park, she heard another car pull into the car park behind her.

The rain was heavy now, lashing down in thick blanketed sheets.

The car was driving too fast, she thought, as she heard the roar of the engine, the vehicle skidding as it moved across the tarmac. The driver going way too fast.

'Bloody idiots,' she murmured, spinning around to get a good look.

She waved her arms at the clueless driver as she noted their headlights were out, too.

What kind of moron raced about at such speeds in this rain? They'd end up bloody killing someone if they weren't careful.

But, too late, she realised that was their intention.

As the car hurtled towards her, rapidly now, Louise didn't even have time to think.

It wasn't going to stop.

It was coming at her. Deliberately aiming for her.

It all happened so quickly, so unexpectedly.

No sooner had the panicked scream escaped her mouth, the metal slammed into her. The impact so brutal that her body was sent flying through the air.

Her screams were suddenly silenced as her body landed with a thud on the cold, wet tarmac.

Her body twisted and broken, she whimpered, then, for the driver to get out and help her.

Only the driver didn't move.

Instead, they just sat there underneath a blanket of darkness. Watching.

*

She stopped the car.

Steadying her shaking hands she gripped the steering wheel tighter. Keeping her gaze fixed on the reflection in the rear-view mirror.

It was dark outside, and the rain was so heavy that she could barely see the road.

But she could see her.

Staff Nurse Louise Langton.

Or at least, the blurred outline of her silhouette on the ground behind her.

Her colleague's twisted form. Face down in a puddle.

Her neck twisted at a peculiar angle from the rest of her body. Broken?

She wouldn't have survived that, surely?

She was dead.

She had to be.

She'd killed her.

Her eyes were wide and alert now, as the realisation of what she'd done dawned on her.

Her heart pounding loudly inside her chest. Beating so hard that it echoed inside her head, inside her ears. The blood rushing.

BOOM. BOOM.

Her whole body was shaking. As if it was physically moving by the surge of adrenaline alone.

It was such a shame, it really was.

If only Nurse Langton had left things alone.

Still, she wasn't finished yet. She knew what she needed to do.

Pushing the gear stick into reverse, she slammed her foot back down on the accelerator and shot the car backwards.

Wincing as the car jolted, her body lifting from the seat as she slammed into Louise Langton's body for a second time.

Spinning the wheels, then, on top of her for good measure.

Before finally turning the car around, facing the entrance of the darkened car park.

Stationary once more. Before she glanced around to make sure that there was no one watching. That there were no witnesses.

She looked back down at the floor then. At her colleague's mangled body, splayed out on the ground.

Unrecognisable now.

The puddle around Louise's pulped body looked black in this light, expanding as it filled with what could only have been blood.

It had stopped raining now, as quickly and dramatically as the downpour had started.

Shit! she thought to herself sadly as she realised that Louise Langton was really dead.

That she'd done this.

Cursing her temper for getting the better of her.

The memories of her father, flooding her mind.

How he'd hurt her and Cassie. How she'd made him pay, too.

She winced again. Pushing the vivid recollection from her thoughts.

She always did that. Went too bloody far.

She could have hurt her, broken the woman's legs. Only, clouded with venomous anger, she'd killed her.

That was such a shame.

Worse still, it could have all been prevented. If Louise Langton had only stayed out of Marie Huston's business and hadn't insisted on poking her nose into things that didn't concern her.

First thing tomorrow morning she was going to report her, that's what she'd said. She'd meant it, too.

Only now Louise Langton would never get that chance.

She took a deep breath in the hope of steadying her nerves, the pressure inside her head finally subsiding as she pressed her foot back down on the pedal once more, before racing out of the car park before she was seen by anyone.

Pushing all thought of the woman far from her mind.

There was no point on dwelling on it.

It was done now.

Louise Langton was dead.

Stupid woman.

Nothing and no one would stand in Marie's way now. Not when it came to Daniel Byrne.

CHAPTER TWENTY-FIVE

'Are we going to see your friend today, Grandaddy? The lady who likes the hot chocolate, the same as me?'

Walking towards Richmond Park playground with his great-granddaughter's hand tucked away tightly inside his, Michael Byrne nodded, before placing his finger on his lips.

'Remember though, we don't tell anyone about Grandaddy's friends. Especially not Nanny Joanie, or Nanny Colleen. She's our secret, okay?'

'Okay, Grandaddy.' Scarlett Byrne nodded. Only too happy to share a secret with her grandaddy, especially as it meant that this was the third trip to the park they'd gone on this week.

Michael dug his hands deep into his coat pockets then. Letting Scarlett off, so that the child could skip on, just ahead of him as he walked.

Alone with his thoughts, he couldn't ignore the stab of guilt that consumed him.

He'd tried to convince himself that there was nothing to it, that he was just meeting a friend in the park. But was it any wonder that his conscience was eating away at him?

He knew damn well that he shouldn't be keeping secrets from his Joanie again, and he certainly shouldn't expect Scarlett to either. But he knew how the woman's mind worked.

How she'd see this as something more than it was.

Technically, he wasn't doing anything wrong. It wasn't a crime, was it? To sit on a park bench and drink hot chocolate, while putting the world to rights. But because his new friend was a female, and attractive, well that changed everything, didn't it?

So far it really had just been about companionship. Nothing more than that and he certainly wasn't doing any harm. It wasn't as if he was getting up to no good.

Chance would be a fine thing! Michael Byrne grinned to himself.

And there it was. The truth. The real crux of his guilt.

This was the reason he hadn't told Joanie about the woman he'd been meeting up with in the park.

Because Michael Byrne actually liked this woman. He had the hots for this new friend of his, and in his defence, he didn't know a red-blooded male that wouldn't.

Far too young for Michael though, of course, not even thirty he guessed, but still, they'd somehow struck up a peculiar friendship of sorts. Talking of everything and nothing at all, so easy in each other's company.

Completely harmless.

Though Joanie wouldn't believe that for a second, especially if she clocked eyes on Michael's new crush.

There was no denying that the girl was simply stunning. She had the looks of a model – a glamour model at that – and a wicked sense of humour, he thought, feeling that familiar stirring in his loins as he recalled their last encounter together just a couple of days ago when he'd had the craziest notion that, despite the forty-year age difference between them both, that she felt some kind of attraction towards him too.

Maybe it was just wishful thinking on his part, only he wasn't convinced.

They certainly had a chemistry between them, he was sure of that. And the way she'd looked at him before he'd said goodbye – with such intent. Her hand 'accidentally' brushing against his knee as she spoke. He smirked. Aware that he was getting carried away with himself.

Though that was easily done, he figured, after living like a monk for the past four years; what with Joanie not interested in sex anymore, and him curbing his gallivanting ways, he'd been completely celibate.

The most affection the man ever got these days from Joanie was an awkward peck on the lips, or a stilted hug. The woman wasn't interested in sex in the slightest. Michael wasn't sure she'd ever been really.

His Joanie did love him though, he knew that. She must do, seeing as she was still with him after all these years. By rights, Joanie should have upped and left him years ago. Especially with all his carry on behind her back with all the other women over the years.

All his 'indiscretions'.

The past four years though, he'd really made an effort to stay loyal to her. After their Jimmy had passed away, and Scarlett had come into their lives, he'd stepped up, finally committing himself to his wife at long last. Michael Byrne was a family man now, and he vowed to himself that he'd stay faithful. Even if he did feel hornier than a dog with two dicks.

'Wait by the railings, Scarlett!' Michael shouted out as he approached the entrance of the park. Turning the corner, he saw her sitting in their usual spot, waiting for him.

She'd made a real effort today, he noted, in a short navy dress and matching heels. Her long hair, straightened. Smiling at her, as she threw him a wave.

'Can I run on to the swings, Grandaddy?' Scarlett screeched excitedly, as Michael laughed.

'Go on then, I'll be over on the bench.'

Walking towards her, he figured that even if she was one of those gold-digger types, what's the worst thing that could happen?

That they'd flirt and maybe share a fumble. Until she found out the truth.

That every penny that Michael had ever owned went through his wife before it got to him. That his family might be as wealthy as fuck, but personally, Michael Byrne didn't have a penny to his name.

Still, his new friend didn't need to know any of that.

If she genuinely liked him for him, then that wouldn't matter anyway. And if she was only after him for his money then Michael would be quids in either way.

Especially if he managed to get his leg over in the process.

'Michael! You made it.' Jess Green stood up, and hugged him, standing back then, her eyes twinkling with delight. 'I started to think that maybe you weren't coming.' She placed her hand on the man's arm as if they were old friends, lovers even.

Michael Byrne grinned. She was definitely flirting with him. Maybe it hadn't been wishful thinking after all?

'Of course I did. Couldn't stand up a pretty young thing like you, could I now?'

Even if Jess was just after his money, which of course, he didn't have, the only one hitting the jackpot would be Michael Byrne.

Either way, he couldn't lose.

CHAPTER TWENTY-SIX

'Scarlett, darling. Are you okay playing there in the sandpit? Grandaddy's just going to nip to the loo. I'll be five minutes, okay?'

'Okay, Grandaddy!' Scarlett said, already filling her plastic bucket up with sand. 'When you come back can you build a sandcastle with me?'

''Course I can, darling. I tell you what, I'll build you ten! How does that sound!'

'Ten? Wow. Okay, Grandaddy! I'll make the ground all flat ready for them.'

Michael smiled then, before skulking off to where he knew Jess was waiting for him inside the toilet cubicle.

This beautiful young woman. Fancying him? What were the chances? Slim to none that's what they were, so there was no way he was going to pass this opportunity off he decided, pushing down the guilt that he felt about leaving Scarlett alone. He refused to let his conscience get the better of him.

Reaching the door, he gave the playground one last glance over, checking that the mother playing with her child on the other side of the playground wasn't watching as he followed Jess into the toilets.

The last thing he needed was any unwanted attention from any of the do-gooder mothers around here. Casting aspersions on him for leaving his great-granddaughter unattended. Or worse, labelling him as some dirty old pervert.

Though there was no one looking. Nobody paying him the slightest bit of attention.

He looked at Scarlett then. Happily patting the ground with her spade, and scooping up heaps of sand.

Five minutes max. That's all he'd need.

He almost giggled out loud then, knowing how long he'd gone without sex, and how hot Jess was. He'd be lucky if he even made it past three minutes, let alone five.

*

Stepping into the toilet block, he saw Jess and smiled, before she pulled him inside the cubicle and shut the door behind them, kissing him intently, as he groped at her small pert breasts through the material of her dress.

All thoughts of his great-granddaughter were very quickly banished from his mind. Jess Green was not only stunningly beautiful, funny and kind. But the girl was a real goer too, it seemed. Fuck knows why, but she'd seen something in Michael that Michael didn't even know was there himself.

Kissing her back passionately, he couldn't believe his luck.

Michael Byrne was getting carried away with himself.

Just the sight and smell of Jess pressed up against him in the tiny toilet cubicle was almost enough to make him go off like a starting pistol.

He had to pace himself, he thought, show the girl that despite the age difference, he still had stamina.

Though that was easier said than done, groping her firm young body. He tried to think of anything he could to stop him from finishing the race before he'd even begun.

Train crash. Train crash.

Though, it helped that they were in a grotty toilet cubicle he figured. The lingering smell of human excrement and toilet bleach helped to bring him back down to reality.

Jess didn't seem to notice any of that, or at least she hadn't at first.

'I can't…' she mumbled, pulling Michael's hand back out from beneath her skirt, looking as if she was starting to have second thoughts.

'What's the matter?' Michael said, worried that Jess had somehow come to her senses and realised that Michael was nothing more than an old, wrinkly man. Pawing at her.

'Is it me?'

'No. God, no. Sorry. It's just this place,' Jess said, wrinkling her nose up at the rancid smell in the air and trying her hardest not to look down at the crusty brown skid marks that lined the inside of the toilet. 'It's just so grotty. Sorry. It's really putting me off, if I'm honest.'

'That's okay.' Michael nodded, relieved that it wasn't him that had killed the mood.

This place was pretty disgusting to be fair.

'Maybe we could do this properly? Somewhere else?' Jess said, stroking Michael Byrne's face as she talked, letting him know that she was still interested. 'How about back at yours?'

Michael shook his head then, suddenly regretting all the lies he'd told Jess. About how his wife had passed away suddenly and that he now lived on his own in a big old house in Richmond.

Another part of his big lie.

The rich widower.

'We can't really go back to my place…' Michael said, trying to quickly think of a reason to justify why. 'My house is being renovated. I've got builders there at the moment.'

'What about a hotel then?' Jess grinned, pressing herself up closer to Michael. Knowing that he would be easily persuaded.

'Well, I guess that's doable,' Michael said then, feeling hot under the collar as he tried to contain himself. The longing inside him was becoming almost too much.

'When?' Jess asked, her breath hot on his neck, burying her head into his chest.

Michael took a deep breath.

Joanie. Joanie. Joanie, he thought to himself, hoping that thoughts of his wife would bring him back down to earth again. And somehow ease the throbbing sensation that he was feeling inside his underpants right now.

'Tomorrow?' he said, his voice coming out in no more than a squeak.

Fuck knows how he was going to get around Joanie and manage to make a hotel booking without the woman getting wind of it.

Joanie held all the purse strings in the house, and every penny was accounted for.

In the bank accounts anyway, he thought, recalling the stash of money he knew she kept in the back of her dressing table drawer.

He'd take some of that. Joanie would never notice, and even when she did, he'd have more or less got away with it by then.

She'd never need to know what he'd done with the money. He could make out that he placed a few wagers on the horses.

It would cause an almighty row, but looking down at Jess, feeling the want and longing radiating from the girl, Michael knew that it would be more than worth the risk.

'Tomorrow then.' Jess smiled, happy that they'd made it a date. 'I'll meet you here, the usual time?'

Michael nodded.

'Okay! I'll sneak out first. Give me a few minutes and then you come out. We don't want to get any of the other yummy-mummies out there gossiping about us, do we?' Jess kissed Michael on the cheek. 'Looking forward to seeing you tomorrow, Michael, don't be late!' Jess said, playfully wagging her finger in Michael's direction before blowing him a cheeky kiss.

Watching as Jess stepped out of the public toilets, closing the door behind her.

Taking a deep breath, he pressed his hand up against the wall to steady himself. Still unable to believe his good fortune. As he tucked his shirt back inside his trousers in an attempt to make himself look less dishevelled, he stared at his reflection through the smears in the mirror, unable to wipe the smile from his face.

He still bloody had it, after all these years!

There was life in the old dog yet.

'You lucky, lucky bastard!' he said then, chuckling to himself as he realised how smug he looked.

It was crazy to think that underneath all of his wrinkles and lines on his skin, he still felt like a young man. As if he was thirty years old.

Especially on days like today, when he was with Jess.

Even if she was after his money, he'd happily settle for that.

Despite the fact that by the time the poor cow realised that not only had he lied to her about that, that he had a wife too.

One who was very much alive and kicking, and likely to string him up by his testicles if she even suspected that Michael was back to his old ways.

Still, what Joanie didn't know wouldn't hurt her, and by the time Jess found out that Michael had nothing to offer her, nothing of any monetary value anyway, it would be far too late for her to do anything about it.

Michael would have already got what he wanted from her by then.

He smirked, staring at the stony blue eyes looking back at him.

Yep, there he was. Still in there somewhere.

Michael Byrne.

Just as young and self-centred as he'd always been.

Ahh, well. Fuck it, you only live once and you're a long time dead, he thought to himself as he stepped out of the toilet cubicles with a spring in his step.

Ready to build those ten sandcastles he'd promised Scarlett.

He might be getting on, but that didn't mean that he couldn't have a bit of fun once in a while.

*

'Scarlett?' Michael Byrne said, as he eyed the empty sandpit and wondered where his great-granddaughter had got to. Spotting her bucket and spade discarded on the floor next to the empty sand box.

Annoyed then, that Scarlett had simply wandered off, when he'd told her to stay in the sandpit.

That he'd only be five minutes.

Kids!

Looking over at the climbing frame he breathed a sigh of relief as he caught sight of the two little girls sitting at the entrance of the slide. Scarlett in her florescent pink jacket.

'Scarlett! I told you not to wander off,' he muttered, making his way over just as both girls shot down the tube slide.

Still, at least she was okay.

He'd panicked for a second. Thinking that something bad might have happened. That Scarlett had wandered out into the main road, or something even worse that didn't even bear thinking about.

He scolded himself then, as he watched the first child come shooting out the bottom of the slide.

Leaving Scarlett to play on her own was a stupid thing to do. If anything had happened to her, he'd never have forgiven himself.

He decided that he'd make it up to her; that not only would he treat her to a nice hot chocolate today, but he'd buy her a slice of cake too.

Watching as the second child shot out of the slide and onto the rubber mat, his panic quickly resumed.

'Scarlett?' Michael said, realising straight away that the child wasn't his great-granddaughter. She just had the same coat.

'Are you okay?' the mother of the children said then, a curious look on her face as she spotted Michael approaching her daughter.

He held his hands up, showing the woman he meant no harm.

'I'm looking for my great-granddaughter,' he said, spinning around and scanning the park, shaking his head, and muttering loudly to himself as he realised that she was nowhere to be seen.

A little boy was on the swing, his mother standing behind him pushing him as he squealed in delight. Another woman was walking her two Jack Russells just outside the playground's borders.

'Have you lost her?' the woman said, again. Trying to be helpful; only stating the fucking obvious wasn't what Michael needed right now.

Yes, he'd lost her!

Michael looked as if he was about to cry then.

'I only left her for a few minutes. She was here.' Michael was panicking. Pacing the playground. Cursing himself for leaving her alone like that.

'She's wearing the same jacket as your little girl. Except my Scarlett's a bit younger. She's only four. She was here a minute ago. Over there in the sandpit. Are you sure you didn't see anything?'

'No, sorry. I didn't see a thing.'

Shit!

'Scarlett?' Michael started shouting then, frantically screaming out Scarlett's name. Sweating and shaking with anxiety, as he ran round looking inside the tunnel slides and behind the climbing frames, in case the child thought this was some kind of a game.

'Scarlett, if you're hiding from Grandaddy, it's not funny. Stop messing around, love, and come out!'

Silence.

She wasn't there.

He eyed the main park gates, wondering if perhaps Scarlett had got bored and decided to make her own way home. Or the woodlands next to the park, with its thick lining of trees.

She wouldn't have gone wandering in there, would she?

'Do you want me to call the police?' the woman said now, the expression on her face looking almost as concerned as Michael's.

He shook his head.

The first thought that came to his mind was Nancy.

How she'd bloody murder him when she found out that he'd left Scarlett all alone. Joanie would be next in line, of course.

Between the two of them, they'd have him hung, drawn and quartered before he'd even taken his coat off.

Shit!

An awful feeling in the pit of his stomach as he thought about some of the stories he'd read in the paper recently. About paedophiles that hang around parks. Getting off on watching the little kids that play there.

What if Scarlett wasn't playing? What if she wasn't hiding?

What if someone had taken her?

Blind panic set in then.

'Scarlett? Scarlett?' Michael was bellowing now. Shouting his great-granddaughter's name at the top of his lungs.

Michael Byrne pleaded. Not knowing what else he could do.

Go home and face the wrath of Joanie and Nancy, or call the Old Bill.

Though as soon as he called the plod, Jack Taylor would find out that his child was missing; so either way, Michael was royally screwed.

'Yes. Please, call them,' Michael Byrne said then, changing his mind and nodding.

He was going to need the Old Bill for his own protection, if anything, once his family got wind of what he'd done today.

'Scarlett! Scarlett!' He continued searching the park, screaming her name, until ten minutes later, when the police turned up.

Only Scarlett Byrne didn't answer back.

The child was gone.

CHAPTER TWENTY-SEVEN

Screeching up the driveway, Nancy Byrne pulled up outside her house.

Though how she'd managed to get here in one piece, she had no idea. With no recollection of the journey, she'd no doubt just driven across London like a woman demented.

She was still in shock.

The phone call that she'd received from Jack just twenty minutes ago, still replaying over and over again in her head.

Jack had made a mistake. They all had, she thought, as she eyed the row of police cars that lined the driveway outside her house.

Switching the engine off, Nancy ran into the house.

'Jack? Nan?' she shouted, making her way in to the kitchen where everyone was. She threw her bag down on the floor and stared at Jack.

Willing him to tell her that it was all just a huge misunderstanding.

That Scarlett was here. That they'd found her.

'Where is she?' Nancy said, as the room fell silent.

A sea of faces turning to look at her.

Jack stood up, making his way towards Nancy. His arms outstretched. The solemn look on his face only confirming that it was true.

That her worst nightmare had been bestowed upon them.

'No, Jack. Please. She's here. She has to be,' Nancy said, her voice a high-pitched wail. No longer giving a shit that everyone in the room was looking at her. That they could all hear the fear in her voice. The underlining panic that was so evidently there.

'Nancy. We're going to find her,' Jack said now, his tone full of a confidence that Nancy was certain he couldn't have really felt.

Not when their baby was missing.

Their Scarlett, out there in the world without them, on her own.

'She can't have just disappeared. Are you sure that you checked the house properly? She could be hiding,' Nancy said, suddenly figuring it out. That's what had happened. Scarlett was playing hide-and-seek.

She was playing with them all.

Only the game had got out of hand, and now everyone was worried, and the police had been called.

'She's scared!' Nancy said. 'She probably thinks we're all going to shout at her.'

Jack looked at Joanie then, alarmed that she didn't seem to be taking anything in, but before he could say anything else Nancy turned and ran from the room.

Racing up the stairs, she began searching in all the bedrooms. Throwing herself down on the floor, and checking underneath each one of the beds, before she started looking inside the wardrobes then too.

'Scarlett, baby, Mummy's here. No one's going to shout at you, darling. No one's mad. Just come out from wherever you're hiding and show Mummy that you're okay.'

Jack was there then, standing in the doorway.

His heart breaking as he watched Nancy, so adamant that she would find Scarlett when nobody else could.

'Nancy!' he said softly, as she pushed past him.

Purposely not listening to him as she continued dragging out each room. Pulling out the contents of cupboards and toy boxes.

Until there was nowhere else left to look.

'Where is she?' She was crying now. The realisation hitting her that it was true.

That Scarlett really wasn't here. Her little girl was missing.

'Jesus, Jack. Where is she?'

Sinking down onto her knees and letting a sound escape her mouth that sounded like that of a wounded, scared animal.

And Jack was there then. Wrapping his arms around her, and holding her tight.

'We're going to find her, Nancy, I promise,' he said, as he hugged Nancy to him, letting her cry. Letting her get all her pain and worry out.

Before he helped her back to her feet.

'Come on, let's get you back downstairs. You need a drink,' he said, knowing that the shock would be setting in now. 'Come and sit with Joanie while I go back to Richmond Park. We're going to do another search of the entire place. I only came back in case she'd made her way back here…' Jack said. Trying to sound like he had everything in hand, like this wasn't his darling daughter he was talking about. That this was just another case.

'The park?' Nancy said, feeling as if she was floating as Jack led her down the stairs. Her legs were trembling with every step, and she felt sick to her stomach.

Bile at the back of her throat threatening to explode from her.

Remembering that Jack had told her that's where she'd gone missing.

That she'd been at the park with Michael.

'I don't understand?' Nancy said. Locking eyes with her grandad, as the man sat at the kitchen table. His head down; he hadn't said a word.

He couldn't. What could he say?

Instead he sat there, shaking. Holding his hands tightly around the mug of sweet tea that one of the police family liaison officers had just made him.

'How did you manage to lose her, Grandad?' Nancy said then, unable to keep the accusation from her voice. 'How did a four-year-old child manage to just vanish into thin air when you were supposed to be looking after her?'

Michael mumbled something. Clearing his throat he spoke up, louder, so that Nancy could hear him.

'She was playing in the sandpit, Nancy. I took my eyes off her for probably seconds. I was reading my paper, that's all. Only when I looked up, she'd gone…'

Michael was openly crying now. Wracked with guilt that Scarlett had been in his care, that she'd been his responsibility.

That this was all his fault.

'That was it?' Nancy shook her head. 'You looked down at your newspaper and then she was gone?'

Nancy didn't believe it. Not for a second.

She must be missing something. They must all be missing something.

Scarlett might only be four years old, but she wasn't the type to just wander off.

She was a good kid.

Michael knew that too.

How his story wasn't adding up. How they would all find out his guilty little secret soon enough.

He was simply buying for time. Praying that Scarlett turned up.

'I swear, Nancy, as soon as I realised she was gone I turned the whole place over. I searched every inch of that park, and then I called the police. When Jack turned up, we both raced back here. Thinking that maybe she'd come home. That maybe she'd got bored of… I dunno…'

'Bored of what?' Nancy said confused. 'Playing on the swings and in the sandpit? Why would she be bored of that?'

Michael shook his head, shrugging his shoulders. The pressure of lying to everyone almost too much to bear – only the repercussions of his family finding out the truth would be far worse.

'I don't know, Nancy. I don't know.'

Nancy looked at her nan then. Joanie was suspicious too, glaring at her husband.

Up until now, she'd been so consumed with worry herself that she hadn't even realised that Michael wasn't just crying with worry, the man was wracked with guilt.

It was radiating off him in waves.

'If there's something you're not telling us, Michael, now's the time to say it. Our great-granddaughter is out there somewhere and we need to find her,' Joanie said. Trying to control the rage she felt building inside her, as she kept her tone neutral. The last thing Nancy needed right now was them arguing and adding to the drama.

Michael was hiding something. Joanie knew that look.

Though fuck knows what it was. But she knew her husband well enough to know when he'd been up to no good.

'For Christ's sake! Don't you think if I knew anything else, I'd tell you?!' Michael shouted then. 'Don't you think I feel bad enough as it is?'

And he did feel bad. He felt awful.

He felt physically sick that Scarlett was missing and that it was all his fault.

He should never have left Scarlett alone. Not even for five minutes.

And he couldn't shake the awful feeling in the pit of his stomach that he'd somehow been set up.

That Jess was somehow involved in all of this.

It was too much of a coincidence, her befriending him over the past couple of days then Scarlett going missing as soon as they were both otherwise occupied.

And Jess had suggested it, hadn't she?

She'd been the one to advocate them both nipping into the toilets and having a few moments together, alone.

He winced, thinking about how she'd told him that she didn't have children. That she couldn't. How she'd have loved one, given the chance.

Maybe that's what this had all been about.

Jess taking her chance. Her one opportunity when the coast was clear, and snatching Scarlett.

That's what this had been about all along.

Jesus! What had he done? He'd never learn, would he? He was just a stupid, worthless, pathetic old man.

There was no way that Michael could tell his family the truth. No way in the world.

'Will you stop with the dramatics, Michael? Jesus if anyone should be shouting and crying, it should be Nancy. She's the child's mother. How do you think she feels huh? Pull yourself together,' Joanie muttered, irritated at her husband's snivelling. Michael sitting here acting all sorry for himself was only making matters worse.

Joanie only had to look at Nancy's expression to see the worry that was etched across her face. Her poor granddaughter was out of her mind and rightfully so.

'They'll find her, Nancy. Soon,' Joanie said; worried sick herself, she prayed to God that she was right. That their little Scarlett was safe. That the child would be found soon.

'Is there anywhere you can think of that she might have gone, Nancy? Anywhere at all that Scarlett might have wanted to wander off and look at, or someone she'd want to visit?' the family liaison officer said then. Trying to calm everyone down. To focus their attention back on the search.

Only his patronising tone instantly got Nancy's back up.

'She's four years old. Who the hell would she want to visit?' Nancy said, then as an afterthought she quickly added. 'Colleen?'

Looking at Jack, wondering if maybe that's where Scarlett had gone.

Jack shook his head.

'I rang her already, she hasn't seen her. She's on her way here now. She's beside herself too.'

'We need to go back to the park,' Nancy said then, pacing the kitchen, unsure what else she could do. 'I can't just sit here doing nothing. We need to keep looking.'

'There's officers there, Nancy. I'm going back there now too. Why don't you wait here in case she comes home?' Jack said. 'Can you make Nancy a cup of tea?' Nodding at the family liaison officer then.

'I don't want to sit around drinking fucking tea. I want to find my daughter. It's getting dark, Jack. We need to find her. If she comes home, Nan's here. She can call us. I'm coming with you.'

'Sometimes kids simply wander off. They get some crazy notion in their head that they want to go and look at some ducks or something. Or perhaps a family member who lives nearby, and off they go. Scarlett's probably safe and sound,' the family liaison officer said, trying to reassure Nancy now. Though he instantly regretted his poor choice of words.

'*Probably*?' Nancy said glaring back at the man. Her vision blurred by tears that threatened to fall. 'But what if she's not? What if somethings happened to her and she's lying somewhere hurt? What if she's lost? What if someone's taken her?'

Unable to stop her tears from falling then, as she said the one thing that none of them wanted to say out loud, Nancy grabbed her car keys from where she'd flung them down on the kitchen side.

'Come on, Jack, we need to go.'

Michael stood up then, heart sorry for the pain he'd caused them all today, as he reached out to touch his granddaughter on the arm.

'If anything's happened to her, I'll never forgive myself,' Michael said, blubbing once more.

'Well, you better start praying to God that we find her then,' Nancy said, wiping the tears from her face and throwing her grandad a parting shot, 'because trust me, Grandad, if anything has happened to Scarlett, I'll never forgive you myself. In fact, I'll be holding you personally responsible.'

CHAPTER TWENTY-EIGHT

Being led into London City's command control centre, by a fellow officer, Nancy Byrne made her way over to where Jack Taylor was sitting with a CCTV operative.

After spending hours earlier this evening scouring Richmond Park and all the surrounding areas in the hope of finding some clue as to what had happened to Scarlett, they'd both come away completely deflated.

Though no sooner had Nancy returned home to her house, and switched off her car engine, than Jack had rung her mobile phone, summoning her here.

'Have you got something?' Nancy asked, her voice full of hope that somehow Jack had finally found a lead.

Up until now they had nothing else to go on. It was as if Scarlett had simply vanished into thin air.

The officers had questioned all the other parents and passers-by in and around the park, and no one had seen her.

She hadn't made her way back to the house.

Nancy knew that this wasn't looking good.

She could see the concern on Jack's colleagues' faces. They were thinking the very same.

The clock was ticking and the longer this went on, the more dire her fears about her child were.

'You better see this. Here, take a seat.' Jack nodded. Pulling out a chair next to him, before asking one of the junior officers to get Nancy a hot drink.

She looked awful, her skin deathly pale, the worry etched across her face.

'We've managed to get hold of some CCTV footage that covers the corner of the playground. It's grainy as fuck, and it's mainly focused on the toilet cubicle. So we don't really see Scarlett.'

'You've got her on camera?'

Jack held his hands up. Not wanting to give Nancy any false hope, he shook his head.

'Barely. The camera angle is off. Forty grand they spent on this system. Monkeys must have installed the thing. It should have been facing the playground and the gates to the park. All we've got is the toilet cubicles. Look, down here in the bottom left of the screen. That's the corner of the children's sandpit.'

Nancy nodded. Half hoping that she would get a glimpse of her daughter. As if somehow that would make her feel better. Seeing her on the screen.

It would make her feel as if they were finally getting somewhere.

That they were heading in the right direction if nothing else.

Though now, listening to Jack's tone, suddenly him summoning her down here, didn't sound like this was a good thing at all.

'Keep watching,' Jack said, as he waited for a few seconds and then got the CCTV operative to pause the tape. He pointed then to the screen.

'There. You see her?'

Nancy stared. Her eyes fixed on the flash of red hair. A bright pink coat in shot. On the screen for just seconds. It was her, Nancy was certain of it.

'Colleen bought her that jacket. Everything that woman buys her is bloody florescent pink,' Nancy said, her heart beating hard then inside her chest. Her breath shallow, as she stared at the screen as the operative replayed the last few seconds so that Nancy could be sure. 'That's Scarlett. A hundred per cent.'

Jack nodded in agreement.

He wasn't disputing that at all. It was the rest of the recording that Nancy needed to see.

'Keep watching,' Jack said. Not able to bring himself to say anything else. Nancy had told him that she wanted to know every single detail about this investigation, and that he wasn't to hide anything from her. He had to respect that.

Nancy watched the screen. The picture blurred and grainy in places, just as Jack had warned her. But clear enough to just about make out the silhouette of a woman walking past the sandpit.

'Who's that?' Nancy said, wondering if the woman was even relevant. Unable to catch a glimpse of the woman's face, her back to the camera as she stepped inside the public toilets.

Nancy watched as another figure went into the loo then too. This time a male. Reaching the toilet door he looked towards the sandpit, as if he was saying something to the child that was playing there. His face in full view of the camera then.

'That's Michael,' Nancy said, narrowing her eyes, as she watched her grandad follow the woman into the female toilets. 'He told me he didn't take his eyes off her. What the fuck…?' The penny dropped then at the reason he'd gone into the toilets in the first place. No wonder he'd kept this to himself. Nancy was furious then.

'He couldn't lie straight in bed, that man. I'm going to kill him for this…'

Biting her lip, they waited in silence.

Anger building inside her as she realised her grandad had left Scarlett out there playing on her own.

Watching the clock.

That fucking man. No wonder he was so beside himself back at the house.

She knew that there had been more to it.

He was guilty as sin, because sinning is precisely what he'd been up to.

'That lying bastard,' Nancy said, impatiently, keeping her gaze fixed on the toilet door between constant flickers to the bottom corner of the screen.

To the sandpit where her baby-girl was playing all on her own.

Scarlett was barely in shot for most of it, but every now and again, Nancy caught a flash of pink, as her daughter moved about.

Impatient, Nancy shook her head. Watching as the minutes on the screen passed them by.

'What's he doing in there?'

'I'll give you one guess. Looks to me like your grandad is up to his old tricks again. Getting his rocks off with some fucking brass in Richmond Park bogs, while our daughter is left unattended in the fucking playground,' Jack spat, angry now too. The vein pulsing in his temple. His fists clenched so tightly together that his knuckles had gone white. If Nancy didn't murder the bastard for this, he personally would.

Hearing the hard tone to his voice, how angry and upset he was, Nancy knew that this was really bad. Jack had already seen this footage, he knew what happened next.

'Tell me, Jack, what's happening?' Nancy said, too impatient to wait now.

She just wanted to know where the fuck Scarlett was.

But Jack wouldn't tell her.

'Keep watching,' he said. Unable to find the words. How could he tell the mother of his child that her worst fears were about to come true?

So they stared at the screen in silence. Both continuing to watch the footage play out, the silence in the room palpable. The only noise, a loud hum of the monitor playing the CCTV imaging; the occasional click of the keyboard as the operator paused the footage hoping to get a better view of Scarlett, every time the child came into shot.

Jack hated to put Nancy through this, but he knew Nancy well enough to know that she needed to see for herself. First-hand.

'There. Pause it,' Jack instructed the CCTV operative. 'Go back a bit. There.' Pointing down towards the dark shadowy figure at the bottom of the screen.

Nancy looked closer.

The operative pressed play again.

A flash of pink again. Scarlett's jacket.

So sudden that if Jack hadn't pointed it out, Nancy would have probably missed it.

Then another figure. Moving quickly.

'No, please God, no!' Nancy wailed. Her hands over her mouth, her eyes fixed on the screen in front of her. Unable to shift her gaze from the figure standing over her daughter.

'Pause it,' Jack instructed.

They both stared at the screen.

The operative zoomed in.

The only image in front of them, of someone's hand wrapped around Scarlett's arm.

Too dark to make out if it was a man or a woman.

Too grainy to see any features.

Just a shadowy silhouette, reaching down for Scarlett.

The bucket and spade are thrown down on the floor beside the sandpit.

Then as quickly as both figures had come into view, they were gone; the camera still focused on the now empty sandpit.

'Please, pick it up. Pick it up,' Nancy muttered to herself, transfixed on the bucket and spade that Scarlett had just been playing happily with.

But she wouldn't pick it up, would she?

Because she wasn't there anymore. She was gone.

'Oh my God, Jack. Someone has taken her, haven't they?' The words that left her mouth were spoken in barely a whisper now. As if saying them any louder would somehow make them too real.

Only this *was* real.

Clasping a hand over her mouth so that she wouldn't scream with anger and fear, or worse, throw up.

'We don't know anything yet, Nancy, so don't jump to any conclusions. We need to keep watching. We have to keep our wits about us, Nancy,' Jack instructed. Knowing how hard it was to watch, how hard it was to take in the fact that their daughter may have been abducted. Determined to stay professional and calm, so that he wouldn't lose his head too. 'Keep watching, Nancy. It's important.'

Nancy saw another movement then.

The toilet cubicle door opening.

Jack Taylor tapped the screen.

'Watch. She comes out first, shortly followed by Michael. Seven minutes they'd been in there in total,' Jack said, talking Nancy through it. Keeping her focused. 'She looks in the sandpit, and sees Scarlett is gone, but she just keeps walking,' Jack said, convinced that the woman may be involved. 'Don't you think that's strange? She must have known that Michael had left Scarlett to her own devices, yet she doesn't seem worried not to see Scarlett there. Maybe she expects it?'

Nancy stared, narrowing her eyes.

'Hang on a minute. Go back,' she said, as the woman stepped out of the cubicle. Her face visible to the camera now too.

Not a hundred per cent clear, but Nancy could just about make her out.

Sensing something familiar about her.

'You know her?' Jack asked, scrutinising the image himself.

'I don't know, maybe. I think I recognise her,' Nancy said, shaking her head. Unsure then; the image was hazy. She's probably just clutching at straws. Trying to see something that's not even there. 'She looks familiar, but I can't place her. I don't know. Play the rest of it.'

A few seconds later Michael steps out of the toilet cubicle too.

The panic on his face evident as he eyes the empty sandpit. The discarded bucket and spade. Standing for a few seconds, completely still, before he moves quickly out of shot.

'That's it,' Jack said then, turning the CCTV footage off. 'That's all we've got so far, Nancy. We've checked for cameras along the main road leading into Richmond Park, but so far, this is our only lead. But at least we've got one. We just need to get back to the house now and find out what the fuck your grandad's been up to, and who the fuck this woman is. She's part of it. I'm sure of it.'

Nancy nodded.

The feeling of trepidation in the pit of her stomach.

Her mind replaying the image of the hand locked around her daughter's arm.

That one minute, Scarlett was there and the next minute she was gone.

Standing up to follow Jack out of the room it was all too much.

Her legs gave way.

The tears came then too. Engulfing her entirely as she realised that her worst fears had indeed come true.

Some bastard had taken her baby.

CHAPTER TWENTY-NINE

'Oh Joanie, stop harping on at the man. Can't you see he's distressed enough as it is?' Colleen Byrne said, feeling heart sorry for Michael Byrne. Ever since she'd got here, an hour ago, all Joanie Byrne seemed intent on doing was beating the poor man down with all her accusations about what he'd *really* been up to today.

The woman just wouldn't let it go.

Quizzing him and questioning the man, as if she was trying to catch him out somehow, as if Scarlett going missing today was personally his fault, when anyone with two eyes in their head could see that it wasn't anything of the sort. Michael adored Scarlett. He'd never put her in any harm.

'Today wasn't this poor bugger's fault. He's told you a million times what happened. The same as he's told all the officers here too,' Colleen said, nodding to the family liaison officer who was sitting with them all. Who appeared to be keeping well out of the two ladies' minor dispute.

'It's not your fault, Michael. It could have been any one of us that took Scarlett to the park today,' Colleen said, wanting to believe what she was saying more than any of them.

The poor guy looked like a broken man, sitting at the table in silence. Hanging his head as if he had the weight of the world on his shoulders. Which, Joanie was making sure, he did.

'Scarlett will probably turn up here any minute now. We all just have to try and stay positive. Kids wander off all the time.'

'What? Like the night Nancy did her Houdini act?' Joanie scoffed. 'She was younger than Scarlett was at the time. Do you remember? When they found the poor mite wandering around Richmond High Street with no shoes on. The night you were supposed to be keeping an eye on her, only you were too busy trying to flush out your other baby with drugs and alcohol,' Joanie spat, her venomous words loaded with intent.

How dare Colleen turn up at the house in the state she was in.

Drunk, though she was trying ever so desperately to play it down. Only Joanie had clocked her, staggering as she got out of the taxi and made her way up the driveway. If it wasn't for the family liaison officer hanging around the place like a bad bleeding smell, Joanie would have battered the woman on first sight.

Even now, the blatant audacity of the woman, sitting here and trying her hardest to disguise the slur in her words. Pronouncing each syllable painfully slowly. Which, despite her best efforts, only had the opposite effect and gave the woman away.

She was trying too bloody hard, and she wasn't fooling anyone.

And neither was Michael. Joanie didn't care what Colleen thought she knew, Michael was keeping something from them all and Joanie was going to make it her business to find out what it was.

Her great-granddaughter's safety depended on it.

'You don't know what you're talking about, Colleen. Spouting all your shit about her just coming home. What if Scarlett didn't just go wandering off? Eh, what then? What if someone did take her?' Joanie Byrne said, unable to hide the tears in her eyes.

She was sick of Colleen sitting here, spouting her drunken crap, and all her useless wishful thinking and cliche sayings.

Convinced that any minute now Scarlett would turn up at the front door. That the search would be called off. That her precious little great-granddaughter was safe and their nightmare would all be over. Only this was the real world, and sometimes it didn't work out like that.

'The vodka's clearly numbed your brain, Colleen!' Joanie said, before turning back on her husband. 'There's something you're not saying, Michael, and whatever it is, I will get to the bottom of it,' Joanie warned again, glaring at her husband who had gone a pale, deathly white at the eminent threat that lingered in Joanie's tone.

Something bad had happened. Joanie was sure of it. She could feel it deep in the pit of her stomach.

And still Michael didn't speak; he didn't bother to so much as open his mouth and defend himself. Another sure sign that the man was guilty as sin.

In fact, other than when he'd been bawling earlier, the minute he'd set eyes on Nancy, the man had barely said a word all evening. Well, Joanie had had enough.

'You're better off telling me, Michael, before I find out from someone else,' Joanie said again. Shaking her head ruefully. 'And I will find out.'

She knew how stubborn Michael could be. The man was an expert at his conniving and selfish ways. As much as he'd made out he was a changed man this past few years, Joanie knew, deep down, he was still the same.

'I know you, Michael, and I know the lengths you'd go to, to try and save your own arse. Well, let me tell you, if I find out that you're hiding something about our Scarlett, something that might help us find her, then nothing and no one will save you, do you hear me? I'll unleash merry hell on you myself.'

'Joanie, for Christ's sake will you just give it a bloody rest!' Colleen said then. Losing her rag, as Joanie's voice echoed through her. Just the sound of it, so nasty and condescending. Reminding her of all the times the woman had spoken to her in exactly the same way.

'No wonder the man's a quivering wreck. It's okay, Michael. She doesn't mean it. She's just worried about Scarlett, that's all. We all are.'

Watching as Michael broke down once again.

His shoulders shaking violently, as he hung his head. The tears running down his face, dripping onto the kitchen table that they all sat around.

Colleen reached out and touched her father-in-law's arm.

The kind gesture, seemingly only making Michael cry more.

'I'm surprised poor Michael wasn't the one committed to a bloody mental hospital!' Colleen said then, the alcohol in her system making her feel brave. 'The amount of giving out to him you do, the poor man's a nervous wreck.'

'What? As opposed to me being the one in a mental hospital? Is that what you're getting at, Colleen? 'Cause let me tell you, you don't want to be going there, love! Not if you want me to keep my mouth shut,' Joanie said, her eyes flashing with fury at the cheek of Colleen using her breakdown against her. The breakdown she'd had because of her in the first place.

If Colleen wasn't careful, Joanie would tell them all. Her expression said as much, her eyes boring into Colleen's.

Only Colleen waved her hand at Joanie dismissively, too wasted to care. She'd spent the best part of the day stuck in her flat alone. Stewing on the fact that Joanie was going to hold what she did over her head forever.

Well, fuck Joanie.

'Do it, Joanie. Tell them. I don't give a shit anymore,' Colleen said then, challenging Joanie. Playing the woman at her own game. She wasn't willing to spend the entirety of her granddaughter's life being held to ransom for her mistakes. 'Tell them, and maybe then you can stop hanging it around my neck like a noose. You'll have nothing on me. Nothing to keep me from Scarlett once she's home.'

Colleen had already missed out on enough, she decided.

'You're a state, Colleen. Look at you.'

'Look who's talking, Joanie, Lady Muck herself….'

The two women were standing then, leaning over the table as they shouted at the tops of their voices. Swearing at each other and calling each other names.

Michael was shouting too.

Begging them to both shut up.

They were doing his head in. All this screaming and shouting, as if all hell had broken loose before him.

He couldn't stand it for a second longer.

This was all down to him.

He had to tell them the truth about Jess.

But Joanie would murder him. She'd kick him out of the house. He'd lose everything.

Then he thought of Scarlett.

Sweet, little Scarlett. He owed it to her if nothing else.

It was starting to get dark. Wherever Scarlett was, whoever she was with, she'd probably be petrified by now.

This was all his fault. All his doing.

So what if his family disowned him, if they all turned against him? He deserved everything he got.

'Please shut up!' he shouted, on his feet now. Banging his fists on the table. 'SHUT UP!'

He was crying still, his body heaving with huge almighty sobs, snot hanging from his nostrils, his face bright red.

'It's my fault; Joanie's right. I fucked up big time. This is all my fault.'

The two women stared at him then. Rendered silent, as they saw the pain and guilt etched on Michael's face as he continued. The family liaison officer standing at his side, trying to comfort him, to calm him down; only Michael shrugged the man off him.

'I left her on her own. It wasn't even ten minutes. I swear to God. And she was fine, playing in the sandpit. I said, "Scarlett, Grandaddy won't be long. Don't go off anywhere."' He shook his head remorsefully, ashamed of himself.

Sick to his core.

'And when I came back, she was gone.'

'"When you came back"?' Joanie said, her fists clenched at her side. She knew it. She bloody knew it. 'Came back from where?'

'There was this woman…' Michael said now, as Joanie closed her eyes, instantly feeling as if she'd been punched in the gut, a cry escaping her lips.

'"This woman?" Oh, Michael there's always "some woman" when you're involved.'

'It wasn't like that,' Michael lied. Continuing now that he had started, relieving himself of the guilt that was eating him up inside. Glad to finally unburden himself. 'I think I was set up. Jess was the one who suggested it. That we meet up in the toilets… I should have known…' Michael looked away, ashamed then. Even as he said the words, he knew how ridiculous he sounded.

How pathetic and desperate he must be to have fallen for the woman's advances. To have even believed for a second that she'd really be interested in someone like him.

A wrinkly, old fool.

This had never been about him, he knew that now. This had been about Scarlett.

It had always been about Scarlett.

Joanie knew it too.

'You stupid, stupid bastard,' Joanie shouted, her suspicions confirmed that Michael was back to his old tricks again. Up to no good with some old slapper.

Only this time he'd put their precious little great-grandchild in danger in the process.

'What have you done? You selfish, lying, cheating bastard. What the hell have you done?'

Joanie was on him then.

Battering him with her fists. Screaming obscenities at the man, as the family liaison officer tried to drag Joanie off, as she swung out wildly in the middle of the kitchen, catching Michael over and over on the back of his head, pummelling him to the floor.

Colleen standing there, looking confused at what was happening. Still drunk, and not sure what Michael was admitting to, as if she'd just missed something. Her mind couldn't keep up.

'Are you going to tell our granddaughter what a fuck up you are, huh?' Joanie spat now, pure hate in her eyes.

Her and Michael were done now, forever.

After today she'd never have him back again.

'Are you going to tell Nancy that you gambled with her daughter's safety for some slapper you were meeting in the bogs? Like some dirty old pervert.'

'He doesn't need to, Nan,' Nancy Byrne said, marching into the kitchen followed shortly by Jack. 'I already know. Now you better sit down, Grandad, and tell me everything you know about this woman. And I mean *everything*.'

Seeing the cold hard expression on Nancy's face, Michael knew without a doubt that by the time Nancy and Jack were done with him, he'd have wished that Joanie had put him out of his misery while she'd still had the chance.

CHAPTER THIRTY

'What is it with this family and all your fucking lies? Why can't anyone just be straight for once and tell the truth?' Nancy said, standing in the kitchen, her eyes flashing with fury. 'Who the fuck is she, Grandad? That woman that you met up with?'

She could feel Jack's hand gripping the back of her arm. Holding her off from running at Michael and physically tearing strips off the man.

They needed him to speak, to tell them everything.

Their priority now was getting Scarlett back.

Dealing with Michael could wait.

Defeated now, and heart sorry for his actions, Michael shook his head. Not even sure where to begin, as he sank back down into the chair behind him.

'I'm sorry, Nancy. Hand on my heart, I don't know what I was thinking. Leaving Scarlett like that…'

But he did know.

He'd put himself before the child.

His greedy, dirty, wanton needs before the safety of his great-granddaughter.

And now his family knew it too.

'She said that she liked me, and I don't know, I guess I just got sucked in by her spell…'

'Oh you were sucked in by something all right! A spell? Oh, I've heard it called a lot of things, but "spell" is a new one on me,' Joanie scoffed. Ready to launch herself at the man again; only she could see the urgency in Nancy's expression. She knew that whatever was going on right now, she had to let her grand-daughter get to the truth.

All she wanted to do was batter the man, and as much as that would make her feel better it wasn't going to help get Scarlett back.

'Her name's Jess. That's all I really know about her. She met me at the park a few times. She seemed sweet. I felt sorry for her. When she said she didn't have any kids of her own. That she couldn't—'

'Jess, what?' Nancy said, her tone harder than stone.

Michael shook his head. Realising that he didn't know her surname. He hadn't asked her, and she hadn't told him. And even if she had told him, Jess's sob stories were all just lies anyway.

'I don't know. She didn't tell me and even if she had done, none of it was real, was it? Maybe not even her name? It was all orchestrated to catch me off guard. And I fell for it, too. Hook, line and sinker. Like the old, doddering fool that she'd hoped I'd be.'

Michael felt physically sick then.

The fact that he didn't know anything about this Jess, nothing genuine anyway, finally hitting him.

And now he couldn't even cry. He had nothing left inside him.

A broken empty shell.

He'd done this. He'd let his family down.

They all had every right to hate him. Christ knows, he hated himself.

'That's it, is it? That's all you know about her?' Nancy said, her eyes full of fire. 'All you know about a woman that you were happy to go off and do Christ knows what with in the toilets. That her name was Jess. That's it?'

Michael stared at the floor. Deeply ashamed of himself then.

'Get out,' Nancy screamed. Not even able to look at the man. Just the sight of him made her want to claw his eyes out.

She could see the hurt and the utter humiliation on her nan's face.

'I said get the fuck out of this house.'

Michael didn't need telling twice. He was glad to go. Glad to escape from all the accusing glares, all the angry hateful faces.

He ran from the room, almost knocking down Bridget as she came through the front door.

'Michael? Oh God, what's happened?'

But Michael didn't bother to stop to fill her in.

'What's the matter with Michael?' Bridget asked as she made her way into the kitchen; staring at everyone's faces, she prayed to God that it wasn't what she thought it was.

That they hadn't just had bad news about Scarlett.

All she knew so far was that little Scarlett had gone missing. Jack had phoned the house and told Bridget to keep an eye out. To ask the girls to check everywhere, just in case Scarlett had made her way there.

Not that she would have. The child had no clue how to get to the place, but Jack had sounded desperate. As if he was running out of options. Even Bridget had known that.

'I came as soon as I heard, Nancy,' she said then, almost too scared to ask what had just made Michael run from the house. 'Have you found her?'

Nancy shook her head.

'She was taken, Bridget. Someone's taken her. We saw it on CCTV. While my feckless grandad was busy trying to get his end away with some little tart!'

The tears coming once again.

Frustrated and angry that this was even happening. That her own grandad had caused all of this, with his stupid, philandering ways.

That her precious baby was out there, somewhere, without her. Scared out of her mind no doubt.

'Oh, darling!' Bridget was crying too then. Wrapping her arms around her friend, the two women standing together in the kitchen in a locked embrace.

'Do you know anything else? Who it was? Anything at all?' Bridget said finally, this time directing her questions to Jack.

'We're doing everything we can…' he said with more bravado than he really felt.

Trying to hold himself together then too.

Trying to be strong for Nancy.

'We've got a couple of leads…'

Nancy knew what he was doing. He was trying to placate her, trying to keep her hopes and spirits up. When the truth was they had fuck all to go on really. Nothing.

'*Leads*? Grainy CCTV footage of some shadowy figure in a park? We don't even know if it's a woman or a man!'

Nancy began pacing the room. Ready to tear her hair out in frustration that they were all just standing around waiting for something to happen. To hear some news. That they were pretty much rendered useless. That the fate of her little girl was completely out of her hands.

'Let me make you a tea, Nancy,' Bridget said. Feeling useless then too.

Seeing the distress and fear in everyone's faces.

She busied herself as the women sat down at the table, and Jack went off to make a call.

Handing out the hot mugs of tea, just as Jack came strolling back into the room.

'We've got something, Nancy,' he said, sounding hopeful now. His phone still in his hand. 'One of the residents just outside the park, over at the Sheen Gate entrance, made a report of a car hanging about, around the time that Scarlett went missing. Said that she'd noticed it because it had been blocking her driveway. The resident didn't think too much of it, until one of our officers started doing a house-to-house on that street, asking if anyone had seen Scarlett. That's when the woman mentioned it. She thought the driver had been acting a bit suspiciously. That he'd seemed on edge. Tapping his steering wheel and constantly looking up and down the street. She said that he went into the park, only to come running back out a few minutes later. Followed shortly afterwards by a woman. That they'd both sped off.'

'And Scarlett? Did she see Scarlett?' Not allowing herself to get her hopes too high. It wasn't much to go on.

'She doesn't remember seeing a child,' Jack said, wishing that he had something more solid. But this was a start. This was something at least. 'But get this, Nancy. She said that because her car had been vandalised twice last year, she'd invested in some CCTV cameras of her own. She reckons she's got the car on camera. My officers are there now, seeing if she managed to get the car's registration number. This could be our lead, Nancy. We might finally have something.'

'Or it could be nothing.' Not feeling hopeful, Nancy wasn't convinced.

Another beep then, from Jack's phone.

'They got it. The car is registered to a Kyle Boyd?' Jack said looking at Nancy half hoping that she might recognise the name. Only she shook her head.

'Doesn't ring a bell.'

Another beep.

'They've got an address for him. He's clean, he hasn't got any previous.'

'He might have nothing to do with it,' Nancy said then, annoyed that they seemed to be just going around in circles. As if they weren't getting anywhere closer to finding Scarlett.

Another beep then. This time Nancy closed her eyes.

What was the point in all of this?

They should be out there, combing the park and the surrounding streets. Checking every house, every car. Not digging up information on some random bloke who more than likely had nothing to do with any of this.

They were just wasting precious time.

'This is him…' Jack held it out for Nancy to see. 'They managed to get a clear image of him from the woman's CCTV when he got out of his car.'

A young man. Nothing untoward, tall and well-built but other than that he was average-looking.

Brown hair, brown eyes. His face pale and unshaven.

Nancy had never seen him before in her life.

'Fucking hell!' Bridget said, almost dropping her cup on the kitchen table, as she leaned in closer to get a better view. Certain her eyes were deceiving her. 'I know him.'

Her blood running cold as she got up and snatched the phone from Jack's hand, staring at the image. Making sure that she was certain.

And she was.

'That's him. He's been in your house, Nancy. He's the guy from the security company. The fella that we hired to do the alarm system. The first time around.'

'Fuck! Are you sure?' Jack said then, before grabbing his phone back and making a call to his colleague. Demanding Kyle Boyd's listed address.

'Hang fire on heading over there,' Jack instructed his colleague, not wanting any of his co-workers to go around to this fucker's place of residence and interfere.

Jack Taylor was going to sort this fucker out personally.

Chances were that this man had his daughter.

It had to be him.

It was too much of a coincidence for it not to be.

CHAPTER THIRTY-ONE

'Let's get the hell out of here!' Jess Green ordered as she slid into the passenger seat of her boyfriend's Ford Mondeo, glancing back towards Sheen Park gates to make sure that Michael Byrne wasn't following closely behind her.

A week of buttering up that dirty old git was all it had taken for Jess's plan to come into play.

Men! God may have blessed them all with both brains and a cock, but the flaw in the big man's grand design had been that he hadn't given them enough blood supply for both to be operated at once.

And Jess had been counting on that.

Fuck, she'd made a career out of it.

Michael Byrne had, just as she'd hoped, taken the bait. Unable to resist her charms, he'd been only too happy to leave his precious little Scarlett unattended for a few minutes, and that was all Jess had needed.

Shuddering at the thought of Michael Byrne's grubby hands roaming her body, Jess pushed the memory of their sordid little encounter to the back of her mind. She never wanted to think about Michael Byrne again.

'Come on, Kyle, get a bloody move on.' Jess looked impatiently at Kyle Boyd then, wondering why he hadn't even started up the engine.

He looked awkward. His hands tightly gripping the steering wheel, his eyes fixed straight ahead of him.

He was avoiding eye contact with her.

Her heart sank.

She knew straight away.

'Oh God!' Jess turned to check the seat behind her, expecting to see little Scarlett Byrne sitting there, under the blanket, just as they'd planned.

Only the seat was empty. The large blanket they'd brought with them to conceal the child, unused, still screwed up in a ball in the middle of the chair.

'Where the fuck is the kid?' Jess said, gritting her teeth, glaring at Kyle, confused now.

She'd checked the playground herself, and Scarlett had definitely gone.

Jess had even smirked to herself as she'd stepped over the child's abandoned bucket and spade that had been discarded down on the pathway, before getting her arse out of there quick time too. Not wanting to hang around and witness Michael Byrne's melodramatics when the dirty old bugger finally waltzed out of the toilet cubicles only to discover that his beloved great-granddaughter had gone on the missing list.

But something had clearly gone wrong.

'You have got her, haven't you?' Desperate now, Jess's last hope was that maybe the kid had been a pain in the arse, and had kicked off, so Kyle had put her in the boot? Though she couldn't hear any noise coming from back there. No crying or banging to get out. And the fact that Kyle wouldn't even look at her told her all she needed to know.

'Fuck! You didn't get her, did you?' she shouted then. Smashing her hand against the dashboard with pure rage.

Typical Kyle. He'd fucked up yet again.

'I'm sorry, Jess… I did what you said, but…' he started.

But Jess stopped him in his tracks.

Her voice high-pitched, laced with hysteria.

'You're sorry! You're sorry? Oh please, spare me, Kyle.' This could not be happening. Not after all the groundwork she'd put in to get this right today.

And to think that she'd just let that filthy pig, Michael Byrne, paw all over her, for nothing.

Squeezing her eyes shut, at just the thought of what she'd let that man do to her, the thought of his wrinkly, saggy body pressed up against her. The memory of his shrivelled-looking penis in her hand making her want to gag.

Jess had more than done her bit.

And for what?

So that Kyle could fuck everything up for her, just like he always did.

'I know you're not going to believe me, but it wasn't my fault.' Kyle Boyd was stuttering now. Knowing full well how much this job meant to Jess; not only that but it had been his chance to make it up to her. To prove that he was up to the job. That he was sorry for fucking up the last attempt he'd had at getting their own back on Nancy.

He knew that Jess wasn't going to take the news well.

He'd been sitting here for a full five minutes preparing what he was going to say to the woman. Only now she was sitting in the car next to him, glaring at him as if she wanted to throttle him, Kyle Boyd was positively shitting himself.

'What do you mean "it w-w-wasn't your f-f-fault"?' Jess said, mimicking Kyle as she repeated back his broken, stuttered words, her beautiful face contorted with such anger and venom that she looked almost unrecognisable.

'Whose fucking fault was it then, Kyle? Not fucking mine, that's for sure. I stuck to my side of the deal,' Jess shouted. 'You really are a fucking useless moron, do you know that, Kyle!' Jess Green said then, her temper finally getting the better of her. She struck out and smacked the man hard around the back of his head.

Which Kyle just took. Just as he always did.

He knew better than to react. If he made any attempt at trying to defend himself, it would only anger Jess even further.

He felt ashamed then. Blinking back his tears. Jess was five-foot nothing and tiny compared to his giant form, but the woman was ferocious. Kyle had never met a woman like her. So full of anger and hate, so reactive. She thought nothing about jumping on Kyle and beating the man repeatedly around the head if he pissed her off, and Kyle never fought back. He couldn't. Not only had he never hit a woman, Jess Green genuinely scared the shit out of him.

'Why can you never do anything right? You had one thing to do, Kyle, one bloody thing.' Jess spat, carrying on her tirade of abuse as she shook her head at the pathetic man sitting next to her. The bloke was a bitter disappointment. Just like they all were. He may be six-foot tall, and built like a proverbial brick shithouse, but his looks were just about all the charm that Kyle had to offer her.

The man was as soft as shit.

If Jess wanted something doing, then she knew that she would have to do it herself. Just like she always did.

'Seriously. Is there anything that you can actually do right, Kyle?!' she said, biting her lip so hard that she almost drew blood. Her brain working overtime. 'Go on then, what happened? And please don't tell me that you let her run off?'

That wouldn't surprise her. If Kyle had freaked the kid out and the child had done a runner.

'It wasn't my fault, Jess. I didn't do anything. Literally,' Kyle said then. Annoyed with himself that he sounded so whiney and pathetic. That Jess could have this effect on him. Reducing him to nothing more than a quivering, nervous wreck. 'I did exactly like you told me. I waited until you and that Michael Byrne went into the toilet cubicles and then I went to get the kid. But someone else beat me to it.'

'You what?' Jess raised her eyes at that. Wondering if one of Michael's family members had been hanging around. His wife maybe? Or maybe the child's mother herself.

'Scarlett didn't look too happy to go either. She was practically dragged away.'

Kyle stared at Jess then, letting her know that he was telling her the truth. That this really wasn't his fuck-up.

That it had been out of his control.

'I'm telling you, Jess, as God is my witness. I didn't fuck it up. Someone else got to the kid before us!'

'Get off me,' Scarlett Byrne shouted, struggling to break free of the nasty woman's firm hold as the lady tried to force her into the back seat of her car.

The woman was becoming annoyed now. She hadn't expected the child to be so difficult and defiant. Nor had she thought that the little brat would try and fight back.

'Your mummy said I need to bring you home to see her right now, Scarlett. She's waiting for you. So get into the car and be a good little girl, like I told you.'

She was pushing her again, pinching her flesh between her bony fingers, making Scarlett scream out in pain.

Scarlett turned, ducking down under the woman's arm, trying to make a run for it.

But the woman was one step ahead of her. Blocking the child's way, she grabbed Scarlett tightly, both arms wrapped around her.

She felt an almighty pain then, as the child sank her teeth into the woman's arm.

'You little bitch!' the woman screamed out, batting Scarlett off her.

Tired of the games now, her patience worn well and truly thin, she lost it. Shoving Scarlett face down on the back seat of the car, she used all her weight to pin the girl down, despite her convulsing and kicking out.

'I told you to behave, but you just wouldn't listen, would you?'

She reached through the gap in the two front seats, feeling around for the bag on the passenger seat. Fumbling around inside, she felt the syringe.

Her backup plan.

With one knee digging into the child's back, she dragged her sleeve roughly up her arm, searching for a vein.

Ignoring the child's cries and pleas now, she pushed the needle deep into Scarlett's flesh.

Waiting a few seconds for the child's writhing to stop.

For Scarlett to go completely still.

She quickly scanned the street then, making sure that no one was watching.

Why would they? she thought.

From a distance she looked like any other mother struggling with a difficult, tantrumming child.

The kid was quiet now.

Anaesthetised.

The woman took her chance to rearrange Scarlett's posture. Propping her into a sitting position, leaning her head against the windowpane, so that she looked as if she was simply taking a nap.

Then tightening the seatbelt around her, not taking any chances for anyone to pull her over now. She ran around to the driver's side and started the engine.

Looking down at the red welt on her arm. The tiny teeth marks that had pierced her skin.

The smear of blood.

She shook her head.

Oh, the little brat was going to pay for this.

But first, she needed to get out of here before she was seen, and fast.

Driving around to the front gates of Richmond Park, Kyle Boyd scanned the streets in search of the woman that he'd seen just five minutes earlier. If Kyle was right, then she couldn't have got very far, not with a struggling young child in tow. The chances were that she was probably still in the area. And if she was, then Kyle needed to find her.

This was his one and only chance to redeem himself. To prove to Jess that he really hadn't fucked up. That he could put this all right.

'Stay down,' he ordered, scouting the park's main entrance, relieved that there was no sign of Michael Byrne there, before putting his attention back onto the road.

Eyeing the pedestrians walking down the footpath.

The mothers walking hand in hand with their children. A big group of teenagers all messing about and laughing as they walked. An elderly couple, walking slowly past them, intimidated by the noise and scuffling.

Carefully observing the road, desperate to catch a glance of the woman and Scarlett.

Nothing.

Then finally, he spotted her.

'There!'

Jumping in the driver's seat of a blue Peugeot 205, the woman pulled out into the oncoming traffic as if she hadn't even bothered to look. Almost crashing head on in to another car that had been coming the opposite way.

She screeched to a halt in the road, before steering around the shocked driver and speeding off.

'Bingo! That's her.' He grinned. 'You can sit up now. We've gone past the park. There's no sign of Michael Byrne, but I've got eyes on your woman.'

Doing as she was told, Jess looked ahead on the road, trying to work out which car in front of them they were now following.

'That blue one, two cars in front,' Kyle said, as if reading her thoughts. 'I thought we should stay back a bit, out of sight. So we don't arouse her suspicions. She's already driving like a headcase as it is. We don't want to lose her.'

Jess nodded. For once, Kyle seemed to actually be on the ball.

Both of them glued to the car as they made their way through the London streets.

Following the car up Hill Street, before turning left onto Bridge Street, and crossing the bridge across the Thames.

'Where the fuck is she going?' he muttered, following the car through the streets of Twickenham.

Making sure he kept his distance. Several cars back, until they finally made it to George Street, where ahead, the blue Peugeot came to a stop.

'Stay back,' Jess said, ordering Kyle not to go any further. They pulled up at the side of the road and watched as the woman parked outside a block of flats further down.

Abandoning the car on double yellows, the woman got out.

Going to the back of the car, she stood scanning the street once more. Checking to make sure that there was no one around, before leaning into the back seat and picking Scarlett up, holding her against her body, like any woman carrying her sleeping child. She hurried inside the flats.

'What the fuck did she do to the kid?' Kyle said, suspiciously.

He'd seen Scarlett kicking and pulling to escape from the lady, now she was fast asleep? It didn't add up.

Jess couldn't agree more. Something definitely wasn't right.

'I'm going to follow her, and see what flat she goes in. Wait here,' Jess said, going for the door handle, ready to jump out of the car.

But Kyle quickly pulled her back. Holding her by her wrist, he shook his head.

'You can't go on your own, Jess,' he said then, a concerned expression on his face. 'We don't know who the fuck she is. For all we know she might be delivering that poor kid to some fucking paedophile ring or something. We don't know what we're dealing with…'

'I'll be careful,' Jess said, recognising the concern on Kyle's face. Though right now she didn't need concern, she needed to move her arse, and fast.

'Sit tight, I won't be long.'

She was gone then. Running down the pathway at the side of the road, making a point of keeping in close to the large wall that lined the block of flats so she wouldn't be spotted.

Reaching the main entrance of the flats then, she scanned the grey drab concrete stairwell, eyeing the floor numbers above the lift until one of them lit up.

Third floor.

Jess took the stairs. Kicking off her shoes so that she could run faster, careful where she stepped.

This place was disgusting.

Christ knows what she was walking in, the floor sticky and stained a mass of yellow and browns. The acrid stench of piss on puke that lingered in the air. As long as she didn't step on glass, or worse, a needle, then she didn't care. Above her head, she heard the balcony door open.

Hurrying, to catch up.

The door still swinging wildly just as she got there, she peered out through the tiny crack where the two doors met.

Eyeing the woman as she stood outside one of the doorways. Jess made a mental note. *Flat number 9.*

Struggling to retrieve her key from her back pocket, the woman gripped the child tightly as she finally managed to push the door open widely.

Finally, she was in. She turned then, taking one last look around the flat's walkway as if to make sure that no one was watching her, causing Jess to duck inside the stairwell once again. Worried that she'd been somehow seen, she stayed still, pushing herself up against the wall, out of sight. She held her breath, petrified that the woman would come looking for her, her heart beating rapidly now. Pounding as if it would burst out of her chest.

It felt like forever had passed when in reality it could have only been minutes at the most. Jess looked out again.

The door of Flat 9 was firmly closed, no sign of the woman now. She hadn't seen her.

And more importantly, she hadn't wanted to be seen.

Jess smirked then, as she made her way back down the dingy stairwell.

Her plan today hadn't been completely ruined, she figured.

Whoever it was that had taken Scarlett, might have royally fucked up her original idea. There was no denying that, but maybe, just maybe, not all was lost.

In fact, the more Jess thought about it the more she was inclined to think that whoever this fucker was who had just taken Scarlett had actually done her a favour.

Because now, they'd be the ones having to do all the hard graft. They'd be the ones having to physically look after the kid. Feeding her, and taking her to the toilet, and putting up with her whingeing.

And to all intents and purposes, they'd be the ones taking the rap too, if the plan went tits up and the police ended up tracking this woman down.

In actual fact, thinking about it, things couldn't have worked out much better.

All Jess had to do now, was make sure she got to Nancy with her ransom before whoever this fucker was did.

It was that easy.

And she was certain that Nancy would pay through the nose to get Scarlett back.

Of course the woman would.

Today, she'd had the most precious thing in the world snatched away from her.

She'd be frightened, terrified, in fact.

A feeling that Jess had known too, once, only too well.

Jess grinned to herself then, as she ran to the car where Kyle was waiting for her.

An eye for an eye and all that.

The way she saw it, Nancy Byrne owed her big time and it was high time that bitch finally paid up.

CHAPTER THIRTY-TWO

Sitting back on the bed, she scanned the tiny room.

A bed, a chair. That was it. Other than that, the room was bare.

It was getting dark now and the curtains were drawn.

She didn't like the dark.

At home, she had a little night light by her bed. In the shape of a mermaid. Sometimes her nanny Joanie would press it and it would play her a funny song.

Here, her only focus was the small stream of yellow that shone in through the gap underneath the bottom of the bedroom door.

Every now and again, she saw movement. The light broken up by a black shadowy figure.

The bad woman.

She was out there. Moving around. Scarlett could hear her. Only just though.

The woman was so quiet that for a while Scarlett had wondered if she'd been left in this place all alone.

She was scared of the lady.

The woman wasn't very nice, and she'd hurt her arm when she pulled her away at the park. Dragging her up and out of the sandpit.

Dragging her into the back of her car.

Her arms were still hurting now. Both of them bound together tightly. The rope cutting into her wrists. Making her skin red, and hot as if it was burning.

She'd given up trying to wriggle free.

She wanted to scream. To call out, shout so loudly so that her mummy and daddy could hear her. So that they could come and get her, and make the bad lady go away.

Only, she couldn't shout. The bad lady had put tape across her mouth. She'd pulled it so tightly that it was pinching at her skin.

Her mummy and daddy didn't know where she was. They weren't going to come and save her.

She started crying again. Leaning back against the cold wall behind her.

Thinking about home now.

Home with her parents. With Nanny Joanie and Grandaddy Michael too.

Grandaddy Michael.

He'd be looking for her. He'll be worried about her now.

He told her not to move. Not to leave the sandpit. He said that he wouldn't be long.

But he did take long.

And Scarlett had done as she was told. She hadn't moved. Even when the bad lady tried to take her.

Her grandaddy would probably be cross with her now. When he saw that she wasn't there.

But it wasn't her fault.

It was all the bad lady's. She'd taken her and forced her into a car. Made her lie down on the seat, and when Scarlett had tried to scream for help and kicked out in a bid to escape, the woman had screamed at her to be quiet.

Then she'd stuck something sharp in her arm that made Scarlett scream out in pain.

She couldn't remember anything else. Only that she'd woken up here.

But she didn't know where *here* was. All she knew was that she didn't like it.

She was scared, and all by herself.

Just her and the bad lady.

Shivering now from the cold and shock, unable to pull the blanket up around her because her hands were tied. Scarlett closed her eyes.

Her body exhausted, and trembling wildly.

Maybe she could just go to sleep?

Maybe when she woke up, she'd realise that this was all just a bad dream.

Like the dreams she sometimes had about the scary monsters or the hairy spiders, or the ones where she thought she'd lost her mummy and daddy somewhere and she woke up in her bed crying out for them.

Those dreams always seemed so real and frightening, even though when she awoke her mummy told her that they hadn't been real at all.

Maybe this wasn't real either. Maybe it was just a nightmare.

She squeezed her eyes tightly together and counted to ten.

Opening them again.

Her eyes blinking through the darkness. The curtains still drawn, the small ray of light still beaming in from under the door.

Then she started to cry.

It was real.

She was still here.

Still scared and trapped in this house with the bad lady.

CHAPTER THIRTY-THREE

'Argh, my head's killing me,' Daniel Byrne said, coming out of the bathroom, looking like death warmed up. His face shining from all the special ointments and lotions that he had to apply daily to stop his scaly, scarred skin from cracking open.

'Did you sleep?' Marie asked, knowing that he had.

She'd checked on him when she'd come in a few hours ago. Standing at the end of the bed, watching him sleep, as she so often did.

He was so peaceful when he slept.

It reminded her of all the time she spent with him at the hospital, when he was in a coma, and she'd sit at his bedside. Just the two of them.

'A little,' he said, rubbing his head, the pain behind his eyes excruciating. 'I need some more of my pills.'

Today was a bad day.

He could feel it already.

His anxiety building inside him. His body and mind already exhausted.

He'd been in bed for most of the morning, though he felt more fatigued now than he had when he'd first lain down.

Tossing and turning and flitting in and out of sleep.

When sleep had finally come to him, he'd found himself trapped inside his nightmares.

Now he remembered, he remembered it all. Over and over again. Every waking minute of the day, and in his sleep too.

It was as if, now, his brain was forcing him to relive every moment of his horrific ordeal. As if it was on repeat.

The fire. The torture.

How his sister Nancy had set him up. Handing him over to Alfie Harris, like a lamb to the slaughter. The pair of them leaving him in that derelict warehouse to die.

'I'll get them for you,' Marie said, nodding, glad that Daniel wanted his meds again.

Happy to assist, like the dutiful girlfriend, she went to fetch them from the kitchen cupboard. Coming back carrying a glass of water too.

She handed the tablets to Daniel and watched as he swallowed them down in one big gulp.

'Thanks,' Daniel said. Slumping down on the sofa and trying his hardest to hide his irritation that Marie was still hanging around the flat, despite the fact that he'd been in bed for most of the day. She still sat here waiting for him.

It was pathetic really. How she hung on his every movement. His every word.

Yet she seemed unable to take the hint that he just wanted to be on his own.

Apart from the medication, Daniel wished that she'd just fuck off home and leave him alone. He was struggling today as it was.

But Marie didn't take hints. The woman had skin a rhino would have been proud of.

She knew that her only use to him was the medication too. That's why the evil cow dangled the pills just within his reach. Making out as if she could only get a couple of days' worth at a time.

Painkillers, sleeping pills. High-grade stuff, stuff the doctors had tried to wean him off.

It was Marie's way of staying relevant. Of thinking that she was indispensable in his life. Always there lurking in the background, obsessed with him. Suffocating him.

She'd mistaken him for a fool.

Whoever this Robert Parkes was, that she thought she knew, it wasn't him.

He was Daniel Byrne.

His father had been the notorious Jimmy Byrne.

He knew everything now.

How he'd been well on his way to firmly setting himself up on the gangland scene. Working with Gem Kemal to bring in drugs to The Karma Club nightclub. They had been set to make a fortune together.

Daniel had been about to prove himself to the world, to that bitch of a sister of his too.

He'd been about to take it all from her.

His father's business, everything the man had worked for. He'd been about to show her and everyone else that he was capable, just as much as Nancy was.

Only Nancy hadn't liked that idea one bit.

And once she found out that he had murdered their dad, she'd done everything in her power to wipe him out. Handing him over to that psycho Alfie Harris so that the bastard could torture him, set fire to him. Leaving him like this, a mere shell of a man.

But even that couldn't keep Daniel down.

Marie didn't have a clue who or what she was dealing with here.

Daniel didn't have the slightest interest in her. He never had. Remembering his past relationships now. He could never be interested in Marie, because he was gay.

All of this, this grotty little flat, his paltry boring life, none of it belonged to him.

That's why he'd never settled, that's why he'd always felt as if he didn't belong here.

'Are you not going to ask me about my day then?' Marie said, interrupting Daniel's thoughts. Unable to keep her secret from Daniel a minute longer.

'How was your day?' Daniel said, bored now of playing Marie's games. Of all this pretending to be cordial and polite when deep down he couldn't stand the woman.

Just being around her made his skin crawl.

She was everything he hated in a woman. Needy and desperate and weak.

He was going to have to get rid. He decided. Marie Huston might find herself having a tragic accident. That's the only way he'd truly be shot of the woman.

This charade had gone on for long enough.

Fuck knows how, but he'd have to sort out his own way to get his hands on some meds himself.

He'd do this on his own, without her.

'You know what you were saying the other day about wanting to get your revenge on your sister?' Marie said, her eyes boring into Daniel's, not noticing the way the man's jaw was locked, how he was gritting his teeth.

His eyes had glazed over, barely listening to her as she spoke. Well, she'd soon have his full attention.

'What about it?' Daniel said, wishing now that Marie would just let all this shit about his sister drop.

He was sick of all her questions about Nancy. Where she lived, where she worked. Of Marie trying to find out every last detail. It was as if, suddenly, Marie Huston was just as obsessed and occupied with Nancy as he was.

'I want my fucking vengeance on the woman, Marie. I want to hurt that bitch, just like she's hurt me.' Isn't that what he'd said? After one too many drinks. Still in shock at his memory returning, of him finally remembering the truth of what had happened to him.

He'd opened up to Marie, that was the problem. In a moment of his own weakness, he'd bared all his family's secrets.

Marie knew it all. Every last sordid little detail.

Only now she wouldn't let it go. Like a dog with a bone, she was just gnawing away at him. Acting as if because she now knew everything, that, somehow, she had become part of it.

As if by Daniel confiding in her, they'd somehow got closer.

When in actual fact, he couldn't have felt further away from her as he did right now.

She repelled him.

Her neediness and desperation made him feel physically sick.

'Well, I've done it,' she said smugly. Sitting down on the sofa next to him. Her hand twitching with excitement as she restrained herself from reaching out and grabbing his. 'I've got you your vengeance.' That crazy look in her eyes as they sparkled brightly now.

She was drinking him in, desperate to see his reaction.

To hear his praise.

'What the fuck are you talking about?' Daniel shook his head inching away from the woman. She was too close. Invading his space.

He had no idea what she was going on about either.

She wasn't making any sense.

'I told you that I'd help you in any way that I can, Daniel. Didn't I?'

She got up then.

Nodding for Daniel to follow her.

A sickly feeling of dread in the pit of his stomach at whatever it was Marie was about to reveal she had done. He followed her to the spare bedroom.

Marie smiled then, as she reached out for the door handle.

This was going to fix everything.

This would make everything right between them again, she thought smugly.

When Daniel saw what she had done for him.

What lengths she would go to, to keep him happy.

The risks she'd taken.

And he'd be thankful to her forever for getting it for him.

She opened the bedroom door.

Smiling as she watched the expression on Daniel Byrne's face as she switched the light on, and flooded the room with a bright yellow hue.

Disturbing the sleeping child.

'Holy fuck!' Daniel said, his mouth wide open in surprise.

As he took in the sight of the small child lying on the bed. Her hands and mouth taped up.

Squinting at the bright lights, she looked up at Daniel and Marie, her eyes suddenly becoming wide with fear.

'Is that who I think it is?' Daniel said, unable to believe what he was seeing.

'It is indeed,' Marie said triumphantly. Daniel needed vengeance and Marie Huston was determined to help him get it.

Now he knew that Marie would do anything for him. Anything at all.

All his secrets were safe with her.

They were in this together now. Until the very end.

'You said you wanted to make your sister pay for what she'd done to you. Well, here's your golden ticket. Daniel, meet your niece, Scarlett Byrne.'

CHAPTER THIRTY-FOUR

'This is it!' Jack said, pulling up just down the road and staring over at the average-looking two-up two-down set in the middle of a dingy little council estate in Clapham.

They were so close now to getting Scarlett back.

'We need to play it carefully, Nancy. I know you just want to wade in there and break the man's legs, but we need to make sure that if Scarlett is in there, that she isn't in any danger. We don't want to cause this arsehole to do something that might hurt her.'

Wincing at Jack's words, not even able to comprehend that someone would be capable of hurting a child. Her child. Nancy nodded. Jack knew her too well.

Break the man's legs? If that animal so much as laid a finger on a hair on her baby's head, she was going to strangle the last breath out of the bastard with her own two hands.

'We need to get into that house quickly and catch the man off guard. It's the only way.'

Jack didn't want whoever this fucker was inside to get wind of them coming to get Scarlett first, because then he could use their child against them in his bid to escape. They'd end up with a hostage situation on their hands, and Scarlett being used as some kind of pawn for the man to use to get away.

The element of surprise was all they had going for them.

Nancy had refused his offer of backup coming to the scene. Typical Nancy. She wanted to get her retribution on this bastard her way.

Without involving the police.

And for once, Jack actually agreed with her.

'Once we're in, we can deal with this fucker, then we can get Scarlett back. I want you to go around the back. Try the door there or a window. Force the lock if you have to. I'm going to go in through the front. Two minutes, okay?'

Nodding, Nancy hurried. Making her way down the side alley and in through the back gate into the pokey little garden.

Scanning the garden, and making sure the coast was clear, she peered carefully in through the kitchen window.

Staying down, as out of sight as possible.

The kitchen was clear too.

Pulling at the window frames then, in a vain bid at seeing if any of the windows had been left open. She was out of luck.

They were locked.

Bending down, crouching low to the floor, she made her way over towards the back door then.

Trying the handle, she sighed with relief as it moved in her hand and the door clicked open.

She was in.

Quietly, creeping inside the narrow dingy kitchen now. Nancy scanned her surroundings. Her heart thumping inside her chest as she looked for a sign of Scarlett being here.

The place stank.

Hygiene clearly wasn't this man's main priority, she thought, as she eyed the sink full of dirty dishes. Caked in congealed food on the plates, all swimming in stagnant water. The bin was overflowing too. Dried food all down the side of it.

She could hear the TV somewhere off in the background, towards the front of the house.

Someone was home?

Scarlett?

Looking out through the hallway, she could see Jack's silhouette through the glass panel of the door. A second or two later, she watched as Jack stood back and then started to kick the shit out of it.

An almighty crash, as the door slammed hard off the wall behind it.

They were both in, though they'd alerted whoever was in the house with them now.

'What the fuck is going on?' Kyle Boyd said, half asleep. The noise had scared him half to death. So much so, that he'd almost fallen off the sofa in shock. Someone had broken in to his home. He was fuming. Only as soon as he clocked eyes on Jack Taylor and Nancy Byrne standing in his hallway, Kyle knew that he was in the deepest of shit.

'Fuck!' he said, panicking now. Sweating profusely at the sight of Nancy and Jack standing there glaring back at him.

His stomach churning with fear.

How the fuck did they find him?

He had only two options: run, or come clean and beg.

So Kyle started begging.

'Look, I know why you're here and I'm sorry, okay? I know you won't believe me, but I swear on my mother's grave I never meant to stab that woman. She made a lunge for me. I was trying to get her off me.'

'You what?' Nancy said, having no idea what this bloke was talking about. They'd come here for Scarlett. That's all she was interested in.

'I didn't even take the money. It was all just one big fuck-up. A mistake. If I could take it all back, I would. Please. Please, believe me.'

Nancy glanced at Jack then, unable to believe what they were both hearing; she looked back at the man in disgust. Realising what he'd just confessed to.

'You're the one who broke into my place the other night? The man who stabbed Bridget?'

'Well yeah, I mean no. I didn't stab her, I told you. She came at me.' It was Kyle's turn to look confused then. 'That's why you're here, isn't it?'

'Where is Scarlett?' Jack said, not in the mood for this man's games.

'Scarlett?' Kyle Boyd said, feeling as if his bowels were going to release themselves involuntarily.

How the fuck could they possibly know that he and Jess had been planning to snatch the kid?

He was shitting himself now. Everything Dennis Watkins and Louis Blackwell had told him about these nutters must be true. This Nancy bird seemed to have eyes and ears everywhere. Nothing got past her.

They were on to them?

'We haven't got her. We didn't take her—'

'*We?*' Nancy said, her question interrupted by a loud crash upstairs.

They heard glass breaking, then a bang.

'Stay with him,' Nancy shouted, running up the stairs.

'Scarlett, darling? Mummy's here…' she said, following the sound to the small bathroom at the back of the house. She pushed the door open, scared at what she might see.

'Scarlett?'

But instead of her daughter she was met with the sight of a woman. A woman who was, at this second in time, doing her best Houdini impression and trying to escape out of the narrow bathroom window.

'I don't fucking think so, darling!' Nancy said, grabbing at the woman's leg and pulling her back down.

Jess held on to the window frame then, refusing to do anything that Nancy Byrne told her to do. She fought back, kicking out in a rage, glad when her heel caught Nancy in the face, sending the woman flying backwards against the wall behind her.

Momentarily stunned, as she held her battered cheek, Nancy flew at her again. Grabbing hold of her top this time.

'Get the fuck off me,' Jess ordered. Trying her hardest to break free, to get the hell out of here.

She'd already heard her idiot boyfriend spilling his guts out about stabbing one of Nancy's girls. It wouldn't be long until he told them everything about Scarlett too. Bloody idiot.

Well, Kyle might be a gutless fucking moron, but Jess had no intention of sticking around for that fallout.

He'd done all of this.

If he hadn't been so incompetent in the first place, these fuckers wouldn't even be here right now. Kyle had led them straight to them.

She hadn't even had time to make contact with Nancy and demand a ransom yet.

No thanks to Kyle, this was all just one great big fuck-up.

'You're not going anywhere,' Nancy said, again grabbing the girl by her top, and pulling her down with her entire body weight as Jess stumbled back, crashing to the floor in a heap.

'Get up!' Nancy spat, annoyed now that they were dealing with such scumbags. That these were the people responsible for taking Scarlett, a pair of down and outs no doubt.

Amateurs. As sick and twisted as they were thick. Which in truth, was one of the most dangerous combinations as far as Nancy was concerned.

'Where's my daughter?'

Hauling herself up off the floor, Jess Green stared at Nancy then, hate radiating from her. Their moment of reckoning.

She wasn't sure what she expected from Nancy.

Shock? Surprise?

Instead, she got confusion.

'Do I know you?' Nancy said, narrowing her eyes.

Certain it was her, the woman from the CCTV footage.

But Nancy was convinced that she knew her from somewhere else too, only she couldn't pinpoint where.

The woman's vagueness was only another colossal insult as far as Jess was concerned.

'You don't even remember me, do you?' Jess Green spat then, as Nancy was trying to piece parts of the puzzle together.

She laughed, the sound hollow and laced with bitterness.

'You ruined my fucking life. You destroyed me. And you don't even remember, do you?' Jess shook her head incredulously.

She'd imagined this moment so many times over the years. How it would be to stand before the notorious bitch that was Nancy Byrne and put the woman to rights. To get her revenge for all that she'd done to her.

Only Nancy had never even given her a single thought.

The stupid bitch didn't even know who she was.

CHAPTER THIRTY-FIVE

'What the fuck are we going to do with her?' Daniel said, pacing the flat, the shock of what Marie had done finally sinking in.

She'd taken the child! Nancy's fucking child.

Scarlett Byrne was here in his flat.

'Well, I didn't bring her here for you both to play fucking Monopoly, did I?' Marie Huston said, fuming now. 'What do you think I brought her here for? So you could have your revenge on your sister. Isn't that what you've been saying? How you want to screw Nancy over. Well, now's your chance. You've got her most precious possession.' Marie Huston was beyond pissed off.

After everything she'd done today. All the risks she'd taken and yet it still wasn't good enough.

Instead of being happy about her plan, Daniel looked like the Antichrist, annoyed at her for taking it upon herself to just snatch the child. To kidnap Scarlett without even consulting him.

'You stupid fucking bitch! Nancy will cause murders over this. Our fucking murders. You have no idea what you've brought upon us both. No idea at all.'

Shouting now, Daniel paced the flat, rubbing his head frantically. This was just one big headache. One big mess.

'How the fuck did you manage to get her?' he asked, wondering how careful Marie had actually been when taking the child. If she'd been spotted by anyone.

Nancy wasn't stupid.

If Marie left any sort of a trail, they could count on a visit from his beloved sister any minute now. She'd be hot on their tails.

Daniel knew first-hand how vicious and unforgiving his sister could be. He was living testament of that.

'It was easier than I thought it would be,' Marie said, wanting Daniel to know that she was confident that her plan couldn't go wrong. That she'd got away with it, scot free.

She'd spent hours listening to Daniel ranting and raving about his past life. How he'd repeated every detail of what had happened to him, every word. About their fancy home and all the businesses. And she'd taken it all in. Locked it away inside her mind to help her work out what she was going to do.

How she could help Daniel get his own back on his sister.

Then it dawned on her. How easy it would be to make the woman pay.

All she had to do was take the kid.

So she'd done it. While Daniel had been asleep.

'I went to your family home. The one you told me about, in Richmond,' she said then, eager to make Daniel realise that they had the upper hand now. This was a good thing. That, more importantly, she'd done good.

'I was just going to keep watch for a bit, see if I could catch a glimpse of Nancy…' Marie spat the woman's name. The woman that had caused her Daniel so much pain.

The woman that had made him like this.

So angry and empty and full of pain.

'I wasn't even there twenty minutes when I spotted the older man.'

'My grandad?' Daniel said. 'Michael.'

Marie nodded, remembering how Scarlett had called out for him as Marie had dragged the small child away.

'He left the house with the kid in tow, so I followed them both. Ended up in Richmond Park. And that's when I knew. If I took her, for you, you'd have the upper hand. You'd finally have your revenge,' Marie said now, her voice sounding suddenly excited at the prospect of them both being in this together. Of her and Daniel, a team. Against Nancy. Against the world.

'I thought the difficult part would be to get the child on her own, that I'd have to try and lure Scarlett to me somehow; but your grandad left her all on her own. Can you even imagine? What sort of person does that? Sneaking into the toilets with some tart.'

Marie shook her head in disgust.

'He must have had a right shock when he came out and saw that Scarlett was gone. But if you ask me, the old boy deserved everything he got for leaving her on her own. And so will Nancy. For everything that she has done to you, Daniel.'

Marie meant it too. She wanted Nancy to pay, dearly. Not just for the physical damage she'd done to Daniel, but for fucking up his head too.

'Can't you see, Daniel? By taking Scarlett, you can finally get to your sister. You can have your revenge. You can make Nancy suffer now, where it hurts her the most.'

Daniel didn't speak; he just kept on pacing the flat.

The idea of a small kid in the room next to him made him feel on edge. He didn't want her here. Not in his home. He wasn't mentally prepared for this. For any of it.

'You should have told me,' Daniel snarled, still angry at Marie for poking her nose in. For taking things into her own hands without consulting him.

This was his problem, his business. She had no right to get involved in matters that didn't concern her.

'Well, I didn't tell you, did I?!' Marie shouted back now, sick of Daniel's attitude. 'Do you know what, Daniel, you can be so bloody ungrateful sometimes. After everything I've done for you. Well, fuck you!'

Marie'd had enough of being used and spoken to like shit. Daniel Byrne could learn the hard way to show her more respect. Shrugging her coat on, she was off.

See how he liked that!

Being left alone with the little brat, and without his meds too. He'd soon realise that couldn't treat her this way.

He'd be sorry then.

Just like Louise Langton had been. And her father too.

They'd both learned the hard way, hadn't they?

'Where are you going?' Daniel asked, realising that Marie was leaving.

'I'm going to work, Daniel,' she lied, not bothering to look the man in the eyes. Her feelings hurt. Though instead of tears, all she could feel inside her was a hot pool of rage.

The last place in the world she'd be going right now was back to that hospital.

Especially now that all her do-gooder colleagues would have heard about Louise Langton.

But she needed to get the fuck out of here.

Away from Daniel, away from this flat. Away from that bloody kid, crying constantly in the background. The noise echoing inside Marie's brain.

'But you can't?' he said then, realising that he was going to be left alone with Scarlett. 'You can't leave me with the kid?'

'Why not?' Marie said, her tone almost challenging. 'She's your niece. You deal with her. I've got to go to work. I can't do everything for you, Daniel. I'm not just here at your beck and call. I have a life too. Besides if I keep calling in sick, they'll get suspicious or I'll end up losing my job, and then you'll never get your medication.'

He didn't argue with that, just like she knew he wouldn't.

His meds. The only hold she really had over him. As long as he was dependent on them, he'd be dependent on her.

'I'll be back when my shift is over, okay? Just make sure you feed her, and give her something to drink. Oh, and don't forget to make sure she goes to the toilet. You don't want her wetting that bed. Or worse…' Marie said, enjoying the look of panic on Daniel's face.

Smirking as she picked up her bag from the floor, she shot Daniel one last parting glare.

A little time alone with Scarlett would be just the thing that Daniel needed to remind him how much he depended on Marie.

So that he'd realise how much he needed her.

CHAPTER THIRTY-SIX

Grabbing his head, Daniel rocked back and forth on the sofa.

That wretched noise.

The kid in the other room, snivelling away and crying for her mother.

It was doing his head in. He couldn't stand it.

'Shut up! Shut up!' he shouted finally, launching the mug of tea that was down by his feet. The liquid exploding out across the wall. The cup, smashing to pieces and landing on the floor.

Still the kid cried. She wouldn't stop.

She just wouldn't fucking do as she was told.

If anything she was worse now. Louder.

As Daniel began pacing the room. Stomping around the flat, agitated. His whole body felt as if it was on fire.

And the pain in his head. Banging constantly. Thumping.

He needed his pills.

Fucking Marie! She'd done this to him on purpose. This was her way of punishing him.

Leaving him here like this, in this state. With the kid.

He had hours yet until she finished her shift. Until she said she'd be back. That's if she even came back? He wouldn't put it past the mardy cow to make him sweat this out for as long as possible.

That's what Marie did. She played mind games with him. Couldn't help herself. Controlling him. Causing him the ultimate head-fuck. Using the only leverage she had against him. His meds.

Only this time she'd thrown the bloody kid in the mix too, just for good measure.

ARGH! When was this pain in his head going to stop? It was banging. Pounding. As if his skull was being crushed.

He thought of the kid then.

His niece. His blood.

But blood meant fuck all to him. It was nothing, he reminded himself.

Sitting back down and rocking once again. He had to keep moving. To keep his mind from focusing on the agony he was in.

His brain was going into overdrive now, as his thoughts turned to the rest of his family.

All of them cunts. His father, his sister. His grandad too.

Selfish fuckers the lot of them.

The only people he actually gave two fucks about were his nan Joanie and his mother. And even they would put this kid before him if they knew that she was here.

Given the choice between Daniel or Scarlett, they wouldn't even blink an eye.

Scarlett would win hands down.

He was nothing to them, they'd made that perfectly clear.

It had been almost five years since he'd seen any of them, and in that time, none of them had come looking for him. None of them had seemed bothered.

They didn't give two shits about him; of course they didn't, they would have found him by now if so.

It wouldn't have been that hard, would it? If they really searched.

Only they'd left him to fend for himself.

Left him all alone, a broken shell of a man.

Well fuck them. Fuck them all. This kid too.

This spoiled little brat of Nancy's that the whole world and their wife was out looking for now, according to all the newspapers and the articles splashed everywhere on the internet.

Anyone would think that Nancy Byrne was a fucking saint the way the press was suddenly portraying her. Like some celebrity IT girl. Some posh yummy-mummy type.

When that couldn't be further from the truth.

There was no mention now of Nancy being the daughter of a violent gangster. A criminal. Of Nancy being one too, these days.

Instead the headlines used words such as 'devastated', 'beside herself' and 'heartbroken'.

They'd used pictures of Nancy and Scarlett laughing together. The same haunting green eyes. That fiery red hair.

No mention of the fact that his sister had brought this all upon herself.

For being so ruthless. For being such a callous, heartless bitch.

That she deserved everything she had coming to her.

Daniel was up on his feet again then.

He didn't want Scarlett here anymore. Nancy's little fucking clone. Not here in his home. In his personal space.

Marie was right about one thing. Daniel needed to get rid of the kid.

For good.

He needed his revenge.

That's why Marie had brought her here in the first place, so that Daniel could do what he needed to do with her. So that he could make Nancy pay.

Then it was done. This would all be over.

He'd finally be able to get on with his life, knowing that he was the one that had caused his sister a whole world of pain. There would be no more games.

It was time.

Pulling his trainers on. His coat too. He paced the floors. Trying his hardest to pluck up the courage to go into that room.

Come on, Daniel. Get your shit done. This is a fucking kid we're dealing with here. A child.

Opening the bedroom door, he saw Scarlett physically jump with fright, pushing herself back on the bed, away from him, those piercing green eyes of hers looking up at him wide with fear.

Her snivelling had finally stopped, his presence in the room quickly silencing her.

Daniel bent down and undid the rope around her wrists, not looking at the child now, not daring to. Because he knew what he'd see reflected in her eyes. The shock and horror and disgust at the sight of him.

Him. With his scarred face and missing eye. The monster in the room.

'Do what I tell you, Scarlett, do you understand? I'm going to take the tape off your mouth now, and I want you to promise not to scream. If you scream you'll be punished, do you understand?'

If this was going to work, then Daniel had to make the kid believe him.

So he took her one and only last bit of hope and dangled it before her.

'I'm going to take you home, Scarlett. You want to go home, don't you? To your mummy?'

Scarlett nodded, yearning for his words to be true as Daniel pulled her coat around her.

'Be a good girl then and I'll take you home, okay?' he lied, glad that Scarlett seemed to believe him. Surprised at how easy it had been.

He watched as the kid stood there so deadly still, not saying a word, just as they'd agreed.

Obedient. Compliant.

Doing only as she was told.

She looked positively terrified, Daniel thought to himself, as he led the child out from the flat.

And so she should be.

CHAPTER THIRTY-SEVEN

'You haven't got a clue who I am, have you? But I remember you,' Jess Green said, standing in the small bathroom, watching the expression on Nancy's face as the woman tried so desperately to place her.

She could almost feel her brain whirring, as she tried so hard to work it out. To piece this all together. It didn't take her long.

She finally got it.

'Ruth?' Nancy said, narrowing her eyes, finally able to place the girl.

She'd only encountered the girl once. Almost five years ago now. When she'd worked over in Bridge Street, back when Nancy had first taken the place over. 'I threw you out. After I caught you stealing from me,' Nancy said, still confused, still wondering what this was all about.

She barely knew this woman.

Only she was getting the impression that this Ruth knew a hell of a lot about her.

'Ruth Lewis. That's my real name,' Ruth said then, her face screwed up with anger. 'Though, I don't go by that anymore, not after you tried to ruin me.'

Again Nancy narrowed her eyes. Shaking her head then, as if she was missing something. *Ruined her*?

She'd caught her stealing and had thrown her out on her arse. Out on the street. Hadn't even let the girl put her clothes on.

Nancy had purposely humiliated the girl, to make a point to all the others, but that was all.

'You really have no idea, do you?!' Ruth said then, the familiar anger raging inside her once again.

How Nancy could stand there, in front of her, and act so blasé, so unaware of the damage she'd done to her.

The harm she'd put her in.

Well, Ruth was only too happy to educate the woman now that she had the chance.

'I couldn't get any work after you'd put the word out on me being a thief. After you told all your contacts across London not to touch me.' She clenched her fists down at her sides. Trying her hardest to contain her anger.

To not lash out.

Not yet, anyway.

'They all did as you asked. No one within a fifty-mile radius of you would even entertain the idea of employing me. Not a single brothel or strip joint. Not even the real seedy back street places. They were all too scared of the repercussions. Of you putting the hard word out on me. So I was forced to do whatever it took to survive. Walking the streets to tout for business. Getting in cars with strangers.' She shook her head then, as if trying to shake the memory from her mind. Snarling. Seething now. 'You know how dangerous that is, walking the streets of London? Selling your body for sex to any bastard with the money to pay for it. Bastards who know they can treat you however they please because you haven't got any form of backup. 'Course you don't. You wouldn't have a clue about any of that. Because you're the other end of the scale. Mrs Moneybags. Nothing more than a glorified pimp. Look at you, dressed in designer clobber, your fancy diamond earrings. Reeking of your expensive perfume. All that money you have, all made from girls like me. You couldn't even begin to imagine the sort of shit I've been subjected to over the years. Sleeping with some of the most depraved and disgusting punters imaginable. Sickos using my body like a toilet, to simply empty their body fluids into. Degraded and used time and time again.'

Finally after all these years, this was her chance to lay it all out there and tell Nancy Byrne how much she hated her. How much she'd cost her.

She was physically shaking now.

Her words pouring out of her, hurting her with their memory.

'This is what you did to me. You did this,' Ruth screamed now, lifting her top up. Revealing the deep, jagged scars of her back, where strips of her skin had been gouged out that night she'd been attacked.

Wanting Nancy to see them.

Wanting her to know the damage that had been done on that fateful night, when some sadistic fuck had taken it upon himself to rape and mutilate her in the alleyway that stretched down the side of The Ten Bells pub in Spitalfields.

How the sick bastard had almost killed her.

Ruth's hands were shaking violently now. Feeling her tears running down her face, she quickly wiped them away. Angry with herself for allowing this bitch to see her pain.

At least Nancy knew now. That this was what Ruth's grudge was all about.

It was good to finally say it out loud. To speak about something that had caused her so much pain.

Of course, Kyle had asked her about her scars numerous times. Sickened by the thick gouges that had been sliced out of her back. The slashes across her arms and her legs, where that maniac had sliced her up after he'd raped her.

But Ruth had never wanted to talk about it.

Kyle wouldn't have understood. His tiny, hollow brain couldn't even comprehend what she'd been through. He couldn't even begin to try.

And the scars had been a constant reminder. Unable to hide her disfigured body from punters and boyfriends.

She was damaged goods.

Damaged beyond repair.

Nancy Byrne had seen to that.

It was all her doing, all her fault.

'That's right. Look away! What is it, Nancy? Is it too much for you to stomach? Too much for the woman that claimed she was so fucking high and mighty. The woman with the power to make or break someone. Someone like me? Because that's what you did, Nancy. You left me no choice but to fend for myself, and because of that you fed me to the fucking wolves,' Ruth said, as Nancy had the good grace to look away then, her eyes fixed on the floor.

Ruth smirked. Happy that they both finally knew where they stood.

That Nancy had been well and truly filled in.

'How does it feel, Nancy?' she laughed, showing Nancy that she wasn't scared of her, and she wasn't going to tell this woman shit. 'Not to be the one with the power? It isn't very nice, is it? Having something so precious taken from you.' Ruth was laughing now. 'You want me to tell you where your kid is, right? Well, you can rot in hell, Nancy. And so can your precious daughter.'

*

'Where is she?' Jack said, as he watched a dishevelled Nancy drag the woman into the room and shove her down on the settee next to Kyle.

Nancy looked fit to kill, fired up, eyes blazing. Her cheeks burning red.

He'd never seen her so angry, so enraged.

'She won't tell me,' Nancy said, glaring at Ruth Lewis, ready to launch herself on her any second. She'd physically beat the living shit out of the woman to get her to talk if she had to. Though she was done with playing games.

She wanted her daughter back, and this bitch knew where she was.

There was only one thing for it.

Reaching inside the back of her waistband for her gun, she pointed it straight at Ruth's head.

'Shit, Nancy,' Jack muttered. Realising how quickly things were escalating. How out of hand events were turning.

Though Ruth didn't so much as flinch. Determined not to.

'Go on, I fucking dare you!' Instead she stared down the barrel, as if goading Nancy to do it. To shoot her.

Nancy moved the gun across, aiming it at Kyle, who closed his eyes and started praying silently to himself, recognising that mad, crazy look in Nancy's eyes. There was no doubt in Kyle's mind that Nancy would use it.

She would. He could see it in her eyes. How she'd shoot him right here in this lounge. She'd happily blast his brains all over the wall behind him.

He started to cry, which only seemed to irritate Jess even further.

'Oh here we fucking go. The weakest link,' she said, beyond annoyed with Kyle. This was all his fault.

He'd brought Nancy and Jack to their door.

He'd fucked everything up yet again.

'I want you to tell me where my daughter is, and I want you to tell me now. Do you understand?' Nancy said, her patience wearing thin.

It was dark outside now, and all Nancy could think about was how terrified Scarlett would be.

Wherever she was, whoever she was with.

The not knowing was making her feel sick with nerves.

And these fuckers knew.

They knew where Scarlett was but they were withholding it from her.

Leaving her no choice but to drag it out of them. Whatever it took.

'I want my daughter back. Tonight. Now. Or blood will be spilled.'

'We didn't take her,' Kyle began. Stuttering again, nervously. He was petrified now, as he felt the cool metal lip of the gun being pushed into the side of his head as Nancy stood over him.

The look on the woman's face told him that she was capable of doing it, of pulling the trigger and snuffing out his life.

And no one would stop her.

Remembering what Dennis Watkins and Louis Blackwell had told him about her having the pigs in her pocket too. That her boyfriend was a DI for the Met. This man right here. A cop.

Yet still she pointed the gun.

He and Jess were royally screwed. The only way they'd come out of this alive is if they told the truth and gave Nancy what she wanted.

Though Ruth had other ideas. 'Just shut the fuck up, Kyle,' she said, digging him hard in the ribs. Her eyes not leaving Nancy's. 'Don't tell her jack shit.'

'It's dark outside, I bet your little one is really scared. Out there all on her own,' Jess sneered. Wiping the trail of blood with the back of her hand. She hoped that Nancy was dying inside. That the pain of not knowing where her child was, was killing her.

Nancy reacting like this meant that she was making the bitch stew.

'Or maybe she's inside in the warm huh? In someone's house or flat. Keeping some old pervert or paedo company for the night—'

Nancy smashed the gun in Ruth's face then, hitting her so hard that her head snapped back, blood trickling from her nose.

It still wasn't enough to deter her from winding Nancy up.

'At least you won't have to worry about her getting cold, eh?'

Nancy hit her again. Harder this time. Bringing the gun down on Ruth's head with such force that she knocked the woman clean out.

Ruth slumped backwards against the chair. Out cold.

Nancy turned to Jack then.

'You know who this stupid bitch is? Ruth Lewis. From Bridge Street. Remember the skank that I threw out that time for stealing from me?'

Vaguely recalling the night he'd seen two of the girls rolling around on the floor at the brothel, trying to kill each other over some missing money, Jack nodded.

Kyle butted in, confused. 'Why are you calling her Ruth? Her name's Jess?'

Nancy shook her head. 'That what she told you, is it? Well, she spun you a pack of lies, mate.'

She almost felt sorry for the guy. Completely gormless. Sucked in by Ruth's spell.

Which was exactly what his appeal to the woman would have been. Men like Kyle were easy pickings. All muscle with not a lot going on upstairs. They looked the part, but they were simple. The perfect combination for a woman like Ruth to control and manipulate.

Well those traits would work in Nancy's favour now, especially seeing as Ruth was out cold.

Kyle being every bit as weak and pathetic as he looked was what she was counting on.

'I'm going to give you one last chance, Kyle. One last chance to tell me where I can find my daughter. And if you don't tell me, I'm going to lodge a bullet firmly inside your skull, do you understand?' Nancy said.

Her steel eyes boring into the man.

Her voice calm and neutral. Her words cold as ice.

'Then I'm going to do the same to your friend here. And then Jack here, is going to take your bodies off somewhere that no fucker will ever find you. He'll bury the pair of you and no one will be any the wiser. Do you understand?'

Kyle started crying again then.

As he felt his bladder go. Wetting himself now. He could see that Nancy was more than capable of going through with her threat.

He had no choice but to talk. To tell Nancy Byrne everything he knew. Maybe then he and Jess had a chance of getting out of tonight alive.

'We didn't take her. I promise you. We were going to…' Kyle said again. Stuttering so badly now that each of his words came out in a slow juddered delay. 'But some woman got there first. She took her. She dragged her out of the sandpit, and forced her into a car. We followed her.'

'What woman?'

Kyle shrugged.

'Where? Where did she go?'

'To a flat; Twickenham. On the Drakewell Estate, off George Street. Jess followed her up to her floor. She said that they'd gone into flat 9?'

'Swear. Swear on your girlfriend's life,' Nancy said, pointing the gun back down at Ruth then, aiming it at the woman's head.

'Please. I swear to God. I'm telling you the truth, you have to believe me. We didn't take her.'

Nancy looked at Jack, who nodded. Convinced that Kyle was telling them the truth.

The bloke sounded distraught, the panic in his voice evident for them both to hear.

Turning back to Kyle, Nancy brought the gun down hard then.

Slamming it against his skull. Smashing him hard on his temple.

Knocking him out, he quickly slumped lifelessly to the floor.

'You wanted backup? Make a call to your colleagues and get these two dealt with. We need to get round to this flat, pronto,' Nancy ordered Jack, before stepping over the unconscious man.

Unable to look at this scum any longer than she already had.

'I'll wait for you in the car.'

CHAPTER THIRTY-EIGHT

'I'm cold,' Scarlett said, as she took in the dark night skies that loomed over the embankment. The trees swishing together loudly at one side of her, as the wind whipped violently through them. Just as it cut through her too, right down to her bones.

She shivered.

Glancing to the other side of the pathway she was standing on, she looked down at the murky waters of the river, the water so dark now that it looked almost black.

Scarlett didn't like the dark.

All she wanted was to be back at home, with her mummy and daddy. Wrapped up in bed with her Ariel dollies and her special night light that played funny songs.

'Are you still taking me home?' she asked, though she knew he wasn't.

This wasn't the way home.

She'd never been past the river before in order to get home and the man kept stopping, checking around them.

As if he's looking for someone?

He'd stopped again, only this time walking over to the river's edge. Looking down into the black water, before getting all angry and shouting to himself.

Scarlett waited patiently, not wanting to make him any madder, before they moved on a little further.

It was so cold out here now that her teeth were chattering. Her skin like ice, even underneath her lovely pink coat that her Nanny Colleen bought for her.

He lied to her, the man.

Telling her that he'd take her back to her mummy. He wasn't going to. She just knew it.

He wanted her to keep walking. To follow him further down the river.

They were here, alone now. There was no one around. No other people. No houses nearby.

Just her and the man.

And he hadn't said a word to her for ages, since they'd left the flat.

Taking her by the hand as they walked, he'd gripped her fingers hard inside his. Hurting her as he'd marched down streets and through the maze of passageways and walkways. Over the river's footbridge until they reached this embankment.

And she hadn't complained. Not once. She hadn't dared.

She was being a good girl, just like he told her to be. So that he would take her home to her mummy and daddy.

But that was all a lie, wasn't it?

'I want to go home,' she said then. Finally saying the words out loud that were going around and around inside her head.

Only for him to ignore her.

He was standing just a few feet ahead of her now. Scarlett stopped and watched the man walk in small circles. Faster and faster. His hood up, concealing his scary-looking face.

She'd made him mad again, hadn't she? Only she didn't know how.

She'd been good. She tried really, really hard.

He looked really cross, smacking himself repeatedly across the head. Swearing. Saying all kinds of bad words.

'Just fucking get it done.' 'Do it.' He kept saying, over and over again.

Get what done? Do what?

Scarlett didn't know what he was talking about but he was scaring her now. She looked across the pathway, to the tall row of trees. In the distance, far back between the gaps in the leaves she saw the tiny glimmer of lights whizzing past. Twinkling amongst the shadows.

Cars? People?

She thought about running, as fast as she could.

She could hide from him then.

Only the man was probably faster than her, he'd catch her.

And even just thinking about it now, she knew that her legs wouldn't move. They were stuck to the spot, frozen there.

Trembling beneath her from the cold and through fear.

'I want to see my mummy and daddy. You promised,' she said then, loudly. A plea now.

Hoping that he'd hear her, that he'd stick to his word.

She should have made him pinky promise; that's what she does with her daddy and he always keeps his promises then.

'Can you swim?' the man asked suddenly, walking towards her. Standing close. Too close.

She looked up at him and shook her head. Wanting to cry again.

Why is he asking her if she can swim? Does he want her to go into the dark black water?

Why? Why does he want her to do that?

She's bawling now. Terrified.

'I just want my mummy. You said you'd take me home.'

She feels sick now. A horrible bubbling feeling in the pit of her belly as she scans the path, for a way to get away.

Hoping to see another person.

Someone she can call to help her.

But there's no one else around. It's just her and the monster.

And the river.

And the dark.

And she's got a horrible feeling that something bad is going to happen to her.

Something very bad.

She doesn't like it here, and she doesn't like the man.

She's sobbing uncontrollably now.

And the man is shouting. Louder and louder, telling her to be quiet. To stop making this so difficult for him.

Only she didn't mean to make anything difficult.

She doesn't even know what she's doing that's making him so mad.

She can't stop crying, she's too scared.

She should run.

Even if her legs won't move. She should force them to.

Only it's too late for that, she realises, as he swoops down towards her then.

Grabbing her by the scruff of her coat. Dragging her down the grassy bank. Towards the river.

Towards the black, murky deep water.

Kicking out, desperate to escape.

But she isn't strong enough.

Scarlett starts to scream.

CHAPTER THIRTY-NINE

'She's not here!' Nancy says, collapsing on the floor of the empty flat, once again giving in to her tears.

They'd been so close, she could feel it. Only to be led to yet another dead end.

'Where is she, Jack? Where's my baby?' She felt useless.

Like everything was spiralling out of control. She couldn't fix this.

She didn't know how to.

'Did he lie to us?' Nancy said, thinking about that bastard, Kyle. He had sounded so certain, so convincing when he'd told them that Scarlett was being held here.

Maybe he'd been a better actor than she'd given him credit for, telling her some random bullshit, just to save his arse.

'This is hopeless! I just want her back. Where is she, Jack?'

Jack didn't reply. He couldn't, not only because he didn't have the answer, but he couldn't find the words either.

He felt every bit as scared and hopeless as he knew Nancy did, only he wasn't going to voice that to her. He couldn't.

He had to stay strong, to at least pretend that he had this all in his control. Otherwise he'd lose his head too. And he couldn't do that. Not if they had any chance of getting Scarlett back.

Nancy was right, it was hopeless.

This was all they had to go on.

They had nothing now.

And the sight of Nancy breaking down, sobbing so uncontrollably now as she sank to her knees on the floor was enough to break his heart all over again.

Jack wanted to go to her, to hold her in his arms and tell her that everything would be okay. Only he couldn't do that because all he had right now were empty promises.

His instincts were telling him that Kyle Boyd had been telling the truth. He'd looked so scared, and sounded so convincing.

Maybe Scarlett had been here?

He had to keep searching, to stay focused. Rifling through the cupboards and drawers, he pulled out endless bottles and packets of empty pills. A whole cupboard full of them. All without labels.

Then he began searching the drawers. Pulling out a pile of utility bills, he held them up to Nancy, raising his eyes questioningly.

'Robert Parkes?'

Nancy shook her head. The name meant nothing to her.

Jack picked up his phone and called it in. Making sure his colleague at the station did a thorough search on the address and the occupant, before continuing to tear the place apart.

Stepping over the broken mug on the floor, the tea marks sprayed all down the paintwork, he ran his finger across the stain, still wet. Still dripping down the wall.

Whoever had been here had only recently left.

Jack made his way into the main bedroom again, having only glanced in the room quickly when they'd arrived, to check that no one was here. Now he was looking for clues. Something, anything that would tell him that Scarlett may have been here.

He scanned the room. Wrinkling his nose up at the stale stench of sweat that lingered in the air. Bare of any personality, just a filthy-looking duvet on a double bed. A few items of clothes scattered on the floor beside it.

He went into the smaller bedroom, saw the bedding all piled up on the single bed. A cup of water down on the floor. Untouched.

Lifting up the duvet, and throwing it to the floor, his eyes came to rest on the length of rope on the mattress. The duct tape stuck to the headboard.

Then he saw the tiny purple hair clip, still clasped together tightly, inside, a few wispy strands of vibrant red hair.

'Shit!' he said. Louder than he'd meant to.

Alerting Nancy, who seconds later was standing in the room just behind him.

'What is it, Jack?' she asked, the urgency in her voice laced with fear.

He closed his eyes. Then taking a deep breath, he turned to her. Stepping aside so that she could see for herself.

'Oh God!' Nancy said. Recognising the hair clip from a set that she'd bought for Scarlett. She picked it up and ran her fingers along the strands of hair.

'She was here?' Nancy asked, already knowing that she had been, though she needed to hear Jack say it.

Jack nodded.

Then she saw the rope. The duct tape.

Her hand went to her mouth, trying to stifle the scream that threatened to explode from her.

The vomit too.

Some bastard had tied her baby up. They'd kept her here, in this dingy shithole of a flat. In this room. On this bed.

What the fuck had they done to her?

It was all too much to bear, too much to even think about.

Nancy leant over the end of the bed and threw up the contents of her stomach all over the floor.

She was crying now, sobbing uncontrollably as Jack took her in his arms, holding her tightly to him. Wishing there was something he could say to ease her fears; but he felt them too.

His phone ringing then, interrupting him before he could try and offer Nancy any words of reassurance.

Which was just as well, because they'd only be words. Empty words. He was way past the point of making them sound convincing.

Nancy watched as Jack took the call. Nodding, barely speaking. Before closing his eyes tightly as if trying to shut out whatever new information he was being told.

He ended the call and went silent, unable to find his voice and repeat what he'd just heard.

'What is it?' Nancy asked reluctantly. Suddenly too scared to hear his answer, the anxiety in her stomach churning, her legs starting to shake.

Preparing herself for the worst news possible.

Please God no, not my baby! Have they found her? Has something happened to her?

'Robert Parkes,' Jack said. His face a deathly shade of white. 'He was a burns patient at Chelsea and Westminster Hospital almost five years ago.'

Nancy shrugged. Not sure where Jack was going with this. Why she should care.

'He was in a coma for almost a year, his body so severely burned that they didn't think he was going to survive,' Jack said, repeating what he'd just been told. 'He was housed here when he was discharged. My colleagues made contact with Robert Parkes's social worker. They're getting his file sent over as we speak.'

'Okay,' Nancy said, wrinkling her brow, not understanding what any of this meant.

What did it have to do with Scarlett? What was Jack trying to say?

'Robert Parkes isn't his real name, Nancy. He lost his memory. He doesn't know who he is. Or perhaps he does.'

Jack could see Nancy piecing it all together. Trying to work it all out.

'Five years ago. Around the time that Daniel went missing. Apparently a dog walker found him outside a disused railway shed out in King's Cross's badlands. It's him, Nancy. It's got to be.'

Nancy couldn't speak then. Feeling as if she'd just been kicked in the guts.

The wind knocked out of her.

The badlands of King's Cross. Near Alfie Harris's club?

Recalling that last fateful night she'd laid eyes on her brother. When she'd handed him over to Alfie Harris, knowing full well that she'd never see her brother ever again.

'But it can't be? Alfie Harris dealt with him. He told me himself?'

Only she knew that it was him.

That somehow, Daniel must have survived.

All this time. He wasn't dead after all. Her brother was alive. And without a doubt it was him, she knew that now for certain.

Daniel was the bastard who had taken her baby. He had Scarlett.

CHAPTER FORTY

Placing the phone on the kitchen side, Bridget took a seat back down at the kitchen table.

'Well? What did they say?' Colleen asked, sensing by the tone of conversation and the disappointed look on Bridget's face that they hadn't found Scarlett yet.

It was doing her head in all this sitting around and waiting.

She felt the same as everyone else. Useless. In limbo. Jumping every time the door went, or the phone rang.

'It's not looking good, Colleen,' Bridget said, keeping her voice down. She glanced behind her to make sure that there was no sign of Joanie back from the loo.

The poor woman was at her wits' end, and Nancy had told her specifically not to mention any of their conversation to the older woman. For fear that it would send her nan over the edge again.

Joanie wouldn't have been able to take it.

But Bridget had to tell someone though, as even she couldn't get her head around what she'd just been told.

'They found the place where they think Scarlett was being kept. A flat over in east Twickenham…' She faltered then. Not able to say the rest out loud.

So many disgusting, disturbed thoughts going through her head as she thought about what Nancy had said, about the child being tied to the bed.

She'd been trying to stay positive up until then, for poor Nancy's sake more than anything, but the longer Scarlett had been away, the harder it had been to keep up the facade. And now she knew the rest, she knew that it really wasn't looking good at all.

'They found rope, Colleen. And masking tape. In one of the bedrooms,' Bridget said finally, shaking her head. 'A child's hair clip too. Jack had some officers out there taking samples so that they can check for DNA, but Nancy's almost certain that it's Scarlett's.'

'No…' Colleen gasped. Her hands shaking. Her own tears escaping her then at the thought of her poor baby granddaughter's harrowing ordeal.

God, she needed a drink so badly now.

'What sort of sick fucker does that? Snatches a child from the park, and ties her to a bed. Tapes her mouth up with masking tape…' Bridget mumbled to herself, unable to comprehend what had happened to Scarlett. She didn't expect an answer. They both knew exactly what sort of a person did that.

An animal, a monster.

Colleen knew it too.

'What did you just say?' Joanie was there, standing behind them both in the doorway. Listening to every word that had been said.

Only she couldn't comprehend what she'd just heard.

'Tied to a bed? Who, not Scarlett? Please Jesus tell me you are not talking about our Scarlett?' Joanie was falling then. Her legs giving way beneath her. Collapsing on the floor. Her chest wheezing as she struggled to gasp for breath.

Gulping at the air, trying to draw some oxygen in; only none of it seemed to be reaching her lungs.

'She's having a heart attack?' Bridget cried. Running over to the woman. Trying to help her to sit up, panicking. Not knowing what to do.

She should never have opened her bleeding big mouth. She should have kept quiet, just as Nancy had told her.

'Call an ambulance, Colleen. It's okay, Joanie, you're going to be okay.'

'It's a panic attack,' Colleen said, rushing to her mother-in-law's side, knowing the signs well, having suffered spates of attacks herself for years. 'It's the shock. She's hyperventilating.'

Holding Joanie carefully the two women picked her up and guided her over to one of the kitchen chairs.

'Breathe, Joanie. You're all right. We're here with you. Take it easy and breathe.'

Doing as she was told, as Colleen guided her. Talking her through her panic until Joanie managed to catch her breath again.

The wheezing stopping. The colour gradually coming back into her cheeks.

Though her stricken expression remained.

'What's happened to my Scarlett?' she said then, tears in her eyes as she searched Bridget's. But she didn't want to hear the truth, she only wanted to hear lies.

Sweet, beautiful lies that everything was all right. That her baby great-granddaughter hadn't been harmed. That the child wasn't in any real danger.

She wasn't able for anything other than that.

She had to believe only the good.

Bridget knew that too.

'We don't know anything, Joanie. Nothing's been confirmed. We don't even know if Scarlett was in that flat. Jack is just ruling everything out. You know how thorough he can be, and even more so now that he's looking for Scarlett. He'll find her. You know that, don't you, Jack won't rest until he finds her. Nancy too.' Speaking so convincingly now, Bridget wanted to believe her own words herself.

She smiled then.

'Scarlett is a Byrne, Joanie. She's got fire inside her. Just like her mumma. Just like you. She's going to come home, and do you know what? She's going to be okay. This is just some big misunderstanding. You'll see.'

Joanie nodded, grateful then.

Feeling calmer.

She needed to believe Bridget now, more than ever.

'I think I need to go and have a little lie down.' The day's events had got to her. Exhausted. She just wanted to close her eyes and make all of this nightmare go away.

To stop churning thoughts of her beautiful great-granddaughter's plight around in her mind. The hate she had inside her for Michael, for being the one to cause all of this.

Until her dying day, if anything happened to Scarlett, she'd never forgive him.

He'd gone off to spend the night in a B&B, according to Colleen, and as far as Joanie was concerned the bastard could stay there.

'Come on then, I'll come up with you,' Bridget offered, holding out her arm.

And without so much as a protest Joanie took it, still unsteady on her feet.

Glad of the help and the company.

'I'll make some tea,' Colleen called after Bridget, as the woman led Joanie out of the room.

Colleen looked around her then.

Overwhelmed by feelings of utter despair. She didn't know what to do with herself.

Picking up the cups, she began cleaning up the kitchen, anything to keep her mind off what was going on around her.

The madness of it all.

Placing all the cups in the sink, as she filled it with hot soapy water.

Glad of a few minutes alone. The peace and quiet.

She glanced at the door and, checking that the coast was clear, she opened the pantry. Reaching up to the top shelf for Michael's secret stash of malt whiskey.

Unscrewing the cap, she took a huge swig.

Gulping the liquid down, resisting the burn.

Placing the bottle back up on the shelf, she waited.

For something. Anything. To happen.

That warmth, that heat.

But the alcohol wasn't touching her tonight. Not anywhere near.

She was too numb for even that.

They all were.

CHAPTER FORTY-ONE

Sitting on the wet muddy riverbank, as the rain lashed down around him now, Daniel stared straight ahead. Looking further down the river. Way off into the distance, his eyes fixed on the silhouettes of unlit objects – barges and low footbridges.

He sat still, as if in a trance. An eerie silence all around him. Broken only by the sound of lapping water and the heavy downpour of thick heavy rain. The droplets hitting the water's surface, sending large ripples circling outwards. The rhythmic motions mesmerising to watch.

He was crying, he realised, as a low strained screech escaped his mouth from somewhere deep at the back of his throat.

Looking down into the murky water.

The deep, dark depths of the Thames.

What had he been thinking?

Killing a child? A little kid. His niece.

He leant over then, throwing himself onto the wet grass beneath him. Vomiting violently until there was nothing left inside him. Just the remnants of hot bile burning at the back of his throat as he dry-heaved.

All he could think about now was Nancy, and how much he hated her.

For everything she'd done to him. For everything that she was and that he would never be.

She deserved to suffer. Isn't that what he kept telling himself all evening? His mantra tonight, to help him justify his sick and twisted actions.

That his sister deserved to feel pain, so acute, so soul-destroying that she'll never be the same again. Just as she had done to him.

That Nancy should have everything taken from her that she ever gave a shit about. That she should have her entire world ripped out from beneath her. That Daniel should be the one to do it to her.

Her and that two-faced hypocrite, Jack.

Spitting a mouthful of acidic saliva out, Daniel tried to get rid of the nasty taste that lingered in his mouth.

DI Jack Taylor. The bent copper, the family confidante. The snake.

It was ingenious really; Daniel was actually impressed. The fact that the bloke had managed to get Nancy up the duff. That he'd wormed his way so tightly into the family, securing his place there.

It was all so fucked up and twisted that it was almost hysterical.

The funniest thing of all was that Nancy didn't have a clue.

His poor, naive, pathetic sister.

Jack had been there that night. The night that Daniel had killed their father. Jack had taken a cut of the money too, in return for his silence.

His dad's very own best mate, the bent copper. Everyone had their price it seemed, even Jack.

He'd duped Nancy the night of their dad's funeral too. When Nancy had been attacked.

How clever she thought she was, when, all along, it was Jack who had set that up, to stop Nancy from getting any closer to the truth.

To stop her from digging any further into what had happened. Jack had done that to save his own arse. Because she'd got close to finding out everything, and then she would have found out that he had been involved too.

And then he'd only gone and impregnated her. It was impressive, Daniel had to give the man that.

The lengths that Jack would go to, to save himself from being caught out. To get what he wanted.

And now, he was there, with all of them.

The Byrne clan. Playing happy families. The doting father. The loyal partner to Nancy. When the reality couldn't be further from the truth.

Daniel laughed, wiping the tears that poured down his cheeks, his mood lifting slightly.

Nancy had got her comeuppance already, and the ironic thing about it all was that the stupid bitch had no fucking clue about it.

He looked at the river's surface once more, noting how the rain was easing off. He wasn't sure how long he'd been sitting here. Just staring into space. Trying to slow his racing mind.

The water's erratic movements becoming suddenly still as the rain gradually began to stop.

He wondered how deep the riverbed went, what else was down there tangled amongst the reeds and rubbish and God knows what.

What other secrets the river kept from the world, left for dead, floating in the waters with all the sewage and discarded waste.

He shivered. It was time to get going. Daniel got to his feet, wiped the mud off his hands. Smearing it down his trousers.

Noting the blood. Congealed now, all down his arm.

He wiped that too, only it had dried already. Stained his skin.

The jagged cut from the sharp rugged tree branch that stuck out of the water. He'd scraped his skin along it when he'd reached out into the water. His hands desperately clutching at the bright pink coat.

As he hauled Scarlett back out of the water.

Full of regret and remorse at what he'd been thinking of doing. He turned to her then.

The child. Sitting there silently just a few feet further down from him on the riverbank.

Freezing cold. Her clothes soaked through, stuck to her.

Her eyes staring at the river. Those same piercing green eyes that mirrored Nancy's.

Her trembling lips, an icy shade of blue.

She'd gone into shock, he realised. Her whole body jolting, shaking violently.

Walking over to her, he took off his jacket and wrapped it around the child, scooping her up in his arms. Holding her to him. Close now.

Out of necessity, not love.

He only wanted to warm her up. To keep her alive.

Walking back down towards the footbridge then. Back towards Richmond.

Tonight his lesson well and truly learned, he thought, as he took the steps of the bridge one by one. Looking out across the London skyline.

A thousand twinkling lights all sparkling under a thick blanket of darkness.

And as much as he hated his sister, as much as he wanted her to pay for what she'd done, even Daniel Byrne had his limits.

He might be a lot of things, but a child killer wasn't one of them.

CHAPTER FORTY-TWO

Washing up the cups, Colleen Byrne placed them down on the draining board. Glad to make use of herself tonight; she had a feeling it was going to be a long one.

Staring out of the window, into the courtyard at the back of the house, she was lost in her thoughts.

There was no point in going home now.

She wouldn't get any sleep tonight, and as much as deep down she wanted to, she'd only drink herself into a coma.

She couldn't do that. Not tonight of all nights. Nancy would never forgive her.

She needed to stay busy, to keep her head, in case Nancy called with news of Scarlett.

She needed to put her daughter and granddaughter first today.

But all this waiting around, feeling useless, was killing her.

About to put the kettle on and make herself and Bridget a pot of tea, she leaned closer to the window, peering out into the blackened courtyard, and staring at the doorway on the side of the garage.

Open now?

It hadn't been a minute ago, she was sure of it.

Or was she?

That big glug of whiskey she'd just knocked back a few minutes earlier and all the worry and drama of today had left her feeling emotionally and mentally exhausted. Still, with everything that was going on right now, they all needed to be vigilant.

Colleen stared into the darkness as if someone would suddenly just jump out and reveal themselves.

Of course they didn't though. There was no one there. Backing away, berating herself for being so paranoid, she stopped dead still as she caught a movement out of the side of her eye.

A quick flash of white.

Inside the garage. She was sure of it now.

'For fuck sake!' Colleen said, shaking her head annoyed then as she realised what was going on.

It was that family liaison officer from earlier.

It had to be. The cheeky beggar. He'd said that he was going to have a wander around the house, and check that everything was secure. But Colleen knew what he was really up to.

Typical Old Bill. Only that lot would stoop so low as to take the opportunity of Scarlett going missing, so that they could have a snoop around their home, and poke their nose in with things that didn't concern them.

The plod really were the fucking pits.

Always looking for something to catch Nancy out with. Just like they'd done with Jimmy for all those years. Hounding this family, even now. Today of all days when her child had gone missing.

Incensed that they'd be trailing through all of their personal belongings, at a time like this, Colleen wiped her hands down the front of the apron she'd put on, ready to go out there and give the nosey bastard copper a piece of her mind.

And she'd make sure Jack did too, when he finally got wind of this.

Marching out across the courtyard, Colleen stepped inside the garage.

'What the fuck do you think you're doing, snooping around in here?' she said, met with only darkness.

She reached up to switch on the light, but the place still stayed in darkness, the bulb blown, she realised. She couldn't see very much, the only sliver of light streaming in from one of the courtyard's lights outside the back door.

There was nobody here, just the highlighted silhouette of Jimmy's beloved Bentley parked up in the middle of the garage floor, still covered with a dust sheet. Jimmy's pride and joy, that none of them could bear to drive, nor sell since his death.

Other than that, the garage was empty.

Silly old fool, she thought to herself as she realised that she was imagining things now. That maybe the garage's side door had been open all along.

She was getting as crazy as Joanie. Turning to leave, Colleen reached the door, just as a movement to her left caught her eye.

Something lurking in the shadows in the corner of the room.

A figure.

'Michael?' she said, turning to look and catching his build. 'Jesus, Michael. You gave me some fright. Skulking around in here, just because Joanie's banished you from the house. And with good reason too, I hasten to add. I thought you were staying down the road at a B&B?'

Only Michael didn't answer. Instead the man stepped forward.

Closer now.

A hooded jumper covering his features.

Until he turned to face her, the light from the courtyard trickling in through the window.

Lighting up a distorted, scarred face so damaged and scarred that Colleen opened her mouth, ready to scream for help.

Stopping in her tracks the second that she heard the sound of his familiar voice.

'It's all right, Mum! It's me.'

'Daniel?' she said then, her voice thick with emotion 'Son? Is it really you?'

But she knew, without a doubt, that it really was. Daniel. Her Daniel was home.

Colleen stared at Daniel's disfigured face. The thick scar tissue that replaced the perfect complexion he once had. The patch covering his left eye. The awkward limp as he walked towards her.

It didn't look anything like Daniel, but it was him.

Her child, her boy.

She had missed him so much over the past five years that it had physically pained her.

'Daniel?' she said, overcome with emotion. So happy to see her son here in front of her, in the flesh. After all these years. Though he didn't look well. He didn't look well at all. 'What happened to you, son?'

Even with his hood up, in the dimly lit room, Colleen could see that whatever injuries had been inflicted upon him were catastrophic.

He was unrecognisable, even to his own mother.

'Nancy,' Daniel said, then. No longer willing to cover things up or soften the blow for his sister. His mother needed to hear the truth tonight.

All of it.

No matter what the outcome.

'Your darling daughter did this to me. Or at least, she handed me over to someone else to do her dirty work for her,' Daniel said, no real emotion in his voice.

He'd lived with this knowledge for long enough now that it almost sounded matter-of-fact. It was long overdue that his mother knew it too.

'No. Not Nancy. She couldn't. I mean, she wouldn't…' Colleen said, shaking her head. Not wanting to believe what Daniel was saying was true.

That one of her children could inflict so much pain on the other.

That they were capable of hating each other so much.

'But Jack? He said you had gone travelling around the world. He tracked you down. To Ibiza. He said he'd found some transactions from your bank cards. That he'd seen footage of you on camera?'

'Did you see the footage?'

'Well, no…' Colleen said. 'But he said. He told us all…'

She trailed off as she realised how foolish she'd been, simply taking Jack's word for it. But why would she have questioned him? Jack had no reason to lie.

'He's in it with her, Mum. They both wanted rid of me. Nancy, for what I did to Dad…' Daniel paused then, waiting to see the shock on her face, the realisation of what he was admitting. 'But then, you already knew that, didn't you, Mum?! Seeing as you were the one that initiated it. That night of Nan Edel's funeral. When you got so drunk that I had to take you up to your room. Do you remember? You told me everything about Dad then. The truth. About all the terrible things he'd done. To you. To me. To all of us. All of his lies.'

Daniel spat.

Colleen shook her head. Straining to remember, to think.

Her mother's funeral had been the most heart-rending day of her life, and of course, Colleen had ended up getting blind drunk. Stuck in the house with Jimmy and Joanie glaring at her. Whispering about her. Her own kids then too, Nancy and Daniel, who had barely bothered to go near her all day.

She'd lost it.

Shouting and screaming in front of all of their so-called friends and family.

And Daniel had helped her.

He'd walked her from the room, Colleen remembered, because for once he seemed to be genuinely looking out for her. An act so kind, so compassionate, just when Colleen had needed it most.

She couldn't remember much else then.

Only that when she had woken, Daniel had gone. But he'd always seemed softer towards her after that night.

'You told me you wanted him dead. You poured your heart out to me. Telling me all about what he'd done on your wedding night. About the men he'd been with behind your back. You asked me to kill him. Surely you remember telling me that?'

Colleen shook her head. As if trying to shake the memory out of it, but she couldn't hide it anymore.

She thought she'd dreamt it. Really she did, up until this moment, when Daniel was finally saying it out loud. Colleen honestly thought she'd dreamt it all.

But she had asked Daniel to do it. That's how desperate she had been. That's how much she'd hated Jimmy.

The man who had broken her completely, who had taken everything that meant something to her in her life and turned it into crap.

When Jimmy had died, Colleen had just known that it was her son that had pulled the trigger. She'd always known.

Because she'd given the order.

'I did it for you, Mum. And for me. For how he always treated me. With such contempt. As if he couldn't stand the sight of me. Irony huh? Look at the state of me now. Now nobody can.'

Colleen was crying then, heart sorry for the mess that her family were in.

They were all just one great big fuck-up, the lot of them.

And she'd caused it all. Playing them off against each other, using Daniel as a muse, she'd known how vulnerable he had been back then. How unstable he was.

She knew because he reminded her so much of herself.

Weak, and easily manipulated.

How she used to be.

'Nancy left me for dead. She did this to me.'

'I'm sorry, Daniel.' Not knowing what else she could say, what could make any of this better. Nothing could. Colleen knew that now.

'I don't want to hear it, Mum.' Daniel shook his head.

He meant it too.

He wasn't here for sympathy, or an apology.

Tonight he was cutting himself free.

He was done with this family, done with them all.

'You need to know that Jack was part of it,' Daniel said then, needing to get everything off his chest. To unburden himself by telling his mother the truth.

'Your trusted police officer was hiding away, watching, when I pulled the trigger that night. He was happy to take half the money from me too. Blood money.'

He could see genuine shock then on his mother's face.

She really did have no idea.

'He was the one that arranged the attack on Nancy the night of Dad's funeral too.' He laughed then. Glad that he was getting vengeance on Nancy in spectacular style.

'Why are you telling me all of this?' Colleen said, shaking her head. Confused. Wondering what Daniel's motive was.

If he wanted to cause Nancy a world of pain, he'd deliver this news to her himself, wouldn't he? Why was he telling her?

'Because I want you to tell him, to keep them away from me, Mum,' Daniel said, honestly.

'Keep him away from you? But you're back now. Why would I keep him away?'

'No, Mum. I'm not coming back. Can't you see? We're all way past that now.'

He'd lost his family five years ago. After the fire.

He didn't want any of them back. Not now. Not even his mother.

He wanted to be set free. For whatever life he had ahead of him. The misery, the constant pain.

He'd do it alone. He didn't want or need any of them.

Now that Daniel knew who he was again, knew his strength, he'd cope. He was sure of it.

'They'll never let me be free. That's why I want you tell Jack that you know everything and that he needs to stay the fuck away from me. That's the collateral. When they get Scarlett back. They both owe me that much, Mum.'

'"When they get Scarlett back"? How do you know about Scarlett?' Colleen said then, wondering how Daniel could know anything about Scarlett. For a few seconds earlier, she'd wondered to herself if Daniel even knew that Scarlett had been born. That Nancy and Jack had a child together.

He knew that Scarlett was missing?

'Do you know where she is, Daniel?' Colleen asked. The urgency in her voice that he'd been waiting for.

The child was all this family cared about now.

They'd chosen her over him, just as he knew that they would. They always would. There would be no forgiveness for him.

He was walking towards the door then. Needing to get away. To escape. The walls closing in on him.

His mother's pleading look on her face was too much to bear.

'Will you do it, Mum? Will you tell him to stay away? Please, for me?'

Colleen nodded then, at a loss at what else she could say. She had to respect Daniel's wishes, even though her heart was breaking in two.

Then he nodded towards the car.

'She's in there,' he said.

And then he was gone.

CHAPTER FORTY-THREE

He held his breath.

Not just because he'd hidden away inside the putrid smelling bin cupboards underneath the stairwell, surrounded by the stench of rubbish and filth.

But because he could see her.

Coming down the stairwell opposite him. Just a few feet away.

Running now, she'd obviously just heard the news that Colleen had found Scarlett.

That her daughter was home safe and sound.

She'd aged, he thought to himself, pleased at how rough she looked. How haggard and tired she seemed.

Little Miss Perfect.

She looked as if she was ready to fall apart. That pristine persona she put on for all the world to see, gone now. The mask had slipped.

It was all just a show with Nancy, anyway.

All of it fake. Just like her.

She was suffering. That much was real. He could see it in her expression. In the way she held herself.

Her skin looked blotchy and lined. Her eyes were heavy with bags and shadows.

He'd tormented her.

Not enough though, not anywhere near in comparison to all she'd done to him, but she'd suffered all the same.

That would do for now.

She swept past him so closely, so near to him, that he could have reached out and touched her.

He could have grabbed her if he'd wanted to.

Dragged her in here with him and smashed her skull off the cold, grey concrete floor beneath them.

Only he doesn't do that.

Instead he practises restraint, unwilling to reveal himself, and give himself up to those pieces of shit. Why should he?

So that those two fuckers, Nancy and Jack, could have any glory?

They'd both punish him forever then, for something that he didn't even do.

Because they'd never believe that it wasn't him that had taken Scarlett, would they?

When it came down to it, it was his word against Marie's.

And of course, she'd win.

She was that type.

She'd throw him under the bus to save her own skin.

Marie the great fucking manipulator. The fucking fruit loop.

She'd caused all of this. Dumped the kid on him and then fucked off out of it, leaving him to pick up the mess.

Where the fuck was she now huh? While his home was ransacked. Ripped apart by the police. As they swarmed the place in search of him.

In search of him, not her.

Daniel The-Fuck-Up Byrne, with his grudge against Nancy. All of the evidence pointed straight at him.

Of course it did.

And Scarlett would say it was him too.

He'd been the one to push her into the river after all. He'd been the one that had tried to drown her.

And it wouldn't matter that he'd changed his mind at the last minute. That his conscience had got the better of him, and he'd pulled her back out from the water again.

So he stayed where he was, standing in amongst the shadows, keeping out of sight.

All the time watching. Waiting.

He saw Jack then too, close behind Nancy, the pair of them running from the building, another officer behind them both, carrying a clear plastic evidence bag with some of his belongings inside and loading it into the back of the police van.

'They've got her!' another officer shouted, from higher up in the building.

There was a flurry of movement then as officers ran down the stairs. Car doors slamming. Loud, jovial voices filling the communal stairwell.

Scarlett Byrne had been found.

All was well with the world again.

Squatting down then, his back against the cold brick wall. Trying to breathe out of only his mouth so he wouldn't gag on the stench of rot from the bins around him. He waited it out.

They'd leave eventually.

They had to.

There was nothing here for them now.

They'd found Scarlett.

All he had to do was wait it out.

*

Making his way inside the flat, Daniel could see, even with the lights out, that the place had been completely ransacked. The fuckers had searched through everything. Even his bin was upturned. Rubbish and bits of food all over the floor.

The cupboards all empty.

The last of his medication gone.

Most of his personal possessions and clothes had been taken away for examination, he noted. Walking around, amongst the debris.

In search of his laptop. Gone too.

More evidence. They'd only have to look at his search history to know how obsessed he was with his sister, now that he'd regained his memory.

All the articles he'd been analysing.

Articles about Jack too.

He had nothing now.

He couldn't stay here.

They'd be back for him soon. He'd have to leave.

But he had no form of ID now that they'd taken all his personal belongings away, and it wasn't as if he could just blend in, was it? The damage to his face was far too distinctive.

All he could do now was go underground. Live rough on the streets and seek solace at the homeless shelters until everything died down a little.

Until the police ran out of leads.

Until his mother spoke to Jack and told him Daniel's terms.

That he was to let Daniel go free. Not to look for him.

That was the deal. He'd delivered Scarlett back to them, unharmed.

And all Jack had to do was stick to the plan, then, for now, his secrets would all be safe. As long as he did what Daniel had said.

And no doubt he would.

Jack had everything to lose and nothing to gain by tracking him down now.

And Daniel trusted Colleen.

His mother.

He knew that she'd ensure that he was okay.

In some weird warped way, they were both two of the same. Two very fucked-up people.

Victims of their circumstances, casualties of their own fucked-up family.

Colleen would speak to Jack. Daniel could count on that.

She'd be the woman of the hour now. Being the one that had discovered Scarlett tonight.

Scarlett's saviour. The one to give everyone the good news. That Scarlett was home. That the child was safe.

Maybe then, Nancy would cut the woman some slack.

His nan Joanie too.

Colleen wasn't all bad. She was just damaged, that's all.

Damaged, just like him.

Kicking a pile of rubbish down at his feet, he sent the contents of the spewing bin bag flying across the room. He needed to get the fuck out of this place. This grotty cesspit that for the past four years he'd called home.

This wasn't ever his home.

He never belonged here.

It was time to break free of it all.

His family, this flat. Marie.

And he would survive, somehow, no matter where he ended up.

He knew this because already he'd been through much, much worse.

He owed himself a fresh new start now.

Grabbing the very few clothes that had been left behind, Daniel looked around in dismay at what his life had finally come to. Just a few rags scrunched up inside a carrier bag. That's all he had to his name.

He shook his head sadly, before making his way back out of the flat.

Creeping down the stairwell.

Unable to shake the feeling that he was being watched.

He wouldn't put it past that lot. The police. Staking out the place, setting up some kind of a trap, waiting for him upon his return.

A noise behind him, startling him. Making him turn.

His intuition right all along, he wasn't alone.

Only he wasn't quick enough to see who was there.

Who would be the one to turn him in to the fate that awaited him? A torturous life behind bars. A child snatcher. A monster. A freak.

All he felt was an almighty thud against his head, as he was struck.

A female's voice then, ringing out in his ears.

Nancy?

It couldn't be?

Then there was nothing at all, as he fell to the floor and was swallowed up by the darkness.

CHAPTER FORTY-FOUR

'Nanny, Nanny, can you do my new puzzle with me? Pretty please?' Scarlett Byrne said screeching around the room, in her element that her whole family were here together.

Spoiling her and giving her gifts as if it was her birthday.

'Nanny, Nanny? Which one?' Joanie laughed.

'Both of you!' Scarlett said, pulling at her nanny Joanie's arm, before reaching out for her nanny Colleen too.

'Ohh, I think we can manage a puzzle, don't you, Joanie?' The two women at ease with each other. Their quarrelling days well and truly put to bed now that their granddaughter was back home again, safe and sound.

Suddenly all of their rowing and bitterness felt so petty and pointless.

They both had this little fireball in common.

It made sense to get along. To join forces. Lord knows they needed each other's morale with the amount of energy little Scarlett had.

'Er, what about your doddering old grandaddy?' Michael Byrne said, trying his luck. Still wracked with guilt and acutely aware that he'd only been invited here today by Nancy for Scarlett's sake. Because the child had wanted so desperately to see him. 'Do I get to help?'

He smiled at Scarlett. Deeply ashamed of what he'd done. For all of it. For cheating on Joanie, or at least he would have done given half the chance. But more so for putting Scarlett in such risk.

For leaving her alone like he had.

There was no fool like an old fool, isn't that what they said? He just hoped that in time his Joanie would forgive him. Until then, he was just happy to be given the time of day. To see with his own eyes that little Scarlett was okay.

'Yes, you can help too, Grandaddy,' Scarlett said, after a couple of seconds' consideration. Then not wanting to leave anyone out, she added. 'You can all help me. Come on.'

'Oh we can, can we!' Nancy said, as she watched Scarlett tip the jigsaw puzzle out all over the floor. Her family all sitting around her, obediently sorting through the pieces as Scarlett gave them all instructions.

Nancy couldn't help but smile then.

Still unable to believe their good fortune, that she had Scarlett back.

Her baby, safe at home, where she belonged.

The last few days still raw in her mind.

She still couldn't believe the ordeal that her poor little girl had been subjected to.

That Scarlett had been some part of Daniel's warped, fucked-up kidnap plot.

Her brother, the bastard.

All to get his own back on her.

How could he have done it? How could he have brought himself to push Scarlett into the river? To attempt to drown her. A small child. His own niece.

Even if he had pulled her back out again.

He'd still done it. He'd still sunk so low as to almost kill a child. *Her* child.

When Colleen had called her and Jack to tell them that Scarlett was home. That she'd found her in her dad's car in the garage, blue with the cold, and she'd gone into shock; she'd called for an ambulance, but she'd told them that Scarlett was safe. That she was home.

Nancy and Jack had raced to the hospital in record time.

Amazed after they'd found out what had happened, that Scarlett hadn't suffered with hypothermia.

Daniel, the gutless bastard, must have brought her back to the house and dumped her inside the car. Listless and barely moving. Not giving a shit that she might die.

He must have left her there, on the whim that she would be found.

Colleen said she hadn't seen anything untoward. She'd only gone in there because she'd seen the side door ajar.

That's when she'd found her.

Scarlett. Their little fighter.

Glad to be home with her parents, she seemed to be coping with the entire experience a lot better than they were. Nancy couldn't even sleep. Every time she closed her eyes, all she could envisage was the image of her daughter's small body being swallowed by the dark murky waters of the River Thames.

Refusing to let Scarlett out of her sight now, she wouldn't rest until Daniel was found. And they would find that bastard.

She'd made Jack vow to her that no matter what they would track him down.

She would catch up, eventually, with her brother the fucking vanishing act that he was – and when she did, she would personally annihilate him for what he'd put Scarlett through.

What he'd put them all through.

She'd take great pleasure in personally wiping him from the face of the planet.

'Hey! You all right?' Bridget said then, passing her friend a glass of champagne. Recognising the distant look in Nancy's eyes.

Nancy was a million miles away again, lost in her thoughts, still in shock over everything that had happened.

'She's okay, Nance,' Bridget said, pulling her mate close and rubbing her arm. She knew how traumatic Scarlett going missing had been for Nancy.

Scarlett was Nancy's world. The woman loved her daughter more than anything.

'Look at her, Nancy, she's coping better than all of us. I said to your nan and Colleen earlier. She's got fire in her belly that one. She's just like her mumma. She's going to be just fine, and so are you. You all are.'

Nancy nodded then, trying and failing to hold back the single tear that escaped as Jack walked over and pulled her close to him, hugging her tightly.

The two of them were in this together.

And Nancy allowed him to hold her. In fact, she wanted him to. She wanted to breathe him in, to keep him close to her.

This man that had stood beside her through the most harrowing times in her life.

She was in love with him.

She had been for years, only she'd been too scared and vulnerable to admit it. Even to herself.

Jack was her rock.

The one person who through all of this had somehow managed to keep her sane.

And what's more, he adored her too.

He looked down at her then and caught her eye. Smiling at her, both of them knew.

As bad as everything had been the past few days, it had brought them together.

United them as one.

They were a family now, and Nancy had decided that finally she was going to put her fears behind her, and give the man a chance.

He'd already proved himself to her in every way. Over and over again.

Leaning up towards him, Nancy kissed him back.

'Oh, Jesus!' Bridget rolled her eyes then and laughed, trying to lighten the mood. Made up for her two friends that they'd finally realised they were made for each other and put themselves out of their never-ending misery. 'Would the pair of you get a room? Neither of you have kept your hands off each other all day and, if I'm going to be perfectly honest with you both, it's a bit sickening to watch.'

Jack grinned then. Looking like the proudest, happiest man in the world.

'How could I possibly keep my hands off this one huh? Look at her, she's just amazing.' He leant down then and kissed Nancy tentatively on the head.

Her emotions were so raw, so overwhelmed by the past few days' events that this only made Nancy cry.

'What's the matter, Mummy?' Scarlett said then, looking up, and catching her mummy wiping her tears away, as her daddy held her in his arms.

'I'm just so happy,' Nancy said, breaking away from Jack and bending down to reassure Scarlett. 'To have all of this. To have you. I'm just so, so happy.'

Scarlett looked at Bridget then, and rolled her eyes dramatically.

'It's only a jigsaw puzzle, Mummy!' she said, before turning her attention back to her great-grandparents, who were still in the process of putting the thing together for her.

'See!' Bridget giggled then, as if Scarlett's mindset only proved her right.

'She's forgotten all about it already. She's stronger than you think.'

Nancy smiled then.

As much as she wanted to believe that was true, she knew it wasn't.

Even at only four, Nancy could see it. How Scarlett bottled everything up inside her and just got on with it. How she hid her true feelings from the world.

Nancy knew, because Bridget was right, Scarlett was just like her.

Well, from now on her daughter was going to be her only priority. The businesses could take a back seat.

If anything, the last few days had shown her exactly where her priorities lay.

With her family. Her daughter.

The businesses could practically run themselves. Nancy had enough people around her, working for her, that she could trust. It was time to step back.

Scarlett might not be over her ordeal a hundred per cent, but Nancy would do her damnedest to be there for the girl from now on.

To make everything all right.

'Right. There's four pieces left to go. Auntie Bridge, Mummy, Daddy and me,' Scarlett said, bending back down on the floor before passing out the last remaining pieces of the puzzle.

'I'm doing the last bit though, okay!' Scarlett announced, picking it up and placing it in the middle of the picture.

'Of course you are, darling. You're the final piece of the puzzle. The bit that holds us all together,' Joanie said proudly. Beaming at the child that reminded her so much of Nancy when she'd been that age.

Scarlett seemed happy with that.

Standing back and admiring the joint effort that her family had all made.

'Okay, everyone. Good job. Give yourself a round of applause.'

They all laughed then. Clapping away as Scarlett Byrne did a little curtsey in the middle of the room.

In her element to be back home, surrounded by the people she loved the most in the world.

The people that made her feel so safe.

'Nanny Colleen's going now, Scarlett. Give her a kiss goodbye, and Daddy too. You'll be in bed by the time he's back from dropping her home.'

Doing as her mother told her, Scarlett kissed her grandmother and father, before running up the stairs to where her Auntie Bridge had promised to read her a story from one of the new books she'd bought her.

Nancy shook her head, smiling still.

Glad that Scarlett was still taking this all in her stride.

'It's been lovely having all the family here together. Just the tonic she needed,' Nancy said, hugging Colleen to her, and planting a kiss on her cheek. 'Thanks for everything. I'll see you tomorrow, Mum,' she said then, before giving Jack a peck on the cheek and following Scarlett up the stairs.

'Well that's a turn up for the books,' Colleen said. Her palm going up to her cheek. To where Nancy had just kissed her. Startled at her daughter's rare show of affection, she followed Jack, as he led her out to the car.

As Jack, ever the gentleman, pretended not to notice her tears.

Letting her have her moment.

Mum. She hadn't heard Nancy call her that for years.

Not since Nancy had been small, probably about the same age as Scarlett was now.

Colleen being the one to find Scarlett, to tell Nancy that she'd found her, had somehow broken the curse between the two women.

Nancy was eternally grateful, and Colleen really appreciated that.

For the first time in a very long time, there was hope. Maybe, just maybe they could start building bridges between them now.

Getting into the car, Colleen leant her head back against the seat, as Jack drove in silence.

Glad of the quiet. Colleen was lost in her thoughts.

She'd barely even noticed that they'd pulled up outside her flat in East Sheen until Jack turned off the engine.

'You all right?' Jack said, seeing the raw emotion etched on the woman's face. The tears still in her eyes.

She shook her head.

'We need to talk.'

Jack nodded. He'd known that this was coming. He'd been waiting for it, in fact. The past few days, so swept up in getting his daughter back, and making sure that everyone was okay. But he'd seen it in Colleen's eyes.

How the woman was suddenly looking at him.

There was a coldness there now that he'd never seen before.

'Is there something you want to say to me, Colleen?' he said then, convinced that there had been more to the story that Colleen had fed Nancy about just finding Scarlett inside Jimmy's car. That she hadn't set eyes on Daniel.

Jack had known straight away that wasn't true.

'You saw him, didn't you?' he said then.

Glad that at least Colleen had waited. That she hadn't simply blurted out whatever Daniel had told her about him to the rest of the family. To Nancy.

'I did, Jack,' she said sadly. Not bothering to add the state that Daniel had been in. Jack didn't deserve to know how much her son had suffered. He didn't deserve to know a single thing about him.

'He told me all about you, Jack. I know.'

He nodded. He didn't expect anything less from Daniel if he was honest.

Already bracing himself for that fact.

Colleen's cold hard stares eating into him the past few days.

That knowing look in her eyes.

'I know that you were there when Jimmy was killed, and I know you were behind the attack on Nancy.' Colleen spoke so directly now. Glad that they were finally alone. Glad that she could finally ensure that Jack knew his place.

Jack closed his eyes.

Knowing that this was coming, though it didn't make it any easier to hear.

Daniel had told Colleen everything.

Even now, after all of this, he still wanted to ruin any chance Jack had of not being found out, that he'd been in all of this too.

'I love her, Colleen. Genuinely. Like I've never loved anyone before.'

He stared straight ahead of him. His eyes fixed on the busy high street. The blur of headlights that passed them both. The people walking on the pathway next to them.

'I didn't know that Daniel was going to kill Jimmy. You have my word on that. I swear.'

'But you were happy to take half the ransom money. Blood money, as Daniel called it,' Colleen spat, shaking her head.

Jack put his head down then, his voice low. Full of remorse.

'A lot has changed since then, Colleen. I need you to know that I'd never do anything to hurt Nancy. Not ever. You have my word on that…'

'Your word means nothing to me.'

Jack took a deep breath.

Of course, why would it?

He'd lied and cheated his way into this family. Acting as if Daniel was the monster in all of this, when he wasn't completely innocent himself.

Colleen had every right to hate him, to out him.

'I'm not interested in your word, nor am I interested in your pathetic excuses. But there is something that I want you to do.'

Praying that she wasn't going to ask Jack to walk away from Nancy, from his daughter too. That she wasn't going to force him to lose everything he cared about.

Jack braced himself for the worst.

As long as it wasn't that, he'd do anything.

Anything so that Nancy never found out the truth.

'I've never been the best parent, that's no secret as you well know. And I've lived a lifetime regretting my choices. One thing I've learned is you can't go back. You can only go forward. I know my Nancy makes you happy, and Christ knows, you do her too. She lights up around you.' Colleen shook her head. Remembering that feeling so well with her Jimmy. How she'd fallen under his spell. So unaware of everything he was deep down inside. So oblivious to it all.

'Nancy and Daniel are both my children. My blood, and I need to do right by them both. So I'm asking you, as of tonight, to set Daniel free. Stop looking for him. Whatever you have to tell Nancy, however you have to do it, leave him be. It's time for this family to stop fighting. To stop the constant feuds. To let the past lie where it needs to be, behind us all.' She may have been a shit mother, but Daniel and Nancy were both her children and this war between them needed to stop before they both ended up dead.

'From now on, you do right by my daughter. No more lies. No more secrets. And you leave Daniel alone. Stop searching for him. Then and only then will your secrets be safe with me,'

Colleen said, laying down Daniel's terms, though this was her insurance policy too.

This way no one would ever find out, not even Jack, that she'd asked Daniel to pull the trigger on Jimmy all along. That she was the real person who initiated Jimmy Byrne's murder.

Sealing their agreement, Jack nodded at Colleen's veiled threat, watching as the woman got out of the car and closed the door behind her, before disappearing into her flat.

Aware that Colleen had just thrown him a lifeline, that this was his last and final chance.

As much as he begrudged the fact that Daniel was still out there somewhere, that the bastard had got away with everything once again, Colleen was right.

Scarlett and Nancy were his priority now.

Daniel could have his freedom.

As long as he stayed the fuck away from Jack and his family.

They were the only things that mattered now.

CHAPTER FORTY-FIVE

He could hear a noise.

A strange far off beeping.

Though somehow he knew he wasn't here alone in the complete darkness.

He was lying down?

Aware of the heaviness of his body, numb, as if it was being weighed down by something.

He was trapped somewhere?

Trying to get up, to roll on his side, to lift his head, only he couldn't move. He couldn't even open his eye.

Where the fuck was he?

He started to panic, claustrophobic then.

The darkness all around him, swallowing him up. Engulfing him.

His heart beating rapidly, as he felt someone's presence nearby.

Someone was here with him?

He could sense them. So close to him that he could almost feel their breath on his skin.

Yet they seemed so far away too. So far that he couldn't get to them. He couldn't reach them.

Nancy?

Was she here with him?

That bitch.

What had she done to him?

What had that bitch done to him?

Trapping him here. Wherever the fuck here was.

He felt something then. The light touch of skin.

Warmth. Then a sharp, short, electric shock sensation. Like a jolt. Something stabbing him in his arm. Scraping at him, before being sunk inside his flesh.

A needle?

Everything around him melted away then.

The noises in his ears gradually subsiding. Slipping off, far into the distance.

The darkness getting bigger, expanding all around him until it swallowed him entirely.

Until he was gone.

*

Marie Huston took the syringe out of Daniel Byrne's arm.

Robert, she reminded herself again.

His name was Robert Parkes. She should know. She had been the one who had named him, after all.

And it was the perfect choice. Robert suited him.

Much better than Daniel ever did.

She smiled then, as she stood next to his bedside. Watching her Robert lying there, in his drug-induced coma, so peaceful now. As if he was merely asleep.

He looked just the way he had done that very first day she'd met him. Lying peacefully in his hospital bed, on that fateful day, working at the High Dependency Unit at the hospital.

Comatose once again, unable to move or speak.

It was a shame really. Unfortunate that it had come to this, but it was for the best all round. Marie understood that now.

She hadn't really cared much for Daniel Byrne if she was completely honest.

He hadn't been a very nice person.

With his demanding ways and his volatile temperament.

The way that he spoke to her with that constantly irritated tone; the way that he bristled at the idea of her wanting to get close to him. For them to be together.

He'd always fought it.

The inevitable.

As soon as Robert had started to remember who he was, it had got worse. Much worse. It was as if, suddenly, Daniel Byrne had invaded Robert Parkes's body. Taken him over. Daniel had filled Robert's head with all sorts of nasty, angry notions.

Obliterating the man that Marie had first fallen in love with until there was almost nothing left.

Only Marie had saved him now, hadn't she? She'd saved him from himself.

It had to be this way.

It was the only way they could be together again. Properly.

Here in her new flat.

Where no one would come looking for her. All these months of paying the rent here, of keeping this place a secret. Putting all of the official paperwork and tenancy agreements in a false name. Tricky, but not impossible. And worth it now it was done.

They'd be safe here. No one would ever find them; they wouldn't even know what to look for.

It was just the two of them, together now. Soul mates.

Surrounded by the beeping machinery. The monitors and equipment that had been painstakingly slow and difficult for her to steal from the hospital.

The fact that she'd had to take each item singularly. To sneak it out after her shift and hide it in the back of her car.

Piece by piece, over the course of the last six months.

Things went missing in hospitals all the time. Moved around, placed in the wrong ward.

Still, she had taken her time so as not to draw any attention to herself, or raise any suspicions.

Though of course, that nosey old cow Nurse Langton had started to suspect her. She'd made it difficult for her then.

Poor Nurse Langton. Rumour had it that the woman was killed in some random hit-and-run.

Such a shame.

Silly woman!

It was bad enough that she'd suspected Marie of taking the medication, yet the woman wasn't smart enough to connect her with all the equipment she'd stolen too.

The stupid woman had thought that Marie was stealing to make Robert feel better, to take away his pain, when in actual fact she'd been preparing for this.

For her Robert's homecoming.

Keeping him with her, in an induced coma.

Here with her, forevermore now.

Marie looked at the photo then, that she placed carefully on the cabinet beside Robert.

Her and her baby sister.

She'd lost Cassie, but she wasn't prepared to lose Robert too.

She wasn't prepared to live the rest of her life alone.

She closed her eyes then, the pain still so raw.

Cassie wasn't even supposed to be home that day. There had been no way that Marie could have ever known.

She'd thought her sister had gone to school. *She should have been at school!*

Her father was doing his usual of taking his mid-morning nap.

Exhausted, the poor man. Such a tiring job, living on the social and sitting on your big, fat arse watching TV all day, before spending all night in your youngest child's bed.

Striking the match, Marie had watched the flame flicker with fascination at first, as the stick began to blacken. The heat licking at her fingers, as if encouraging her to do it. Egging her on. Forcing her to drop it down onto the sofa and start the fire.

She had no time to think after that.

It was done.

The flames growing quickly, lapping wildly against the fabric, spreading up the wall behind the chair.

The heat becoming so intense that she could feel the warmth on her face.

The crackling noise growing louder, as the flames got higher. Hitting the ceiling then.

The curtains catching light too.

That had been her cue to leave.

Locking the door firmly behind her.

The room would be up in flames soon, an inferno.

By the time her father realised, it would be too late; he wouldn't be able to escape. He'd have to come through the lounge to get to the front door, but he wouldn't be able to pass through the wall of fire that she'd created, and the door was locked.

He'd be trapped here, inside. Eight floors up. With no way of getting out.

The fire would get him, the smoke choking his lungs, the intense heat cooking him from the inside out.

Just as he deserved.

To burn in hell for all that he'd done to her and Cassie.

She'd waited then, further down the street, keeping out of sight, watching as the plume of black smoke poured out from the eighth-floor window, as the fire engines roared past her, and people gathered outside at the front of the flat. Other residents, passers-by, all staring up at the inferno in horror.

She imagined him in there, choking slowly to death.

His skin blistering from the heat. Dying in the most painful way possible.

She'd waited for what felt like hours.

For the fire to be extinguished. For people to gradually start moving away.

For his body to be brought out.

Only there had been two bodies inside the flat that day.

At first she'd thought that her eyes were deceiving her when the second trolley had been wheeled out. A second body, hidden away inside a black body bag.

Smaller. Like that of a child.

Marie knew instantly, her legs going from beneath her, as she let out a heart-rending scream.

Cassie.

She'd been in there too.

Her father must have had her in his bed, instead of sending her into school that day.

Marie had run then, towards the chaos and smoke. Towards the paramedics, towards her little sister. Desperate to bring Cassie back. To make things right again.

But it was too late. Her father and Cassie had gone forever and Marie was left all on her own.

Blinking away fresh tears, Marie looked down at Robert then and forced herself to smile.

She wasn't alone any more though. She had Robert now.

Beautiful, perfect Robert.

She'd known that from the very second she'd set eyes on him.

How caring for Robert would be her way of making up for what she'd done to her beautiful Cassie.

How this was her chance to make everything all right again.

She smiled as she began running the comb through the small patch of hair that remained on the right side of Robert's head.

Then she used a warm flannel, gently placing it over his skin, ever so lightly so that she could wash his face, before slathering

on all his special lotions and potions. All the creams that he liked
to use, to stop his skin from splitting and getting sore.

She loved these moments. When her hands roamed freely
across his body. Touching him, caressing him lovingly.

'I've missed you, darling.' Leaning down, Marie Huston kissed
Daniel Byrne gently on the lips.

And he didn't dare tell her not to now.

He didn't dare complain.

He was compliant now. Just as he'd been when she'd first laid
eyes on him.

'But don't you worry. I won't let anyone take you now. You're
safe now. You're home.'

A LETTER FROM CASEY

Thank you for taking the time to read *The Forgotten*. I've loved writing about the dysfunctional, feisty family that is The Byrnes and I really hope you've loved reading their story too.

To keep up to date with the latest news on my new releases, just click on the link below to sign up for a newsletter. I promise to only contact you when I have a new book out and I'll never share your email with anyone else.

www.bookouture.com/casey-kelleher

If you fancy leaving me a review, I'd really appreciate it. Not only is it great to have your feedback (I love reading each and every one of them!), but adding a review can really help to gain the attention of new readers too. So, if you would be kind enough to leave a short, honest review, it would be very much appreciated!

If you enjoyed reading about Nancy and the rest of the Byrne family – a twisted family if ever there was one! – and you want to read more about Jimmy and Colleen, and where it all began, please check out *The Betrayed* and *The Broken*.

I'm currently working on the next book so if you'd like to stay in touch and find out about the next release, or you just want to drop by and say 'Hello', I'd love to hear from you!

Casey x

OfficialCaseyKelleher

@CaseyKelleher

www.caseykelleher.co.uk

ACKNOWLEDGEMENTS

Many thanks to my fantastic editor, Keshini Naidoo. Your brilliant ideas, suggestions and editorial skills have really helped to make *The Forgotten* into the book that it is today.

Thank you so much for everything! As always, it's been an absolute pleasure working alongside you!

Special thanks to Noelle Holten. Social media superstar and one of the nicest, supportive women in the industry. I can't wait to read your book, Noelle! Thanks also to the rest of the Bookouture team Oliver Rhodes, Kim Nash, Lauren Finger and Leodora Darlington for all their continued help and support. Biggest shout out to the Bookouture authors too, that I've been so lucky to meet along the way. For all the giggles, and for keeping me sane!

Huge thanks also to all of those at the scene of the crime. You guys are the best :)

Special mention to Lucy, my bestie, who this book is dedicated to. For everything, (but especially for holding my gin at festivals ;) Also to Laura – wish I could write as fast as you read!

Thank you to Peter David Hodkin for all your help and advice on the legalities of constructing a new Identity. Special mention also to fellow author and Staff Nurse, C. Leslie. For all your information and advice on burns patients, care and procedures. You were a great help!

To all my fantastic readers, thank you so much for all your kind words about my books. You are the very reason I write, without you, none of this would have been possible. I love receiving your feedback and messages, so please do keep them coming!

As always, I'd like to thank my extremely supportive friends and family for all the encouragement that they give me along the way. The Coopers, The Kellehers, The Ellis's.

My Bestie, and all my girlies.

Finally, a big thank you to my husband Danny.

Our three children Ben, Danny and Kyle.

Not forgetting our two little fur-babies (Princess) Sassy and Miska (Boy).

x x